I0524208

FIRE & FROST

THE CANENS CHRONICLES BOOK 2

KELSIE ENGEN

Litera Scripta Manet

The Seven Kingdoms
Merise
Avium
Canens
Abbatia
heia
heia
Ostium
Ardor
Edormisco
Tepor
Nubilus
Merise
Canens
Manor
Ardor
Nubilus
N
W
E
S

FIRE & FROST

PROLOGUE

WINTERBERRY

The Queen has ignored the King's Curse. She attempted to kill me, even knowing the Curse will take her own life if she succeeds.

She stops at nothing to keep the throne. Killing is nothing, not with her goal in sight.

I thought I was safe—safe from death at her hands at least. Instead, she shows me just how unpredictable she is and how far she will go to keep my throne and call it hers. She won't stop, she will risk everything, and she will never surrender.

She seeks us all now. She wants far more reverence than I ever imagined. There will be no stopping her, should she succeed.

The throne has taken her completely.

But I cannot let her win. I will not.

PART I

1: WINTERBERRY

ROYALTY

In two days, the hunter has not stopped hunting us.

We rode through the first day and into the night as long as the dancing lights above allowed. All along, there was a pale figure upon the horizon following.

It doesn't stop; it only falls out of view behind dips in the snow or under the cloak of darkness.

He's there. The Queen's Huntsman.

I shudder. The cold penetrates deep into my bones despite my heavy fur cloak, fur-lined tunic, wool stockings, and fur hat and mittens. There is no escape from this chill, for it exists inside of me; it has become a part of me.

My memories after the wolf attack are faint, jumbled, but one thing I do recall is waking to a soft, glowing light and two men holding vigil over Elaina and me. I'd found Elaina's throat covered in blood but no visible wound. I remembered the wolf pressing on my own throat, hovering over me as I couldn't breathe. But I can't remember what happened to the others or why Elaina and Rus were covered in blood.

I can't remember how we survived. Or why Elaina has not

woken if she is not wounded. But we run...no faster than the man who chases us, keeping ahead of him, halting when we must.

Instead of lighting a fire when we stop, we huddle together for warmth, keeping Elaina in the middle. I do what I can to push warmth into her, hugging her slender frame close to my own thin body. Reminded of Des and how I failed to keep her warm, to keep her alive, I constantly check Elaina's throat, reassuring myself with the slow, steady thump there. The cold drains me, making my bones ache, siphoning out my energy.

On the second morning, I nearly weep when Elaina's eyes open and she pulls away from me as though she just woke from a heavy night's sleep.

I almost fall back into the snow in shock, then I lean forward and grip her arms in mine. "Oh goddess, Elaina. I thought you were going to die on me."

She offers a cheeky but slightly confused grin. "Die on you? Whatever gave you that impression?" Raising her mittened hand, she scratches at her cheek and frowns when she lowers it, staring at the dried blood upon it. "Did I cut myself?"

Taken aback, I pause before answering her. "What do you remember?"

Shaking her head, she frowns at the snow, searching the area around us. "I remember Cito and Rus... Where are they?"

"They went off to see about hunting a couple of hares we've seen." I point past one of the horses toward a small, snowy copse where they remain just within sight. Thankfully, or else I'd not be able to talk to her at all without the judgment radiating from her icy brother and his slightly warmer friend.

"Oh." Her brows dip toward each other above the wool swathed across her mouth and tip of her nose.

"It's all right. You're all right now."

"We—" She turns to me. "All right? What happened?"

"You and Cito and your brother found me in the *oubliette*."

"I remember that," she says slowly. "But after that it's a bit fuzzy. I remember insisting they save you, and we dragged you up from the depths." Forehead wrinkled, she shoves her scarf down and reveals cheeks, lips, and chin marred with blood.

My stomach lurches. I hadn't dared to use snow—the only water we had available without a fire—to wash the blood off her face while she slept. Rus had cleaned himself off with the snow, but I'd been too afraid to freeze Elaina further, like I had Des. Canens is unforgiving...Des' death taught me that better than any history lesson I'd learned as a child. Yet my own hands are numbed from checking Elaina's pulse so often.

"What is it?" Elaina raises a mittened hand to her face. "Am I hurt?"

"No, not anymore," I say firmly, putting a smile on my lips. "But you have some blood on your face. You'll want to clean yourself off."

She frowns, craning her neck to inspect herself, pulling at her bloodstained tunic. "What happened?"

"We were attacked by a wolf." I inwardly grimace at the half-truth. That was no wolf. That was my stepmother, the Queen of Canens, who attacked us in wolf form. I am not quite sure how I know, only I'm certain that it was no ordinary wolf, and not an enchanted wolf either. It was her. She came to finish me off. And, because of me, the three who saved me nearly got killed.

"Helena?"

I start at the name. It's only been a day or two since I told Rus and Cito to call me Winter, but I've already grown accustomed to it. "Call me Winter," I say now. "It's my true name."

At that, her lips twitch. "I know. Winterberry, right?"

Shock dulls my senses; I can only gape at her.

"You're Princess Winterberry, aren't you?"

"I—" Rocking back onto my heels, I give a quick glance to Rus and Cito, but they remain crouched in the woods. "How did you know?"

She shrugs. "Something you said when we met. And knowing how to speak Heian. I had a feeling you were royalty."

"And you…who are you really, Elaina? You aren't just some Heian girl are you?"

"Ah." Her eyes light up. "You know our secret, too. Excellent. I hate secrets unless I get to keep them."

I want to chuckle, as inappropriate as it seems at the situation we're in. "Well? Who are you?"

Wrinkles crease her youthful forehead. "I'm Princess Elaina Kara Solem of Heia."

Her answer takes my breath. "Oh. And so, your brother…" I glance back at the woods, locating the tuft of his red hair peeking out from under his white, fox-fur hat that he's traded his beaver hat for.

"Is the Crown Prince of Heia. Bonifaas Ruslan Solem." Elaina stands and stretches. "He goes by Rus."

"Right." I breathe out my disbelief. Why not? It's no stranger than the heir to the Canens throne becoming a slave.

"What's that?" She points back the way we've come.

I follow her finger and a shudder runs through me. Grabbing her by the shoulder, I say, "You'll have to tell me your story some other time. I'll fill you in as we ride." I push her toward the horses. "Rus! Cito!"

A loud curse is my answer.

Half shoving Elaina against the saddle, ignoring her protests, I spare a glance at the men to see a white hare bounding away and Cito's arrow flying into the snow, missing the hare by a foot.

"We must go!" I yell at them. There's no point in remaining quiet. We have a half day's ride to go to reach the border, and still he comes, only a few miles distant. "Now!"

They exchange a glance, and whether gaping at Elaina mounting the gelding, or at me and my urgency, they stumble toward us.

"Elaina, what—how—?" Rus gasps as they near, wading through the deep snow. "When—?"

"Mount up and we'll talk," I command, trying to keep the fear out of my voice. "He's near. Too near for us to linger."

Rus turns and the flush drains from his face as he spots the huntsman. "Right. Ride. We must ride as fast as we dare." He pulls Cito out of the snow behind him.

The taller, but thinner, man struggles through the soft snow that reaches his knees. "You don't suppose the orb can drive away the man like it did the wolves?" he asks Rus.

"I don't know. Maybe if it were fully powered—but it seems dead now anyway, after reviving us."

I pause in mounting my horse, my hand on the back of the saddle and my other in Elaina's. "What orb?"

Rus doesn't answer, and Cito wears an expression as though he's accidentally told a secret. Rus all but shoves Cito into his horse's saddle then swings into his own as I repeat my question.

"What orb are you talking about?"

"Don't concern yourself with it now," Rus says. "Just ride."

Scowling to myself at the terse answer from a man I still don't trust, I realize we don't have time to stand here arguing. Instead, I swing into the saddle and nudge our horse forward before I ask again. "What orb? Is that why you didn't tell me how we lived through the attack?"

He shoots me a glare. We can't gallop through the snow, and we ride as fast as we can, which isn't very fast. But the huntsman cannot go fast either. We are all limited by this cursed winter.

"Well?" I demand, glaring at Rus. Of course he won't tell me, if he's a prince he'll think he's entitled to keep secrets from me, a lowly—wait. Elaina knows my identity—does he?

"It was an orb a man in Ostium gave him," Elaina answers.

I crane my neck to stare at her. "What?"

"Is that what saved us all?" she calls over to Rus. "The orb again?"

"Orb? Again?" A shudder rocks through me that has nothing to do with the chill. Magic? They're using magic? Heians using magic? Magic obtained in Ostium? Who are these people?

"Some old man in Ostium gave Rus and Cito a magic orb," Elaina continues.

"A magic orb?" Dread drags me down. "They're using magic? You've used magic on us all?"

Rus shoots me a glare. "It's the only reason you're alive. It's saved you twice now."

Bile rises in my throat at the thought of magic touching me, even as I realize it makes me a hypocrite to think so. I clench my fists around the reins. "You should have let me die."

"Believe me, I wanted to," Rus mutters.

I narrow my gaze at him, but feel a surge of amusement when he kicks at his horse's side as if he doesn't go fast enough. "I can't believe you used magic."

"Why do you hate magic so much? What's so bad about it?" Elaina asks, but doesn't wait for my answer before pressing on. "No one can ever tell me why it's bad, but I've heard them complain that Queen Blanche has magical abilities. The way I see it, magic saved our lives. Heians don't trust magic, and we don't let it in our borders, but I'm not going to quibble about something that's already been done," she finishes as if that answers all of her questions and puts an end to our argument.

"Magic corrupts," I say loud enough for Rus to hear. Elaina flinches from the nearness of my mouth to her ear, and I lower my voice only to insert more of a growl. "The more you use it, the more corrupted you'll become. How long have you had the orb? How much have you used it?"

Rus rolls his eyes. "I'm not corrupted. Believe me, I'm the same as I was when we first received it."

I glare at him around Elaina's shoulder. "You would be the last to realize your own corruption, you know."

He shoots me a glare. "Just ride. Whether it's corrupted me or not, it's too late now. And whether you like it or not, it's saved you already."

"Twice," Elaina reminds me. "You're grinding your teeth again. I can feel it."

Forcing my jaw to loosen, I take a breath and count to three before saying, "Using magic is dangerous. You never know when too much is too much. It corrupts. It steals from your soul."

Rus rolls his eyes and nudges his horse again.

"Stop doing that," I snap, "the poor animal is already going as fast as he can in this snow."

At that, Rus turns his face to me. "Why did we rescue you again?"

"Because of my charm," I retort. "You saw me in the slave sales and couldn't stop thinking about how you could own me."

After a moment's pause, he snorts then turns his face away, whether to hide his disgust or his smirk, I can't tell.

"No, it's because of me," Elaina says cheerfully. "And he secretly likes you more than he's letting on, I know it."

I glance at her, then back at Rus. To my shock, I think I spot a flush crawling up from under his scarf toward the apples of his cheeks. It's almost impossible to tell in this cold, for all our cheeks and exposed skin have reddened. "Just promise me you won't use magic again, Rus. Not for anything."

This time, when he faces us, there's a darkness to his face and a tightness to his shoulders that I didn't catch before. His gaze slides to Elaina, who picks at our gelding's frosted mane with a mittened hand. "I have no desire to use magic."

"Good." I give a sharp nod, remembering the burn of magic in my fingertips when I touched Elaina.

That's what it always was, you know.

At the voice in my ear, I jolt so violently that Elaina grips my knee with her hand. "Are you all right?"

"Yes. Sorry. Just..." I trail off, and Elaina lets it go.

This time, when the voice speaks, I'm ready for it.

Magic, it whispers. *Magic is what it was when the light helped you out of Blanche's prison. And magic it was you saw in the* oubliette. *Magic that called to them and rescued you.*

I stiffen. "Why?" The word leaves my mouth so softly that I barely whisper it at all, and though I know the voice hears me, it doesn't answer. And despite stewing on these thoughts for the rest of our ride south, I can think of no good answers to give myself either.

INVITATIONS

A strong sun burns the layer of Ardorian cotton into my skin as I heft my end of the heavily laden cart up and push it over the manure pile. A rogue bit of manure rolls down to land upon my toe. I pause in my humming to scoop it back up the hill with my shovel before I store the wagon and survey my hard work.

One task down on today's mental checklist.

Smiling in satisfaction, I brush the dirt off my practical men's leggings and tunic before straightening and arching my spine to stretch the often-abused muscles of my back.

But a grimace pulls at my lips when I sweep away a strand of hair and catch sight of my hands and arms. A wash might be in order.

A quick walk around to the front of the stable delivers me to the well, where I drag up a cool bucket of splashing water. With sleeves turned up to my elbows, I scrub my face and arms in the icy water.

Arms dripping, I study the clear, blue sky. I have dozens of other things to do, but I simply cannot stand here without enjoying the privilege of this view. The cloudless sky, the green pastures, the white fences, the lines of apple trees with glints of shiny red apples pulling down the branches. The constant rich scent of horse and grass along with a sweeping breeze wrap around me like a warm blanket. I wouldn't trade this for anything.

An eruption of loud barks behind me startle me even though I recognize them. The oldest of the huge mastiffs who guard the stables, Gus is also the leader of the pack and the first to send up the alarm when something happens. His bark is a warning, an announcement bark, for he doesn't rise from his position, his arthritic limbs perhaps protesting his decade-long job.

A younger dog emerges from the shadows, darting toward the dirt road leading up to the stables. An unfamiliar bay horse with a well-dressed rider trots up.

"Custos!" I call to the younger dog, who skids to a reluctant halt but locks his gaze on the uninvited guest.

The rider stops his horse, eyeing Custos warily. After two more barks, the mastiff plops down in his place, but doesn't look away.

I approach the rider with Gus beside me. "I'm so sorry," I say, though guard dogs like Gus and Custos are expected at Gelu stables. Some of the more well-off stables even have armed guards on staff that practically hold approaching riders at sword point before allowing them into the stable.

"They won't bother you, I promise. Can I help you with something?" As I speak, I inspect the horse before the rider, for in many instances the horse tells me more than the rider will. This impeccably groomed Gelu Rigens wears a supple saddle and bridle with a square blanket underneath the saddle embroidered with *Greggory III*. Upon two heavily laden saddlebags is branded the King's insignia: one rearing horse and one rearing unicorn pawing an apple tree between them. It's a familiar image to all Ardorites, but especially to me as a stable owner who reports to the King's Gelu Rigens Crown Inspector every month. This man, however, I realize quickly, is not one of them.

"A message from the King," he says. "I knocked at the house, but there was no answer." Annoyance shadows his face.

"I'm sorry." My stomach squirms and drops. Questions I dare not voice rise on my tongue. They can't be here to take the property from me, not yet.

I purse my lips together into a thin smile. "I can accept any message you have, sir."

Peering down his nose at me, the man frowns at my men's clothing. After a long moment's examination, which I flush and shift under, he begrudgingly flips open the saddlebag at his knee and digs through it to pull out four rectangular, thick envelopes closed with a thick wax seal.

The squirming in my stomach eases only to turn into calmer wiggles of curiosity. If there are four envelopes, that means one for each member of my family, and no message regarding Aeneas Stables would cause the King to send a message to all four of us.

"There are three maidens and their mother who live here, yes?" The messenger's brow arches as if to imply that I cannot possibly be one of the four he mentions.

"Yes, sir."

"The King and Queen are throwing three masqued balls to celebrate the return of their son, Prince Brann, from university. All noblemen and noblewomen of Ardor are invited to attend." He sniffs slightly, as if to imply that what he sees here doesn't suggest anything noble at all.

My mouth tightens. After Father died, the fees on keeping the stable doubled or tripled, as customary for any woman-run business. Instead of upgrading the stables and paying for flowers or things to pretty them up, I chose to put the money into things that might increase my capital like studs and new stock. The Crown requires me to show increasing profit yearly, and flowers won't do that.

The man holds out the envelopes. "I trust you can deliver these to the proper recipients?"

"Yes, of course."

I reach for the envelopes and, with one more scrutiny of me, he drops them in my hand. They fall with the weight of dog's paw into my palm, and I grasp them just as firmly as I might while shaking Gus' paw.

Without another word, the messenger turns his horse and nudges him into a trot.

I watch the horse's movements, the slight swing inward of his right back leg as he jogs. Maybe a hint of lameness or stiffness or an old injury.

Gus whines beside me and nudges my hand until I relent and pet him, his reward for protecting us. When the messenger and his horse reach the far gate, I finally look at the envelopes. Thank the Lord I just washed, though I missed some of the dirt under my nails. I thumb through the four invitations. Carmen Saevus, Haydée Saevus, Eleanora Saevus, and Lady Eleanora Saevus, each labeled with "of Cruesa House" beneath the name. I hate seeing my name written out in full, so easily confused with my mother's.

Sensing my mood, Gus growls at the road.

"Don't worry, Gus, he won't be back."

He shakes his head, his ears flopping and spittle flying.

"Gus," I complain in good humor, bending my head away but shielding the envelopes with my body.

He snorts and plods toward the shadows of the barn.

I follow him with my gaze for a moment, then turn it toward Cruesa House, perched above the stables on a slight hill. A shadow so heavy falls over me that I glance upward to check the sky for clouds but find none. I shake my head, knowing it's my thoughts that lead me to blaming the weather. Though no one answered at the house, someone could still be there, watching. Guiltily, I hurry after Gus, not stopping until I reach the side of the stable hidden from view of the great house.

There, I tuck the three envelopes for Mother and my sisters under my arm, then slide my finger between the flap and the red wax seal. Four pieces of parchment spill into my hands. Three look identical, while the fourth sheet is a personalized letter in elegant script.

You are cordially invited to three masques in honor of His Royal Highness Prince Brann Tatius of Ardor. Enclosed within this envelope, please find three invitations which must be presented for entry to the balls. Formal dress with full mask required.

My jaw drops as I peruse the three invitations, each with my name on them, just as promised. Only the dates differ, with the first a week from today. My heart leaps with excitement, then plummets with biting disappointment.

Mother will never let me go. And next week? I have so much to do with the auction coming up the following week, I don't think I can manage an evening out dancing with a prince.

I grin. Dancing with a prince. But as I tuck my invitations and letter back into the envelope, my smile slips. I lean against the barn wall, tilting my head back and sighing. What wouldn't I give for just one night of feeling like I belonged? Of feeling like a woman, or even daring to feel like a princess, rather than a servant in my own home or a groom at my own stable.

I straighten. No matter. I don't much like balls anyway; I'd rather be riding.

Denouncing my own pang of regret, I slide my envelope into my tunic pocket and shift the other three to my hand as I step away from the sanctity of the barn. I'll have to deliver these sooner rather than later, before my mother or sisters hear of the news from others and have a chance to wonder why I haven't immediately notified them.

Inside the stable, a horse neighs, and I tuck the other envelopes into my pocket alongside mine. The invitations will have to wait at least until I can turn out the horses.

THE CROSSING

We reach the frozen lake at sunset. A glance behind tells me we have no time to rest, no time to pause. The huntsman is almost upon us.

Rus' face pales when he looks back. His breath escapes with such force it seems to cloud his vision for a few precious seconds. His chest shudders, then he lunges from his horse. "Dismount; the horses can follow."

I slide from my gelding's saddle and turn to help Elaina down. For all her earlier cheerfulness, she's still weak from her ordeal. I'm not certain why, but Blanche's wolf attack seems to have affected her more than the rest of us.

Ice sprawls out between us and freedom, clear enough to see the blue beneath its surface but stretching on for miles. Occasional cracks collect opaque snow, demonstrating the ice's depth. It should be safe... Still...if it's safe for the seven of us, four humans and three horses, then it's going to be more than safe for the huntsman to follow. And if it's not...

I refuse to entertain the remainder of that thought.

Concentration mars Rus' youthful features as he stares across the frozen water. It seems like he's aged even since I first saw him, and that's been mere days, weeks at the most. I would have thought him to be looking younger now that he has found his sister after his months of searching. Instead, it seems his concern has only increased the farther we travel.

And the nearer the huntsman comes.

I shake my head. In ordinary times—whenever those would be—I might have thought him handsome with his unusual dark red hair and skin a few shades darker than most Canensians. I had, for a brief moment at the slave preview where I first saw him, thought him so. Then he had been unforgivably rude. My cheeks still burn at the words he had said. "If all women smelled as such, we'd die out." He had gained himself some laughter at the comment, perhaps some confidences—at my expense.

Of course, he's a Heian prince, and Heia has long been one of our enemies. Arrogant, entitled people they are, considering their small country. Yet Elaina has shown none of the same hatred, despite all the reasons she has been given. She has every right to be angry and hateful toward me, yet she has been nothing but gentle, cheerful, and generous. She has conducted herself like a true princess.

I give Elaina a thoughtful glance. If I have to choose between whom I can save… She doesn't deserve any of this, not with her generous heart.

"I'll go first," Rus says, jerking my attention back to him. "Although this ice should be thick, we shouldn't all go at once but spread out."

"It is thick." I turn and survey our group. Three horses, each laden with some supplies and their tack, then the four of us, with only our thick clothes. While Elaina and I are thin and small, the men are tall. Cito is slender, but Rus is thicker. But it will be the heavier horses who break through the ice first.

"Exactly, so we should be—"

"We should send the heaviest one first," I interrupt.

Rus shoots me an annoyed look. "That's what I said. I'll go first—"

Before he can finish, I take the flat of my hand and slap the haunches of my large gelding. He starts, slipping ahead onto the ice. Loose reins flapping against his neck, he trots fifty feet out on the frozen lake and stops, peering back at us in confusion.

"Winter—" Rus growls my direction, but his eyes remain on the gelding, who stands with all his fifteen hundred pounds on four small spots on the ice.

Ignoring Rus, I scrutinize the lake, chewing on my lip and waiting for the ice to crack or creak or for something more dramatic. When nothing happens, I aim a grin Rus' way. "Guess it's safe to there."

He narrows his eyes at me. "Horses are expendable to you? We lose these horses and we die, too."

I shrug. "Better than your sister falling through the ice, isn't it?"

He snorts through his scarf at me but doesn't answer.

I grin at his annoyance and confidently step out where the horse traveled. There's still a chance the gelding could have weakened the ice, but we can't stand here forever.

My leather boots slip as I leave the snow and find the ice.

"Rus, why do you have to make things so complicated?" Elaina's voice is light with the teasing laughter she often uses with her older brother.

Halfway to the gelding, I turn to catch him shooting her a softened look that is half glare and half exasperation. He meets my gaze fleetingly before turning on his sister. "Elaina, if any of us fall through the ice, you keep going to Ardor. Don't wait for any of us, understand?"

Elaina slips into his arms for a quick hug. "Rus, you traveled across Canens to save me—do you really think I'd ever leave you behind when we're so close?"

"Elaina!" he snaps in frustration.

Hiding my grin, I turn back and follow the path to my horse. At his haunches, I softly lower my foot. In answer, the ice creaks loudly. I freeze, holding my breath and dart my gaze to those on the snow. Elaina's expression changes from amusement to fear in a blink. Rus takes a step forward only for Elaina to grab his arm.

The creaking echoes over the land and frozen water, then something snaps far away. The gelding snorts and steps backward, toward me. I put a hand to his rump, but he keeps coming. I hold my breath while the gelding snorts and lifts a back leg only to put it down in the same spot, a mere step from my foot.

Then, as suddenly as the creaking began, it stops. I stare at the ice, but no cracks appear. The tension in my limbs eases, and a nervous giggle escapes me. "I think it's safe."

Rus' answering breath is ragged without relief. Behind him, Cito looks as though he's going to collapse.

"Send the rest of the horses," I tell them. "I'll try to get the gelding going again."

"But—"

"We can't let the horses be our downfall, not when they could save us."

"Winter…" Rus begins, then trails off to add, "Be careful." The last words are almost buffeted away on the wind.

"I'm next!" Elaina calls out, and I turn just in time to see her run onto the ice as though it's all a game. My heart leaps into my throat with such force I think it won't ever go back to place.

But the ice holds, even with the other two horses leading the way before her, spreading out over the lake and following my brave gelding.

"Walk over there," I warn her, pointing to a path several feet away that Rus' horse has forged. "Not too close to me."

In this manner, we begin our journey. Elaina giggles and slides a few more times, but soon enough the thrill wears off, especially when another ominous crack fills the air.

I go as fast as I dare, keeping a steady pace of catching up to the gelding and then smacking his haunches to drive him ahead. Elaina does the same with her horse, and then Rus and Cito follow the third horse. Cito trails behind Rus, but every time I glance back, I read the terror in his eyes.

Regardless, we fall into monotony where our walking becomes nearly no different from traveling upon the snow. As we reach the middle of the lake, the skies begin to clear before us, but a dark cloud storms behind us.

My feet grow heavy as I trudge along. Elaina, several paces away, missteps and falls to her hands and knees. She doesn't move.

"Elaina? Are you hurt?" I call out, keeping my position, though the ice remains silent.

"Yes. I—" She breaks off and lifts her hands, staring at them in confusion. From them, something plops back to the ground in little droplets.

Water.

I suck in a breath and hold up a hand to stop Rus and Cito's advance. The gelding she follows continues plodding along, lifting hooves dripping with water and placing them back down with a small splash. I flinch every time he sets his hooves down, expecting the ice to crack under him and for him to go plummeting into icy water. Instead he continues, steady as can be, supported by the weight of whatever ice is underneath the melted layer atop.

"All right?" Rus calls out after a minute of us watching the animal stride on.

Elaina and I exchange a look.

"We're fine," Elaina answers. "Just a little soft over here."

"You'd better come this direction…" I trail off, looking ahead. Patchy, mushy puddles litter the ice now, some large, some small.

Elaina spots them too, her eyes widening before turning back to her own path. "I guess it's all like that." Excitement takes over the surprise. "We must be getting close to Ardor." She grins and finally rights herself, this time stepping around the puddle and following the horse.

"Let's press on. I can see Ardor's grassy shore from here." Rus turns, waving Cito on.

I squint in the direction of Ardor. I can't see anything. I'm about to tell Rus so when I see the terror on Cito's face. My heart twists, bleeding for him. I slap my horse ahead and take a step toward Cito when the ice gives an almighty crack.

"What was that?" The terror in Cito's voice is nearly as loud as the crack.

The sound echoes over the air. A dozen smaller cracks answer.

The horse in front of the men gives a nervous neigh and trots toward the green shore, his eyes showing white.

I take another step toward Cito, but Rus glowers at me. Opening my mouth, I begin to roll my eyes when the sight behind Cito stops me. The huntsman is less than a mile from us, tracking us across the ice...*riding his horse* across the ice with boldness that surprises even me.

All of our options run through my mind at once. Abandon caution and run, stand and fight, or plead for their lives and go with him.

I hold my breath.

Then, decision made, I stride toward Rus.

He frowns and opens his mouth.

"Take Elaina and run," I tell him. "Follow the horses' paths, you should be safe enough if they are." I shake my head. "You know that." I brush past him, and he grabs the edge of my cloak.

"Wait, what are you doing?" His fierce gaze slips from my face to over my head, and the skin around his eyes tightens before he drops his gaze to my face again. "You can't go back to him."

I glare my most withering glare at him. "Let me go. I'm going to help Cito."

"Help Cito?" Rus' eyes round, then flick in the direction of his advisor.

Cito has spread himself out on the ground, sprawled nose touching the ice, and the sound of a murmured prayer reaches my ears.

"*Some*one has to help him. I don't think he'll move on his own." I tug my cloak free from Rus' grasp and turn.

"No." Rus grasps for my cloak again.

Incredulously, I face him. "No? You would let him die? He's followed you through your enemy's land, and you would abandon him?"

Rus closes his eyes and lets out a little breath through his nose, releasing a cloud of mist that clings to his scarf in wet droplets. "No. You take Elaina. Help her."

I step backward in shock. "She doesn't need—"

"You get her safely to Ardor, do you hear me? No matter what happens to Cito and me, you get her safely into that country and get her to the palace." His glare would cow a weaker person, I am sure, but I stand firm.

"The palace?" I frown. Why in the Seven Kingdoms would I go running straight to my enemies? Only…it's not her enemy, is it? She's Heian. It's only me they would be delighted to kill.

"Yes, to the palace. She'll know why. Just take her there, and don't surrender to the Magister—ever. If you care about your country and the Seven Kingdoms, do not surrender to him or Blanche. Ever." He tugs my cloak toward him, hard enough to pull me off balance and step toward him.

"Go after her, Winter," Rus murmurs down to me as I search his softened expression for answers he won't give. "I'll protect Cito; I can't leave my most loyal friend at the mercy of"—he pauses and gives me sweeping glance—"of my enemy."

At his choice in words, my irritation with the arrogant prince returns. I tilt my head and give him a withering glare. "But you'll leave your sister to her instead?"

He snorts. "You have more to worry about than she does. Now go! He's coming!" He grabs my arm and pushes me in the direction of the shore.

I am half a dozen steps away when he calls out, "Keep her safe, Winter. I'd hate to have to exact my revenge on you."

His words bring a grim smile to my lips. "No promises!" I look back to see his expression, but he's striding toward Cito, and with the huntsman already a quarter of the way across the lake, I don't wait another second but dash toward Elaina as fast as I dare.

4: WINTER

THE EARTHQUAKE

laina slips as I near, falling to her knee with a splash that has my heart falling to my toes. The gelding ahead of her is a few hundred strides from shore, water biting at his knees as he hurries away from us. Nearby, the other two horses are jumping from the ice into the water, which laps at their stomachs, swallowing the stirrups hanging below and groping at our supplies.

Focusing on making my steps light, I follow Elaina. "Are you all right?" I call to her as she clamors back to her feet.

"Yes. A bit cold though."

I grin. "Just get to the shore and it'll be warm soon."

"Right?" She returns my grin and walks on, her feet sinking through the softer ice above only to be caught beneath.

Though I can't see the shore, Elaina walks confidently on, clearly not expecting to plunge under the ice with every step.

The farther I walk, the more I expect my heart to calm and my eyes to see green grass, but neither happens.

My heart thumps harder, faster. I don't fear the ice; I don't fear falling through it anymore, but I do fear death because it means she wins. It means I leave Canens in Blanche's care. I

28

glance behind at Rus pulling Cito toward the shore, then gasp in surprise as I step forward without looking and fall up to my thigh into the water, then plunge waist-deep as my knee buckles in surprise. My hands slap at the water's surface, trying to catch me from falling, but they simply fall through until my chin touches the water. I jerk upward at the shock, and the sound of giggling reaches me.

"Pay attention, Winter," Elaina teases. "We're almost in Ardor."

I stare at the water lapping against my hips, my thick cloak floating on top of water beside melting ice chunks. "I think we already are." I pull off a mitten and scoop it into the water. The water is both cold and warm, as if a warm current mixes with a cold one. Lifting my gaze, I gasp.

Tantalizingly near ahead, is the land of Ardor. It's land unlike any I've ever seen or imagined. Trees laden with bright orange, yellow, green, and red leaves wave in a gentle breeze. Dark dirt meets their trunks, stretching toward the water, interspersed with rocks, clumps of green plants, and bright flowers.

"Come on, Winter," Elaina calls as she drags herself and her floating cloak through shin-deep water toward the shore. But the shore...I never imagined in all my imaginings—

"He's gaining on us."

Her words jolt through my body. I glance back. She's right; he'll be on top of Rus and Cito in a minute if Rus doesn't get Cito to hurry up. I hesitate, torn between obeying Rus' wishes to save Elaina and returning back to help them.

"Come on!" Elaina splashes up ahead, and I turn my attention forward again. She stands in shallow water and the horses are already on the grassy shore, gathered together and looking uncertain where to go next.

During our mad dash from the Manor across the snow and ice, I hadn't considered what Ardor might look like. Spread before me is a sight like I've never seen before. Tall, bushy trees have wide leaves on every limb. Plants emerge from the ground everywhere it seems, except for a shore of variously sized rocks along the shore of the lake. Even that only lasts a few feet before it turns to brown dirt and is overtaken by green. Grasses and plants, none of which I've seen in real life before, sprout from the earth. I can already smell them, the dirt, the plants, the very scent of life itself sprouting from the ground in the way I've only seen in Blanche's growing houses.

But this is far more beautiful.

My knees weaken; I can't speak. I continue to drag myself toward the shore, drawn to it through my daze.

"It's…it's…"

"Ardor," Elaina says, her tone odd.

"Yes," I answer. "It's amazing." Something crawls down my face. I put my fingertips to my cheek, and they come away wet. I'm crying.

"Are you all right?" Elaina asks.

I can't answer. In the water near the edge of the lake are round green things the size of my hand. Plants. Pink flowers rise from amongst them. Elaina's on the other side of them, standing atop a rock twice as big as her, holding out a hand toward me.

"Come on," she says. "We can gather the horses for Rus and Cito." She darts a glance over my shoulder, reminding me of my purpose here and pulling me out of my distraction. There will be plenty of time to admire Ardor later. Well, if we get a later. If we escape the huntsman.

I drag myself, soaked furs, cloak, dress, and water-logged boots toward the shore. Elaina has already ripped off her cloak, revealing the Canensian peasant's gown beneath.

"Almost here." She squats down and reaches for me as I near.

The vibrancy of Ardor's colors draw my gaze again, and when I am a few feet away from her, I trip on something under the water and sprawl toward the rock she sits on. My hands, one mittened and one bare, collide with the stone. Under my hands, the rock shudders and shakes. Elaina wobbles and falls back onto the shore, falling heavily on her bottom with a squeak of injury. The horses neigh and scatter toward the towering trees behind them. I go to my knees, gripping the rock with my fingers.

The entire world is shaking. Behind me comes a mighty crack.

Elaina shrieks, scrambling back up to her hands and knees to look behind me, terror alighting her features.

The world roars as if it's a dragon waiting to swallow me whole, hungrier than any dragon woken after hibernation. What have I done?

The thoughts surge through me, burning my skin so I release the rock. But the world continues shaking.

"What's happening?"

"An earthquake," Elaina calls from her position above me, where she's crawled and extends a hand to me.

"Why?" I beg her with my eyes to answer my question, as if she could possibly have the answer for the wrath of the gods.

She grabs my hand with hers, gripping tight so mine doesn't slip out and pulls me onto the rock with her. She falls back and I fall forward, half on her. When we disentangle ourselves, she shrugs. "I don't know. They happen now and then. I remember having one when we visited Ardor the last time. But it was nothing like that one."

As she speaks, I realize the earth has stopped shaking. The horses are scattered amongst the tree line, two together and one trotting off deeper into the woods.

I point to him. "We have to catch him."

Elaina says something in Heian that I think is a curse. As she climbs up, her gaze strays to the lake and goes white. "Rus."

"What?" I follow her gaze, and my heart falls to my wet boots. "Oh goddess."

The lake is fractured. A gaping split in the ice, perhaps a quarter mile away, flashes dangerously blue against white. A few feet behind the gap is the huntsman, desperately trying to control his white horse. I squint. Is that Ice, the horse I had attempted to ride to freedom as a slave?

As I gape, another crack fills the air. Elaina shrieks. "Rus!"

The divide deepens between the huntsman and Ardor. Between us. But where is Rus? Where is Cito? I scan the ice for them and my gaze stutters to a stop on a dark spot halfway between the crack and the shore. They've fallen through.

"Stay here!" I yell at Elaina.

"What?"

"Stay here! Gather the horses."

"*What?*" Elaina repeats, coming after me.

"Stay!" I demand. "I can't save all of you. Not again."

She slides to a halt under my insistence. Then says, "Fine. But if you return here without him, I *will* kill you."

I meet her golden eyes and answer with one, sharp nod. Then I scramble onto the ice and begin my search.

MOTHER

On my way to find Mother, Haydée, and Carmen in town, I pick up a few yards of fabric scraps from the village seamstress to use for horse bandages and stop by the apothecary's to replenish my salve ingredients. I finally find them right where I expect: admiring fabrics and jewels in the town square market stalls.

Lady Eleanora stands, her long, golden hair twisted back intricately into the two braids she favors. Expensive red cotton brushes the cobblestones of the ground and hides her shoes, which are undoubtedly of the most expensive Teporian silk, despite our modest coffers. An elaborate new brooch on her bust catches the sunlight, glinting back at me, while a delicate gold necklace hangs from her neck, and rings sparkle from her fingers. I sigh. My sisters aren't much better, though they wear fewer jewels and less ostentatious pale lavender and pink.

Guilt stabs me at my thoughts, and I'm tempted to turn around and walk away, perhaps visit the temple and calm my temper before approaching, but Haydée turns to say something to Lady Eleanora and her eyes light up. Her mouth goes round then forms a little smile.

"Why, Ella, what a lovely surprise," she croons at me.

"Ella?" Mother turns so fast that she puts a hand to her neck as though she's put a crick in it. There's a mean glint to her eyes.

Oh no. This won't go well at all. Holding my breath, I stride up to them with confidence I don't feel, reminding myself that they'll want these invitations. They need good things in their lives after Father's death, just as I do. My heart softens toward them. Mother, though she might appear harsh and unloving, desperately sought Father's approval. As did my sisters, who were often jealous for reasons I never understood.

"What are you doing here?" Lady Eleanora asks, her gaze on the display of expensive brooches, almost as though she's trying to pretend I'm not here at all.

Haydée leans toward me and wrinkles her nose in disgust as if she caught a whiff of something unappealing. I automatically glance down to see if I've got a smudge of manure on my breeches and frown to find myself in a dress. When I lift my gaze, Haydée is smirking knowingly at me.

"Well?" Lady Eleanora prompts through tight lips, turning away from me to pick up a large, silver brooch with several green gems in it.

The stall owner fidgets, trying to pretend that he doesn't sense the storm brewing before him. I give him a smile, but he averts his gaze and rearranges the other jewelry on the table, pulling back some of the smaller ones and pushing forward some larger. I frown.

"I'm sorry, Lady Eleanora," I say, addressing my mother with the title she prefers and ignoring Haydée and Carmen. "But we received a messenger from the King this morning, and I thought you would want to know as soon as possible." I withdraw the three invitations and hold them between us.

My sisters' eyes widen and dart toward each other, then quick smiles break out on their faces. They lunge toward me, ripping the invitations from my hands.

"Wait—" I protest, but they don't listen.

Lady Eleanora has somehow ended up with one of the envelopes, and she is as quick to open it as her daughters. Her smile is smug, but I think I detect a bit of relieved worry as well. She must have heard of the masques and...feared not getting invited? It's too far-fetched to seem possible, but I know my mother's expressions, and there is definite relief in it now.

"Girls!" Lady Eleanora's eyes widen as she reads the letter. "Darlings, this could be your chance to catch the prince's eye!"

I blink at the expectation Lady Eleanora has for her daughters and bite back a surprised laugh or gasp—I'm not entirely sure which. The prince has met the princesses of Tepor or Ostium, some of the most beautiful women in all of the Seven Kingdoms, and might even have invited them to his masques, or even become betrothed to one of them. And yet, Mother is right: my sisters are pretty enough to compare, especially when draped in beautiful cloth and jewels.

"Three masques!" Mother's voice quivers as she reads the message. My sisters squeal, their eyes lit up.

I look away from their excitement across the square. Colors swirl from the lightweight summer dresses the women of Nubilus wear and the colorful displays of cloths, leathers, and other goods spread out on tables, peeking through the crowds inspecting them. Some vendors are already preparing for the autumn auctions with flags and signs above their shops.

"And where's *your* invitation?" Lady Eleanora's voice jerks on my attention just as I jerk on a lead to snap my horse out of a distraction.

I give her my most innocent expression, one I practiced on the way here. "I did not receive one, my lady." I almost grimace; lies do not come easily to me.

"Ha ha!" Haydée crows, leaning over to laugh with Carmen.

But Lady Eleanora narrows her eyes. "Why would they not invite you?"

"They must have made a mistake and forgotten me."

"Hmm." She raises her chin to peer down her nose at me again. "Or perhaps they didn't."

"You can't honestly think them forgetting you was accidental." Haydée laughs.

Carmen smiles at the joke, but her round face pinks when I catch her eye.

Although Haydée's comment helps my argument to Mother, my sisters' laughter still cuts through my heart. Ashamed of both my lie and my embarrassment, I duck my head. "Yes, my lady."

"Go home, Ella. You must have many things to do. And so have we. I think a trip to the bank first…"

I lift my chin before I can stop myself and catch the greedy glint in Lady Eleanora's eyes as she surveys the market stalls.

"Does this mean we buy new dresses for the masques, Mother?" Haydée asks eagerly.

"Yes, can we?" Carmen asks, her delicately featured face lit up.

Lady Eleanora inspects her younger two daughters. "Of course. If we find something that we like, darlings, of course we will buy them."

Panic churns my stomach, and I fight to keep from sticking my hand into my pocket and gripping the cloth bag there. She can't take the money I set aside for the auctions, because it's not at the bank. My nerves still tremble. Mother always finds a way.

But what can I say or do? Not only will no one listen to me, they will only ridicule and abuse me.

Lady Eleanora throws me a disdainful glance. "Why are you still here? Go. I have no desire to see you in town again unless your news is equally as good."

Cheeks burning at her cold dismissal, I find my sisters already three vendors down, admiring fabrics we'll never be able to afford. My sigh almost escapes this time, but I turn my back before I can release it.

With a pat to my dress pocket to make sure my envelope is

still there, I make my way to The King's Inn. I tie Flora in the
back alley and head up the path. The back door swings into a
darkened hallway, but a light ahead glows in the doorway to the
kitchen. The scent of baking bread and light smoke from the
cooking fire draws me there, and I dart through the low
doorway.

"Oh!" The girl in the room, about two years younger than my
nineteen years, jumps back from the open fire where she's stirring a huge, cast iron pot with a wooden spoon. "Faery's teeth,
Ella, you scared me!"

I giggle, earning a confused glare from my honey-haired
friend. She blows it back from her face impatiently, then swipes
at her face with the back of a hand and leaves a streak of something green across her forehead.

"Oh hush." She crosses to the large table in the middle of the
cavernous kitchen, slams down her wooden spoon, snatches up a
towel and points it at me. "I've got too much to do to let you
distract me today. I slept in." Annoyance creasing her nose in a
way that almost makes her look childish, she wipes her hands on
the towel, and tosses it down next to her spoon. Then she turns
to the table and pulls a heaping fistful of dough out of a large
bowl. She tears it in two and rolls each portion into a small log,
then sets them aside on a flour sack cloth. "What are you doing
here right now?" she asks while she works the dough.

Fighting the urge to help her, for my hands are dirty with
horse, I pull up a stool at the table and watch her work her magic.
Her skin glows white against the dark, classic rye dough Nubilus
is well known for. Dalia has put her own spin on it, of course,
sweetening it with honey and bringing out the richness of the
flour, the same flour and honey she feeds her yeast.

"Don't you have something to do? Like horses to ready for the
auction?" Dalia's tone bites just a little as she sets another two
mini loaves next to the first two.

"I have plenty of time still." I wave a hand through the air and then, beaming, pull out my invitation from my pocket and hold it out before her. "Look."

She darts a glance at it, then tosses another two loaves in line. "So?"

"So? Don't you see what this is?"

With one eye on the envelope, she shrugs a shoulder. "Something from the King to Lady Complains-A-Lot?"

Realization washes over me. "Oh! You thought—?" I hold it up again. "No. This is for me."

Forehead creasing, she pauses her dough shaping to inspect the envelope more fully. "To *you*?"

My grin widens. "Yes."

"Bu— why? How?"

"The prince is returning from his schooling in western Ardor, right?"

"Any day now. They haven't said exactly when." Dalia shapes another two loaves. The stew in the pot over the fire spits and bubbles, splattering against the back of the cast-iron stove, but she ignores it. "What does that have to do with an invitation to you?"

Quickly, I read the letter in the invitation to her.

"Masques?"

"Yes. Three of them."

"And you…wish to go?" Dalia's hands are slower this time in her task.

"I think it might be fun… But…"

"Lady Eleanora," Dalia finishes.

"She'll make it miserable for me."

Silence falls between us as Dalia realigns her loaves. Then she casts me a mischievous grin. "Maybe you won't tell."

"How would I attend?" I roll my eyes. Trust Dalia to always insert a bit of mischievousness in my life.

Dalia raises a brow. "It is a *masque*."

"They'd recognize me. A masque doesn't cover my hair or my

figure or dress. And she'll find a way to humiliate me." A shudder works its way down my spine.

Dalia's shoulders sag in momentary defeat. "You're right."

I chew on my thumbnail.

Dalia tilts her head. "You know, I make my own dresses."

My gaze flicks down her body in consideration. Her dress, although the color of pale dirt and made from simple flax, is expertly fitted to her body and the stitching is invisible. It's better fitting than my own, certainly.

"Don't judge me on this one." She puts her floured hands on her hips.

I open my mouth to argue but then shut it; instead, I meet her glowing gaze and smile. "And you're skilled. But I've got to go." I give her a wave and turn to leave.

"And plan on going to the masques!" she calls after me.

I laugh.

"I mean it!"

Leaving Dalia, I head toward the bank on Flora. I shouldn't even want to go to the masques, but I do. Just one. Though I am not of the caliber of women who will attend… No prince would want to dance with a woman who mucked stalls that morning.

Tying Flora at the front door, I pause to give her a pat on the neck. I fill my lungs with one last breath of the city air, breathing in the lingering scents of fresh-baked bread, rich stews, and sweet, Ardorian ale.

I release the breath with a rush. If I don't go through with this now, if I start to think about the costs too much, I'm not going to do it at all. And I can't afford to make that choice.

INTO THE LAKE

A mist descends with the rapidity of a sudden snowstorm. I squint, but can't see more than a half dozen feet in front of me. The seconds tick on, my heart loud in my ears as I search the ice for the hole that must hold Rus and Cito.

I speed up. For all I know, the huntsman could be just beyond it. He could be watching them die right now.

The cold has returned with a bite through my wet clothes, drawing out a bone-rattling shiver.

"Rus! Cito!"

The mist surrounds me now; I can't see far to any side. Tentatively, I advance. I've already revealed myself and gotten no answer from those I seek. Is the huntsman just beyond, waiting for me to walk into his deadly embrace?

My foot slips, and I fall to my bottom, barely managing to force my body backward instead of into the open water before me. Then I see it. At the edge of the hole, a hat bobbing in the water. Oh goddess have mercy.

Cito stands at the opposite side, frozen in fear.

His face says it all.

"Stay here!" I command as I tug off my cloak and shimmy out

of my wet boots.

Cito doesn't speak, and I jump into the water. Unlike the water nearer the shore, with its mix of warm and cold currents, this water is a thousand knives attacking me at once.

I bound upward with a shuddering gasp. Then I force air into my lungs and dive before doubt and fear overtakes me. I owe him my life.

Submerged, I open my eyes and wave my hands in the water to turn around. The water is clear; everything within a dozen feet is visible.

Yet no Rus.

My stomach clenches. I turn around and swim lower. The bottom looms toward me. No one. Then at the end of my turn, I see him.

Surprise steals a bubble of air from my lips that bobs toward the surface. Though my lungs burn, I strike out for him. It's been years since I swam the ice lakes, something that all kids do at least once. It's a quick way to bathe in Canens, although a painful one. It was always the hot baths afterward that I wanted.

In seconds that feel like years, I've grabbed Rus' arm, and I let buoyancy take us back toward the surface, kicking to aid it.

"Ow!" My grunt comes out in a water gulp as my head collides with the ice.

I turn onto my back, my body so cold my muscles begin to seize. My fingers weaken, and Rus' arm slips through my grasp. No. I force my stiff, reluctant fingers to tighten. I kick at the ice with my stockinged feet, but it's unrelenting.

I won't let him die like this. I won't die like this.

I crane my head around, searching for the hole we came through.

I kick to bring us a little ways away, but my lungs burn and my body stops obeying. Weakening further with every second, I claw at the ice with my fingers, dragging myself toward the hole —the hole that never seems to get any closer.

Something dark moves above me. Hope stirs in my gut.

"Here!" My words come out as small bubbles. My body weakens every second, seizing into ice. Blackness nudges at my existence.

I can't have come so far only to die like this, under the lake on the edge of Canens. I cannot die now, not when I have seen the escape Ardor offers.

An ache unlike any I've ever known before begins in my chest.

Where is the light to help me now? Where has it gone? When I need it, it abandons me?

A thump above me. I'm too tired to even lift my gaze. Still, I hold Rus' arm. I won't let him die like this; I can't.

Save me. Please save me.

With blinding force, the water around me erupts in light. My eyes creep open; I'm almost past caring.

You come too late this time. Too late to do anything but watch us die.

It's you, the light answers. *You call me, and I come. I am in you. Don't slumber, Winter. Rise and fight. Rise and break the ice that surrounds you, that infiltrates you. Your companions depend on you now. Your country depends on you.*

I blink and turn slowly to face the prince in the water with me. Illuminated by the light is a face—and it's relaxed in unconsciousness. No! Despair jolts through me. Above us the ice shatters.

Warm water sends hot coals into my exposed skin.

The shadow above reaches for us, hands grabbing and pulling. The light remains, but now illuminates me from the inside out. The ice seeps from my veins, burning from my chest out to my fingers and pouring onto the ice beneath. The shadow moves next to me, to Rus, pressing on his chest, pulling at him.

I want to tell it to stop, to leave him alone, but the blackness threatens again. Then there's pressure on my chest, pushing and releasing.

"Winter!" A voice close to my ear screams. "Wake up! We don't have time for you to—"

Breath rasps over my lips and tongue. A cough breaks free and won't stop. Rolling, I spit onto the ice, hacking until hands yank me up.

Someone else—Rus—coughs. With a hand on my shoulder, Cito leans over me, face dark with concern.

"What was that?" Cito asks warily. "In the water."

"What?" I wheeze and aim a wet gaze, teary from the efforts of my coughs, his way.

"That light," he says.

"What light?" Rus croaks, an accusatory note in his voice before bending over in a fit of coughs that has his entire body shaking.

I hesitate, allowing another coughing fit to overtake me to give myself time to answer. The light is in me. Is that what it said? A shudder runs down my arms, but it's not a chill. I feel warm but exhausted.

My skin burns as though in fever.

I force myself to my feet.

"Rus, we have to get you out of this cold." Cito steps over me and drags at the taller man. "Come, Ardor is close."

"Wait—" I choke out.

"For him to catch us?" Rus demands through a cough, his anger at me flaring back to life.

"You mean surrender to the huntsman?" Cito asks.

"The huntsman?" I blink in confusion. What has he to do with — Oh, yes. He's after us… I turn, scouring the Canens horizon, vaguely realizing that the fog has lifted, perhaps while I was under water. I shake my head. "He won't come after us. Not for a while."

"What? Why not?" Cito pulls Rus to his feet.

I lift a hand and point toward Canens' shore. "He can't follow past that."

Both men follow my finger, and their eyes widen.

Between us and my homeland is a twenty-foot crack splitting the ice. On the other side, a quarter mile away, the huntsman stands watching us atop his white horse.

His hard, determined gaze injects a chill into my spine and the burn of fury in my gut. I clench my fists at my side. If this light is in me, maybe I can use it to hurt him or hide our trail from him. Maybe it can do more than bring others back from the dead.

"Winter." Rus' voice is cold and wary. "Why are your hands glowing?"

I look down and turn my palms upward. In them is light. Two glowing orbs hovering atop my skin. It doesn't burn. It's not fire. It's simply light. I focus on it and it burns brighter.

"What are you doing?" Fear laces his words now.

"Stop, Winter," Cito says softly.

"I—" I shake my head at my hands. "I don't know what this is."

"It's magic; any fool can see that." Rus pauses to cough, nearly doubling over, his lungs rattling. He peers back up at me. "And it makes you a b-bigger hypocrite than I."

At his words the light flickers and dies in my hands. "I don't— I *don't* have magic."

Rus glares at me. "You have s-s-something." He gives a mighty shiver, and Cito grabs for him before his knees buckle.

Alarm flares in my gut. "Are you all right?"

Shivering, Rus groans and crumples to the ground, despite Cito's help.

"Here, let me help." As I reach for them, Rus recoils, putting up his hand to stop me.

"Don't touch us."

I freeze. "I—I didn't mean anything."

He glares at me. "Y-y-you made me f-feel guilty about…using the orb, Winter. And what m-m-magic have you been…h-hiding all along?" He grunts and drags himself upright with Cito's help.

"Let's get you to shore, sir, it's warm there," Cito says, holding him up.

Without another look my way, they start toward the Ardor shore.

"I'm sorry, I—"

Rus turns to silence me with a cold glare only marred by the chattering teeth below it. "I-I thought that…Elaina was r-revived with the o-or-orb, but maybe it was you. If magic c-c-corrupts, how c-c-corrupted are you? H-h-h-how m-m-much have you c-c-corrupted her?" He weaves in place, his anger only managing to help him force the words out, not warm him, if the blue tinge to his lips are any indication.

"I'm not—" I protest. "I don't know what this is. I do *not* have magic."

I follow them, reaching to take Rus' other side, but Rus yanks his arm away so hard that he falls into Cito and my hand grasps upon air.

I huff out an angry breath. "Please, Rus, don't—don't do this."

At his answering snort, I stop walking and let them draw ahead, surprised by the tears of frustration that prick my eyes.

Why am I begging? He has so obviously resented my presence from the start. He didn't want to rescue me from the *oubliette*; he doesn't want me now. I am a hindrance.

I trail them until they reach the spot where the ice drops off. Together, they stumble off the mini-cliff of ice into the water before I can warn them. They splash forward, Rus' dead weight dragging Cito almost down to his face in the water. Hurrying forward, I grab Rus' arm and lift his head from the waves.

I gasp. "Rus, you're ice."

His eyes barely parted, he peers up at me, too weak to pull away or even show his hatred of me.

On his other side, Cito disentangles himself from a wet cloak, scrambling to get it off his face and out of the water. He'll probably never go into the water again after this whole fiasco.

But if Rus isn't warmed soon, he'll die, I know he will.

I seize my chance and touch Rus on the face, holding his head out of the water.

Light, I don't know how to do this, how to summon you, but...he needs help. Even the warmth of Ardor isn't going to be enough to drive this chill from him.

Nothing inside me answers, and my hands remain lightless. I close my eyes and try again. "Please," I whisper. "Save him." I imagine a flame inside me driving outward into Rus like a fire's heat warms a room. It doesn't work.

I drop my head.

Then without warning, heat explodes within me. I choke on my breath as my eyes fly open. My hands, still pressed against Rus' cheeks, burn from within my bones.

Don't kill him!

Rus gasps. His eyes burst open, panic lighting them from within.

I cannot pry my hands away, and the light enters him so that he glows, just like Elaina did. And as abruptly as it began, the glow dies and my hands slip from his skin. Energy trembles through my skin, revitalizing me. A wave of dizziness drapes itself over me. I grit my teeth and wait for it to pass.

Rus coughs in my face and slumps onto my shoulder. Grunting, I stagger and grab his elbows, holding him upright. This time, he doesn't glow, and nor do I. But his eyes open and he blinks down at me as Cito hurries over and grips his other arm.

"Winter? Wha—? What happened?" He glances to Cito, then back at me, standing straight and tall, no longer leaning on either of us. "What happened?" He glances over his shoulder. "Did we lose him?"

My gaze slides to Cito, who stares at me with an expression I can't quite name. "Yes. We lost him. He's stuck in Canens."

Rus' body sags in relief. Then a slow frown creases his forehead.

"Come on," I say, turning, not wanting to see him remember

his hatred of me. "We need to get to shore."

I slosh through the water toward the rocks. The heat swells inside me, almost as though my body bloats with it. Is it because I used more of the light? I won't call it magic. Because I can't use magic. I cannot give in to it.

Yet it's so tempting to fix all our problems with one request…. Power warms my veins with every surge of my blood. If I asked it, it would answer, I know it.

No. I won't.

I steal a glance behind me. It doesn't matter that I'm saving lives with it; it will corrupt me until I begin to take lives, just like Blanche. If there is any hope of saving Canens—and making all my efforts worth it—then I cannot use magic of any kind. If I do… I pause. If I do keep using magic, I can't be a fit ruler; it would be impossible. But it still would be better than Blanche in power, a small voice in the back of my head whispers.

As I near the shore, I hesitate at sight of the rocks. The last time I touched them, the entire earth shook.

Rus pushes past me and climbs up the boulder. Atop it, he turns and offers Cito a hand. He narrows his gaze at me, still standing foolishly in the water. I try to read the emotions in his eyes, but I can't.

I drop my gaze, suddenly ashamed of myself for saving him. Ashamed of giving into the magic's lure again.

Should you have let him suffer instead? Die? the voice asks snidely.

As my gaze reaches his feet, a motion catches my eye. He extends his hand, fingers red and angry, and offers it out to me.

I hesitate but step nearer. I put one hand on the rock instead. It stays still.

"Give me your hand," Rus says impatiently, leaning down.

Finally, I allow Rus to half drag me up the boulder. He releases my hand as soon as both of my feet are on the dirt and small rocks littering the shore.

"Where did you leave her?" Rus asks, pulling off his cloak and holding it out like a dead animal. I don't know if the disgust in his tone and in the sneering curve of his lips is for the fur he holds between his fingers or for me.

"I—I told her to gather the horses."

He drops the cloak on the boulder we climbed and peers around.

"She's not here. Where is she?" Rus demands as if I should know.

Dread clenches my stomach. There's no way the huntsman could be here before us. He's trapped. Isn't he? But all I see before me are two horses tied to a tree. The third horse, along with Elaina, is missing.

"I don't know," I whisper.

Rus rolls his eyes and strides past Cito, heading straight for the woods.

Panic flares inside me, and my light responds. It's almost becoming expected, normal...familiar. My breath comes faster, and the light burns hotter. I gasp.

"Winter!" Cito reaches for me.

My skin flashes a warning, pricking me with danger. "Stop! Don't touch me, I—"

Cito holds up both hands, palms raised toward me. "It's all right. You're all right."

"No, no." Tears prick at my eyes as the light burns, swelling within me and seeping out. I clench my eyes shut. "I can't —stop it."

"Winter," he says calmly. "Winter, open your eyes. Look at me."

More out of control than ever before, I pry open my eyes. Tears leak down my cheeks as I stare at him. "Cito—"

"I know. Just take some slow, deep breaths."

Something sparks out of my fingers and I shriek.

"Shh, shh." He reaches out.

"No! Don't! You'll get hurt," I plead.

"Trust me, Winter," Cito says.

I look at him. He does invite my trust, alongside his calm tone.

"Trust me," he repeats. "I know what I'm doing."

I search his face, looking for hint of a lie, but I can find none. My heart beats as fast as a rabbit's within its bone cage.

"Take a deep breath, Winter. Stare into my eyes and breathe deeply."

I obey. The first breaths are hard, air only goes in a little ways to my lungs, then the next breaths are easier. With each filling of my lungs, the fire dampens, the light dims. Cito keeps talking, telling me how good I'm doing and how to focus on the air flowing over my tongue. Finally, my heart beats its normal rhythm. Tearing my gaze from Cito's, I inspect my fingers and find them normal. Relief courses through me.

"How did you know to do that?" I ask him.

He busies himself unbuckling the clasp from his cloak.

Voices drift over from the woods, washing over me with familiarity. He's found her.

Expression a bit relieved, Cito looks over his shoulder to where Rus and Elaina emerge from the trees.

"What were you thinking?" Rus demands, grabbing the reins of the horse above where Elaina holds them and slowing both her and the gelding.

"I had to grab the horses!" she retorts, snatching back at the reins. "You know, I've survived without you for the past several months!"

"Yes, and that's your own doing!" he answers.

"In Canens, no less!" Elaina adds.

Rus responds with something I can't hear.

Cito sighs and moves toward them, his weary expression mingling with relief, like he's tired of breaking up arguments between the royals but grateful they're back safe.

Without a look at me, he moves off toward his charges.

Toward the Heians. I'm the outsider, the one unworthy of a response. None of them wanted me with them, and I've almost gotten them killed several times.

Canens is dangerous enough with me. They defied the odds surviving, and then they saved me. We're in Ardor now, but the huntsman won't stop; he'll keep coming after us. Me.

I should leave them. And now, with my magic—or whatever this light is inside me—I *must* leave them.

Behind me, is the lake, and the huntsman is gone. Before me, the woods, dense and an unlikely exit. Between the two, a thin border of grasses and dirt that looks well enough defined to follow like a trail. If my knowledge serves me right, that way is east, toward the capital of Ardor, and toward the sea.

One of the horses approaches me. The gelding has tugged himself loose from his tree. I take him by the reins just under the bit.

He gives me a gentle look with his liquid brown eyes. "I know I know, I ought to leave them, but should I? Can I leave them?"

I look over at the trio from Heia again. They are happy amongst each other. Well, they will be once Rus and Elaina realize he's just happy to have found her safe.

They don't need me. Nor do I need them.

If I stay with them, I'll get them killed.

Yes. To stay with them is death for us all.

I shift the reins to my left hand and throw my left foot into the stirrup, my right over the saddle. Gathering them in my hands, feeling the horse bunch under me, I direct one more glance to Elaina.

She will be safe with them. Safer than I could ever make her by myself.

Finding that thought not as reassuring as I would like, I don't give myself time to doubt.

I spur the gelding into the surrounding trees.

SIR BIRCH

I push open the door and step into the mayor's warm office, wrinkling my nose at the heady scent of sweaty bodies and old food. In one corner is a table piled with a dozen dirty dishes, as if the mayor and his staff has been too busy or too lazy to bother cleaning up after yesterday's lunch.

"Catalus, where is that file I asked you about?" A fatherly looking man calls into the next room, his back to me as he rustles through a pile of papers on the sprawling desk. He mutters under his breath some words I don't catch when he doesn't receive an answer.

I let the door shut behind me, and the man straightens mid-mutter to turn at the sharp click. His face lights up, his eyes sparkling behind his half-moon wire reading glasses.

"Miss Ella, what a lovely surprise!" Sir Erik Birch drops the thick, leather ledger onto the desk behind him. "What brings you in today? I hope you have good news?" He spreads his arms out to me as if greeting a good friend or a daughter.

"Good morning, Sir Birch."

Approaching with the apparent intention of wrapping me in

his arms, he widens his eyes as I step back. He stops with a slight frown creasing his forehead and lets his hands fall to his sides.

"Hmm. Not the news I was hoping for then?"

With a gentle smile, I say, "If you don't mind, Sir Birch, I'm here on business."

"Oh? Business?" His expression turns to confusion, and he motions to the door adjoining the bank and his mayoral office. "Don't you want next door? Or the constable's down the way?"

I frown. "Why would I want the constable's?"

"Oh, I thought maybe your stables might have been mistakenly targeted in the break-ins."

"Break-ins?" I echo, stepping forward as my stomach clenches into tight knots. "Have any horses been stolen yet?" I need to warn Gavin, and then look into hiring a human guard. The dogs are great deterrents, but Gus is getting older, and—

"Not yet. Of course we deal with this leading up to every auction, so the bank has been busy with insurance claims and the constable with reports of suspicious activities." He shrugs as if it's not his problem, though if too many horses are stolen, or even one of the most anticipated horses of the auction, the entire event could suffer. And if the auction suffers, then Sir Birch and all of Nubilus suffers—and through that every one of Ardor's twenty-four Gelu Rigens breeders.

"Has the trespasser been found yet? Has security been offered to the stables in the auctions?" Perhaps I can get an armed guard for Aeneas Stables if they are making such offers.

"They haven't suggested that yet. But you'd have to be in the auctions for them to worry about you, my dear." Sir Birch's patronizing smile slides into place. "And you enter only the spring auctions. So what can I help you with today? Is it what I'm anticipating?" His eyebrows waggle up and down.

I bite my lip, having hoped that he would forget his son and his son's all-too-frequent mentions of marriage. I take a small breath of strength and step forward. "I'm here to enter the autumn auctions, Sir Birch."

His mouth drops open. "Excuse me?" He shakes his head as if he realizes how unmayoral he appears. "I mean, of course, Miss Ella. But you—are you sure your stock is qualified for it?"

The accusation stiffens my spine. "Yes, I'm sure, Sir Birch."

He purses his lips and considers me, his gaze lingering on the toes of my boots that peek out from under the hem, dirt still clinging to them. It travels to my dirty fingernails, and continues upward. I hide my hands in the folds of my skirt, but raise my chin defensively; when he meets my gaze it's to find determina-tion there, I hope.

"I don't wish to be indelicate, Miss Ella," he says in what must be an intentionally condescending tone, "but do you have the finances for entering the autumn auctions?"

"Yes, Sir Birch." My lips twitch up on the edges.

"Hmm." He narrows his gaze at me. "All of it?"

"Yes, Sir Birch."

His eyes round; he scans me again. "With you?"

"Yes." I motion to his ledger. "Perhaps we can start with the paperwork? I'd like to get this finished, as I have much to do at home still today."

"Oh, right." He aims a frown my way but walks around to the backside of his desk. For the next couple of minutes, he bustles around, moving papers back and forth, muttering to himself as if he doesn't know where he's placed something.

"You know, I spoke to Sallust just the other day about you."

I bite back a sigh and stare at his desk. A ledger lies open upon the table, displaying messy columns of numbers.

"He said he hasn't received your answer to his offer yet." Sir Birch raises his gaze to peer at me with that scolding, over-the-glasses look again that I've come to despise in my visits to him. "I know you don't have a father anymore, Miss Ella, so I feel it's my duty to tell you that it's not ladylike to keep a man waiting so long."

I crook a brow up, and then my tongue carries me away. "Isn't that something of which a mother might inform her daughter?" I want to clasp my hands over my mouth at the words, ones that might get me locked in my room at home, but I barely refrain from covering up one mistake with another.

Sir Birch's lips purse again, this time under eyes full of surprise. "Yes, well, some mothers and daughters don't have the relationships they ought either."

At the obvious chastisement, my face grows hot, and I drop my gaze.

He turns back to his desk. "Ah, here we are." He pulls out a sheet of paper that he's been shuffling around for the past five minutes. "It was there all along," he adds cheerfully.

I grind my teeth.

"I'll just need to see your deposit?" He frames it as a question, implying again that I don't have the funds.

Mutely, I reach into my secret pocket and pull out the cloth bag, my heart pounding with nerves. I have been shamefully secretive about this stash, having to slowly, over the months, trade coin for paper money at the bank next door or have Dalia do it for me—without Lady Eleanora hearing of it. If she knew, this money would never be safe, which is exactly why I couldn't keep it in the bank at all. Any money left there is money that she takes or money that shopkeepers can claim with her notes of debt.

My teeth grind in my ears, and I force myself to relax them. This money has stayed safe for months, thank the Lord, but now it's time to use it for its intended purpose. Still, a part of me aches handing it over, fearing that it still might find a way into Mother's grasping hands.

Surprise mingles with that glint of greed in Sir Birch's eye that I have never cared for. A shimmer I have seen even more often in his son. One more strike against Sallust. I don't think he cares so much for me as he does for the money and glory my stable might bring him. As one of only two dozen lawful Gelu Rigens breeders in the country, it will take marriage or an edict from King Greggory III in order to give Sallust and his father the illustrious career in breeding Gelu Rigens they hint at wanting. I've read the laws myself, and it's the only way to transfer a current breeding license, such as the one I've inherited from Father.

"Let's fill out this paperwork first; I'll need to know how many horses you plan on entering." He flips a page on his ledger where I can see the names of horses entered for the autumn auctions listed by stable and number.

"I have six." I pull out a piece of paper from my billfold and pass it to him. "Here are their names and information."

"Six? Are you sure?" He crooks an eyebrow up at me.

"Yes, sir."

He takes the money from my hands and flips through it. "And everything is in order with Aeneas Stables?" He pauses at a paper. "Your inspection is out of date, Miss Ella." He frowns over his spectacles at me again.

"I have supplied a certified copy of the most recent one, Sir Birch, and as soon as this month's inspection is completed, I shall have the Crown Inspector supply you with the newest copy."

He nods once over the inspection paperwork, where information as to the quality of my horses, the number of stallions, geldings, colts, fillies, broodmares, and pregnant broodmares are listed, along with their current training status and their bloodlines. Information regarding upgrades to the stables, employees, servants, and all other things associated with Aeneas Stables are listed on another sheet. I have supplied him with the full version, the legal requirement for me to enter any auction. Only because I am a woman running my father's business after his death am I required to abide by the convoluted and complicated laws of Ardorian inheritance.

As if he's read my mind, Sir Birch clucks his tongue. "This would all be so much simpler if you married, Miss Ella."

I suck a breath in through my nose and position a smile on my lips. "Yes, sir. But I haven't."

His lips tighten before he taps the papers into place together. "Running out of time though."

He sets about filling out paperwork and noting my horses in the ledger while my stomach squirms at the sight of their names going under the heading "Autumn Auctions." Still, I can't help but smile just a little.

"How much is the fee?" I hold up my pouch. Sir Birch points to the number he's filled out on my papers, and I carefully count out each bill, the equivalent of seventy-five silver coins for each entry. It's twenty-five more than the spring auction fee per head, but I've prepared for this. Seeing so much of my hard-earned and harder-saved money heaped on Sir Birch's desk with no guarantee of it coming back to me makes my forehead break out in sweat.

"The rules are a little different for autumn auctions, Miss Ella," he says. "No refunds after ten days before auction and you cannot change any of your entries after that date, no matter the reason. If you do, or if you remove your horses from sale, you will be penalized for one calendar year and unable to sell in Nubilus or at any of the King's auctions." He pauses to peer over his glasses at me once again. "Are you *certain* you'd like to enter? While the average sale price *is* higher than the spring auctions, are you *certain* your horses can command that kind of attention?"

"Yes, sir, I know my stock to be—"

He holds up a hand. "Don't mistake me, Miss Ella. Of course I believe you have excellent horses. But this is the autumn auction.

It's much different, much more competitive than the spring auctions. You might not have the support that you've found at the spring auctions. The clients expect the best. Not every stable is of the caliber to enter. Entries come from all around the country. And the entry fee is non-refundable. As a first-timer, you must expect that at least one of your horses won't sell, especially if they don't draw well."

"I'm certain." My horses are just as good as any other entered, I guarantee it, regardless of the auction position they draw. But let Sir Birch think what he will.

"Well, if you're sure," he says in a disappointed tone. He bends over the ledger and slashes a few ink marks across the top and bottom. I watch as he heats a stick of wax over his lantern's flame and smears two spots of wax on the paper, one on top and one on bottom, which he presses his pinkie ring into. Then he rips the paper in two and delivers the bottom half to me. "Your copy, Miss Ella."

"Thank you." I read over it, making sure everything is correct, from the date to the number of entries, to my name and my stable's name.

"A word of caution, my dear," Sir Birch says. "Unless you have bred all your mares to a stallion from Lord Sarcina's stable or from an even more magnificent stable I've yet to hear about, your animals will struggle to stand out from the rest. You can braid all the pretty bows into their manes and tails that you like, polish their hooves until they shine, but we will have colts and fillies from every stable in Nubilus up for auction, including Lord Sarcina's own.

"Are your animals descendants of Argentum like his are?" His patronizingly raised brows drive spikes of fury into my gut. He spreads his hands before him and shakes his head like the puppets used to entertain children in the town square.

"No," I force out.

His sympathetic smile widens. "It's not too late to withdraw." He puts out a hand for the paper he's given me. "You can go buy a few pretty dresses for the masques. Perhaps your luck will be better there, if you insist that my son is not good enough for your hand in marriage."

"I never said that, Sir Birch." His provocation is making it hard for me to stay calm. In truth, I have been cautious to give Sallust Birch any type of answer at all, refraining from any hint at yes or no. But as time marches on, it's harder and harder to hold him at bay, not only due to his father's interference, but due to the fact that time before my twenty-second year grows short.

"Maybe you could put it aside for a dowry?" he suggests. "It's not much, but some might take you for it, coupled with the stables."

My mouth parts. How dare he?

"Sallust has asked me to remind you of his offer, Miss Eleanora. He is willing and ready to marry you, even without a dowry; he is simply awaiting your answer."

Teeth grinding, I try to hold back my frustration at his determination. I'm sure he's merely concerned at his son's future, as well as his, but I don't want to marry Sallust. And, at the moment, I don't want to marry at all.

"Is that all, Sir Birch?" I manage through tight lips.

"What?" His forehead creases, almost as if he's uncertain as to how I might be offended. "Oh, yes, if you insist on your entry, that will do. Don't lose that paper, Miss Ella."

I carefully fold the paper and place it in my cloth pouch, then return the moneybag to my pocket. "No, sir. Good day." Fuming, but oddly satisfied, I stalk from the mayor's office, grateful that my courage at least hasn't failed me today.

I only make it to the middle of the square before a sudden bump from the crowd sends me staggering two steps aside.

"Oh, I'm so sorry, Miss Ella, I didn't see you there." Sallust

Birch holds my elbows in his hands as if to steady me, though I am quite steadied on my feet.

I put a proper amount of distance between us and say politely, "Good morning, Sallust."

"I see you just came from my father's office." He smiles, his wide face spreading wider.

"Yes, I did. I just spoke to your father." I wince almost as soon as the words emerge from my lips. *Why* did I say that?

"Oh you did? That's wonderful news!" Sallust fixes me with an earnest expression. There's something hopeful in him that I don't want to crush, but as soon as that thought flashes through my head, he scrutinizes me, reminding me of how he makes me feel like he's imagining a breeding between a prized mare and his best stallion.

I know Sallust; I watched him grow up from afar. He can flatter like the best nobleman, loves to hunt, fish, and waste his days in sport, tagging along with dukes and other titled gentry instead of learning his father's business. I know that he has flitted through many of the young women in Nubilus—so many that I don't want to be the next. But he knows nothing of me except that I own a stable he would love to control.

"What were you talking to Father about?"

"Oh, nothing really," I answer.

"Nothing? Did Father not speak to you of anything in particular?"

Innocently, I shake my head, and not wanting to lie again today, change the subject. "I'm sorry, but I must be going. I have so much work to do."

A line cuts into Sallust's brow, his expression turning from eagerness to something else. If I knew him less well, I might consider it hurt. But he is too arrogant to be hurt. Instead, the hard glint in his eye suggests something nefarious to me.

"Excuse me," I say, for he blocks my path.

Finally, Sallust steps aside, his eyes dark in thought. I bob my head at him but avert my eyes from his attentions; as soon as he talks to his father, he'll want to know why I lied. There is no winning here for either of us; I will not marry him, and he must stay disappointed.

I must remain single as long as I can. I must.

8: MAGISTER

LAKESIDE

I drop to my knees at the edge of the grass. The only time I tracked anything through dirt and grass and over rocks and rivers was when the Queen sent me on a quest for a few special ingredients that she couldn't acquire in Canens. I have eaten strange things in my quests. It is my habit to avoid people as much as possible through those journeys, to hunt and survive off the land if at all possible. Rarely was I forced into villages and towns, except to discretely ask for information regarding my quests.

I stand and brush half-heartedly at the knees of my brown trousers.

Tracking animals is not like tracking humans. And tracking over these conditions is nothing like tracking over snow.

Although the Queen detested my decision to return to the Manor and speak to her before pursuing her stepdaughter, it afforded me the opportunity to properly pack.

Irritation brews in my chest. I almost had them. Then that girl's witchcraft broke the ice; there was nothing else it could be. When has the ice between Canens and Ardor ever cracked? Not only cracked, but severed all the way through and moved apart from each other, leaving a gap that even my Gelu Rigens horse couldn't jump. It would have been death to one or both of us to attempt so.

Her witchery forced me to return and ride around the lake while those I hunt fled into Ardor without pursuit.

A chill ripples over me as if a cold breeze blows in, but it's only my unease. I vaguely remember an oft-quoted prophecy of the countries becoming one and barriers between them being severed; I wish I could remember it more clearly. The Queen has long considered her stepdaughter's life and death to be foretold in prophecies. But could this severing be a precursor to what the prophecies foretell?

I push aside my thoughts and the chill that comes along with them, determined not to let it interfere with my decision making. Prophecies are an uncertain mixture of falsehood and facts. But here before me is true evidence of their flight. A few days old, but there nonetheless. None in all the Seven Kingdoms have my ability as a tracker, and now I need every last skill in order to determine these events.

On the grassy bank beside the Ardorian lakeside, I scrutinize the scattering of prints both human and horse. There are far too many to make sense of them, but if I move toward one of the paths leading away from the lake, there are tracks where several horses have ridden off into Ardor's forest. Continuing my search, I trace one trail leading from the lake's shore off alone between the forest and the frozen lake. Deep in thought, I return to the other tracks and follow them a little ways before coming to my conclusion.

They have split up. And I cannot tell which horse the princess has mounted and which the others have taken.

I blink back the image of Her Majesty's fury as I confessed my failure in killing those she left alive by sheer necessity. I cannot fail again. I will not return to her empty-handed. She asked for her stepdaughter's heart; I will give it to her.

At the lake's edge, I squint at the ice as if it can tell me something I missed, something the earth does not. The ice stops about twenty feet out, where large bergs float, bobbing ominously. The lakeside is still, and water lilies dot the edge, nestled safely against the rocky shore. Frogs and fish live amongst them, despite their proximity to death should they travel just a few dozen feet away.

The sun catches a spot of blue on the surface of the ice. Dark blue, the color of the frigid water.

The girl's witchcraft broke more than just the chasm between Ardor and Canens. Perhaps someone fell in. I can only hope so. And hope that it was not the one I seek. If I return without the princess' heart, the Queen will take mine instead.

I cast my lot. If the group separated, it was because the princess did not care about her rescuers and they cared too little to follow her. She will have gone off alone.

A small smile plays on my lips as excitement flames the fire inside me.

This is the hunt.

This is my purpose.

ARRIVED

I cannot stop; I don't dare stop.

Even though I know magic exists in me now—some strange ability to heal or something of the kind—I fear the huntsman even more now than ever before.

If only the lake had swallowed him whole.

I have not seen him. Yet. It's the absence which, surprisingly, frightens me more than seeing him approach did. There he was a man following me, but with him gone, he becomes a spirit, a warlock, a demon with me in his sights.

Could Blanche have given him magic? Could he have returned to her and could she have cast a spell? With such skills, he could be waiting for me ahead.

Now that I recognize magic and realize the ease of its capabilities, which Blanche always hid from everyone, I fear it more than ever before. Why did she not perform her spells openly and subdue everyone with displays of her greatness? Surely Blanche is more powerful than me? What does she fear? It was my father that hated and feared magic, not her. She can make her laws however she pleases; she could subdue the people of Canens, and yet she hides her abilities and rules through stealth and manipulation.

I worry at my lips, chewing on them until they are a raw, bleeding mess. I must continue until he cannot follow me. Until I am safe. Yet when and where will that be?

As the sun sets at the end of a hungry two days, we crest a hill. At the top it offers views that I thought myth: green grass and patches of towering trees, fields of flowers and crops, and spread out amongst those fields, are Ardor's famed Gelu Rigens. Beyond them is a gray city on another hill in the distance. Farther still is a blue blur with white clouds streaked above it. The sea? It must be, although even squinting at the sight doesn't make me sure.

As we descend the hill, I inspect a field of horses, eyeing the man mounted nearby just as he eyes me. He shifts his weapon from his shoulder to his thigh. None of the Gelu herds are ever alone. Every time I have passed a field of the famed horses, there has been at least one rider armed with bows, arrows, sword, and knives. Each looks formidable, usually a man I would avoid passing in the street; they are armed guards.

I glance down at myself. I am dry now, but my appearance is bedraggled and unkept at the least. I've kept my fur cape, for I have used it as a pillow and blanket with the chilly nights, but my white gown is tattered and thin, contrasting with the thick boots that make my feet sweat. I have tied a square of fabric I found in the saddlebag around my head to keep the heat off my scalp, but I still sweat and itch at the sun's glare.

Under the guard's prolonged gaze, I feel naked and ashamed. I avert my gaze, duck my head, and ride on. The gelding—Raven, I call him, to remind me of Blanche's pursuit—plods on like the nag he is compared to these animals.

Still, the horses themselves are enviable enough that I sneak another glance. They are so valuable they are guarded from their own people. Of course, Father once told me that stealing one Gelu in Ardor is equal to a lifetime imprisonment and sometimes even death. I discretely inspect the guard's horse. Although modest, and suffering knock knees, it looks like the ones in the fields. It makes sense he would be mounted atop a Gelu Rigens, the fastest horses in the Seven Kingdoms, for if someone stole another, how else would he chase them down?

That's what the crossbow is for, I answer myself. Why chase them down when you could shoot them in the back instead? That must be the "punishment by death" Father was talking about.

I chuckle dryly under my breath and feel relieved at my ability to laugh given my circumstances. It's a very good thing I stole my unremarkable gelding straight off the Ardor coast from three Heians instead of Ardorites. I permit myself a little grin at the thought.

My stomach growls, interrupting my enjoyment. I haven't found food in all of my travels. I haven't dared go into any town yet, but I must soon, for I've eaten all the food the saddlebags offered.

We pass a bush with bright red berries. My mouth waters, but I resist the temptation to try them, for they might as well poison me as nourish me. I know far too many berries that are deadly, thanks to my stepmother and her growing house, but I don't know enough about any Ardorian species to know which ones here will kill me. And this type is one I've never seen before.

"I won't eat anything I haven't seen anyone else eat," I tell Raven's twitching ears. "Not that we have that chance, do we, boy?"

His ears flick forward again.

Sighing, I drag a hand down his mane and lift my gaze to the horizon. The sun is setting behind us as we ride east toward the sea and the capital. If I can make it to Nubilus, to the palace, I can find the King and Queen of Ardor and ask them to ally with me against Blanche.

My stomach clenches as it does every time I think of the approaching confrontation. Will they believe I am who I say? And that I should be trusted?

But they're the only hope I have. And chances are, I will run straight in to the very three I just left. Rus said he wanted me to bring Elaina there should he and Cito die. Yet, maybe since all three of them live, they will simply return home and not say hello their family.

I chew on my lip and wince. I'm not sure if that's the better solution or the worse. At least they could vouch for me, tell the King and Queen who I am, confirm me to be the princess and rightful heir to the Canens throne. On the other hand, Rus hates me and they might not choose to. He probably cheered to find me gone. Perhaps he's upset I took the third horse though.

I pat Raven's neck. He snorts. Probably wishing he'd never walked up to me and put the idea in my head.

Perhaps it would be best if Rus and Elaina showed up in Nubilus before me. I am so ignorant of court life and royal proto-col. My father never taught me much, my mother died during my birth, and I only had a nanny until Father married Blanche. Soon after, she had sent the woman away, convincing Father that my nanny taught me lies. As soon as Father died, Blanche locked me in my room, halted all my studies, and made me her prisoner. She certainly succeeded in crippling her truest enemy.

I sigh. Even with my limitations, I must be able to convince the King and Queen of Ardor that I don't mean to betray them as soon as I return to the Canens throne. They have been betrayed by Canens for far too long, but I won't be the one to do it again. I have to convince them that Canens is worth saving and that our curse is worth breaking. We still have the adamas mines in the north, more accessible if the curse falls. I might be able to convince the King and Queen to ally if we offer them gems from the mine. I'd agree to that for the next hundred years if they would help dethrone Blanche.

I would agree to nearly anything at this point if it meant a better life for the people of Canens. It's not that I desire to be a queen; someone else could do a better job. But I am the rightful heir. If protecting Canens means marriage to Prince Brann, I will offer it. If it means being queen consort to the prince and never reigning at all, I will do it. I just need King Greggory and Queen Ada to believe me. They must believe me, or I can do nothing.

If only I knew how to use magic like Blanche, I could disguise myself and—

No! I gasp aloud at my own thoughts, clapping a hand over my mouth so loudly that it echoes in the woods around me like a slap and Raven jerks up his head.

"How can I even think that?" I ask aloud for his ears. "I will not allow this magic to corrupt me. I will not become Blanche, deceiving everyone at every turn. No. I am not her. I will not become so."

The gelding snorts long and rattling. His step is lagging, and the sun is almost completely gone now. We need to find a place to rest tonight. It'll be another long night under a tree, I suppose.

"Come on, Raven, just awhile longer, and then you'll have oats tonight."

His ears perk up.

Our emergence from the woods a few minutes later takes us both by surprise. Raven halts with a jerk, and I lean back at the sight before us. It's almost completely dark now, but city walls are only a few miles before us, stretching out from one side to the other. It must be Nubilus. We can just reach it before nightfall.

"Let's go." I nudge Raven forward. "Before they close the gates for the night."

He shakes his head but seems to understand and picks up his pace. Just before full dark, we slip through the gate into Nubilus, and it closes behind us.

INSPECTION

I am up far before the sun, lighting a lantern and splashing cold water on my face while a full moon shines, unabated by clouds, through my window. It's going to be a beautiful day ahead.

Gus, the only dog allowed inside the house, greets me with a wag of his tail before I climb out of bed. The loyal dog has been my friend for almost ten years now, and after Father's death, I wouldn't have survived with him.

When Father died, Gus saved me from my loneliness. And, for a short time, a secret friend I met in the woods. It was strange, but I was out riding one day when my horse threw me. She was a silly little horse, prone to startle, and caught me by surprise. But the true surprise had been when a boy just a few years older than me returned her to me minutes later, as I sat nursing my twisted ankle. After a bit of a rocky start, we began chatting, and by the time we parted, we were close friends. We met every day until he moved away for schooling. It almost felt harder to let him go than it was to lose Father. I clung to him and wept, and I swear that his tears mingled with my own.

My lips turn down as they do every time I think of Hadwin

and our long-lost friendship. He wrote to me for a little while, but I haven't heard from him in five years now; he's forgotten me, like everyone else in Nubilus seems to have done. Everyone but Sir Birch and his son...

And Gus. The dog pads behind me toward Father's study, where I set down my lantern on the desk and sink into the leather chair behind it. Every time I sit here, I remember Father laughing over something I'd said or walking in to find him bent over his books with a deep furrow between his brows.

Lantern glowing upon the desk, I pull the thick stable ledger for this year toward me and begin my task of triple-checking the numbers while blinking sleep out of my eyes. Not long later, Gus whines and nudges my hand, reminding me that he hasn't been outside yet.

"All right. You're right. I need to take care of morning chores early anyway. The Crown Inspector will be here soon enough." Standing, I sigh and stretch, then leave the ledger on the desk to take Gus outside.

As soon as we step out from the house, Gus strolls off to lift his leg. I continue toward the stables; Gus will catch up later.

The sun is just nudging over the horizon, and the sky is barely blushing above the sea, making the water sparkle with pink smudges. Even tense with worry over the inspection, I pause to enjoy the sight before resuming my journey to the stables. The other dogs greet me with friendly snuffles, informing me that nothing is wrong and no one has visited overnight.

When I open the stable door, the familiar almost-silence of horses breathing in the early morning greets me. I set to work unlocking stall door tops and waking the horses. Before I'm done, Gavin emerges from his room beside the tack room, rubbing a hand over his eyes.

"Morning," I say to him. "The Crown Inspector is here this afternoon."

He nods, stoic as always. I think I told him yesterday anyway.

Smothering a yawn, he trudges past me and off toward the opposite end of the barn. I let him take over opening up the doors while I turn to the feed room and begin mixing breakfasts. Though I will change before the inspector arrives, I won't have time for a full bath. And he will want to see me looking proper and well kept. Like a lady. I bite back a snort at that. No other lady in Ardor runs a stable.

I focus on my tasks for the morning, and soon the horses are fed and watered, the stalls are clean, and I'm leading one of the pregnant broodmares to the pasture when hoofbeats sound on the dirt road to the stable, and Gus sends up his alarm. My heart leaps into my throat at the sight of the Gelu Rigens Equine Crown Inspector riding his immaculately bred and groomed gelding my way.

I glance at the sun low in the sky, remnants of a sunrise still lingering. He's hours earlier than he usually is. Even as my heart flutters in my throat so fast I think I might faint, a smile rallies to my lips, and I lift a hand in a wave. Only then do I realize which inspector has arrived this morning, and my heart sinks to the ground, where my broodmare trods on it. Two Crown Inspectors hold the position that can inspect my stables, and one is more forgiving than the other. Today I've been assigned the one who believes that no woman should run any business, and that I have no right to take advantage of the laws as I am doing.

"I'll just be a moment, sir. I must put Tono out to pasture here," I call out to him.

He barely dips his chin my direction, his attention already on the stable behind me, but then his gaze darts back to me, and his eyes widen only to narrow.

Though my practiced smile stays in place, I grown inwardly. I had intended to change in the hour before his arrival. Maybe if I detour around back, I can still—but no. My dress is up at the house, and there's no way that I can get to it and back without him noticing. He won't allow Gavin to show him the stable either. By law, it must be me.

Oh well. It's only one mark, and I need twenty-four more to fail me.

I unhook the lead from the mare's halter and steal a moment to watch her lumber away. Wishing I could go with her, I turn and trudge back up to the stables. The inspector has not dismounted, as if waiting for my return.

"Good morning, sir. You're earlier than I expected." Trying to keep the chastisement out of my tone, I step up and hold his horse's reins.

His already thin lips grow thinner as he pauses to give me a glare before dismounting. I flip the reins over the gelding's head. And when I look back at him, my eyes round. He's stepped in a pile of manure that I swear wasn't there when I put the mare to pasture.

"Oh no," I whisper.

Disgust dripping from his features, he glares down at his boot, then makes a show of walking to a nearby fence post and scraping his boot on it. "Well this morning seems to be starting as expected."

I cringe. Two marks against me already, one more thing I'll have to clean later, and we haven't even begun the inspection. "Would you like me to stable your horse?"

"Yes." He tugs his formal riding jacket down over his hips. "And some oats, if you would. We were rather rushed this morn-ing." His golden eyes narrow at me.

Oats? He expects me to feed his horse for him?

"Of course, sir." Somehow, I manage not to choke on the words.

But if oats are all it will take to pass this inspection, I will gladly feed his horse. I pat the animal's neck. He shouldn't suffer because his owner didn't plan ahead.

I run my hand over the gelding's smooth, trimmed muzzle.

"I'll go do that now. You can, of course, begin the inspection while you wait."

"Just a moment." He reaches into the saddlebag and pulls out a small leather book and a charcoal pencil. "All right. Go ahead and take him. I'll start making some notes."

"Of course. If you give me a few minutes, I'll make sure Gavin knows you're here as well." Scraping the bottom of the bin for my remaining politeness, I smile at him again then turn and walk his horse into the stable. I keep the smile on my lips until they ache, for if I let it go, I might not get it back again. I put him in an empty stall with clean straw, which I readied last night for this purpose.

It takes me a few minutes, but I water the gelding and feed him breakfast, resigning myself to his owner's request as I do. The inspector knows my finances down to the last copper, but he demands I feed his horse, a horse boarded at the King's stable. He could give his gelding all the oats he could eat there.

I find Gavin walking by the tack room and tell him of the Crown Inspector's early arrival.

His eyes widen with alarm.

"It's all right," I say though it's anything but. He's caught me unaware, and it's clear to all of us.

Gavin's gaze flicks up and down my body, lingering on my hair. It must be woefully out of order with the wind this morning and my rush out of the house.

"I suppose I'll get a mark down for my appearance, but everything is in order, right? Go ahead and finish up with the chores you can. I'll try my best to finish with him quickly."

Concern written on his face, Gavin nods. He clears his throat. "Mistress Ella, your sisters appear to be on their way down from the house."

I groan. "Honestly?"

He nods.

"Well, I assume they wish to ride then. Intercept them if you can, and tack up Midnight and Moonlight for them, should they ask. At least that will get them out of my hair when we go up to check out the books." I pause as Gavin hurries off to prepare for their arrival.

Speaking of hair... Frowning, I smooth my hand over my head and realize with a groan that I put my ugliest rag over my hair this morning in order to keep it clean so I might a good impression on the inspector. I tug the rag from my head and clench it in my fist. That didn't work.

Frustrated, I plaster a painfully forced smile onto my lips and head back outside to the Crown Inspector.

On the way through the stable, I see five violations. The water trough hasn't been filled yet and is under the halfway mark (it's required to be no less than halfway full at all times), the pile of manure his gelding left hasn't been cleaned (the entry to the stable is always required to be in pristine order, ready for the King's visit), the dogs have mysteriously disappeared (we are required to have no less than five guard dogs on duty and/or one armed guard for the stable), one of the lantern's glass has a crack in it and yet it's still burning (no cracks in the glass are allowed for fear of fire), and, perhaps worst of all, I'm not dressed like a lady (the owner of the stable is required to be dressed like a lady or gentleman at all times).

Usually it's only the last item in that list which I never fully meet. I think the rule is there just to keep women from running a stable at all. What woman can groom a horse in a full skirt and proper shoes? I scoff. I'd rather take the failing grade on that requirement, as I always pass on everything else.

I find the Crown Inspector at the paddock nearest the stable entrance, scratching his pen against his notebook. As I approach, patting one hand over my head again, I realize I still hold the rag in my fist and stuff it into my tunic pocket. Then I try to pretend that everything is in order.

The Crown Inspector doesn't look up at my approach but

continues to jot notes in his book, so I clear my throat and wait for his attention. Finally, after several long moments of scribbling, he turns to me.

"Well. Shall we start down here at the stables? I've already begun, so I might as well finish."

Inside, I wince. Just where all the violations I just saw are. "Perhaps we should work from outside in?"

He narrows his eyes but shakes his head. "No. It's a bit too chilly for me out here. By the time we get through the stable, I'm sure the sun will have risen more fully."

"Of course, sir. Let me take you on the tour. Not much has changed since our last inspection, though."

He sniffs and turns up his nose before scribbling down something else.

Within minutes of stepping inside, he's found everything I saw on the way to collect him and a dozen more violations.

Unlike the other inspector, who chooses not to inspect the little things on every single visit, this inspector is downright merciless. Technically, the Ardorian Possident Law requires the inspector to check off each stall as properly mucked, to measure the distance between the muck pile and the stable (for health reasons), and weigh the feed to confirm a month's supply is on hand to last until next inspection.

This inspector steps into the feed room and pulls out a scale, then settles in to make his own calculations.

Judging by the scribbles in his notebook, this is the worst inspection Aeneas Stables has ever had.

11: BLANCHE

CEARA

"Troublesome girl," I mutter at my scrying mirror. "Why won't you appear for me?"

At my words the fog in the mirror swirls and thickens. I watch a few more minutes, hopeful that the princess will appear after my searching for her image for more than a quarter hour.

Nothing but fog. Gritting my teeth, I step away before I lose my temper and lash out at the mirror—physically or magically. Scrying requires patience, and my patience is at an end with that girl.

Mirrors of all shapes and abilities reflect my image within this room, a dozen queens of unsurpassable beauty gazing back at me. For a moment, I hold my crowned, golden head high and survey myself, then as I take a step and wince, the beauty of the images shatter.

Blasted girl. If only I had killed her when I had the chance a few weeks prior. Then I wouldn't be searching the Seven Kingdoms for her now. Though the King's Curse foretells death to any who kill a Canens royal heir, and I was wise not to tempt that fate. All is lost if I die, after all. But if only I had been able to treat my wound faster so the muscles weren't so damaged before I could attend them with my healing herbs.

If only I had enchanted some other wolves to kill her. Perhaps she would be dead instead of a thorn in my side now.

I'll find a way to heal them, and then I'll be better than new.

A gasp escapes me as I put my weight on my injured leg too fast.

"Still hurts?" A familiarly smug voice drifts through the room to my ears.

Halting, I look up and around, but I can't find the owner of the voice. "Reveal yourself!" I demand in my most imperious voice.

"Tsk tsk," the voice answers, clearly amused. "Nursing a less visible wound from that fight, aren't you?"

"If you want my help finding your ingredients, you'd best stop tormenting me," I snap, suppressing the urge to set my hands upon my hips like a petulant child.

"Fine." The voice sounds both exasperated and amused now. There's a faint click, then a swish, and a woman dressed in a pale blue dress with small gems stitched upon it materializes a few feet away. Her hair is curled and past her shoulders today, her skin gleaming and pale, and her eyes match her dress, making her look every inch the Great Fae she is. "But it's not my fault you got injured, you know." She crooks an already arched brow at me. "Not my fault at all. Had you done as I instructed—"

"As you instructed?" I laugh darkly while waving her words aside. "You didn't instruct anything, that's the problem." I narrow my eyes at her. "Why don't we have a little heart-to-heart? And you can tell me what I really need to know."

"Well that depends. Have you caught your princess yet?"

I clench my jaw for the briefest of seconds. "My huntsman has tracked her to Ardor. They made it across the lake."

"Yes, well that's not news."

"He's tracked her to Nubilus."

The faery puts her hand to her chin in thought. "Ah. I wonder if the girl thinks she has friends there." Ceara the Great Fae laughs a mocking laugh. "What a thought! A Canens princess being welcomed by her worst enemies."

I allow myself a smile. "Well the girl is naïve. She has no idea what we've done to the country of Ardor in the past. None at all."

"Of course, that puts your huntsman in a rather difficult spot too, doesn't it?"

"Oh, he can care for himself; I'm not worried about him."

"No, probably not worth your time."

"Let's be done with this banter, faery. Tell me what I need to know. Last time you kept things from me, and I won't have that again. Not if you want my help."

The faery gives a crooked smile and waves her hand through the air. Two large glasses appear before us. "Take one." She nods to the one closest to me.

Becoming more annoyed at the faery's continued distractions, I snatch the glass from the air and hold it. "What do we need to break the Canens Curse? You told me we needed the princess' blood, but not for what or how much or even how to collect it. And that's your mistake, not mine."

"Drink, drink, Queenie; I didn't poison it."

Gritting my teeth, I consider throwing the drink in the faery's face, but what would that accomplish? We've taken a blood oath to complete this task together. Making an enemy of her would be foolish indeed.

Reining in my temper, I take a small sip. At the sweet, cherry flavor, warmth floods through my body, starting at my tongue and traveling down my throat, burgeoning out from my stomach and toward my toes. It fades as slowly as it began, and I stare into the glass. "What is this?"

"Not poison," Ceara replies, toasting me with her glass. "I find it to be a wonderful restorative brew when the aches of too much spell casting become overwhelming or I endure a difficult fight with a monster."

Raising a brow, I move toward her. I stop. Look down at my leg. The pain is gone. I lift my gaze to the faery.

The faery smirks. "So, down to business then?"

"Yes, please." I sip from the glass again to cover up my impatience, but also because I'm curious if the drink will continue to heal my body. I have so many injures from past fights that linger. "And I need all the information about these potion ingredients. Why I need to collect them, how we will use them, and—"

"Everything. I understand." Ceara sits down on the edge of a table that holds a heavy mirror which I have been repairing in my spare time and gazes down into it. "You want to know all my secrets."

"No." I shrug with feigned carelessness. "Not all of them. Just what is needed to break the Canens Curse."

"Of course." She gives me a slanted look over her own glass. "I wouldn't dream of polluting your mind with information you don't need to know."

I snort into my drink, then toss back the last of it.

"Well that's quite an unqueenly sound to make."

"I tire of this banter. Tell me. I don't have any more patience."

"And that is your problem, Queenie!" Ceara exclaims. "You don't have the patience you need. You didn't wait for me to tell you what to do with the princess, and so now we must find out what to do to fix your mistake."

"My mistake?" I demand through clenched teeth. "We've already established that my only mistake is trusting you and your half-told information. You don't have a spell, do you? If you did, we wouldn't be fooling around with—"

"I have a spell," Ceara says stiffly. "But I don't need you. If you won't help, I'll simply find someone else."

I study the faery from her perfectly coifed hair to her elegant gown and slippers. "You do need me. If you didn't, you wouldn't be here, asking for my help. And you wouldn't have tricked me into a blood oath."

The faery doesn't answer, but turns aside to pick at a gouge in the table she perches on.

"What are you getting out of this?" I narrow my eyes. "Why help me?"

"The truth?" The faery points her finger at my glass and the liquid swells up from the bottom toward the top. "There are certain limitations the Fae endure."

"Limitations?"

"Of course. We are not invincible, despite what humans think." She shrugs, but there's a tension in her motion that belies her nonchalance. "All magic has limitations, all magic casters have limitations."

"Well of course. For humans." I frown at Ceara. "I thought the Great Fae didn't have such limitations."

"*All* magic has limitations, Queenie."

My face heats at the nickname. Ignore it. Ignore her taunts. "Well tell me why you need me then."

"There's a pesky little Fae kingdom law, the *regina maledictum* —you've heard of it?"

I smile smugly. "Yes. I've done a little research on the *regina maledictum* since you last mentioned it."

"Oh?" Ceara rubs her palms together in apparent joy. "Do tell."

"Well," I begin, a little discomfited at her eagerness. "The laws of the Fae are notoriously difficult to uncover."

The faery's smile turns smug now.

"But I did find a book on the subject. Or rather, I realized I already had one."

Ceara's eyes widen. "Really? Wherever did you find such a thing?"

I smirk. "Ah, well, that's my secret."

She narrows her eyes. "Hmm. Well, do share. Tell me what you've learned. I love a good student."

"It appears the *regina maledictum* is a spell that the thirteen Great Fae cast after humans appeared on the Island of the Seven Kingdoms."

The faery's brows rise in expectation.

"Apparently something happened—my source was unclear on what, exactly—and the thirteen Great Fae decided that it would be better for all future Fae and human generations if it could never happen again. So a sort of...group leadership...was born for the Great Fae. There is no king or queen—"

"There never was a faery king," the faery snorts. "We never needed one."

"Then how do you exist?" I ask calmly.

"Tell me more of what you discovered," Ceara says instead.

"Well...a spell was cast that prevents any of the Fae from ruling any of the Seven Kingdoms," I say with a bit of smugness. It took me days of reading the book I'd stolen from the Canens Witch's cottage, as well as cross-referencing several books I'd found in my own library to figure this out. No source appears to have all the story, and I had to piece it together in bits.

Clapping her hands together in childish joy, Ceara beams at me. "I knew I picked a wise one. I've waited a long time for you to come back to me."

"What?" Come back to her? She's completely lost me, and yet she's so excited that—

"Haven't you worked out why I need you then? How perfect a partnership we are? What we do for each other?" Ceara leans forward in her eagerness.

I frown, my mind whirring over the situation like a small bird hovering in place. "You need me to be your pawn."

The faery, for a moment, seems to await another answer, then finally grimaces and sits back down in disappointment. "Let's not put it like that. Let's just say that I will allow you to rule the Seven Kingdoms—what you want, that is, for I have no desire to be empress after all, but it seems you do. In return, if you allow me but a little spot of the kingdoms when I make you empress, I think our agreement can be...lasting."

I purse my lips as I consider her offer. She wants me to rule as empress and yet not over a small part of the Seven Kingdoms? What part of the land does she value enough to give all the rest to me? Am I missing something in my haste to take the thrones? To free Canens and put it in its rightful place over the others?

"What happens when I die?" I ask. "You're a Great Fae, you are immortal. Or nearly so, as the legends say."

The faery's lips twitch. "Yes. Yes, I am."

"What happens when I die then? Will the kingdoms fall? What happens to your portion of it? Do you think you shall take on Empress of the Seven Kingdoms once I die? Or if I have children, would they inherit? What if I don't? Who shall inherit then?"

"Hmph. You are shrewd." Instead of looking displeased, however, Ceara looks amused. "Perhaps I misinterpreted your motives. You would be content to die like a mere human?" The faery waves a delicate hand in the air. "When immortality is within your grasp, you would be content with humanity?"

My mouth parts.

"Primogeniture? Arranged."

"I—"

"Oh? Female-primogeniture? That's interesting."

I frown and lift my chin. "I highly doubt I would have more than one child. So whatever I would have would inherit, should it come to that, faery."

The faery's mouth twitches. "Honestly, that doesn't matter now anyway. The important thing is that I have information you need."

"And what is that?"

"The location of the most difficult-to-find princess. She's been enchanted with secrecy since birth."

I grit my teeth. "Why do you need me to get the blood for

you? Do you think I have nothing better to do than run all over the Seven Kingdoms to prick a few princess' fingers?"

"My my, aren't you full of questions and demands today?" The faery tuts. "All right, because you found me some information today and have done your homework so well, I'll tell you the truth. That's how things work in the Fae world, you know."

I huff. What information did I find for her? I shared nothing but what I found out about the *regina maledictum*, which she must have known for herself already.

"I need you to do this because the Great Fae are prohibited from 'communicating with, visiting, or otherwise bothering the royals of the Seven Kingdoms except under express invitation.'" She rolls her eyes as if quoting from a law she finds ridiculous. "And princess blood is priceless for all it can do, you must know. It can make a minor spell into one of great power."

I sip from my glass to cover my confusion. "Tell me one thing, faery, and I might just agree."

"What is that?"

"When can I have my immortality?"

Ceara's face doesn't so much as twitch in her surprise. I am starting to learn her ticks.

"You may have your immortality as soon as you bring me the blood of the seven princesses. I think that shall be a decently appropriate task. Starting with the Ardorite princess."

"I thought she died at birth. Do you mean to tell me they kept some of her blood?"

"Ah." Ceara's lips turn into a smug smile. "There's everyone's mistake. They've all been fooled by King Greggory and Queen Ada, the manipulative royals.

"She did not die. She was taken away from her parents upon her birth, stolen by—well, that's not important—but she did not die. And that is whom I have found for you." Ceara grimaces. "Unfortunately, despite her removal from the royal family, she is still heavily protected magically, preventing me from going and gathering the blood I—*we* need from her."

"And all you need is a sample of her blood? How much?" I cross my arms over my chest. "Last time I gathered a princess' blood, you were quite angry and told me it wasn't good enough. Must I kill this one?"

Ceara's smile on her plump lips grows tight. "Yes, well, as you are sitting on the Princess of Canens' throne, hers is a special case."

I force myself not to flinch; she's saying these words simply to get under my skin like vermin. I haven't quite decided yet if she is the vermin she acts like, or if there is something more complex to her.

"In her case, since you have no blood claim to the throne you sit upon, we will need her heart to complete the spell. You must use a part of her to convince the throne itself that it belongs to you, and then you will gather much strength." A wicked smile plays over her plump lips. "You were perfectly right to demand that from your huntsman. How did you know?"

I lift one shoulder. "The heart is the most magical part of the body, Ceara. Surely you know that?"

She smirks but taps her fingers atop the windowsill she stands beside. Her gaze grows distant as she stares out the frosted glass at the scene below. The city of Merise sprawls out in the distance, and the frozen sea to the side in its perpetual stillness.

Abruptly, she turns back, all evidence of reflection gone. "With your lack of blood claim, you must have Winterberry's heart to complete the spell. We need the blood heir to the throne to break the Canens Curse and cast *you* as the new blood heir. The throne must be able to recognize the blood of its queen—this will require your sacrifice as well. It is a tricky thing, which will require certain support from your people." Ceara's eyes narrow. "Surely you realize there is some displeasure in Canens because of you?"

"We have many problems in Canens; I am the least of them."

The faery grins, revealing sharp little teeth. "If things go according to our plan, Queenie, you'll be the shining beacon of the Seven Kingdoms. You'll be the Empress of the Seven Kingdoms, such an empress that has never been seen before—and never will be again."

Even knowing that the faery tells me what I want to hear, my chest swells at the words. I'll be able to save the kingdom from this curse. Break the curse, save the people. They will love me for me—it is even better than feeding them and providing for them through this curse. This would hand Canens back to the people. No one would dare rebel then; no one would think ill of me. I would be their heroine. They would adore me.

I shake away the distracting thoughts. I must stay on task, not get ahead of myself. I face the faery and find her silently contemplating me.

"Where is this princess, and how do I reach her?"

12: MAGISTER

FREED

These thick woods provide the perfect coverage, were I hunting animals in the Nubilus valley. I can't resist leaving the well-worn road into town to prepare myself a quick lunch of whatever I can find in these woods before begin my search for the princess anew in the city itself.

A couple of miles away are enclosed fences with horses scattering the fields. A similar setup was Crystalli's first home. Until I stole him and brought him to Canens, where he could blend into the snow as my hunting companion.

Nubilus is unfamiliar to me; there has never been a reason to hunt upon the edge of the world. The city sits on a cliff above the sea, as far away from Heia as possible. A set of lower stone walls extend from the main city walls and encircle the horses on the hills above guard the city itself. Beyond the sprawling stone, a large castle is a bound, hungry hawk peering down at me as if determining whether I am prey or predator.

My gaze shifts to the tossing sea even farther away. I have never seen such a violent sea, but ships flying flags in a multitude of colors dot the horizon. They must be large vessels to be visible from here, even with my eyesight. Trade or military? I think the former.

Not finding any fresh, small-game trails, I return to Crystalli and pass through a small gate in the outer walls. A young, sparse forest lies on the other side, appearing little traveled. After a hundred strides, I dismount and tie the young stallion to a sturdy tree, then travel on alone in near silence.

A slight rustle catches my ear. I halt and slow my breathing. A tawny deer walks through the space of trees to my right. Slowly, I begin to reach for my bow and pause. To take such a kill without a way to use it all would be a waste. The deer locks eyes upon me, and her nostrils flare before she bounds away into the brush.

I follow her lead, delving deeper into the trees to where small thickets and saplings wind together. Birch and oak trees increase, the brush thickens, and any semblance of trails that I could follow disappear.

Another soft rustle to my left. My bow is ready this time. As a hare jumps from amongst the leaves, I loose an arrow. It flies through the air and through the eye of the hare, dead before the animal falls upon his grassy grave.

Within minutes, I've caught a second hare, enough to make a large meal that will pacify me from my two days of endless pursuit and little sustenance. Before I return to my horse, I skin the animals and gut them, burying their entrails in the dirt out of respect for the animal's spirits.

Automatically, I cast a glance up, looking for the three goddess spirits of the sky, but the sky is bright and scattered with clouds; even the sun goddess is gone. Their absence reminds me of the danger I face from all sides now without their protective presence.

Winding my way back through the woods, I wash my hands and the meat in a quick-moving stream. As I dip the last hare in, my spine prickles with unease. Casually, I lower my bow alongside the stream, next to my knife.

When I rise, my catch in one hand, knife in the other, a voice cuts through the silence.

"Poaching in the King's Forest?" a wry, woman's voice says.

I turn slowly, searching the sparse trees for her. Oddly for me, I cannot see her at all—not until she emerges from behind a small tree trunk. The old woman, her face lined and wrinkled, is dressed in the Ardor custom of a linen dress with modest skirts and blends perfectly into her surroundings. She stares at me with one eyebrow raised, as if the owner finds amusement in our situation.

"Have you not heard of the laws governing these woods? You could be hanged for taking those hares."

"What are you doing out here, old woman? Have you no family to care for that you must attempt to regulate others?"

The woman chuckles and moves toward the stream with surprising grace. Ignoring the armed man next to her, she crouches at the edge and dips a bucket I hadn't noticed into the deepest part of the stream. She delivers me a slanted gaze out of the corner of her eye. "You look a bit warm down here, northerner."

My fingers tighten on my knife and loosen on my hares. "And you look a bit nosey."

Lips pursed, she pulls out her bucket and sets it down at the water's edge, half filled with the cold creek water. "I suppose I do."

I chew on my tongue. She's a harmless old lady. What a waste of time talking with her. I am about to turn on my heel and march off, leaving her to her task, when she speaks again.

"You reek of magic, northerner. Dark magic."

My eyes flash wide.

"But it's not yours, is it?" She continues with her task, dipping her hands into the water and scrubbing them.

"What are you? Some sort of witch?"

She lifts a handful of water from the bucket to her mouth and tastes it, smacking her lips as though she's sampling fine wine. "Some have called me that."

"Away with you then. I have no need of your charms."

She chuckles and surveys me with a thoughtful tilt of her head. "I think you have. Though you know it not."

I adjust the hares on my string, shifting away from her. It's time to be done with this.

Then she rises with a fluid motion and points a dark wand at me. A trickle of something hot runs from the top of my head to the soles of my sweaty feet.

Pressure surges through my body then exits all at once, leaving me deflated. I stare down at the skinned hares in my hand then at the surrounding woods.

Where am I?

Slowly, I rotate in place. My skin flinches to find a bent old woman studying me with a mixture of curiosity and amusement.

"How do you feel, Marcus?" she asks with tenderness in her voice.

I blink. "I—"

"Oh wait, hold still. There are still a few tangled around you." The woman lifts her hand and points at stick at me.

Few? Tangled? What? My brow creases as I try to work through what she means. I squint at her half-closed eyes. Then something cold brushes over me, followed by a warmth that mingles around me and lifts my hair from my shoulders. I shudder. As soon as I do, the imagined breeze disappears, leaving me blinking in a spot of sunlight filtering through the tree canopy above me.

"Now how do you feel?"

"I feel...excellent."

And I do. Like I was weighted down and now am free. I don't remember ever feeling so free, except for a nagging feeling that I am supposed to be doing something else, and except for that feeling, I could lose myself in the woods and be the happiest I've ever been in my entire life.

"I am glad to hear it," the woman says briskly. "You gave me a bit of concern when you arrived so soon after Winterberry. You'll need to be careful though; the Queen will have felt that severing of her curses."

"Yes, of course."

"I'd recommend doing your job—protecting the princess, unless you'd like to return to the job your title suggests, huntsman? No?"

I shake my head.

"Good. But you'll need all the shrewdness you have and what I just gifted you with in order to trick the queen."

I agree; the Queen is a formidable enemy.

The woman tilts her head at me. "You will find the princess in Nubilus, at The King's Inn, but not yet. I don't know exactly when she will reach it in her journey, but when she does, and when you find her, do not reveal your presence to her. She would not yet understand and would flee. If she flees, we have many troubles on our hands, do you understand?"

"Yes, I understand. I won't let her see me."

"Queen Blanche is already on her way to Ardor. When she arrives, you must convince her that you still serve her. She will be suspicious."

"I will convince her."

"Yes, I know you shall." The old woman gives a crooked smile. "Remember where your loyalties lie, Marcus."

Before I can answer, the woman snaps her fingers and disappears in the tiniest shimmer of smoke, leaving no other trace of her existence.

FAILED

By the time the Crown Inspector has checked the stable to his satisfaction and marked several things that must be addressed, it's already past lunch, but my empty stomach has gone from my throat to my toes. I'm certain Gavin hasn't even stopped to eat, as I had no choice but to follow around the inspector and answer all his incessant questions while acting as his tour guide.

No wonder he showed up as early as he did. He's never been so thorough. Did Sir Birch tip him off that I am entered in the autumn auctions?

Everything he can possibly mark me down on, he is. His list of violations is longer than I've ever seen before.

I don't make excuses though. He's right. Every thing he points out is a technical violation. And I know from prior experience with him that if I argue, the penalty grows steeper, and I can't afford to pay a fine today. Perhaps he'll pass me when he sees my ledgers are in order.

After hours of inspection, the man lifts his beady, golden eyes from his notebook, squints at the sun and says, "Well, it looks like we've finally reached the end of the stable inspection. Quite the challenge today, isn't it?" He smirks at my lack of answer. "Ready to go up to the house then?"

Nodding, I swallow back my frustrations. "Yes. Let me show you the ledgers."

As I walk a half step behind him, I pray that Bona has the house in good order today. I don't need him thinking that we're slobs in the house as well. Let this man see that I'm trying to run the stable for a good reason.

But am I? Am I not doing it out of my own sheer stubbornness, determination, and hatred for being told what to do? Because everyone told me I couldn't run the stable on my own without a man to help me, and I have made sure that I do. I've turned down dozens of marriage proposals—some from quite far away—until they stopped being offered at all just so I could do this alone.

And because none of them were men I love, I remind myself. If I loved one of those many men, then perhaps things would be different now. I—no, we—would be facing moderate inspection that all stables go through before the auctions, not a witch hunt intended to keep women from running stables.

I clench my fists in my tunic pockets at the unfairness. I am not like other women. I'm not going to give up on this. Not until… I blink back tears. No matter what I do today or tomorrow, unless I marry and produce an heir, this will all come to an end far too soon.

The Crown Inspector is comfortable in leading the way to Father's study. I remember him from when Father was alive. Then the inspections had happened only every six months, instead of monthly. At first, the two Crown Inspectors, highly educated men with years of experience upholding the laws regarding the Gelu Rigens, tried talking me out of my decision. Now they are like Sir Birch, clearly disapproving but apparently tired of telling me the same thing and not having me listen. At least in that, I've won. I allow myself a small smile as I produce the ledger for him.

"Hmm." He sits down in Father's chair and opens the book, falling silent as he begins his work. I could probably sneak away from him now and go wash up or change clothes, but what's the point? Besides, I don't trust him in Father's study; I only trust him about as much as I trust Lady Eleanora. Instead I quietly begin to shelve a pile of books that haven't been put away. Funny, but I don't remember taking these off. I don't have time to read these days anyway. Though faery tales and romantic stories were once my roughage…before Father died and I had a stable to run and—

"You have a mistake here, Miss Eleanora." The Crown Inspector's voice cuts through my thoughts.

My heart flutters down by my feet somewhere. Another mistake? This day has been nothing but a mistake. I don't know how I'm going to pass inspection at this point. "There is?" I attempt polite concern in my tone, but I think I've failed by the way the Crown Inspector's left brow rises.

He crooks a finger at me, inviting me to come check the error. He moves aside from the desk only slightly to permit me the ability to view the error. Sure enough, as I recalculate the numbers in the column, a sinking feeling overwhelms me. If he weren't sitting in Father's chair, I'd sink down into it myself. Instead, I have to face the fact that I've credited myself two hundred silver coins more than I ought to have.

"You see it then?" the Crown Inspector asks, his lips curving upward.

"Yes, sir," I answer quietly, moving back from the books.

"This is sloppy bookkeeping, Miss Eleanora, there's no way around that." He motions me back and points to the spot across from Father's desk.

When I stand before him, exactly like it was when Father might be scolding me, my chin down and hands folded before me, he resumes.

"In addition to this bookkeeping error, there are a shocking twenty-five violations in the stables. You've also used the wrong ink here in the ledgers, but I've let that slide—"

I raise my chin, mouth open to retort, instead I halt at the expectation on his face. If I argue, he will mark it against me, I'm sure. Twenty-six violations then.

"I see you anticipate bringing in six thousand coins at the auctions. Do you think that should be enough?"

"Yes, I do—"

He slices a hand through the air, cutting me off, but there is a wicked gleam in his golden eyes. "You are just as I expected, Miss Eleanora. Still as proud as ever. You don't let anyone tell you what to do, even when their advice is sound."

I shut my mouth. He has provoked me, just as I knew he would try to do.

"You also grossly underestimated the cost of oats this winter. With the blight and the shortage anticipated, its estimated to increase at least one and a half times to last month's cost. You've made no allowance for that in your ledgers."

I keep my eyes down this time and let his words wash over me as he continues to list my failures. I try to let the words drain away, until his conclusion that has my heart twisting in my chest.

"As a result, I cannot pass you on your inspection this morning. And until you pass inspection, you are not allowed to sell your horses at any auction. You will be reinspected in one week's time, and if all these issues are not addressed, you will be unable to enter the autumn auctions, as I hear from Sir Birch is your plan." He snaps the ledger shut and stands, shoving the chair back so that it scrapes loudly against the floor. "My time is in much demand today. Good day, Miss Eleanora."

All I can do is gape at his retreating back as he shows himself out.

If I can't enter the autumn auctions, Aeneas Stables won't survive the winter.

THE PALACE

Nubilus is vastly different from any other Ardorian village or town I passed by in my days running from the huntsman. At least three times the size of any other town, it bustles with activity from vendors, traders, horsemen, and even shepherds as soon as I enter the inner city walls.

Wandering through the town streets, which are laid out in a maze no doubt to confuse enemies like me, I happen upon a market square that I cannot find a second time. I try to keep the palace in front of me, following narrow streets lined by houses that sometimes rise three or four stories high and have a small front yard where grass sprouts up. Some choose to put a little garden there and have plants growing up in patches of dirt. The more affluent houses take up an entire half a city block or full block and have brightly colored, fragrant flowers growing in boxes underneath the street level windows. When I stop to smell a many-petaled flower at such a house, one of the servants chases me away before I can ask for directions to the palace.

After wandering around the street maze for several more hours, I choose a modest house and gather my courage. I need directions or else I won't make it to the palace until next week.

I knock on a smooth wooden door next to a small garden of carrots and potatoes and wait. After a few moments, I hear footsteps clicking on a hard floor behind the door.

The pleasant expression on the woman's face degrades into disgust that curls her lips when she sees me.

"Excuse me," I say in my best Ardorian, "but I'm looking for the palace—"

Without answering, the woman slams the door shut between us.

Mouth agape, I stare at the wood for a moment, then slap my lips together. If she won't help me, maybe the next house will. But it's the same there. I must look like a refugee or a criminal. With a horse. I snort. Either their homeless criminals are more well off than any I've ever met, or I'm in the wrong neighborhood.

I remount Raven and direct him toward the palace again. "I just want to find the palace," I whisper, growing desperate as the sun dips lower in the sky.

I could help you, you know, that little voice says within me.

I shudder as if a cold hand grasps at me. "No, thank you," I mutter, ignoring the look a woman hurrying by with a small child gives me.

I'll find it on my own, I continue in my head.

Suit yourself.

Forcing away the voice is harder than it should be. It's persistent today. And I think I feel its cold hand guiding me as we wander the streets. I dredge up my courage again and start asking people in the narrow, twisting roads. Finally, one has pity on me and points me down the correct street, telling me which turns to take that eventually get me to the base of a hill with a road cresting up dozens of steps to the Nubilus palace.

Two guards flank the entrance to the stairs and a few Ardorites walk slowly away from the palace as I approach. The smooth, stone turrets at their backs tower over us all. They seem to find its shadow reassuring, but to me, with the darkening sky behind the white palace making it gleam like moonlit snow, I feel a shiver of fear that I tell myself to ignore.

I aim Raven toward the towering building and the closed, wooden doors that must be at least four times my height. I'm probably too late to see anyone today, for my stomach reminds me that it must be suppertime, but I still must try.

"Halt. What's your purpose here?" one of the guards asks as I near.

I hesitate and pull Raven to a halt. "I'm here for an audience with the King and Queen," I answer.

The guard's eyes narrow as I speak. "Come back on the fifth day of the week around midday," he finally says. "That's the only day the King holds an audience." His gaze slips over me. "Though I doubt you'll get in, stranger things have been known to happen."

"What is today?" I clench Raven's reins in my hand, hoping tomorrow is the fifth day.

His bushy moustache bristles as he frowns. "It's the second day."

Sweat drips down my temples. Three days? At this rate, I won't live that long. "But—"

"They might not hold court next week," the other guard adds. "Not with the masques on Sabbath's eve. I heard a rumor they might cancel."

A wave of nausea and dizziness that I've battled for hours threatens to overtake me now at my disappointment. I grip Raven's mane and blink at the blurry outline of the guards, trying to bring them into focus.

"Are you ill?" the first guard asks.

"I—yes. No. Maybe…" I shake my head and weave in the saddle. "Are the palace kitchens hiring? Or the housekeeper? I need food. I'll work."

The second guard raises a dark eyebrow. "Come back at first light. The kitchen hands out today's leftovers to the beggars then.

You're too late today for anything." He eyes Raven. "But your horse looks like he could use a few good meals too."

"Yes. We both could," I say.

"Come back tomorrow," the first guard agrees.

"Where—" I break off, blink at them, then decide to ask. "Do you know of where I might find shelter tonight?"

At this the guards exchange a glance. They seem kind although they guard a vital post and have undoubtedly heard every excuse and story known to man.

"Check the inns down in the town center," the second says. "Sometimes they'll let travelers work for a meal—and let you stay in the stables if they have room."

I turn Raven back to town. If I can find a place to stay, a stable for him and work for me, perhaps I can find him some oats as well, or at least hay.

"Good luck," one of the guards calls from behind me.

I half turn back to see the first guard staring at me with an odd expression in his gaze.

"Thank you," I say. These Ardorites are strange. Either mean or kind, they are unexpected and unpredictable.

Without anything else to do, and unable to reach the palace except through them, I nudge Raven back down the hill, the guards' kindness encouraging me. Even my magic seems to have abandoned me now, the cold grasp gone. Good, for I might give into it if it asked me now.

Finding the town center is easy this time; I just follow the main street from the palace down. I don't know why I lost it so often before, but looking behind me, it seems like the street is narrower than the others surrounding it, some strange illusion that makes the main street disappear into the others and mislead the enemy perhaps.

In the town square, I locate a long, wide street filled with the most delicious scents of baking bread, simmering stews, and braised meats. My stomach reawakens with a lurch, my mouth erupting with saliva. At least I've been able to find water. But I'm half tempted to start eating pretty flowers, even though Blanche taught me not to trust a pretty flower. Or beauty at all. Pretty soon I'll have to sell my tack or even Raven himself, though it would pain me to do so.

Giving him a sad pat on the neck, I acknowledge silently that he's all I have. Even he's lifting his nose at the scent of bread in the air.

I wipe a hand over my dirty brow, then wipe the sweat on my thigh. It's useless even to attempt to stay clean now. My clothes are becoming more threadbare by the hour. Thank goodness for my cloak, as the evenings and nights are chilly enough to make me tremble.

Giving Raven another pat, I tie his reins to a hitching post near one of the inns. I hesitate to leave him, though I know there's little of value to anyone else in the saddlebags, some might still find him worth stealing.

Afraid to hope, I step into the first inn and wait for my eyes to adjust before entering farther. A dozen sets of eyes stare at me. I look a mess, I'm sure. Wobbling slightly on my feet, I step forward and allow the dusky room to embrace me. Candles haven't yet been lit, and the room is brightened only by the setting sun outside. Eyes follow my progress toward the bar. The server, a girl only a few years older than me, pauses in grabbing two tall, clear glasses from a line of upside-down empty ones, and gives me a judgmental look.

"What do ya want?" she says so fast that I almost can't under-stand her.

"I—"

"What?" she demands, setting the glasses down on their bottoms harder than necessary.

"I'm a traveler without money," I say. "Can I work for a meal?"

She scowls at me. "No work here."

"But—" I frown. "Do you own—?"

A man steps out from behind her. There's a familial resemblance around the jawline and short, straight nose. "No work here," he growls. "Try down the road."

"But—they said—"

"No work here," he growls again, his eyes narrowing.

A scrape of chairs behind me makes me look back where two men have risen from their seats and glare in my direction.

My battered heart sinks. "Fine." I turn back to the man. "Why won't you help me?"

"Leave this place now." He slaps his hands on the counter between us with a double crack.

I flinch but keep his gaze, too tired and weak to even care what he thinks of me. The familiar anger at being treated rudely doesn't rise in me, nor does the light. Thank the gods. But at his unyielding glare, and the threat of the owner and his daughter, I turn and begin the long walk back to the door. As soon as the door shuts behind me, chairs scrape and the talk resumes, louder than before.

I trudge back to Raven only to find he's not where I left him.

A jolt of energy surges through me. I search the streets left and right, up and down the road. He's gone.

The street bustles with people going in and out of the inns for their afternoon meals. I grab the nearest person's arm.

"Did you see someone take a horse—?"

"Get off me, beggar!"

I recoil in shock at his tone, but quickly reach for an older woman who looks a little softer. "Did you see a horse? My horse is missing—" My eyes burn with emotion, though I am not hydrated enough for tears to form.

She scrutinizes me as the people milling around the street give us a wide berth.

My hands fall onto her bare wrist and a surge goes through me. I yank my arms back, my eyes going round. "What was—?"

"You lost your horse, dear?" she asks, her expression implaca-ble, but her voice calm and curious.

I wrap my hands in the folds of my skirt. "Yes. He was here..." I motion to the post, glancing back as though he might have reappeared. "Now he's gone. Someone..."

"Stole him?" she finishes for me.

"Yes," I whisper.

"Hmm." Slowly nodding, she examines me as if we are the only two in the street. "Who are you, child?"

"I—" Something about her makes me wary, but I answer her anyway. "Winter. My name is Winter."

A cloud seems to pass over her. Her eyes go distant and something darkens her gaze. "Winter." She closes her eyes briefly and nods as if confirming something to herself. "Yes, you are." She opens her eyes. "I've been expecting you."

Distracted, I shake my head and pull away. I don't need this right now. "Can you help me find my horse? Did you see him?"

"He's gone. You won't find him again in this city." Dark, gentle gaze locked on mine, she reaches out and grasps my hand in hers. Too confused and exhausted to move, I let her. The surge goes through my flesh again. This time, I let it.

"What is that?" I ask in a low voice. I lean back but don't pull my hands away. The feeling was uncomfortable but not painful.

"It's magic, my dear." She tilts her head at me. "You have great power in you."

I rip my hands from hers. "No. No, I don't."

Her brow creases briefly. "It's nothing to fear. Although some might argue." She waves a hand to the street and I follow it. We have a half dozen feet around us in any direction, and I gather from the way the citizens avoid looking at either of us that it's not just me keeping them at bay. When I turn back to her, she's holding out a coin between two fingers. "I don't have much, but here. It will get you a warm meal and a drink to fill your belly tonight. And after you do, go and find The King's Inn."

I stare at the coin, my chest squeezing in relief and wariness.

"Take it." She nudges it toward me. "You won't get a better offer."

Before I can act, she takes my hand and stuffs the coin into my palm, closing my grimy fingers around it. I say a quick prayer of thanks to the gods, and when I look up, she's gone.

A day later, my situation hasn't much improved. The money the old woman gave me is gone, gone with one—albeit large—meal. I'm so tired. I thought Canens was bad, what with the prison and the Manor. But I had a safe place to sleep then. As safe as I've ever been, I suppose. Though I took the woman's money, I hesitate to trust her advice of going to The King's Inn. Instead, I've asked at every other inn for help, and been turned away, though a couple have given me a drink of water or a leftover slice of half-eaten bread.

Wandering down a wide alley behind the road of inns, I peer over the fences to the back gardens. Some of the inns here have gardens nearly as big as a growing house back home. I've become better acquainted with the city since I first entered and roughly know my way around now, but the variety and plethora of gardens still surprise me. To be able to do so much without more than sun, dirt, water, and a few seeds.

My mouth fills with saliva as I pause outside the gate of one back garden. My breakfast of half a bread slice was so long ago. No one would notice if I stole a few carrots. Or whatever's growing in there.

I dart a look up and down the alley, then reach a trembling hand for the gate.

The back door flies open. I freeze, half hidden behind the low stone wall that separates the inn's garden from the alley.

"I'll grab some from the garden, Dalia," comes a cheerful, feminine voice. "Just carrots? Or potatoes, too?"

I can't hear the answer, but the youthful voice calls back, "Fine. Just a minute then."

Footsteps sound, going from sharp tapping against tile to dull wood, then duller dirt. I stand at the gate, half crouching in fear of being caught.

The girl moves around the garden, humming to herself as she completes her task. She doesn't see me peer through the slats of the iron gate. She is slender and about my age, but dressed in men's clothing. Only her voice and her long, blond hair give her identity away as a woman. Young woman. No more than my age, surely. A surge of hope lifts me at the realization.

"I need some more celery." A person appears in the doorway, a small woman silhouetted by the light inside.

"Celery?" the girl in the garden asks, looking up from her task in the garden.

"Yes. Just a bunch will do."

"All right," the girl in man's clothing answers.

Without another word, the second girl disappears back inside. A couple of minutes later, the girl in the garden finishes her task and carries her basket full of produce through the door inside. As she jostles the basket on her arm to open the door, a large carrot falls, unnoticed, to the ground. She disappears inside.

The alley falls silent. No one else emerges from the back; the gardens lie empty, soaking up the sun.

I stand, uncertain. Should I take the chance and steal some food? I could take the fallen carrot…

Or should I try for more?

My head pounds; my sight blurs. Only my grip on the gate keeps me upright. I'm so tired; so hungry.

I stumble up to the back door, falling to my knees once. I have no other hope.

15: ELLA

UNEXPECTED

$\mathcal{A}$ thump sounds on the back door. Dalia and I exchange a look.

"Expecting a delivery?" I ask, putting the basket of vegetables down on the worktable.

"No." Dalia peers into the basket. "Oh, it could be Smitty with the fish. Will you get it?"

"Of course." Returning to the door, I swing it open and blink in surprise. It's not Smitty the fishmonger at all, but a girl so thin and delicate that she makes me look like a fat giant and Dalia appear harsh. Despite her haggard appearance, there's a beauty written on her face in those ice-blue eyes that cannot be hidden. It's positively unnerving.

Her cough jerks me back to the moment, and I realize she's trying to speak.

"What?"

"I need help," she croaks. "Will you help me?" Her eyelids flutter, and I reach out just in time to catch her before she crumples.

"Oof!" The grunt escapes me as she collides against my chest, even though she's hardly heavier than a child. "Dalia!" I call, but there's no answer from inside. I turn my head and call her name again.

"What?" Footsteps follow the irritable voice from the kitchen to the stone hallway behind me.

"Help me." I shift the girl's dead weight in my arms and turn so Dalia can see her. "She just appeared and collapsed."

Dalia's expression changes from annoyance to concern in an instant. "Who is it?" She hurries toward me as I speak, wiping her hands on her white apron. "What's wrong with her?"

"I don't know." I drag her across the threshold into the hallway, relieved when Dalia takes the girl's other arm. I've never carried someone like this before; it's horribly awkward. "She just asked for help and passed out."

"Should we call Doctor Achilleos?" Dalia asks.

"Let's wait." With less of the girl's weight on me, I'm able to shift her arm over my shoulders and mostly carry her myself now, freeing Dalia to swing the back door closed before a stray cat or dog sneaks into the kitchen, lured by the scent of tonight's supper.

"Where should we take her?" I ask.

Dalia grimaces. "We just had someone reserve two nights in the guest room on this level. They don't leave until tomorrow night. So either upstairs or—"

"Your room?" I suggest, knowing she'll hate it. She's notoriously private, but I don't think dragging this girl up the stairs is the right choice at the moment; she needs to lie down.

"All right," Dalia agrees.

Together we half drag and half carry the girl down the hall where Noemì and Dalia's rooms are, one across from the other. Dalia shoves open her door, and I nearly fall in after her, catching myself on the doorway.

As it is every time I've seen it, Dalia's room is neat and tidy, with few personal items are all stowed in their proper places. Her bed is cleanly made, the teal and pink quilt tucked under the edges of the mattress, her pillow perfectly propped against the headboard, just like a properly made inn bed. She's fastidious, which is why she runs The King's Inn so well.

Dalia leads us over to her bed, and we let the girl flop atop it, directing her head at the pillow. With a huff, I bend and drag her legs onto the bed, positioning them so that she looks somewhat comfortable.

Staring down at the girl, Dalia purses out her lips. "What do we do with her now?"

"I'll get her some water, see if I can get some in her. I think she's hungry and dehydrated by the look of it." I point to her dry, chapped lips. "I can try to find some money for the doctor, but maybe he'll take a look at her as a favor instead. I can give his niece a couple of rides on Flora; she always loves that."

Dalia chews on her lip. "I don't know that I can keep her here though. Do you think it's safe? We don't know anything about her."

"No, but look at her." I shrug. "She's sick. Starving, it looks like. We can't throw her back on the street. You know Noemì wouldn't let us do that."

Nose wrinkled in reluctance, Dalia nods. "I can't stay. I have to get back to making dinner for the guests. I'm already running late."

"Of course." I bite my lip and glance at the girl again. I take the cup from Dalia's bedside table and fill it halfway with water from the pitcher beside it. I put it to her mouth, drizzling it over the girl's lips. At first she doesn't respond at all, but once it begins to trail down her neck and I push her lips apart a little with the glass, she gulps it down greedily, all without opening her eyes.

"She awake?" Dalia asks from behind me.

I shake my head. "No. But drinking, and that's good. Perhaps she'll wake soon at this rate."

"Well, I'm going to be in the kitchen. I'll...get some food ready for her." She snaps the door closed quietly, and her footsteps disappear down the hallway, leaving me alone with a girl who looks more like a malnourished young boy. I manage to get another cup of water down her throat before she pushes me away with a groan.

I put the cup down, watch her a few minutes, then leave her to rest.

"She awake yet?" Dalia greets me as I step into the kitchen. She's searing chunks of lamb on the hot griddle while water heats over the fire. My stomach growls; I forgot to eat breakfast, and it's almost lunchtime.

Dalia smirks and nods to a pile of slightly stale-looking pastries on a side table. "Help yourself."

"Thanks. And no, she's not awake." I choose one oozing red filling and bite through its outer dough. "Mmm." Even though the dough is a bit stale, the strawberries are delicious. How does she even have leftovers of these? "Did you get some food?" I search the kitchen and spot a small plate of soft cheese, jam, a little smoked fish, and a small bowl of porridge. "That?"

Dalia shrugs. "It's all I have right now. And she shouldn't eat much if she's as close to starving as she looks." A furrow lines her skin above her nose. "Do you think we should be helping her, Ella?"

The pastry pauses on its way to my mouth. Trouble with the constables is the last thing I need, and this girl is clearly an outcast, a street urchin at the least. But why? Is it because she's done something wrong or just because she looks…different?

Is that all this is? A girl who looks different? And how much different will she even look when she's full and healthy? If she stays that long.

She reminds me of a horse I found, an animal that had clearly escaped bad owners and only survived through my finding the poor animal trapped by her lead, which had become tangled in between two rocks. She'd been there for some time when I found her and brought her home. Luckily, she'd not been tattooed like all Gelu are required to be. Perhaps that was why Father allowed me to keep her. I'd named her Flora.

"She's so weak," I murmur. "I really hope she doesn't die."

Alarm colors Dalia's face. "Do you think she will? In my bed?"

"I— No. I don't think so. I think she's just tired and hungry—and thirsty. We'll take care of her. I'll see if I can wake her with this food, maybe have her eat a little jam and get some sugar into her. Then I'll send Doctor Achilleos here."

"You're going to leave her here with me?" Dalia fixes me with her wide eyes even wider than usual.

"I'll send the doctor."

"But…what if…" She trails off and bends over her work with a shake of her head.

"What if what?"

She bites her lip and murmurs to the table. "What if someone is after her?"

"After her?"

Dalia raises a shoulder and fixes me with an expression that reminds me of Noemi's lined face when she's stressed. Sometimes when I look at Dalia, I imagine that she has experienced a lifetime more grief than I have. Now, I imagine that she sees more of this girl than I do, and because of it, she is more wary of her.

"I don't think anyone is after her, Dalia," I say slowly, resisting the urge to turn and peer out the window behind me. "If so, she would have looked far more terrified when I saw her. Besides, she was so weak, whoever would have been chasing her would have caught her. She spoke simply as though she was hungry." I smile sadly. "She's a beggar. And unless we help her, she'll die on the streets."

Looking unconvinced, Dalia nods at the pile of chopped onions on her cutting board before tossing them in with the seared lamb. "Send the doctor quickly, will you?"

"Of course."

In Dalia's room, the girl is still upon the bed where I left her, her breathing even but shallow. As I lean over with the plate, she cries out so sharply that I almost drop it. She writhes on the bed, twisting her head back and forth.

Then she cries out something in a harsh language I don't understand, followed by, "Certa! Certa!" in a half-sob.

Gaping down at her, I can only blink as I attempt to still my racing heart. She cries out again, and this time I lean forward to soothe her as I might a horse. A hand on her shoulder to calm her and one on her forehead to check her temperature. She's hot but not unhealthily so, and I continue speaking to her until she calms, eyes half parting only to drift shut before she stills.

I sigh and brush away a small smudge of dirt from her forehead. Her hair is so short. By choice? I don't know if I can believe that. Although perhaps she found her beauty oppressive and tried to make herself less beautiful.

I draw up a blanket from the bottom of Dalia's bed and tuck it in around her shoulders. She breathes out heavily but doesn't wake.

Without giving myself more time for thought, I leave her, keeping the door cracked so Dalia can hear if the girl needs her. I say a prayer that she wakes, even if it might bring me more trouble, for something about her has captivated me.

PART II

WOKE

My head is pounding, my mouth is dry, and my stomach is empty. But there's something different, and I know it before I open my eyes.

I smell things. Not the stench of a gutter or rotting garbage or even a fresh breeze. I smell meat. Fish. Cheese. Bread. Ale. And…flowers.

Stomach growling, I pry open my eyes. A low, dark ceiling made out of wide timbers with knotted wood above greets me.

Memories return to me slowly. Visiting the palace and being told to come back tomorrow. Going to several inns and being told there was no work for me there. Walking down the alley between the inns. Walking the streets. Watching a girl dressed in men's clothing in the garden. Knocking on the door. Falling into her arms.

After that, everything is dark until now. My arms won't lift me, so I settle for turning my head left toward the wall, where a small window is half covered with white drapes, and right into the rest of the room where a door is cracked open to a hallway beyond.

The room is almost empty except for a rickety wooden chair

sitting against the wall next to a small wardrobe. The only other things in the room are the bed and a small basket of fabric, along with a few pink and purple wildflowers gracing the top of the wardrobe in a glass ale mug.

Something teases my nose, not wildflowers. Food. Turning my head, I spy it. A plate sitting only an arm's reach away.

I shove myself upright as fast as I can, which isn't fast at all, especially given being tangled in a blanket. I hope this food is for me, because even if it's not, I'm so hungry that I'm going to eat it. Starting with the jam, I spoon it into my mouth without bothering to look for bread to smear it on. I eat everything at once, not even paying attention to the mingled flavors of fish and jam. In minutes, the food is gone and my stomach churns.

I groan and clutch my stomach. Why did I eat so fast? I know better.

Sitting on the edge of the bed, I drop my head to my hands. Pale light filters in from the window behind me, suggesting that the sun is beginning to set. Did I sleep the entire day here? Should I stay now? Is it safe? A part of me wants to rise and flee, to keep moving, away from the Magister. If I stay too long any place, he'll find me. But…I haven't seen him for days, and I might have lost him on the road to Nubilus. There were dozens of others traveling the same road. He cannot be that skilled a tracker…can he?

I swallow and find my mouth dry. Of course he can. He's the Queen's Huntsman for a reason.

With shaking hands, I pour myself a drink of water and force myself to sip it slowly as I wait for whoever put me here to return. When no one enters the room by the time I finish drinking the entire jug of water, I lie down again. Now that I've eaten, and although my stomach still protests its meal, I can feel my exhaustion. All else can wait, even the huntsman.

When I wake next, it's with a jolt and a gasp. Panting, I blink away the image of Certa's last moments hovering before my eyes.

The room is empty, the plate is gone from the bedside table, and the water jug refilled with sparkling clean water. A blanket has been pulled up to my chin again. After another few moments, I roll over and close my eyes, willing my heart to beat more slowly.

When I wake a third time, it's to pale sunlight warming my face, and my bladder aches, but at least my last sleep was dreamless. Sitting up, I groan, my entire body aching as if the last week has caught up with me overnight. A horse must have trampled me while I slept.

"Oh, you're awake!" A cheerful, sweet-as-a-ripe-fig voice says from beside my head.

Gasping, I flinch away then squint at the girl. It's the girl from the garden. Only, she looks like a girl this time. How long have I slept?

She smiles at me, the morning sun falling upon her golden hair and creating a halo upon her head. "You're probably confused and frightened. I know I would be. But please don't be. I'm Ella." She extends a hand.

My shoulder against the wall, I stare at her slender, work-worn fingers as I translate her Ardorian in my tired brain.

She takes her hand away without me shaking it, instead moving it toward a plate laden with a little bread and soft cheese and jams.

"We had Doctor Achilleos come and look at you while you were sleeping. He said you'll be all right if you just rest and eat what you can. He'd like to come back to look at you though, ask you some questions." She peers up at me from spreading a bit of cheese on a small piece of hard bread, but I still don't answer. "When you're hungry, eat small amounts. He said that in a few days, you'll be back to eating like normal."

Her smile is warm—too warm. I doubt very much the doctor said exactly that.

Ella continues as if my skepticism hasn't been noticed. "You can stay here as long as you need, of course. Dalia and Mrs.

Caupo—she insists we call her Noemì though—anyway, they've agreed that you're not to go anywhere. Unless you want to, of course." She frowns at that. "Of course, it will be best for you to stay here and recover. It's a quiet inn, well respected. There's good food—Dalia's an amazing cook—and when you feel stronger, if you want to help out, you can stay as long as you want. I already asked Noemì about that. She's the owner, you know. Well, she runs the business for her brother-in-law, at least. You know how it goes."

I don't, but I don't interrupt, not when she's giving me so much information.

"And Dalia is amazing. She came here and stayed, like you, sort of." Ella gives a little laugh. "If you want to stay that is." Her broad smile transforms her face as she holds out a piece of toast with soft cheese and jam slathered on it.

I hesitate, but my stomach grumbles at me, so I take it with a nod of thanks and try to be dainty in devouring it. She half watches me while topping another slice of bread like the first.

"Do you have any questions? I realize I've been talking a lot and not letting you get a word in edgewise."

I consider her over the last swallow of my bread. "Who are you?" I croak out.

She frowns. "Pardon?"

I swallow again and clear my throat to carefully repeat the Ardorian words. Although I never visited Ardor, I had a tutor when I was young, and I studied the language on my own after Blanche eliminated my tutors. Much of it has come back to me in my time here, and I try to mimic the accent of Nubilus in speaking to this girl now.

"Oh, well, I'm Ella—Eleanora Saevus," she says with a bright smile. "I run Aeneas Stables, which you might have heard of. It's a breeding stable for Gelu Rigens, and I've run it in the seven years since my father died."

Her smile is disarmingly pretty. Her simple linen dress of

dark blue brings out the brightness of her pale eyes. Her skin is creamy but tinted by too much sun, her long golden hair braided back in a way that seems like a half-finished style of a noble-woman, braided up top and tied at her neck to release the waves that cascade across her shoulders and back, almost as though she couldn't be bothered to let her maid finish the braid.

As I stare, slowly I become aware that she's watching me examine her, and her smile is gone.

"I'm Ella. Do you understand me?"

"Yes." I push myself further upright and my head swims. "I just forgot…"

There's a pregnant pause during which I put my hand to my head and try to regain my composure while the girl waits for me to continue. When I don't, she prompts, "Forgot what?"

I meet her quiet, still gaze. She smells of horse, sun, and sweat, like she's spent the morning out riding. "Where am I?"

"Oh. That. You're at The King's Inn. In Nubilus," she adds as an afterthought. "Where are you from? Have you been living on the streets long?"

Where am I from? In all I've been through, I haven't thought of a lie to answer that question. I ignore it and instead ask, "You said I can stay?"

"Well, yes, if you want to." This time her words are a bit surprised, but also cautious, almost as though she is beginning to regret her promise.

Self consciously, I lift a hand to my head, touching my short hair and undoubtedly dirty face. I've not looked at myself in over a week, except for a mottled reflection in a creek. "I have to…" I motion to myself, suddenly embarrassed.

"What? Oh!" She smiles and nods. "Of course. Yes, there's a garderobe at the end of the hallway. I can't have a full bath brought to you now, but perhaps in an hour or two? After break-fast? I've already had Dalia start the water boiling. After the inn guests eat and the tables are cleared away, and before we start prepping for midday luncheon..." Ella trails off and smiles. "We can get you a bath today."

I stare at her. She's far too kind for an Ardorite—for anyone. Or else she doesn't realize what I am.

"Is that acceptable?"

"Oh, yes. Yes. Thank you." I throw my legs over the side of the bed, facing her. I'm still weak; my body is reluctant to obey my commands, and when I stand, I almost fall. Ella is quick to grab me by the arms, holding me upright.

"I can help you, if you need it. You must still be exhausted."

I shake my head. I will never perform those human activities in front of another again. It reminds me far too much of my time in slavery. At least let my freedom give me some dignity.

"Of course." She half glances at me as she lightens her grip. "I mean just walking you to the door."

My cheeks heat at my own misunderstanding, but I shake my head again, and she drops my arm. Like a babe just learning to walk, I cross the room, using the wall for help instead and steady myself by gripping the door handle and pausing when I reach it.

"To the right," Ella says behind me. "End of the hall."

Inching my way down the hallway, I barely make it to a small door. Inside is a wooden chair with a bowl underneath. A washbasin sits on a wooden table with a small pump over top it, clearly to pump water out. But how does it work? I want to inspect it, but my bladder squeezes at me and I turn back to the rest of the room. In one corner is a large tub, most likely for bathing, and it's the most familiar thing in here, although I'm not sure how they plan on filling it. It's huge.

Besides the simple mirror hanging above the basin which reflects a filthy street urchin, those are the only things in this room, and confused, I turn back to the porcelain bowl, which must be for relieving oneself.

Taking a deep breath and using a bit of faith, I inspect it. Pulling at a cord to one side releases a small flood of water. I jump back before realizing the water in the bowl drains down a hole in the bottom. What strange magic is this? My bladder is more than uncomfortable now, and so I take the risk and relieve myself in the bowl. Pulling the chain again is even more interesting this time as I watch the liquid swirl and disappear. Amazing. Done without magic? I wish I could ask Ella about it, but that would certainly reveal my foreignness.

I pump cool water into the washbasin to scrub the dirt from my hands. We have indoor pumps similar to these in Canens, and though this one works a bit differently, I've seen many people in the villages I've passed pumping their water out of them, and I quickly figure it out. When I'm finished, the once-clear water is dingy with the dirt from my face and arms. I glance at the empty tub. I'll have to come back to that later; Ella did promise.

The mirror above the basin now shows me a girl with wide, startled blue eyes and pale skin, with short raven-black hair sticking out every direction. I don't bother to smooth it down; it will just pop up again.

As I wobble my way back to the room a minute later, voices drift from the room across the hall. Pausing to catch my balance, I listen to the conversation.

"You haven't found out who she is then?"

"No, Mrs. Caupo, but she seems terrified. She's very weak as well."

"Yes, I could see that for myself, dear."

"Of course you could. I'm sorry. How are you feeling? Let me fluff that pillow for you."

"Oh, as good as can be expected—oh, you're such a dear, Mistress Eleanora."

"Mrs. Caupo, you know better than to call me that." Ella's tone is warm in its chastisement.

"I'll call you what you've earned, dear, that's it. And I would call you Lady if your mother didn't share your name."

An affectionate sigh breaks the silence. "Well, if titles are what we earn, then yours would be 'mother.'"

A hoarse, surprised laugh issues from the other voice. "Oh dear, you are a sweetheart. You and Dalia both… You'll take good care of her when I'm gone, won't you? I don't think it will be too much longer now."

"Oh, Mrs. Caupo, you'll never die. You wouldn't dare."

The deeper voice laughs again. "You're good for Dalia, you know. You keep her young."

Ella laughs. "She's younger than me, you know."

"Oh, I have my own doubts about that, dear." She clears her throat. "Anyway, you must allow that girl to stay as long as she needs. She looks positively hunted."

"I agree, Mrs. Caupo, that she does."

I don't wait to hear any more. Using the wall for support, I make my way back into the bedroom and shut the door with a gentle click.

Sitting on the bed, I give myself over to my thoughts. So what if they think I'm hunted? I am. But can I trust them? That's the question I must ask myself. They seem to care for me—I don't know why—but can I trust them?

Something burns in my eyes. How can they care for me? They don't know me. They don't know what I've done. Whom I've killed. Who wants to kill me.

I collapse back upon the pillow, turning my face into its welcoming embrace. I killed Certa and Des. I almost got Elaina, Cito, and Rus killed because they tried to help me. Not that Rus couldn't use a little humbling as Canens' enemy, but he doesn't deserve to die for helping me, even if his help was reluctant.

Everyone is my enemy now. How can I trust anyone?

Start small, answers a little voice inside me.

My breath catches on my lips, and I go very still. Start small? I venture in my head. Nothing answers. "Light?" I whisper. "Was that you?"

If you want to call me that, I'll answer to it.

I shudder. The voice is so clear in my head. Am I going crazy?

It doesn't answer.

With a trembling breath, I bite my lip and embrace the crazy. "Where did you go?"

Go? I've never left you. But certain things bring me out more than others. And you don't seem to want me.

"I never asked for you. Why did you come to me?"

"Who are you talking to?"

The voice startles me, making me jerk up on my belly like a fish out of water as I turn to the door.

The petite girl in the doorway raises a brow, her abrasive gaze skimming over me with something close to derision. A dark blond braid trails down one of her shoulders, and her eyes are large and darker green than I've ever seen, almost the color of Blanche's most poisonous plant.

"I—" I fall silent. How do I respond to that? I'm talking to the voice in my head? To myself? What would make me seem less mad?

"I'm sorry I startled you," she says again, this time in a different tone. The suspicion is still there, but it's veiled behind mistrust now. I missed my chance to confide in her, and she has distanced herself. I recognize it because I have done that, and I have also been the one in her position, vulnerable and open until someone shows no excitement to reply. It happened all the time at the Manor, where I was trained to be a slave, and where any slave I confided in disappeared.

The girl enters the room and crosses to the wardrobe, putting a hand on the top of it and looking at me out of the corner of her eye.

I push myself upright and place my feet onto the floor to steady myself. "You must be Dalia."

She pauses in tugging out the top drawer of the wardrobe. "Yes."

"And this must be your room."

A vaguely amused expression lights her dark eyes, but it quickly fades into wariness. "You are quick."

"I'm sorry. If there's anywhere else I can stay—"

"There isn't," she says shortly, pulling a square-folded handkerchief out of the drawer and snapping it closed with a click as sharp as her words.

I fall silent watching her. This is Dalia, the one who is loved by the owner, and by Ella too, it seems. And yet, she seems to be the only one who doesn't want me here.

"I'm sorry for taking your room."

She faces me and puts a hand on her hip, eyes narrowed. "For now, you need it more than me. But as soon as you're recovered, don't think I'm sharing." She leans closer. "In fact, I might just call Brunnea myself and see if she can speed things up."

"Who is Brunnea?"

Dalia's brow furrows, and she opens her mouth to answer when the door to the room opens.

"Oh, Dalia." Ella beams. "You've met. Perfect. I have to go back to the stable. I've got so much to do before the auctions."

I glance between the two young women. A stable sounds more inviting than staying in Dalia's room. Far more inviting, given the hidden barbs in all of Dalia's words. "I could go there with you."

Mouth open in astonishment, Ella shakes her head. "Oh, no, no. No. You couldn't." Her gaze skitters to Dalia, who stands with a slightly raised eyebrow and a downward flick to her lips as if she's trying to suppress a smirk. "You're much too ill—too weak —to go that far. It's two miles." She smiles prettily, but there's a sense of secrecy in her words.

She hides something. The little voice in my head agrees.

I flinch at the unexpected and unwelcome opinion. "Perhaps I could...ride?"

Ella shakes her head. "No, it's best for you to stay here. Safer. I mean, there's more food and it's more comfortable—"

"I don't mind," I say, suddenly desperate not to be left alone with Dalia. There's something strange in her, something I don't—can't—trust. Something that squirms over me.

Dalia snorts. "We have a stable you can sleep in, if you insist."

I drag myself to my feet, using the bedpost to stand. "Of course."

"No, don't be foolish. Dalia, hush," Ella adds, stepping forward and putting out her hands as though to push me back into bed. "You need to stay here at least one more night. Recover your strength and eat as much as you can. Then maybe, if there are no rooms here, you can sleep out there." Ella grimaces. "But I'd prefer it if you stayed inside."

"You could use the help at home more than I can," Dalia murmurs for Ella's ears.

My gaze flicks to her. It's clear the girl doesn't want me here, neither in her room nor inside the inn.

"I want to help wherever I'm needed." I consider them. "You cook for the guests, Dalia? And Ella, you manage a stable?"

Ella shrugs while Dalia nods a bit proudly.

"Yes, she manages a stable. And she has dozens of horses that are the best in the land." Dalia beams, drawing herself up to her full height, though it's nearly a foot less than Ella's stature.

"Yes, well, only because Father died," Ella explains. "And yes, it's true I need the help, but Lady Eleanora would never allow it. She would be furious..." Ella trails off and shakes her head. "I'm sorry, but you have to stay here, at least for now. And then maybe in a week, after the first masque, maybe I can have you help me."

A week? I'm supposed to stay here with a girl that doesn't like me for a week?

Dalia looks as dismayed as I feel.

Perhaps in a week I'll be well enough to leave on my own. I

don't have a week anyway. I have to appear before King Greggory at his next audience.

A twinkle in her eyes, Dalia turns to her friend, switching subjects with ease as she ignores me and shrugs off my troubles. "The prince arrives in a couple of hours. Aren't you going to stay in town and watch?"

Ella narrows her eyes. "You know very well I don't have time for that. I just stopped by to check on Winter."

Dalia chuckles. "That's right, you'll see him in a few days yourself anyway."

"Hush, Dalia."

There's something sweet about the way these two bicker. As if they're sisters. They're clearly not, as despite their blond hair, Ella's is bright, pale blond, while Dalia's is the golden of the sun. Ella's eyes are warm sky, while Dalia's are the green of a dangerous forest. Ella's face is round and short, while Dalia's is long and oval. If I had to liken them to animals, Ella would be house dog greeting everyone with a smile, but Dalia would be a feral barn cat, hissing at those who dared come too close.

Smothering my smile at the thought, I wonder how Dalia got here—and how she and Ella became such friends. It's probably all Ella's doing when Dalia appeared in her life. Capital cities always have a way of gathering foreigners; I know Merise does. The words of Mrs. Caupo come back to me. That she has her doubts about Dalia's age; she looks like she could be either thirteen or twenty-three, depending on which feature you examine. She's petite, but I must admit she's also beautiful.

"Well, I must go. Dalia, will you check on Winter every now and then?" Ella casts me a comforting smile.

At the request, Dalia's good humor drains from her face, and she shrugs. "Of course."

"I can help. Help Dalia, I mean," I say, though just the idea of standing and helping clean or cook nearly makes me collapse.

Dalia snorts. "Well you won't be let out of this room until you get out of those clothes and take a bath. I'll have to find you something to wear. And you'll probably be hungry soon."

My stomach growls in answer, and I clasp my hands over it in surprise. Now that I've given it food, it seems to expect it.

Ella's smile widens. "I'll bring you more food. And there's water heating on the fire already for a bath," she adds. "It won't be the warmest bath you've ever taken, but—"

"It may be," I tell her with a half smile, thinking of icy plunges in Canens and the superstition that getting too hot would make you far too cold and could kill you after you got out of the bath. Although I think the adults told the children things like that to keep the kids from spending too long in the bath or even wanting a hot bath. I blink my memories away and return my attention to Ella. "Thank you, Ella."

She gives me a curious little smile, then nods and steps close to her friend and lowers her voice. "Dalia, please help her."

A faint look of mutiny appears in Dalia's eyes, but she nods. Then Ella leaves with a wave and click of her boots, leaving us alone in the room.

Dalia goes to the door and watches out the hallway a few moments, seeming to wait for something. Then she steps back inside, snaps the door shut, and twists the key in the lock.

My muscles tighten. The light inside me begins to gather, but Dalia doesn't look at me. Instead, she returns to the wardrobe and crouches, pulling open the bottom drawer. There she removes a bundle of beautiful, icy-blue fabric. It appears far too rich for either her or anyone in this inn, but like a fabric a noble-woman might make a dress from. Dalia rummages around for another little bundle, then straightens, goes to the chair, and plops herself down, crossing her right leg over the left without a word.

From a small bag, she removes a threaded needle and begins to turn it in and out of the bottom of the dress. A few minutes pass, during which she avoids my gaze, and I don't dare speak.

My stomach growls, and her lips twitch.

Several minutes later, my stomach rumbles again.

"When is dinner?" I venture.

"The doctor said not to feed you again for another hour." Dalia smirks.

I wrinkle my nose at her wording, as if I'm a horse on a feeding schedule. "Oh."

"He said you might founder."

"What?" Did she read my thoughts?

She snorts and ducks over her sewing.

Oh she is sassy, isn't she? Despite being the object of her humor, I'm amused at her amusement. "What are you doing?"

"What does it look like?"

I shrug and consider how to ask the questions I really want to ask. She seemed secretive about this dress, waiting until Ella left the inn before taking up the sewing, and then locking the door too. "You are making something for Ella?"

She lifts her gaze, stares at me several seconds, then tucks her chin and stabs the dress. "I'm going to get Ella to the masques—all three of them—if it kills me."

"The masques?"

Dalia laughs, a cynical laugh that sounds years older than she looks. "Where have you been that you haven't heard of the masques?"

I give her a look. "Dying on the streets. Where were you?"

Her lips twist into a comical grimace. "Fair enough."

"What masques?" I ask when she shows no sign of going on.

"The palace—the King and Queen—are throwing three masques. I'm not sure why, except the rumors are that the prince needs to find himself a wife." Dalia snorts again. "He'll need a wife soon, I suppose…"

"Why?" Though my mind isn't on Prince Brann finding a wife but me gaining access to him.

"Rumors of the King being ill, and Prince Brann is the only

heir to the throne of Ardor." She gives me a slanted look. "What rock have you been living under?"

"The streets—"

"The streets, yeah," she says with me, as though she'd forgotten when she asked.

I study her as she sews. "Where are you from?"

She doesn't answer, but a wince skims over her skin, and her jaw tightens.

"You don't look Ardorian."

She raises a shoulder. "Nor do you."

That was a stupid gamble; she knows exactly where I'm from. Too bad I can't say the same about her. "I've been a few places," I say. "I don't know what I am. What are you?"

"I don't know either." She chuckles down at her lap. "Just like you."

Silence falls between us. Her needle moves deftly in and out of the fabric, making straight, invisible-to-my-eye stitches.

After several minutes of this, I finally ask, "Is there anything I can do to help?"

"You know how to sew?"

"Yes. A bit. Nothing fancy, but…"

She stands, bustles around for a half a minute, then deposits a pile of mending on the bed beside me. "You can start with that. If you impress me, I might let you help me make Ella's dresses."

Trying not to grin, I set to my task.

2: ELLA

THE PROPOSAL

*D*istracted, I leave Winter in the King's Inn, hoping she and Dalia will get along. Though Dalia is sweet with me and Noemì, she can be acerbic with others. Chances of her playing nice with Winter right away are moderate at best. If they were fillies or mares, I'd put the two in separate paddocks for the first week or two.

I'm so deep in thought that I don't pay enough attention and walk straight into Sallust Birch. Curse him for habitually putting himself in my path.

"Ella!" he says with such unexpected joy that my heart sinks. "I'm so sorry, I didn't see you there."

I step back, putting a proper distance between us again. *Why don't I believe you, Sallust?* But outwardly, I only say, as pleasantly as I can, "Good morning, Sallust."

Not wanting to encourage conversation, I step to the side, but he darts in front of me again, coming closer in the process. My heart twists in my chest. I don't need this right now, not with everything else—

"How are you today?" His wide blue eyes eagerly seek out my face from only inches away.

Leaning back, I plaster a tolerant smile on my face. "I'm doing well, thank you. Very busy though." I try to move around him again.

His face crumples in mock concern. "Oh? What is it you have to do? In the middle of a good novel?"

My mouth parts. I should be used to his not-so-subtle digs at my worth, but I barely refrain from glaring at him now. How dare he insult me by implying I have nothing to do other than sit around and read a book?

I lift my chin. "Actually, I am in the middle of a fantastic novel about a princess who pricks her finger and falls asleep for a hundred years, but I have been too busy to read it lately. I'm afraid I have to prepare for the upcoming auction." I snap my teeth shut as soon as the words escape.

I should not have said that. If I tell Sallust that I'm in the auction, he might tell someone else, and word will get back to Lady Eleanora. She could try to take the deposit money if she catches wind of my entry fee just sitting in there with Sir Birch.

"The auction?" he asks too innocently. "What are you doing for the auction?"

"Oh, just helping out, you know. Keeping an eye on things. As always, considering the Gelu are my business." My smile feels thin inside. Hopefully it still looks natural on the outside. "So I really must be going. I also have chores to complete; night feeds to prepare, and the masques, of course." I'm rambling, not making any sense, but I doubt he notices any difference in me.

"Oh?" His words seem harmless, but there's too strong a wave of interest beyond them.

"Yes," I say almost too eagerly at having something other than the auction to speak of. "I have to help with the dresses and masks for the balls."

His soft curls bounce on his shoulders as he nods, his fitted jacket making him look like a highborn gentleman instead of the banker-mayor's son that he is. "Are you planning on attending the masques?"

I tighten my grasp on the edges of my skirt, burying them in the fabric. "No, I don't believe I'll have the time."

He nods and a calculated smile dawns on his wide face. "Father said he spoke to you the other day."

A chill caresses my body. "Did he?"

"Yes…" Sallust leaves the word up in the air, the thought unfinished, waiting to see what I'll say, I'm sure.

"Well, yes, I stopped in to see him. See who was selling horses in the upcoming auction."

He glances down at my hands as if to reach for one, but they're still buried in my skirt's folds; I know his games. With a false look of concern, he steps closer and ducks his head toward me. "He said he reminded you that I'm awaiting your answer."

"What answer might that be?"

"Ella," he says gently, as though we are lovers. His head is only a hand's span away.

Though he turns my stomach, I refuse to back up this time.

He huffs impatiently. "I tire of you being stubborn about this. You know what I mean."

I brush back a lock of hair from my face. "I'm sorry, Sallust, but I don't—"

"Marry me, Ella." He grabs my hand and pulls it into his, clasping it between his sweaty palms.

"Sallust—" I try to tug away, but his grip is tight.

"Ella, the only thing I want to hear emerge from your lips is the word, 'yes.'"

"Sallust—"

"Ella, I know what Father said to you. And he's right. When is the last time you had an offer of marriage? A real one—one that you might accept? You cannot expect to have any more offers that are halfway decent, not with your situation and age. I am here, offering you my hand. I know horses, and what I don't know I can learn. Father and I have long desired to enter the breeding business, but you know the laws."

"I do." Better than him, I wager, but I don't say that.

"You can either marry now and save your stable, or you can watch your stable go up for auction—all of it, down to Flora and the very saddle you learned to ride in."

I glance away, gritting my teeth.

"You know that's what happens, Ella." His voice grows firm, authoritative, as though he's instructing a small child in the error of her ways.

My teeth grind so loudly that I almost can't hear Sallust's next words.

"You'll lose everything, Ella," he says with feigned gentleness. "Everything. But I'm here, offering you everything you have…and more."

Forcing my teeth apart, I crook up an eyebrow at that and try to keep my voice light when I speak. "More? What might that be?"

"Me, Ella." He shrugs with a self-deprecating smirk. "I'm desirable, so I've been told."

I take a breath. "Sallust, I have no doubt that some women find you very desirable."

His expression begins to rise in hope.

"But I do not." Inwardly, I wince at the words, but I forge ahead. "I am certain that nothing but love will force me to marry. Even if it means losing everything, I will not marry a man I do not love."

"All women think that about their husbands." He gives me a patronizing smile. "You would learn to love me, Ella."

"Sallust," I say, exasperated, "if I have not by now, then I shall not ever."

His eyes darken as his ears turn red.

Immediately, I wish that I could take back the words, but they are out; it is too late.

"You will regret that decision, Ella." His lips thin. "I have offered you everything, and you have denied it."

I straighten. "I am sorry, Sallust. But I do not love you."

The muscles in his jaw tense. "You are a fool."

"Perhaps so. But I cannot see myself marrying anyone right now. And if that means my land will be given to the Crown to be auctioned, then that is the risk I must take. But at least I will have remained true to myself and my father."

"True to your father?" Sallust snorts in disgust. "He demanded—your father discussed with my father about you marrying me. He saw our futures as melded together, melding our families together. You are being stubborn, just as you've been since his death. You are a fool to deny me, and a fool to run your stable into the ground and destroy Aeneas Stables and its legacy forever."

Flinching, I turn my face away. There's just enough truth in what he's saying to make me uncomfortable. Father mentioned Sallust to me once, a few months before he died, but I told Father I didn't like him. Father dropped it, but only after telling me that I ought to consider his best qualities, for he could outgrow his worst. Still, Father never saw Sallust as lord over the stables. He couldn't have. Perhaps as one who was suitable for Haydée or Carmen, not as a man to trust with the legacy of Aeneas Stables.

"I am sorry, Sallust. I don't believe that's true." My words are gentle but final.

His cheeks go as red as his ears, and without so much as a goodbye, he drops my hand, turns on his heel, and stalks away.

My stomach twists and dips. I have made an enemy of him now, of that I am certain.

FOUND

I lost the girl's trail several miles back, but I am certain of her destination now. I simply have to reach her before she can convince anyone of who she is. It would not do for even one person in Nubilus know the Princess of Canens walks into their city. She would put herself in grave danger.

My heart thumps unusually fast at the thought. Already, getting her to believe me and safely away from Blanche is unlikely.

The walls of Nubilus tower before my horse and me. Stone and cold gray, reminding me of Canens and all its grayness, it's rather comforting. Surprisingly so. Some might not appreciate the monotone colors of the north, but I have always found those natural colors soothing. During a hunt, I prefer the strange-colored beasts, the ones that stand out as odd and unusual. Not for their difference in and of themselves, and not because they are easier to find—they often are harder—but to remove the different ones from the world. The world should be more uniform, more like a line of soldiers or well-trained slaves.

For the first time that I can recall, a niggle of unease occurs to me at these thoughts. It has never felt wrong before. Uniformity is comforting, to know what you have and what you will have. To not be surprised by something odd and different. Something like the princess with her blue eyes and black hair and red lips. It was a good thing the Queen removed that hair from her, wasn't it? It marks her as different. Wrong.

I press my own lips together. The princess is different indeed. Queen Blanche is far more appropriate a queen for Canens. She looks just like a Canensian should. But then, she's not the rightful queen, is she?

Annoyed at the confusion of my thoughts, I focus on my surroundings. Here, I am the odd one. Despite attempting to blend in, I am well aware that I don't quite look the part. I have exchanged my heavy clothing for light ones, but my features are too sharp, my beard too long, my skin too pale and pink to be Ardorite. All of which an astute Ardorite will see.

I ride Chrystalli through the streets of Nubilus, knowing that he, at least, fits in here. He will help me look the part. I've changed his saddle and bridle, even his saddlebag and blanket, and now he looks just as any other Gelu Rigens on the street. He draws attention, surely, but that's because of what he is. He tosses his head up and down or arches his neck when eyes fall on him, preening in his arrogant way.

People dressed in colorful gowns and tunics mingle among the streets, chatting under the warmth of the sun. Above them, on the city walls, guards patrol. There are three times as many today. Perhaps they anticipate trouble.

Little good they do, positioned up high with their swords sheathed and flimsy spears pointing at the sky. They would accomplish nothing against invaders. And their skills are under-developed, for when I entered Nubilus through their gates, my horse wore Canensian tack. I shake my head. I could pick them off one by one with arrows from the forest five hundred paces away, and no one would know where the attack came from. Even with triple their numbers, they are useless.

I smirk. Ardorites are as arrogant as the rumors say.

Still, as one's eyes fall upon me, perhaps feeling my scrutiny, I dip my head and turn my horse down a side street. I scan the shadows, trying to peer into the windows for any sight of the princess. The woman had said she would be at The King's Inn. But where is that? And how does she know? She is far too much like the Queen with her strange knowledge.

Hours of fruitless searching later, I'm more than ready to say goodbye to the city of Nubilus and exit for the night, but something stops me. Though I am far more comfortable out in the woods than in a building here, staying inside the walls might allow me—

A sudden fanfare from the city walls sends a jolt through my body. I tense for attack, for sight of my queen. I whirl my stallion and hurry him through the back streets toward the noise.

The fanfare sounds again, joined by cheers in the city center. Earlier I watched merchants decorate their stalls with streamers and flowers, but I kept my search for the girl mostly to the back streets and alleys, which remain untouched. Now, upon returning to the high street, I find the swollen, excited crowds. Someone important is here; a parade is about to begin.

My eye slips to an inn a few doors down. A sign above the door with a kingly crown painted upon it proclaims it to be The King's Inn. Guests pour from its door, adding dozens of people to the bursting streets. Trailing the crowd, a young woman pauses in the doorway, absently stirring the contents of a bowl with a wooden spoon. Amusement is written on her round face. But she's not the princess; I put her aside.

Crystalli tosses his head and prances at the crowds touching him. My attempts to soothe him are useless, and so I ride him into a back alley where he calms. I dismount and tie him to a hitching post. He won't let anyone steal him; no one would get past his own bad attitude and flattened ears.

On foot, I head to the corner opposite The King's Inn where I can see the alley if my horse should bolt out, but also the windows of inn and the approaching parade.

And a princely parade it is. So princely that it might just be the perfect opportunity to find what I'm looking for.

Perched atop a low stone wall, I settle back against a window ledge and scan the faces in the crowd.

PARADE

A day later I graduate from the mending to helping Dalia stitch the laces of the dress she plans for Ella's first masque. With nothing better to do while I wait for the audience at the palace, I might as well earn my keep. All day, I remain in Dalia's bedroom, far from any mess that might mar the fabric or any prying eyes. On occasion, I push the drapes open and peer out into the back garden where Dalia scrubs sheets from the rooms. When I peek out into the hallway, I catch sight of her passing the end of the hallway at times, mounds of laundry or trays of food in her hands.

When Dalia does bring me meals, I don't bother asking her how she obtained these expensive fabrics I work on, but I show her how careful I am with them. The work is mindless and boring, but at least it fills the time better than staring at the ceiling. Dalia has left my midday meal when I'm curled up on the bed, my eyes and neck aching from staring down at the fabric all morning and the sound of hooves clattering outside on the cobblestones drifts through the walls. Voices fill the air, a low murmur interspersed with sharp, excited cries of children.

Hoofbeats sound in the alley behind the inn. It must be Ella.

Hurriedly, I stow the fabric at the bottom of the basket of mending, hiding every inch of the icy blue fabric under the ratty mending of petticoats and handkerchiefs. I grab one of the handkerchiefs and begin repairing the embroidery upon it.

A few minutes later, Ella still hasn't entered the room, and the hoofbeats are louder, more than just one horse, more than just a couple of horses, and not at the back of the inn at all. Cheering fills the streets, filtering in around me, muffled rejoices.

I put aside the handkerchief and stand. After a few decent meals, I'm much steadier on my feet, and I hurry into the empty back hallway, through that and into the kitchen hallway. The kitchen is empty, though the evening's stew bubbles abandoned on the stove. I frown at it and then follow the empty hallway to the front of the inn and out into the dining area. Chairs sit empty with tables holding half-drunk drinks, bowls of half-eaten stew, and abandoned loaves of bread. Outside another cheer erupts.

Cautiously, I cross the empty room to the front window and peer out. People throng through the streets, standing on porches, railings, steps, children on top of men's shoulders, whatever can make someone taller to see. I inch my way out of the inn, and no one pays any attention to me. For once, no one's head turns my way as I appear. And it's rather nice to be ignored.

I nestle in amongst the spectators as horses in fancy livery and riders with button-up jackets and tight breeches prance through the streets. The riders hold fluttering, dark blue banners with bright gold fringes.

A fanfare announces the honoree of the parade, and my attention jerks down the line riders to the stoic man riding up in the midst of another batch of soldiers. I pause.

While the prince is handsome enough in his smooth, tan breeches and his well-fitted dark blue jacket with gold accents, he's not nearly as handsome as Rus, though I can see the familial resemblance. I jolt at the strange turn in my thoughts. Rus? Rus with his hatred toward me and his dark red hair and his eyes that flash with intelligence and humor? Well, humor when he looks at his sister, at least. When he looks at me, there's only hatred.

I sigh, regretting the way I had to leave him, regretting everything except saving them. At least they left me with no more deaths on my conscious.

Prince Brann's coppery horse tosses his head as he prances past me. The prince controls the impressively muscled animal with ease, his hips moving in fluid motion with the saddle, never allowing air between his seat and the leather, even when the animal tosses his head and throws his hindquarters around at a particularly loud shout from the crowd. I remember Caleb pointing those aspects of a good rider out back in Canens as he taught me to ride. Caleb, the gentle giant whom I tried to save from slavery only to have him join me in serving the Magister. Flinching at the memory and all the pain it brings, I pull myself back to the present.

Even with the animal's antics, the prince appears bored with the entire parade. Then his horse spooks, surging toward the crowd with sudden aggression, his ears flat upon his head.

The crowd parts with alarmed cries. The prince pulls on the reins so the animal's mouth yawns open as those before him jump aside to avoid danger. Only a few don't move, foolish—

I gasp. I only see him for a moment, for the merest flash of a moment, then he's gone, blending back into the crowd, leaving me wondering if I've seen him at all.

The Magister. The Huntsman of Canens.

He's here. He's found me.

AENEAS

The morning of the first masque coincides with the official notice of auction entries announced in town. I'm hoping that Lady Eleanora is too distracted to pay much attention to the list of stables announced.

Early in the day, Dalia sends Winter to me with an entire gaggle of children to help out at the stable. I nearly laugh to see their arrival, Winter a head taller than the tallest of them, and her dark, short hair and pale skin making her look like one of the temple goddesses wearing a wig.

Squinting in the sunlight as though her eyes are unaccustomed to anything so bright, she darts her gaze around almost nervously. I reconsider Dalia's concerns of Winter being pursued, but push them aside again. I don't know why, but I trust her. It's the same feeling I get with a neglected horse: she might be sad and wounded, but she's genuinely kind inside, just needing a little bit of help getting back to health.

After I assign the children to their tasks, giving the larger ones the heavy lifting and the younger to help with minor jobs, I turn to Winter and survey her with a tilted head. She gives me a funny look, wariness clouding her face.

"So how are you finding The King's Inn? And Dalia?" I add with a small grin.

Her face relaxes, though she still has that half-wild look in her eye like Flora had for months after I rescued her.

"It is all wonderful," she says in her slightly stilted Ardorian. "I thank you for your hospitality."

I blink at her formality, almost like thanking a person for inviting her to dinner. "Well, of course," I say. "I couldn't let you die on the streets."

Her lips flicker. "Well the rest of Ardor was willing to let that happen."

Opening my mouth to argue, I pause when she lifts her shoulder and continues.

"I can't blame them. You saw me when I knocked on that door."

I smile gently. "True. You were looking a bit…haggard."

She furrows her brow, almost as if she doesn't understand the word, but she simply turns to watch a younger child in ratty clothing carrying a pitchfork too large for her tagging along after an older boy pushing a wheelbarrow full of soiled straw. They work so cheerfully, eager for their reward of food from the inn later. But there's something dark on Winter's face. It makes me feel almost as though I abuse these children in asking them to work for their food.

"Are you sure you're ready to help at the stables today?" I ask Winter. "It's hard work."

"I'm accustomed to hard work." She gives me a slanted look. "And Dalia is sick of me."

I chuckle. "She gets sick of everyone. She likes her own company best."

Winter's big blue eyes crease around the edges in uncertainty at my humor. She's nervous. Though she hides it well, like an animal who doesn't know whom to trust.

"Do you like horses?" I move toward the mare in the nearest

stall and pull a carrot from my dress pocket. With the auctions so close, visitors from town are expected daily, and I have to at least wear my riding slacks or leggings underneath a dress in case of unexpected potential buyers.

I crack the sliced carrot in half and offer a short piece to the mare on a flat palm. She lips it up and snuffles around for more, but I hold out the rest of the carrot toward Winter. "Care to feed her? She's gentle."

Winter glances at my outstretched hand, then the horse, and takes the carrot. Before I can explain how to feed the mare safely, she extends the treat on her flattened palm and the mare snatches it up. Winter runs her hand from the mare's velvety nose and up her cheek to find the spot under her forelock that every horse loves having scratched. The mare leans into the affection, and Winter obliges her.

"You're familiar with horses then?"

Winter's muscles tighten just enough for me to catch. I'm accustomed to the minuscule flinches of my high-strung animals and the way I must stop their tension before they lose control. But with Winter, although I see her reaction, I'm not sure why or to what she's reacting.

"I've done a bit of riding before." Her icy gaze flicks over the stall door.

"Good. Well, you won't ride her. This mare is pregnant, about six months along now, as we traditionally try to have our horses foal a month or two before the spring auctions. I practically grew up on the back of a horse, one like this girl here," I say, stepping forward and scratching the mare's other favorite spot, along her cheek where the halter rubs. "But once the broodmares are six months in, we just turn them out to pasture and don't ride them. It's a tradition going back hundreds of years."

Winter is silent, but I sense her listening with her reserved interest, so I continue.

"I cannot bear to be inside when horses are waiting for me

outside. And I love rides through the woods or along the seashore." My words grow distant as my thoughts turn to my childhood here at Aeneas Stables and my rides over the years, alone, with my sisters…with Hadwin.

The mare jerks her head away and retreats to the back of her stall, where she noses at the small window showing the pastures beyond. When I turn to Winter, I find her staring at me with a thoughtful softness to her eye.

"Dalia said your father died a few years ago and you're going to lose your stable if you don't marry."

I blink at the bluntness of her statement. "Yes. It's true."

"But that doesn't explain why your mother hates you."

Her words tighten a rope around my ribs, squeezing the breath out of me before I press my lips together to stop it. "Who told you that she hates me?" I shake my head at my own question. "I suppose it's no surprise that you would hear that. But I thought —well, it's a long story."

"I have time." Winter's solemn voice, gentle as a whisper of wind, almost brings tears to my eyes.

Brushing my hair away from my face, I walk toward the rear of the stable. As I hope, Winter follows. I don't speak as we pass several of the children cheerfully cleaning out soiled straw from a stall while another drags an entire bale of straw toward it. I give the older girl lugging the bale a faint smile of encouragement. She bobs a little nod toward me, a bead of sweat dripping down her brow. I sense, rather than see, Winter's disapproval at the sights.

Aeneas' paddocks stretch their long, white arms toward the sea a few miles distant. Apple trees line the wide carriage path leading from the rear of the stable to the long barn where we house the carriages and where the dogs often sleep. Beyond that, the path continues down to the cliffside and then the sea, a path I've taken many a time in my life, searching out solace in the midst of unrest.

My heart twists to think of losing all this, of never again being able to walk out of these stables and see this as mine.

Winter catches her breath as Letifer, my silver-colored stud, dashes toward the tall fence and slides to a halt so that his nose stops within an inch of it.

He curls his upper lip and neighs loudly. Then he rears high and slices the air with his front hooves. His feet land with a thump on the grass. He kicks out behind him and dashes off, bucking and kicking.

The day of my father's death flashes back to me in detail at Letifer and his actions. I close my eyes and speak. "I killed my father, and for that, my mother hates me."

6: WINTER

AIDE

"How do they think you killed your father?" I keep my voice calm as I ask Ella to explain her dramatic statement.

She shakes her head sadly and sighs a long sigh that drains the energy from her body so that she slumps onto the stallion's fence. "Father and I went out one morning to break Letifer to saddle. I was thirteen." She stares at the silver animal as she speaks. "Father told me to get on him, and I did it wrong. Letifer spooked and reared." She gnaws on her lower lip, and her gaze grows distant as though she's witnessing the event.

My body tenses, and I blink away images of Certa flashing before my eyes.

"Letifer hit Father with a hoof, and Father fell. He…died in the ring, didn't even make it home to his bed or to the healer." A tear slips down her cheek. "There was nothing I could do."

I unstick my teeth from each other, pushing back the memories that assail me, the faces I couldn't save. What I wouldn't give to have just one. "And so they blame you."

Wiping at her cheek, she straightens and offers me a self-deprecating little smile. "Wouldn't you? But now you know why Mother and all of Nubilus hates me." She shakes her head sadly, her eyes on the stallion who grazes in the distance now. "He's all that I have left of Father, really. Father put all his hopes on him, and I transferred mine there, but as a woman, I cannot expect this to last." She sweeps a hand at the grounds around her. "It's all fleeting, isn't it? I think I'm just trying to enjoy the time I have left here, for who knows what will happen after the Crown forces my hand?"

"I don't understand why they do that," I say without thinking.

"The Ardorian laws of inheritance are complicated, especially when you're a woman. But unless I marry and produce an heir by age twenty-two, I lose everything."

"Everything?"

"Well, I lose the stables and our home and all our ancestral lands. They'll be taken by the Crown and auctioned off, and I'll get a percentage of that money as dowry. Even the auctioning rules in such a case are complicated. I don't know that it's ever happened before, what I've been doing. Most eldest daughters who lose their father choose to either immediately marry or to surrender their possible inheritance to the Crown so they get their dowry money and someone will marry them."

I frown. "So they pay you the money it would bring in?"

"Sort of." She shrugs. "They'll auction off everything." She waves a hand around us. "And then that money is held in trust and enough is given for the young woman's family to live in a modest home with one servant until she delivers an heir, when-ever that might be. If she doesn't marry, she might live simply on dowry money for the rest of her life. She never gets all her money, not unless she has heirs, and then it technically belongs to her son anyway."

"And if they run their family's business?" I ask.

"None before me have desired to run her father's business. Or if they have, they haven't attempted because the rules are so complicated and no one wants to help a young woman do so."

Her smile has deep sorrow and a hint of regret in it. "I chose to do so because of a deep love for the horses. Nothing else could convince me." She shakes her head and pulls a red apple from her pocket. As if smelling it, the stallion lifts his head and turns it our direction. He snorts, then ambles our way.

"And you don't want to lose this."

She watches the stallion near. "No."

"Then why not marry?"

She seems to be holding her breath. "Because I don't want the kind of marriage my father had."

"He wasn't happy?"

"No. He and my mother ended their marriage with hatred. And when she didn't give him a son, well, I think their relationship never recovered."

"I'm sorry."

She shakes her head. "I spent most of my time out here with Father, and I think it was his way and mine of coping with Mother's hatred toward him. Because I chose the stables over her as well, she's hated me for it. But after he died, she changed toward me."

I am silent. I know exactly what kind of changes she means.

"But it has made me stronger. And it's made me even more determined to marry for no reason other than true love."

At that, I smile faintly. If only I had such freedom as well. But all I have to offer the prince of Ardor are my land and me, and I will gladly make that sacrifice. What is my happiness for a country's salvation?

The silver stallion approaches, giving me such a suspicious look out of the corner of his eye that I remain absolutely still. Ella doesn't move, simply holds the apple out on a steady hand. He slowly stretches out his neck and snatches up the treat. Then he moves another step toward her, nudging her hand with his nose, and she obligingly scratches his chin. I watch for a minute, then move to scratch my neck. As soon as I lift my hand, he tosses up his head and bolts.

"Sorry. He's absolutely incorrigible." Ella chuckles affectionately. "Infuriatingly so." With a shrug, she turns and heads toward the stable again.

I follow, curious to see what she might share with me next. One thing is for sure: she is not the young woman I expected.

"The auctions are coming up fast," she says as she walks, "and now I have to be ready for anything. In addition to dealing with the Crown Inspector's instructions, I have to make sure my horses are constantly in the best condition."

"Why?" We walk into the darkness of the stable where the children are finishing up the last stall.

Ella pauses to pick up a sharp rock from the ground and puts it in her pocket. "Well, there's a tradition in the week before the auctions for people to drop by stables unannounced."

"Why? Oh, to see the horses up for auction," I answer before she can. "That makes sense. And that's allowed?"

"Technically, no." Ella smiles my direction. "But it happens every auction, and everyone just looks past it. Honestly, the laws concerning Gelu Rigens need to be revised." Sorrow infiltrates her face. "So many rules are too difficult or too ridiculous to follow."

"You think that it should be legal to sell Geli to anyone? At anytime?" I follow her down the aisle and toward the front of the barn.

"I think that there are far too many restrictions on the breeders. We should keep Geli well regulated, but not simply within the country of Ardor. We lose a great deal of money and prestige by refusing to sell to other countries. We could be a very rich country, which we could use to help the poor and build better roads and—"

I smile at her ideas. She is sweet, kind-hearted, and ultimately a gracious young woman. And yet her ideas are somewhat naïve.

Once the Geli leave the border, their bloodlines would become polluted.

"That's an interesting idea," comes a voice from farther down the aisle.

Ella and I jump at the unfamiliar voice. It's not her groom, Gavin, nor is it one of the children.

I search the shadows but all I can see is a man's outline standing near one of the front stalls. My body tenses.

Panic grows on Ella's face, as though she's said too much before someone that she shouldn't have. "Can I help you, sir?" She walks toward the faceless man.

There's an eagerness in her voice that is almost embarrassing, but given the history she's related to me, I have no doubt that she needs to develop any buyer's relationship she can.

The man steps out of the shadows, and I can't conceal my gasp. It's the prince of Ardor.

7: ELLA

HOPE

inter's gasp behind me steals my attention from the man who's emerged from the shadows before us. I glance at her, confused. Did she trip on something? But she's staring at the man with her icy features more frozen than usual.

Ignoring her, I face the man before us. Perhaps he's a titled man with money scouting out horses for the upcoming auctions and Winter recognizes him from town or the inn.

"Hello, sir. What brings you to Aeneas Stables?" I add a silent prayer asking the Lord that this man wants to bid on all my entered horses and has the cash to do so.

But as the light plays across his face, I find myself distracted from my question. There *is* something familiar about him, but at once, I know that I don't know him. At least, not as he is. His features are too angular, too chiseled, his eyes too pale, and he is far, far too tall and muscular to be Hadwin.

The man standing before me is quite…beautiful. There is no other word for it. His golden hair and skin, coupled with eyes as green as the grass outside, I, quite frankly, lose my words as I stare at him.

Winter nudges me.

"Wha—?"

"She's the owner and breeder of this stable, sir," Winter is saying in her slightly stilted manner. "And there is no one more knowledgable about these horses—or Gelu in general—than Ella."

"Ella? Ella Saevus?" The man's voice is gently curious.

"Yes," I say automatically.

"It's very nice to meet you, Miss Saevus."

A blush works its way up to my cheeks. "I'm sorry, I think I missed your name?"

For some reason, the man hesitates, his gaze flicking from me to Winter and back to me. "Uh, I am Duke Orestes."

My spine straightens. A duke? He's awfully young to be a duke.

"I noticed a remarkable young stallion outside, the silver?"

"Yes, your grace, that's one of our studs," I answer. "Letifer."

He raises a brow. "Is that the stallion people come from all over to catch a glimpse of? The one that they call the Unicorn of Nubilus?"

Chuckling at the almost-forgotten nickname, I nod. "Yes, he is. Have you come to see him?" My face tightens as I await his answer. I hope not. I hope he's here to look at horses for sale, not one of the few horses I could never sell.

"And your father bred him?"

"Not exactly. That's a common misunderstanding. He purchased Letifer's dam, who had been bred to Mythos—unsuccessfully, it was thought."

Duke Orestes' eyes widen. "To Mythos? Truly? How have I not heard that before?"

"It was lucky, since the mare had been thought to be barren." I lift a shoulder. It's not something I usually volunteer, given Letifer's history. "I haven't spoken of it much, merely list it on the papers. But with Mythos' recent death, Letifer and all his siblings have gained some fame."

"Lucky indeed." He studies me with a lingering, sidelong look. "Would you ever sell him?"

I put the required smile of denial on my lips that I use whenever someone asks me that question. "No, sir. I'm afraid I could never."

"Your grace, if you have some time, I'm sure that Ella would enjoy showing you the horses she does have for sale next week," Winter says. "Or I could show you the horses if Ella doesn't have the time."

The duke's attention doesn't waver from me at Winter's interjection. "Yes, that would be nice. Do you think that's possible, Miss Saevus? Would you show me your horses?"

My heart gives a strange thump in my chest, almost as though it's wobbling where it should be and in danger of falling before it steadies itself. There is something so familiar about him. Hadwin's name is on my lips, but...Hadwin would know me, he would remember me. Of my name, I never deceived him.

Hope I didn't realize I harbored inside me plummets to my toes. I reach for a lead rope hanging nearby to distract myself from his penetrating stare.

"I would be grateful for a tour," he says.

"Of course. I would love to show you around," I say, lifting my gaze to his and putting a polite smile on my lips. He might not be Hadwin, but he is a duke. And a young, attractive duke at that.

"I'll direct your helpers through their chores when they finish up," Winter says wryly. "Take your time. Take Duke...Orestes, was it?"

The duke casts her what seems meant to be a lazy look. "Yes, that's right," he says coolly. "And who are you?"

Winter motions to me. "Why don't you show him Letifer while I tack up two horses for you? Which ones would you like?"

"No. Have Gavin do it." I hesitate. "I'll help you."

Winter touches my arm. "We'll be all right. You just show...his grace...the horses."

I release the tension in my shoulders. She's right.

"Where is Gavin?" Winter asks.

"He's around the tack room, I think."

Winter nods. "Of course." With a glint in her eye, and before the duke can ask her anything else, she disappears in that direction.

The duke and I watch her, then I walk toward the exit. "I'll lead you out this way, your grace. We can take a peek at the others up for sale on the way."

"Thank you," he murmurs, falling into step beside me. "How many do you have for sale?"

"There will be six in the auction." As we walk, I point out the other four.

"All impressive specimen," the duke says. "And you bred them?"

"Yes."

"Most impressive." This time when he speaks, his eyes are on me.

I shift my weight, uncomfortable with the intense way his attention keeps turning from the horses to me. It's like he sees me the same way I see the horses.

"And how did you learn all this?"

"My father taught me, your grace." I pick up a misplaced lead rope from a hook off the wall as we pass it.

"A good father to teach his eldest daughter the business."

"Yes. He was." I inject a bit of stubbornness into my words. I believe Father to be a good father. He was. Although he had his own struggles to contend with, he taught me and loved me the best he could. As his eldest daughter, the burden of learning this business landed on me. "I do miss him."

As I speak, I realize I never told him I was the eldest. He turns away from me to peer into the feed room. Perhaps he's simply inquired about me before coming. I examine his profile. He can't be Hadwin. Hadwin was skinny with dark hair.

"I would miss my father should he die, as well," he says, turning back to me.

We emerge from the stable into the sunlight, now at its height. I squint up at it, wishing for my wide-brimmed hat to shield my face.

"This way?" the duke asks, lifting a hand toward the rear of the stables where Letifer roams.

"Yes." I walk alongside him, twisting the metal clasp of the lead in my fingers.

"So if you were looking for a horse in all of Nubilus' autumn auctions, would you buy from you or from another stable?"

I blink at the oddness and abruptness of the question. "I—"

"Be honest now. No false modesty or misleading answers just to spite me."

A laugh escapes me before I can halt it. I fight the urge to slap my hand over my mouth, which would probably be the only thing worse than just pretending it didn't happen as my cheeks heat. His words remind me so much of Hadwin that my heart aches. When I risk a glance at the duke, he's grinning, looking strangely proud of himself.

Smoothing my smile away, I clear my throat. "Well, I haven't seen a full list of the other horses up for auction, but I firmly believe that my horses are some of the best in all of Ardor, not just Nubilus."

"Well, with the son of Mythos here…" He tilts his head at me, but we arrive at Letifer's paddock, and his attention shifts to scan the grass with a frown. "Where is he? He was in here earlier, wasn't he? Did someone move him?"

I step up to the fence and scan the far edge of the fence. "Sometimes he grazes on the clover and sweet grass on the opposite side. But he should be in there. No one else can handle him."

The young duke turns his frown my direction. "No one else?"

Perhaps I shouldn't have admitted that. I bite back my sigh. "He's a difficult horse. I don't dare let anyone else handle him."

Again I feel that disconcerting examination under his gaze but, this time, the duke says nothing.

"He's there," I say a moment later, pointing to the silvery white smudge against the green grass. He nearly blends into the fence and the pale bark of the trees beyond.

He squints in the direction of the stallion.

I give a low whistle and Letifer lifts his head, his neck arched as he looks my direction. He stretches out his neck and shakes his head as if deciding something, then abruptly jolts into a canter toward us.

The duke is respectfully quiet and unmoving at the stallion's approach. I pull a slightly withered apple quarter from my pocket and hold it out between the rails for the stallion. Letifer slides to a graceful halt in front of us, eyeing Duke Orestes before snorting and shaking his head, his long, silvery mane flopping from side to side. Stepping up to me, he huffs on my palm then lips up the offering. He eyes the duke again, then does something unexpected. He stretches out his nose for the duke, blowing his breath into the man's face in an intimate gesture. Abruptly, he turns and gallops away across the pasture.

The duke releases a breath that is half chuckle and half relief. "He's the most perfect Gelu specimen I've ever seen. His conformation, his speed—he floats across the ground." He gapes after the stallion for another minute in silence before turning to me. "Do you have any horses of his for sale?"

"Actually—"

"Please say yes."

"Yes. One."

"Colt or filly?"

"Filly."

He sighs. "Well, it's not what I was looking for."

As I open my mouth to respond, Winter walks out of the stable with two horses in tow. My eyes widen at the two she's chosen. Both glimmer in the sunlight, one a six-year-old stallion and the other a four-year-old filly, Letifer's offspring. I blink at the calmness with which Winter handles the animals. She doesn't even know these horses, and yet they follow her without argument. Perhaps her talents are wasted at the inn. I should have had her help here days ago. She calmly leads both horses to us, taking the long way that has her turning them around a mounting block, probably so that the duke can see the way they walk.

Despite my distraction at Winter's ability to handle them, I don't miss the silent scrutiny the duke gives my horses on their approach.

I meet Winter and take one of the horses. "Did Gavin help you tack them up?"

Winter gives me an innocent look. "Oh, I couldn't find him. I knew the duke was waiting, so I just went ahead."

"That's quite a risk you took. With my horses."

"They were sweethearts," Winter says, giving the usually difficult Retono a pat on the neck. He cranes his head toward Winter and bobs his head up and down.

I take Espoir's reins instead of answering. She's tall for her age and barely broken. I'm astonished Winter could even get the saddle on her. Like her father, she's wary of strangers.

"Miss Ella?"

I turn at the duke's words. "I'm sorry?"

"I asked whom you'd like me to ride."

"You should ride the filly," Winter answers immediately. "I think your personalities will match up quite well." There's a mischievous glint to her eye that suggests maybe the saddling didn't go as smoothly as I think.

"Wait." I hold up a hand. The duke glances between us, and I smile uncomfortably. "How do you know his personality?"

"Just what I've seen so far." She meets the duke's eye before his gaze darts away, and he runs a hand down the filly's neck.

"That's fine," the duke answers. "I can handle any horse."

I wince at the over-confidence he projects. Espoir doesn't respond well to that.

Winter hands me Retono's reins with an almost challenging expression. Why is she acting so strange this morning? First in the barn when the duke appeared, and now trying to force my hand?

"I imagine you'll want to see that filly move under a rider first," I tell him firmly, motioning at her. "This is Letifer's filly. Espoir. I always like to see how they move first and then ride second. Perhaps you'll agree?" I chew on the inside of my lip waiting for his answer.

He smiles graciously and gives a little bow. "Certainly. I will bow to your expertise, my lady."

"I thank you," I answer automatically, then I jolt. Hadwin used to say the exact same thing to me when I corrected him. I lift my gaze to the duke's, and I'm met with a familiarly uneven smile.

CANCELLED

When Ella disappears with the Prince of Ardor, I give the children their instructions for when they finish their tasks and then tell the quiet Gavin that I'll be back in a couple of hours.

He opens his mouth to speak, and sensing that he's about to offer me a horse, I say goodbye and hurry away. After getting my own horse stolen, I don't trust myself to take advantage of Ella or Gavin's generosity. I'll use their help as little as possible and then leave. As soon as I talk to the King, whether he agrees with me or not, I'll let Ella get back to her life.

By the time I reach town, I'm already panting and sweaty under the sun, but I cannot slow. According to the guards, the audience begins around midday.

The palace looms above me as I pass the holy street, or so Dalia and Ella call it. I say a silent prayer for help; I have a feeling I'm going to need it. I rush past The King's Inn a minute later, casting a quick glance its way but otherwise keeping my head down.

The square is almost empty except for a mother watching two young children play in the middle and an older woman haggling over a bolt of fabric. I pause. In Merise or Monticola, children never played like that. If they were free children, they were inside, working to survive. Adding coals or logs to the fire, spinning yarn, mending fabrics, all while shivering under thin wools and furs. And that was the better life than the one I found outside the palace. At least they were free. But children, only a few years older than the ones playing before me, are sold in Canens to work for the rich. Or, like Des, to serve a man's pleasures.

The children shriek and laugh as one catches the other and they go down in a heap in the middle of the bright square. I jolt back to the present. If the King won't ally with me...where do I go? I can't go back home.

As I hurry past, the woman calls the children back to her with the enticement of treats, and they race each other toward the shade of the building.

At the pathway to the palace grounds, I turn to one of the two soldiers standing at either side. Neither is the same as the first time I came here, but I pick one and motion to a spot to the right of the main doors. "Is that where I wait for an audience with the King?"

The soldier barely spares me a glance. "No audience today."

"What?" I point to the crowd. "Then what are they waiting for?"

He shrugs. "No audience today."

I scowl. "Is that all you can say?"

His face remains implacable.

I huff and stride past him toward the small crowd, and the guard doesn't stop me. "What are you waiting for?" I ask a young woman who looks like she could be a baker's wife or maybe the wife of a shopkeeper. Her hair is covered with a large blue kerchief, and she holds a plump baby on her hip.

"I'm here to complain to the King—"

"But they say they aren't holding an audience because of the masque," a man interrupts.

"Then why are you waiting?" I ask.

The mother shrugs. "Maybe he'll change his mind or reschedule if enough people wait." She shifts the baby to the other hip. "I must talk to him about the state of the oats this season."

Nodding, I move off to the next person, who tells me much the same thing, except his complaint regards his neighbor encroaching his land. I don't bother to ask a third but instead settle in to add to their numbers.

"Excuse me," says a voice near my ear, "but do you wait for an audience with the King?"

Surprised at the close address, I turn to find a crooked old woman standing beside me, leaning on an even more crooked stick. "What?"

"Do you wait for an audience with the King?" she repeats in the trade language.

"Yes. I'm hoping he might have mercy on us all."

"Hmm." She lifts her chin and stares at me with a dirt brown gaze that penetrates me to my bones.

There is something oddly familiar about her.

"They won't be holding it today," the woman says.

"How do you know? He might—"

She shakes her head with her lips pushed out into frown. "No."

"But—"

"Come with me, Winterberry."

A chill grasps me, freezing me to the spot. "How do—"

"Just come." Without waiting for my response, she starts down a path leading around the perimeter of the palace.

With another glance at the waiting crowd, I dart after the old woman. "Who are you?" I demand. Falling in beside her, I match my pace to hers, which is surprisingly quick for an old woman.

"The most important thing is who you are."

"I—" My feet slip to a halt on the path. "Who sent you?"

Her simple, dark green dress flutters around her legs as she walks, and although she carries a crooked stick, she doesn't seem to lean on it. "No one sent me, dear."

Catching up to her again, I hiss, "*Who* sent you? Was it Blanche? Her huntsman?"

She doesn't speak but motions her hand through the air as she leads us into a garden with tall hedges. A shimmer ripples through the air, and a shiver runs over my skin. Magic? Dread grips my throat. I ready myself for an attack that doesn't come.

"Where are you taking me? Where are we going?" Tension sends my muscles into knots and awakens the light within me. As she strides around the corner of a hedge, disappearing with a swish of her dress, I fight back the glow beginning in my palms. Only when I forced it back underneath my skin do I follow the old woman around the hedges. If I'm in trouble, it can help me...right? Blanche couldn't have found me so quickly, and the huntsman wouldn't be able to take on her appearance, would he?

As soon as I turn, I jolt to a standstill. The old woman faces me. Only, she doesn't look so old anymore. She stands straighter and seems taller than before. I blink and her face turns youthful, her spine straightens, her hair turns from gray to brown.

"Who are you?" I demand, talking a half-step back and steeling myself. As soon as I say it, I realize that she was the woman who gave me the coin in the streets. "You—"

"I already told you," she answers. "The important thing is who you are, Winterberry. And what you have inside you, aching to escape." She dips her chin at my hands.

Light glows upon my fingertips, and warmth climbs from my nails up my wrists and elbows. I catch my breath but don't bother to try and stop it this time. Let it intimidate her. But no—that's what Blanche would do. That's how magic corrupts. If I give in now, if I use it with such evil intent—

With the greatest of willpower, I clench my eyes shut and

force the light away. Draw it from my hands and arms into my center, where I can absorb it like winking out a candle.

When I open my eyes and fix the woman with a hard glare, the twist of pride in the curve of her lips and brightness in her eyes makes my glare falter.

"Impressive." She claps her hands once in apparent appreciation. "No one's taught you that control, have they?"

I wrap my arms around my middle and don't answer.

"I can teach you."

Something flares inside me—not the light this time, but hope. Suspicion isn't far behind. "Who are you?" I repeat desperately.

"Some call me a witch. Some call me a sorceress. Some call me a faery. Some go so far as to call me a daemon. It depends upon your perspective, I suppose."

"What's the truth?" I try to pin her with my gaze, but she seems to shift out from under it without any trouble. "Who are you *really*?"

"It doesn't matter. But I can help you."

"Help me do what?"

"Why are you here in Ardor, princess?"

"Don't call me that."

"Why not? Aren't you one?"

"I— Of course. But I can't do anything. Not unless someone else will help me. I'm a princess without a country. Without a home." I blink back the sudden emotion pricking my eyes. Exiled.

"And you think that makes you powerless?" The woman motions to my hands. "What about that power?"

"This?" I hold out my hands, palm up. "What does this do but make me unfit to rule?"

She frowns, surprise creasing her forehead. "I don't understand."

"I can't rule until I rid myself of this curse." I almost spit the word at her, the venom in my tongue is so great.

"What—?" She stops herself short, her frown deepening and then relaxing into understanding. "You fear it. Why?"

"Why?" I spread my arms to encompass the hedge around us. "*Why*? What has magic done except corrupt? I shouldn't even be talking to you—you're doubtless as bad as her." I whirl on my heel and take a few strides when her words cut through me.

"Winterberry, that's enough." Her tone reminds me of my father when he scolded me, so long ago, down to the very words she says. It shocks me enough that I stop and turn back.

"What?" I stand, my arms loose at my side, fighting the pang of regret and sorrow that washes over me like an unexpected gust of wind.

"Magic isn't evil. Far from it." Her tone softens, her head tilts to the side. Warmth in her brown eyes reminds me of the tree trunks of Ardor, full of strength and age. "Yes, it can be used for evil, but anything can."

"It is power. And power corrupts," I insist.

"Power can also humble," she answers gently. "Is that your fear? What do you think you'll accomplish by talking to the King of Ardor if you fear yourself so greatly? What do you think you can offer when you are crippled by your own strengths?"

Averting my gaze, I stare at the hedge to my side. Should I tell her what I plan, could I even begin to trust her? I know nothing about her.

"Oh, I see."

I whip back to face her. "See what?" My words emerge defensive and angry, a wolf snapping at another who threatens her prized bone.

"You don't plan to return to the throne at all, do you? That's why you don't call yourself a princess." Her lips press into a thin line that could be either disappointment or sympathy. "Winterberry, no one can take your birthright from you. Only you can surrender."

"Yes, well—"I cross my arms"—that's what I plan."

"Why? Don't you have anything back home to fight for?"

I lift one shoulder in a shrug. Des, Certa, Pia, Elaina, and Caleb all course through my mind. Of those I risked my heart for, two are dead at my hands, one is not even Canensian, one is enslaved to someone unknown, and the fifth is trapped in slavery at the Manor. Emotion boils hot and bubbly in my throat, and I have to fight to keep the light at bay.

You couldn't save any of them, whispers a little voice in my ear. *What makes you think you can save a country?*

"Even if I do, I have no way to fight her on my own," I snap at the witch-fae.

"You intend to offer your throne to the King of Ardor. Your land, your people, everything. Don't you?"

"What else can I do?" The words wring their way out of me, and to my surprise, I find myself honestly asking the question of her. I want her to present another solution, one that won't surrender all the people I've ever cared for in this world to my enemy. If I give my throne to the King of Ardor, I will have no home, no place, no life. But my whole life has been one of misery, one of suffering and watching others suffer. What can I do for those people when I can't even save myself? And yet, I have nothing else to bargain with. I am exiled, and although the proper heir, who supports me? Who even believes me alive?

"Oh dear," she murmurs, stepping up to me. "Dearest Winter-berry, there is much you can do. You have been Fae gifted, don't you realize?"

I lift my head to peer into her warm eyes. "What?"

"Your birth was ordained by the Great Fae many centuries ago."

I laugh bitterly. "Because I'm *cursed.*"

"Cursed? Is that what you believe, dear?" This time it is sympathy that manipulates the woman's expressive face, turning her lips down into a sad twist of her lips. "Oh, my dear, I had no idea you felt this way."

My eyes burn, but I refuse to give in to my emotions before this strange woman. "Who are you? Tell me. Or I leave right now."

"I answer to many things, but my true name is Brunnea." She watches me closely as she says it, as if to see if I recognize her name.

I shrug.

"Oh dear, your education hasn't been what it ought, has it?"

I bristle slightly at the insinuation. "What does that mean?"

"Dearest, only that, as the chosen heir to Canens' throne, you ought to know your history of the origin of the Seven Kingdoms."

I narrow my eyes. "What are you then? Tell me more than your name—"

"I am one of the Great Fae."

I step back as surely as if she's pushed me. "Then—then—Why are you here?"

She chuckles softly at that. "There are thirteen of us, dearest. And we are needed everywhere. But with so few of us for so many people in the Seven Kingdoms, we spread ourselves around." She shrugs. "We stay in some places longer than others. Some of us stay only a short time, other many years. Some have chosen to avoid humans entirely."

"What do you do?" Curiosity pulls the question out of me. Despite my lack of education, I've heard of the Great Fae. They are like lesser gods, guardians perhaps, who protect countries from evil and...I don't know exactly. All I've heard are myths, and I never thought the Great Fae actually existed.

"Do? Well, I suppose I *do* a great deal. I help those who deserve it succeed, and I help those who *don't* fail."

"But... Then does that mean that Blanche deserves my throne? She has succeeded for so long—"

"No, dear." Brunnea sighs. "No, yours is a special case."

"Why?"

"Well, Canens is under a curse. And that curse extends to the Great Fae. Or most of us at least."

"What? Why?"

She purses her lips. "This isn't really what I intended to tell you. All that can come later. But what needs to come now is you."

"Me?"

"Yes, we must teach you how to control that Fae gift of yours."

"But I don't want it. Can't you take it from me instead?"

"Even if I could, I wouldn't. You may not want it, my dear, but you will need it."

I hesitate, rubbing at my neck. "I will?"

"Yes." Brunnea tilts her head at me. "There's a very small chance someone else might be able to defeat Blanche. You are the one who, with the help of your magic, can meet her evenly. You will be able to do it quickest and most efficiently."

Disappointment grips my heart. "Me? In battle? I'm no warrior. I was hoping..." I trail off.

She raises a brow.

"I thought maybe I could give King Greggory information and he would send in soldiers to fight, to...kill her."

Brunnea shakes her head slowly back and forth, but there is compassion in the tilt of her head and the press of her lips. "No, my dear. It will be challenging, but I have faith in you."

"What if I fail?"

Brunnea narrows her eyes as if the thought hadn't occurred to her. "Then I suppose we all fail. And the Seven Kingdoms fall."

"What?" My heart jumps into my throat, and my voice comes out squeaky. "What do you mean? You mean the fate of the entire Seven Kingdoms rests on *me*? Alone?"

"Oh no, not alone. Never alone." She smiles reassuringly and reaches out to pat my hand. Her skin is soft and cool, as comforting as if I have a fever and she is a cool cloth. "You will find allies. You have already found a couple."

"I have?"

"Yes. Did you think we left you unsupervised completely?" She tsks. "Not with the Seven Kingdoms at risk."

"But, Brunnea, there's so much I don't understand, I—"

"Yes, dear, but that's all for another time. We must give you a quick lesson in your magical control. We can't have you erupting into light every time you grow angry or afraid."

My eyes widen. "How did you know—?"

She tsks again. "I'm a Great Fae, dear. We know a great many things."

"Right."

She turns in her spot, inspecting our surroundings, then raises her crooked walking stick and closes her eyes. Her mouth moves silently, and a ripple of something brushes over my skin and around us as though a light breeze rustles through the garden. She lowers her stick. "There. That's done."

I glance around. "What is?"

"A spell of privacy."

"Oh. Is that what you did before?"

She crooks a brow. "No, before I cast a spell so that whatever we said would not be understood. But we need more than that now."

"Oh." I shift on my feet, rubbing at the tattoo on my neck with nervous fingers.

"Now, your first task is to clear your head of all emotion."

I can't withhold a scoff. "That simple?"

She waggles a finger at me. "No speaking back. Just do as asked."

"And how do I clear my head of all emotion?" I shake my head instead. There is too much emotion in me to do so—concern, grief, pain, worry, even excitement for Ella with the first masque tonight and Dalia's determination to get her there.

"Think of nothing. Or think of something that relaxes you," Brunnea suggests when I scoff at her suggestion. "Now we don't have much time, so start now."

"Here?"

"Here." She nods brusquely.

Over the next hour, Brunnea schools me, teaching me to keep the magic under control and keep the light from overtaking me. It's a mixture of control and desire, and it's a difficult balance to find.

"Keep practicing," Brunnea says. "Even when you're walking down the street, you'll have to control yourself, so practice control at all times."

Staring down at my hands, devoid of light but with the tingle of magic in them, I nod.

Brunnea fills my head with knowledge, telling me how it's no wonder my magic didn't appear in full until I left Canens because of the cold's dampening effect upon magic casters. She tells me in the same breath how it doesn't mean I'm not strong and warns me that my stepmother is stronger and more well practiced than I if she casts such powerful spells in Canens.

With her pragmatic words and actions, she gives me hope and takes it away in the same breath. But by the end my time with her, I have cast spells and I have controlled my magic, even when angered and frustrated.

Despite my fear of the magic itself, it is frighteningly natural to me.

"It feels natural to you because it is natural for you. It's a part of you, as much as your hair or your eyes," she tells me. "You were Fae gifted, don't forget that."

"What does that even mean though?" I snap, annoyed at her reminder. My hands flare. I stare at them, willing the light back inside me, but it takes its time responding this time.

"Why, it means a Great Fae gave you the gift of your magic. Usually at a Christening or other official event. But it happens on occasion that a royal is gifted even before birth, such as in your case."

"And how often does that happen?" I shake my head. If

Blanche is more powerful than I, and I have been Fae gifted, what good does it even do me?

Brunnea takes my hand at that. "Darling, Winterberry, it is incredibly rare."

"How rare?"

"Only a half dozen humans have been so gifted with Fae magic."

"Well that's—"

"In all of the centuries," she interrupts. "Only six—ever—have been Fae gifted at all, before or after birth."

At that, my mouth parts. "Who? Besides me?"

Her smile turns a little sad now. "You are one—the only one gifted before birth. And there are two other living now."

For some reason, a chill runs down my spine at the tone in her words. "Who are they?"

"One is a princess, cursed in eternal slumber."

"And the other?" Somehow I know the answer before she gives it.

"Your stepmother. Blanche."

TRACKING

*S*itting atop my quiet palfrey, I push back my damp hair from my face. This heat is oppressive. Every breath I take in feels like I'm breathing through a cup of water.

I've never regretted not using my magic more. While the mornings are cool enough and almost magical with the water droplets that collect on all surfaces, by midmorning that chill wears off, and we're left sweltering, now with water droplets upon us. The heat doesn't disappear until hours after the sun has gone down, leaving me tossing even in my sleep. And now the sun beats down upon my head this evening, scratching my skin.

Coupled with the knowledge that something has happened to my huntsman to sever my connection to the spell upon him, I'm more than irritable.

Behind me, the steady clop of hooves remind me of Baron Silvanus Tueor's presence. I sigh, still doubting my decision to bring him along. At the last moment, I instructed him to come, thinking he might be as useful as his brother once was. Besides, any time spent with a man half as attractive as him must be worth it in the end.

My skin prickles again, but this time not with heat. Or at least, not the heat of the sun.

A few hours later, the city of Nubilus looms out from the shadowed sky like a lighthouse in the sea. I wrinkle my nose. The town seems afire with the sunlight upon it, but it holds not a candle to Merise and its icy sheen. Behind the city lies the sea, where dark clouds have gathered, perhaps for an autumn storm.

The countryside explodes with green, red, yellow, brown, and an assortment of any color I can name, but it looks like a painter threw dozens of paints upon a canvas without consideration for how they complement each other. The hot sun certainly contributes to the thriving colors. I aim a dark glare at the cloudless sky. Couldn't just a few clouds come in to offer some relief?

I tug my brimmed hat down over my face, grateful that we at least changed into Ardorian clothing. The brimmed hat seemed silly at first, but it's far more effective at blocking the sun than the little brim Silvanus has.

Within a few hours, the monotony of the road into Nubilus turns into the city itself, through a long line of short outer walls and through some pastures into the inner walls of the city. Guards swarm the top of the inner circle and stand to either side of the gates but don't bother to ask us one question as we ride into the city.

I scoff silently. Useless. What good are they if they don't challenge anyone or inspect what they bring inside the gates? Foolish guards from a foolish country.

"Where do we go in here?" Silvanus asks from just behind me. His horse tosses up his head at the close quarters of the town as people press in on every side.

"We go to find my huntsman," I murmur just loud enough for him to hear.

Silvanus nods, but I catch the sneer upon his face as he raises a hand to push away a beggar that presses desperately upon his horse. The beggar falls back against the wall of the nearest house, his face a mask of pain, but Silvanus turns back to me. "How will we know where to look, Your—" he breaks off, recalling himself.

"I know exactly where he is."

A frown makes his face appear years older, creasing the smooth skin into dark wrinkles upon his light skin. "How?"

"I'll find him." I add a smirk to cover up my annoyance.

Whatever happened to sever my spell upon Marcus has left traces, but I can't very well explain something like that to someone like Silvanus. He wouldn't understand, nor does he need to. The larger problem is that whatever has destroyed my enchantment upon Marcus could only have been done by a skilled sorcerer or sorceress. Which means it's very likely they are sensing me if I reach out to sense them. They might already be feeling for me, guessing or knowing that I am here. I might follow the traces of my spell to a huntsman enchanted by a very different one. Or I could follow the remaining threads of my curse to a corpse.

My gaze slips from the road in front of me to the palace towering above the city. It's far different from Merise with its black stone. This palace is white and gleaming, surrounding by a glittering city and hills of green with the Geli specking them like silver and gold jewels in an emerald crown.

I tip my chin toward the palace as I lean over toward Silvanus and say in Canensian, "Do you think that palace is as defensible as they say?"

He inspects it, his blue eyes narrowing and his strong brow creasing as he squints through the sunlight to consider the resi-dence of King Greggory III and Queen Ada of Ardor. "Perhaps. It might be accessible to a couple of Ardorites seeking an audience with the King, but as a whole, I think getting an army to the front door is highly unlikely. With the cliff behind it, there's no real way to surround it, and it forces you up to it through the city." He motions to the winding, twisting paths through Nubilus, his gaze slipping over the cobblestones, houses, and shopfronts with their blue and gold flags and streamers, some with the Ardorian coat of arms.

Residents of Nubilus weave confidently through the streets in their brightly colored linen dresses, tunics, leggings and knee-high boots. They disappear around corners and down through alleys or into shops and homes, voles racing through their snow burrows in an endless maze of destinations known only to them. Some servants wash shop windows, others push their little carts down the roads. How they race around with such haste, these strange people and their strangely lush land. They have so much —everything—and yet they work for more?

Silvanus draws his animal closer to mine. "The palace at least looks heavily guarded."

I pull my gaze from the frantic Ardorites to settle it on my companion's strong mouth and jaw.

"And guards patrol the city streets right now," he adds, dipping his head toward a group of people up the street.

This time I follow his gaze to where two Ardorian guards dressed in their blue and gold uniforms roam the streets.

"I've counted a dozen already. And from what I've seen, the Gelu Rigens are guarded almost better than the royals. So if someone happened to attack their much-beloved ruler and flee through the main gates, they might just end up attacked by the armed guards before the next wall." He glances back over at the walls behind us. "Not to mention the guards on the wall that could shoot those attackers in the back."

I nod slowly, having noted all the same, and having already come to the same conclusions. But hearing him say it shows me how he is willing to take the same risks with me.

As we've been inspecting the city, moving along with the crowd, we find a shaded spot along the widest street to stop our three horses and make this assessment.

He turns back to me and half smiles to find me watching him

and not the gates or the guards or anything else he's pointed out. "What is it?"

"I've merely reached the same conclusions as you. Perhaps they have increased their guard for the masques."

"And the auction," Silvanus reminds me as I aim my palfrey toward the castle, easing her back into the crowd.

"Ah yes, the auction…what we're here for." At least, that is our story whenever asked.

"Although I'm sure we could procure a couple of invitations to the masque if that's within your interest," Silvanus says with laughter in his voice.

"Well, that's hardly what we're here for, though it might pose the perfect opportunity for my intentions. Three masques, you said?"

"Yes. One this Sabbath's eve, then next Sabbath's eve is the auction and another masque, then a final auction the following one." Silvanus scratches at his bearded chin. "A lot of activity for three weeks."

"Hmm. Then we have two weeks to accomplish our first task and three to achieve our second." I allow myself a smile. "And masques… How lovely that they expect everyone to conceal their identity already."

Silvanus gives a low laugh that washes over me like a breeze on this warm day, or perhaps a pair of inviting arms.

For a moment, I entertain the temptation simply to fall into his warmth, to let the heat of the day and his warmth combine into something…combustible. I clear my throat. "Our first task, however, is to find your brother."

"And you know where he is?"

I detect the merest amount of skepticism in his tone, but glancing back at him, I see an eyebrow raised my direction. I give him a smirk that tells him he underestimates me.

A sudden tug upon me, as if a rope is tied around my midsection, has me almost gasping.

Finally.

I pull my palfrey into such a sudden halt that Silvanus, his horse, and the packhorse travel past us before he can stop them. A few residents on the streets around us call out in their native tongue, then one says in the trade language, "Watch where you're going!"

I aim an imperious, quelling glare at him, and he blinks before hurrying away like a whipped dog. With him gone, I close my eyes, grasp hold of the invisible rope around me, and follow it.

He is here. He is near.

There.

My head pulses at the pain of the magic's grip. Squinting through half-lidded eyes, I nudge my mare on, guiding her in the direction the rope leads me. Finally, after wandering in the streets for the better part of an hour, the presence of my huntsman is undeniable.

"Looking for a place to stay? Or something to eat?" Silvanus asks when I stop at the corner of a square and scrutinize the line of inns and shops before us.

"Not quite." I search the shadows the setting sun casts upon the town. He must be here somewhere, but he wouldn't be in the inn. Could he be dead? Lying dead in the alleys nearby? It would be odd, strange even, with the pull of magic so strong here. I felt the first tug a full week ago; surely such a clean city wouldn't leave a corpse in its streets for so long.

My gaze skips over the shadows again then returns to an outcrop between buildings. My lips twitch, but I say nothing. Instead, I dismount and hand my mare's reins to Silvanus.

He gives me a searching look, but when I don't answer it, he dips his chin and wraps the reins around the horn of his saddle along with the packhorse's lead.

I move toward the shadows of an inn displaying a masculine crown. I bypass its entrance, ambling toward the shadows, noting the almost imperceptible tremble to the invisible rope as I near.

He knows I am here. And something makes him react. Whether with fear, or relief, or something in between, I cannot tell. But I will.

10: ELLA

HADWIN

*D*uke Orestes' gaze doesn't linger on me, but slips back to inspect Retono, as if our exchange of words is nothing remarkable. Instead, he mounts the stallion as Winter holds the reins.

With the duke mounted, Winter releases Retono and takes hold of Espoir under the chin. I catch the concern on her face as I stand dumbly, holding Espoir's reins, staring at the duke, but she doesn't speak.

Hastily, I turn and mount Espoir. It was just coincidence. It must have been. Or he would reveal himself, wouldn't he?

"Have fun," Winter murmurs to me then releases the reins and steps back.

"So where shall we go?" Duke Orestes asks from the saddle. He looks completely at home atop Retono, and the stallion looks perfectly at ease with his unfamiliar rider.

"I have the perfect place. Near where I saw my first unicorn." I aim Espoir toward the trail and nudge her forward.

"Truly? You've seen a unicorn?"

I hesitate. But after I left Hadwin the final time, I saw an animal so silver that he glowed almost like the moon lowered

177

amidst the trees. I've only told Dalia of the sighting. I don't know what made me say it now. There are too many memories of Hadwin today. I must be sentimental.

"Yes," I say. "Many years ago now, shortly after leaving a friend in the woods, I saw him."

I just catch the duke's glance before I take the lead and direct Espoir toward the seaside path.

"You truly saw a unicorn?" There's a decidedly skeptical tone to his voice.

I shrug. "Yes. But it was a long time now. She's probably long gone."

"A unicorn mare?" The duke's eyebrows rise. "Isn't that supposed to mean good fortune?"

My answering smile is wry. "If it is, I haven't seen much of it. But I've also heard it means a friendship will never be lost."

His brow furrows in thought.

"You seem familiar to me," I say as we ride toward the seaside. "You haven't been to Nubilus before?"

He rubs a hand over his square, smooth jaw. "Did I say that?"

His words are slightly teasing, but also much more amused than I expect from such a comment. "Oh, I..." I trail off, trying to think under his scrutiny. "I can't recall now."

Embarrassment floods my cheeks. His words are not disrespectful or annoyed, but conversational. I twist a piece of the filly's white mane in my fingers. It's like he enjoys our banter and wants to keep the conversation going. I'm not used to having men interested in anything about me but my horses.

I risk a glance at him. His lips flash into a smile before his gaze drops to Espoir's form. He studies me as much as the mare, so I study him. He is a talented rider; he barely pays any attention to the colt he rides and handles him perfectly. Perhaps I shouldn't have doubted, but without any example of his skills before now, I couldn't say for sure. Now I see his control over the colt is sure but gentle. He rides, I think with a sigh, just like Hadwin. I turn my attention to the path again. Perhaps that was what seeing the unicorn was supposed to mean, simply that I would one day meet a man who reminded me of the boy who was leaving, not that I would ever see Hadwin again.

When we come to the beach, I motion him ahead. The tide is out, exposing damp sand a shade darker than the pale, dry sand above. "Would you like to see how the horses move?"

"Yes." With a glint in his eyes, he nudges the colt. "Race you," the duke calls back over his shoulder.

Retono leaps ahead of Espoir, his ears flicking forward in eagerness.

With a half laugh, I follow suit, my filly surging forward in a few strides to draw even with Retono. A few more steps, and we're in front, Retono snorting with displeasure as he tries to reclaim his lead. We cross the beach with the colt's nose at my knee, and at the other side, I pull the filly down and cast the duke a grin I can't suppress. At the tightness of his lips, I wince. A real horse breeder and seller would have let him win, but pride got ahold of me.

He pulls the colt down alongside me, his lips in a twist of something like admiration or annoyance. "You ride extremely well."

My cheeks burn, but I can't resist saying, "Well, sir, I grew up on a stable, breaking, breeding, and training horses. At the very least, I should ride better than almost any man who hasn't done the same."

The duke blinks, then a laugh starts to bubble out of him, shaking his shoulders in such genuine appreciation that it brings a grin to my mouth.

Still smiling, I motion to the colt. "What did you think of him is the question."

He places both reins in one gloved hand and leans forward in the saddle to drag the other down the colt's mane before reaching back up to scratch between the animal's ears. "He's more impressive than I thought he'd be, compared with that filly you ride." He pauses as he delivers another scratch to the colt's ears. "But I'm still more interested in the offspring of Letifer."

"Let's trade mounts then. I merely wanted you to experience both animals." I kick my toes free from the stirrups.

He dismounts quickly and is at Espoir's shoulder to catch me by the waist before I can slide to the ground.

When I turn my face, it's to meet his blue-green eyes; I catch my breath at his smile.

"You were too quick to mount earlier, or I would have helped you up as well." He smiles. "But I believe every lady should have someone help her down from her horse."

"Even a female business owner breaking all the rules?" With a nervous laugh, I press my hand to my lips as soon as the words escape me. What was I thinking to make a comment like that to a potential buyer? He's not going to buy from me now, no matter how much he likes Espoir.

I step out of his woodsy-scented embrace and fiddle with the reins, untwisting them with trembling fingers as I wait for his answer.

"Especially then." His voice has lost much of its laughter, replaced with a genuineness that makes me hold my breath. "If she'll accept the help."

I clear my throat, ignoring the blush that creeps up to my cheeks. "Espoir's got a bit of her father's spirit, so she'll run away with you if you let her. She's like a stubborn child. You have to immediately tell her who's in control and remain calm with her no matter what happens or what she does."

"From what I've seen, you'll handle her just fine." I check the girth as I speak then step back and bump into his chest. "Sorry." I turn, and my breath stumbles.

Why am I acting like my sisters right now? I can't seem to look him in the eye, and my skin trembles. I swear I can feel his exhales on my ear.

"It's clear that your horses mean a lot to you, and that you are important to them, too."

More aware of his nearness than anything else, I smooth down a lock of Espoir's soft mane, even though she cranes her head around and nibbles on my dress when I do. "They're vital to me. They are what I live for."

"It's clear that's why you've stayed on your father's land." He cocks his head to the side. "I admire that."

I jolt at his words and can't form any words to reply with, and after a moment of my silence, he continues.

"I confess myself surprised that you chose to run the stable yourself after your father died. Especially with the laws intended to make things difficult for you."

Espoir paws at the ground with a front hoof.

"The laws are intended to encourage newly orphaned young women whose father left them a business to surrender her land to the Crown and focus on husband hunting for herself. It promotes our patriarchal laws over the historical significance of a family's lineage or business."

I turn and gape at him, eyes wide. Never has a man disapproved of the patriarchal laws of Ardor in my presence. Few women are even bold enough to do so.

His lips quirk as he offers me a little shrug, almost as if to say that he doesn't mean any offense but it's just the way it is. He motions at the horses we rode here. "But you decided to stay and run the stable. And by all accounts, you're doing better than any man would."

My cheeks heat again. I hope he doesn't think I'm a silly girl turned by a quick compliment, for I've been blushing more with him than I have in the past six months alone. "Well, your grace, you have some unusual views. And I don't know if the sales from the auction support that belief."

The duke shakes his head. "Auction numbers aren't always accurate. Especially when there's a woman running a man's business. Some men are bound to be threatened by that, especially when she does it so well." He shakes his head again, but it's in admiration this time. "How do you do it? How have you bred a filly that can move like that?"

Smiling to myself, I run a hand down the filly's face, tickling her nose until she curls her lip at me.

"Why did you choose to run the stable? Given all the laws? And all the risks?" There's something like desperation in his voice, as if he cannot go on without the answer to this question, as though my answer somehow affects him.

I scratch the filly's chin to hide my confusion. Everyone else doesn't ask me why I chose my path, but tells me why I should have chosen differently.

This time, Duke Orestes doesn't speak as the seconds pass, yet I feel his gaze on me, heavy and insatiable.

"I..." Before I even begin, my words trail off. How do I explain my past to someone like him? And explain it in a way that doesn't cast blame upon my mother for doing the best she can within a loveless marriage? "Growing up here, I spent all day every day with my father. The horses were his passion. And they were mine, too. So I learned everything I could about them, from raising them to training them to breeding them."

The filly noses my shoulder, and I realize I've stopped scratching her chin. When I resume, she stretches her neck out, half closing her eyes.

"Father left an amazing stable behind. It might have been in our family for many generations, but he changed it, was bringing it back. And only I knew his plans and knew these horses as well as he did. Entrusting a man who had no knowledge of these animals or how we pasture them or this land..." I shudder.

"Giving power over to a stranger makes no sense. Not when you know the business better," the duke murmurs as if he never thought of it that way before.

A soft breath of a chuckle escapes me. "No. It made no sense—

still doesn't—to me to surrender my father's land and stable to a man who knows nothing of it. Not until I have to." I meet the young duke's gaze. "I've been told since the day Father died that I am a foolish young girl for choosing this path. And every man I've met has tried to convince me of that."

He draws back slightly with a look of shocked innocence. "Me?"

I flush and turn away, only to turn back to him, unable to keep from searching the honest interest I see in his face. "Not you. I don't understand that though."

Espoir stamps a back foot and swishes her tail, impatient at our lengthy conversation.

I peek back at the duke, unable to resist.

One side of his lips are turned up in a crooked smile. "I'm fascinated by you—your choices, I mean." This time it's his cheeks that go pink, and he rubs his jaw as if looking for a beard to scratch. "You could marry, keep the stables, and not have to deal with all the extra laws associated with running a man's—a stable, I mean. Or you could surrender it to the Crown and be free from it and marry anyone you wanted. Would you ever give it up? For anything? Anyone?" He stammers over his rushed words, as if this discussion has put him in a position he's not accustomed to.

I chuckle and offer him the reins to the restless filly. "This is a longer conversation than I wish to have on the ground. Care to mount up, and we can continue?"

"I—" He grins. "Yes. I'll help you up first."

A smile blossoms on my lips at his offer. "I don't need—"

His expression quells my argument. "I know you don't. But I am a gentleman, and I insist. If you'll accept my help. Please."

I bite my lip as my heart flutters at his words. "All right then."

What's wrong with me? He's a buyer, not a suitor. I should turn the conversation back to the horses, not me. Instead, I hurry toward Retono.

With the filly's reins looped over his arm, he follows me to the colt's side and places his hands on my waist. I shiver, though it's not cold, and he lifts me into the saddle with surprising strength. He hands me my reins, his fingers brushing mine. Our eyes lock. A hundred words tumble up into my throat, but I press my lips together. He looks as though he might speak first, but then his lips thin slightly.

I gather up the reins. "Thank you...for the help," I finally murmur.

"You're welcome," he says before swinging himself into the filly's saddle. She prances out to the side, and he rides her in a quick circle, his face slowly brightening with a smile. He looks at me with blue-green eyes gleaming. "She already feels like a dream."

We return to our ride, but the conversation of before lies abandoned on the beach, much like my friendship with Hadwin.

11: BLANCHE

THE CURSE

"Your Majesty." A low murmur comes from a dark shadow amidst the empty alley. "I thought you trusted me."

I halt and slowly turn just my face toward the shadows. As I wait for my eyes to adjust, I fight the urge to use magic to heighten my sight. Until I know what has severed the spells upon him, I cannot risk using my own magic, at least, no more than necessary, and certainly not so near him.

"When have I ever failed you, Your Majesty?"

Now I can see his face enough to tell that he looks at me evenly, his face turned down with exactly the proper amount of reverence. Although one might think he is not looking directly at me, I know him too well to know that to be the case.

"You put undue risk upon yourself to come here, Majesty," he says in that steady, soft voice of his. If I had never witnessed his skills as a hunter, I would find it soothing. But it's the same tone in which he uses to pacify a hunted animal.

"I have other business here," I say coldly. "You know I check on my subjects whenever possible."

His head dips further, but the tenor of his voice does not. "You risk my success by being here, Your Majesty."

"I know." I tilt my head at him, feeling for the magical traces that I left upon him and for any other touch polluting my magic. A full minute later, I can still find no trace of another's touch of magic upon my huntsman. But what then severed the spells?

"Your Majesty?" Marcus prompts. "Is there something wrong?"

Slowly, I shake my head. Perhaps it is simply Ardor. Just as its land seems to enhance my abilities, perhaps it has severed the spells upon him as well. Perhaps it was no enchantress after all.

"Where is she?" I ask instead of answering.

There's a long pause before he answers. "She stays at The King's Inn."

"The King's Inn?"

"Which my brother stands staring at like a fool."

Framed at the end of the alley, Silvanus obtusely gazing at the front of the inn while atop his mount and holding onto two others. I barely hide my grimace. He does look the fool, but easily explained by him waiting for a friend to emerge from the inn.

"Why haven't you killed her yet then?" I ask.

"The opportunity hasn't presented itself."

"You could work your way in and attack."

"How much do you want her heart?"

"Excuse me?"

"If I'm to infiltrate that inn, I'm as likely to be killed as she is before I can complete my task of obtaining her heart for you."

I pause. My curse upon him demanded he obtain her heart for me and return it to me, one way or another. Does he still not recall the King's Curse and the judgment cast upon any who dared kill a royal Canensian? I acted out of anger when I enchanted him, forgetting that I would have to collect the girl's heart somehow if Marcus was struck down by the curse.

"And what does she do inside The King's Inn?"

"Most I can tell, she helps."

"Helps?"

"Gets food from the garden and other such tasks. It does not seem she lies idle at least."

"How long has she been here?"

"Several days. She might not stay much longer."

I roll my eyes at his imprecise measurements. "What else has she been doing?"

There's a moment's hesitation. "I heard her and another young lady working inside talk about making dresses."

"For the masque?"

"It seems likely."

A slow grin works its way onto my lips. Killing the girl myself is out of the question, at least directly, according to the King's Curse. But if I don't raise a hand against her? If it's simply a result of a spell, then I will be safe as I can possibly be.

"That's perfect," I say.

"Your Majesty?"

"She's in there now?"

"No. I believe she is due back shortly though."

I turn to face him. "You said she was in there."

"No, I said she stays here. She left this morning with a group of children. I followed her out of town a little ways, but there was no way to continue following her without being seen, and so I chose to return here and wait for her return. I expect her back at any time, perhaps shortly before dark."

"I see." I glare at him. "Perhaps next time you will be more clear."

He dips his head in apology. "Yes, Your Majesty."

A quick thought is all it requires to shift my plan. "Remain here. And should she return before I emerge from that inn, prevent her from entering." I finger my skirt. "What was the princess wearing this morning when she left?"

He considers a moment. "A simple blue gown, much like any of the lower class residents of the city.

I flick my wrist and feel the change go over me. "Such as this?" I face him, but I am no longer me. It requires a great deal of power to make such a change, but the cost is worth it.

Marcus' eyes are wide as he stares at my face, then slowly he runs his gaze over my body. Her body.

"Her gown is a few inches shorter, the sleeves go only to her wrist, tighter around them, the neckline is lower and square, but a bunched bit of white makes it more modest. She usually returns with dirt under her nails and on her dress."

As he speaks, I perform the changes on my appearance until he has talked my dress into something resembling his memory of hers.

I enter through the back door of the inn, feigning confidence while attempting to act like the timid princess I recall. The door opens into a hallway echoing with noise from the front rooms. A clatter to my left and a following curse from a woman, along with the rich smells of meat and breads cooking suggests that I will find the kitchen there.

A beautiful young blond woman darts from the kitchen with a tray in hand and a wet stain on her sleeve. Her eyes fall on me and widen. She slides to a halt. "Winter?" Her word is quick, but followed by an even quicker frown. "When did you get back?" She scrutinizes me far too astutely for my liking, even as she juggles the tray into one hand with a clatter of silverware atop it.

"Oh, just now." I give her a reassuring smile. "Back early."

"Well, you can help me in the kitchen once you clean up then."

I glance down at myself and resist the urge to smile.

"Hurry up. We've got lots to do tonight, and once the dinner rush starts, I won't have time. Is Ella on her way?"

"Yes, of course," I agree. Whatever will get me into Winter's room quickly.

"Great. Then as soon as she comes in, let me know." Without another word, she pushes her way into the front room and is greeted by a surge of laughter and chatter.

I watch her disappear before inching my way through the other door with a small squeak from its hinges to reveal an empty hallway beyond with four additional doors.

From all the spells I've cast on Winterberry, I can feel her presence within this hallway as surely as if she's a fire burning.

I turn to the one on the left first and listen with my ear pressed to it for a minute. When I hear nothing, I slowly open it. A woman lies in bed, her eyes heavy with sleep. At the sight of me, her eyes start open. "Oh, Winter. Where have you been? Did you bring me some water?"

"What?" I blink. "Oh, no, I...forgot."

"Hurry up girl, my throat's dry as a baked bone. Get the water and your sewing and come back and sit with me."

"Yes, of course." I step back and shut the door. How odd to be spoken to like that. I push the thoughts aside and move to the next door, feeling for the thread of my powers. The strongest one leads outside to Marcus, but otherwise it is a strange tangle of thin and thick ropes as I inhabit Winterberry's body.

I open the second door more cautiously this time, not wishing to find another person asking yet another thing of me. The door opens without protest to a darkened room. The small window inside is covered by a gauzy drape, keeping the room even darker than it should be.

Frowning, I step inside where I find a strange setup that seems to be for bathing and personal needs. It's not here then. I turn to the exit when footsteps in the hall stop me. Light steps, like Winterberry.

My stomach twists in distaste. This girl is so much trouble. She must die. But not yet, not directly at my hands.

From down the hall, the voice of that young girl cook trails down to me, Ardorian spoken in confusion, answering the older woman's voice. They exchange words too rapidly to understand, then the door shuts and moments later, another door squeaks.

When I peek out into the hallway, it's vacant once again. I dart to the third door and open it with a creak that makes me wince.

Inside, the bedroom is empty, and there, lying upon the bed is exactly what I seek. Finally. I quickly check behind me before slipping into the room.

Marcus is right—this dress is far too pretty for a common day in Ardor. Winterberry must have plans to sneak into the masque and talk to the royal family. I pause a moment, considering my options. I could cast a spell that would immediately incapacitate or one that would take effect upon the witching hour. If I let her go to the masque, she might speak with the royal family. But if she does…

I nod. That might work better. What if Winterberry manages to convince the King to ally with her and then dies from a curse I have placed on her? Such a beautiful irony will not be wasted upon the Ardorian royals. They will see my power firsthand and quake in their silk shoes. They will know I have entered their country undetected and can kill whomever I please, even them.

Yes, I think as I point my hand and its now-invisible wand at my dress to the perform the necessary spell. I watch the fabric glow with the power it infuses into every single fiber and stitch. Yes, having an entire audience watch Winterberry die will suit my plans perfectly. In fact, the larger the audience, the better.

DECISIONS

*P*rincess Winterberry exits The King's Inn wearing the same simple gown that the Queen wore when she entered.

A flinch ripples over my skin.

One thing I have realized since meeting that woman in the woods: I am not the same man as I was before. I cannot remember ever having seen the world as clearly as I do now. It's as if a fog has lifted; the edges of everything are sharper, more focused.

If the princess were to die at my hands, I would die of grief. I would only want to die, for the princess has done nothing to deserve death. She is the rightful heir of Canens; she has been betrayed, only she.

I am not quite certain how I kept my trembling hands from betraying me when the Queen approached me in the shadows.

I bluffed her. Her, the sorceress whom no man can fool. But is she fooled?

Now she has done something to harm the princess, I am certain, and all I have done is stand here and keep watch. I have aided her. Again. This time, I have aided her with all my faculties intact. The words of the woman in the woods return to me. *Remember where your loyalties lie, Marcus.*

She knew my name. She knew me in ways only the Queen has ever known. And yet she freed me instead of capturing me.

Who is she?

The Queen, still in her disguise, steps off the path from The King's Inn and walks through the shadow of a building. When she emerges from the shadow on the other side, she is no longer the young princess, but a grown woman.

I suppress a shiver and glance around the street. No one has noticed a girl enter a shadow and emerge a woman. No one but me.

She walks quickly up to my brother, who blinks at her as though surprised at her sudden appearance. He holds out the horse's reins and says something.

In a few moments, I have traversed the distance between us and slip between the horses' haunches.

"Did you find her?" I ask, unable to help myself.

"No, she was not there," the Queen answers, unsurprised by my appearance. She adjusts her peasant's gown and narrows her eyes at me. "Did you think her there?"

"No." I force the single word from my lips without inflection. "I should expect her return then. Are my instructions unchanged? I shall wait for her?"

The Queen mounts her palfrey and arranges the reins between her fingers. "You are to watch for her. But I have changed my plans. Don't touch her. Let…let her squeeze into that dress herself."

My brother hacks a guttural laugh that sends a knife through my spine. Before I can reply, they have nudged their horses away from me, leaving me amongst the shadows.

13: WINTER

MAGIC

"As long as you use your magic for good, it will not corrupt you," Brunnea reminds me. "Now, can you feel the magical trail I left for you? Seek it out. Grab hold of your magic within and ask it to find my trail."

I grimace and close my eyes. As I focus, reaching invisible hands into my middle for my powers. It rustles and rises like a bear disturbed from its slumber. I imagine it going out from me, sniffing out the traces of Brunnea's magic.

"Keep your eyes closed," Brunnea says. "Follow it through your magic only."

Slowly, I walk through the woods, tracking the magic she left for me until it ends in a pool. I reach out to find traces of its path, but I only sense the trail I've already followed. Hesitantly, I open my eyes and find Brunnea smiling at me.

With a sigh at her mute approval, I collapse where I am with a sharp exhale as I let my exhaustion wash over me. Lying amongst the grass and letting the sun wash over me, I breathe deeply, trying to gain some peace.

"How do you plan on speaking to the King and Queen of Ardor, if you don't mind my asking, dear?" Brunnea asks.

"I have no idea," I mutter through gritted teeth.

Brunnea raises a brow at me from down above, a halo of butterflies flittering around her head like a crown.

Still panting slightly, I turn my head to the other side, staring at a bouquet of flowers Brunnea insisted I force to bloom from buds yesterday. It took me most of the day, but I finally accomplished it. And they look no different from when I left them, making me wonder how long they'll live. Forever? Or just the lifetime of a flower bud? I let the thought go like a blade of grass on a quick wind.

Today, I have spent the day learning how to seek out my magic and hold it under my control inside me, asking it to do my bidding in many ways. Unease has clawed at me all day, and now, as I rest under the waning sun, I try to allow its warm caresses to soothe me. Only, I don't know if it's the heat of the magic or the sun that calms me.

The sound of a gentle breeze rustling through the canopy above Brunnea's cottage only helps me relax a little. It's my exhaustion, more mental than magical or physical, that pushes me toward sleep. I want nothing more than to crawl into a soft bed and sleep for a week. But as I close my eyes, Brunnea's words drift through my head. *You must always keep your temper and strong emotions in check, especially if you want to conceal your magic. You can conceal your magic, if you choose, even from others who know how to trace it, but it requires a great deal of practice and skill. But more valuable to you is the ability to trace magic. Most magic-casters don't bother to conceal their magical traces because most people can't trace it or feel it at all and because of how difficult it is to conceal in the first place. But you have shown me that you can. And that will help you find Blanche.*

A bit of guilt eats at me. I'm sitting here, at Brunnea's, learning how to do magic, which is exactly what I told myself I would never do.

"Well?" Brunnea prompts. "Have you been thinking of how to reach the King and Queen? Time grows short."

"I don't know," I mutter reluctantly. "Break into the palace? Have you magically transport me there? You can do that, right?"

"Not quite, dearest," Brunnea says, her tone wry. She moves to stand over me, casting a long shadow over my face as she peers down. "We need to get you ready for the masque."

After a moment's shock, I laugh. "No. Absolutely not."

"Why ever not? You want to get close to the King, don't you?"

"Because it's pointless! There will be so many people there I won't be able to get close to them."

She tuts at me. "Clearly you've not been to many masques."

I pause. "Well, no. I mean, Mother died when I was born, and when Father died, I was still too young..." I trail off and shrug awkwardly from my prone position. "Well, I didn't exactly have a lot of chances to attend a ball."

She simply shakes her head. "With so many people there, the chances of brushing up against a royal is much greater. I could give you a little help, too."

I prop myself up on my elbows to look at her. "You'll take me? Go with me?"

"No. I cannot enter the palace without express invitation from the royal family."

I raise a brow. "What?"

She shakes her head. "It's an ancient law, one which originated when humans were quite angry with the Fae—and for good reason."

"So you can't enter the palace unless a royal expressly invites you?"

"Correct." Brunnea turns away to pluck the bud of a flower off a stem.

"Like the one Ella got? For the ball?"

"No. I need one more special than that."

"One from a royal."

"Yes." She eyes me, holding the bud in two fingers.

"What about this royal?"

She shakes her head sadly. "I'm afraid you don't count, dear. Not unless you're inviting me to the Merisian Palace."

I sink back down to the grass. "Well, it was worth asking."

"Yes, I suppose so." Brunnea holds the bud above my head. "Try again."

I squint at the bud, and it bursts into bloom without so much as a flicker of light from my palms.

Brunnea's lips twitch as she suppresses a smile.

A part of me doesn't want to go to the masque and ask for help. If I do, I reveal myself. If the answer is no, I will be forced to leave, or perhaps have to run for my life. I'd like to stay in Nubilus longer, rest, gain some strength, hone my skills with Brunnea, and get her to answer my questions. But then, every day I wait is a day that Blanche destroys my country.

Heaving a sigh, I push myself back into a sitting position. "I should go, shouldn't I?"

She doesn't answer, but moves away to deadhead a red flower. She turns to me and holds out the expired bloom. I aim the magic required to bloom a bud at it, then frown. It's done nothing.

Brunnea tilts her head and raises a brow. "Let go of your restraint, Winterberry. Accept who you are and who you are created to be."

Biting my lip, I try again, exerting more energy and focusing on asking the withered flower to return to bloom. Reversing the life cycle requires much more energy, but I recall those moments after Blanche's wolf attack, when I brought Elaina back, and then reviving Rus. Elaina's revival required much of me, but I did it… and Rus, well, he wasn't dead, just close to it. And I was in Ardor already, I remind myself. Magic isn't so suppressed here.

The dead flower reverses, drawing life back into itself and bursting into glorious bloom, deep, blood red with the faintest black sheen.

Brunnea blinks at the bloom, then gives an approving nod. "Nicely done."

A little breath of relief slips from me. Accept who I am meant to be. Is it just that simple?

"Brunnea?" I ask.

"Hmm?" she replies distractedly, leaning over a pot of flowers outside her cottage's back door.

"Why don't I use a wand? Or a stick or something?"

"What for?" She moves dark green leaves out of the way as if searching for something specific.

"You know, how you use your stick to do magic, why don't I need one?"

She purses her lips and reaches into the plant. "Well, that's a complicated answer, I suppose. Your magic is different, unique from what I've ever encountered. Before I met you, I thought you would need one, but you've lived so long without knowing of your magic, you've developed a sort of relationship with it."

"What?" I think of the light's voice in my head. "Is that why it hasn't…hurt me yet?"

She straightens, lifting her cupped hands from the plant. "It's quite unusual, I grant you, but then, so are you." She smiles broadly at me over her hands. "Don't worry about magic's effect on you, dear. You're right to think about the consequences of your magic, but believe me, you shall know when magic is the right choice and when it is not.

"The more important thing is what you'll do at the masque tonight. What's really bothering you about going?"

I sigh and rub my neck. "I'm afraid the huntsman will be there."

"The huntsman?" Her smooth brow furrows. She's in her young woman's guise today, but I've grown accustomed to both her images.

"He…" I pause. She seems to know everything else, why doesn't she know about him? "Don't you know?"

"You forget that I'm not allowed in Canens. None of the Great Fae are."

"Right. Um, he's my stepmother's huntsman. Well, she says he hunts for her, but half the time, I think he hunts humans down for her. And enslaves them," I add darkly.

"Oh, dear." She frowns, but her gaze lingers thoughtfully upon me. "His name wouldn't be Marcus, would it?"

My entire body chills. "How did you know that? If you can't go to Canens, then—"

She takes a breath. "Now, don't be angry with me, dear."

"Don't be—" I jump to my feet, and the butterfly in Brunnea's hands takes to the air. "*What?*"

She tuts as the insect flutters away. "Dear, I had plans for that butterfly…a life-taking spell I was going to teach you. Used only in emergencies, all you must do is touch it and take its *anima*. It can save *your* life if you are weakened—"

"Let's get back to why I shouldn't be angry with you," I interrupt, not caring to learn a spell I would never dare use.

"Dear, I promise that—" She breaks off, an odd look coming over her face. Grabbing her staff, she whirls to face the path to her cottage.

"Brunnea!" Following her around the corner of the cottage, I skid to a halt as a man dressed in dark blue rides a white horse toward the cottage. As he lifts his chin, I gasp and recoil.

"Bruen—" His gaze slides to me and then over my body.

He almost stumbles off his horse's back and to Brunnea's cottage on foot.

"What is it?" she asks him, her voice urgent, reading something much more than I can upon him. "What has happened?"

He motions to me. "Princess. Your Highness. You're alive. You are safe."

Flames of fury licking at my body, I charge forward, remembering every thing he put me through. "You. How could you—? I'm not going to be afraid of you anymore, I—"

He stumbles to the ground, prostrating himself before me.

I halt in shock. "Wha—what are you doing?"

"Your Highness—Your *Majesty*. I—I cannot convey to you how much I am in your debt. How remorseful I am of what has happened between us."

My mouth falls open. I snap my teeth together. "What has happened'? You mean how you enslaved and abused me?" I spit the words down at him, my fists clenched at my sides to keep the magic inside. "How you made me kill Certa?"

Brunnea lowers her staff and turns to me but doesn't interrupt.

The huntsman's bow deepens, and his hair parts, exposing the back of his neck to me. "I can say nothing but tell you how grateful I am to see you alive and uninjured."

"What?" The word bursts out of me. "What are you talking about? If I were injured, it would be because of you—"

"Yes, of course, Your Majesty."

"Stop it! Stop lying. Stop pretending like you care about me. You've done nothing but try to kill me. You've followed me from Canens to kill me and now when you find me, you apologize?" My hands burn. I'm losing control. But I don't care if I do, not if it hurts him. He made me kill Certa.

Brunnea clears her throat. "I'm suddenly glad that butterfly got away," she says dryly. "Perhaps you aren't ready for learning that spell."

My palms flare bright.

"He *does* have a bit of an excuse, dear."

"Excuse me?" I accost her with a glare. How dare she take his side?

"Your stepmother's huntsman was under a spell. Quite a few spells, actually."

"What?" I direct this at Brunnea. "You dare to blame his actions on a few spells from my stepmother?"

She cocks her head at me. "Well, yes. Spells and enchantments can be devastating."

"What are you talking about? He's been trying to kill me ever since—since I can remember!"

Brunnea makes a face. "True. But then he's not been himself for some years."

I scoff. My hands burn, flickering with something like lightning. "I don't care," I say. "He— I don't think years of cruelty are excusable by—" I break off, panting at the effort to keep my powers at bay. My fists spark and crackle.

"You have a right to be angry, Winterberry," Brunnea says, her tone severe and gentle at once. "But heed me when I tell you that this man has not been in control of his actions since you have known Blanche. Or perhaps, since she has known Marcus."

Slowly, the crackling in my fists eases. Still, fury licks at me, refusing its hold upon me. "I'm just supposed to expect he's stopped hating me and following her orders because you—"

"Because I say so?" Brunnea interrupts, a bit coldly this time. "Yes. Or perhaps because I broke the spells upon him."

My fists go cold. "You did?"

"Well, dear, I couldn't very well let him walk into Nubilus and kill you, could I? I'd have the entire country collapsing upon itself within the week."

"What?"

"The prophecy, dear, the prophecy."

I shake my head. "Which one? I thought it said whoever killed the heir of Canens will be killed."

"That's one of many prophecies. But don't worry about that, dear. Marcus, what brings you here to confront your princess?"

For the first time since falling at my feet, Marcus lifts his face and looks to Brunnea. "Queen Blanche has cursed the dress Princess Winterberry made for the masque tonight, and I was worried that she was already wearing it."

A chill rushes over my body with the rapidity of a plunge into ice water. "What dress?"

"When did she do this?" Brunnea asks, stepping between Marcus and me. "When did it happen?"

"Several hours ago. As soon as I could, I rushed into the inn, but the princess was not there, and the dress was gone."

"Dalia was going to take the dress to Ella today." I cover my mouth with a hand as I step backward, my feet not wanting to obey.

"What did she do to it?" Brunnea asks, calm but urgent.

"She cursed the laces. Whoever puts the dress on will be suffocated."

My hand tightens over my mouth.

"How much time do we have?" Brunnea asks.

"The curse will activate at midnight, I think."

Brunnea faces me. "Do you think Ella went to the ball?"

I drop my hand. "Well, yes. Of course. I mean, Dalia took the dress to her and—"

She turn to the Magister. "Are you certain of your information?"

"Yes, as certain as possible."

"Then we have no time to waste." Brunnea raises her staff and something warm flows over me.

I gasp and look down. My chin drops in shock. "Wha— I can't. Brunnea—"

She silences me with a glare and then mutters something I don't catch. There's the slightest whistle in the air, and Brunnea puts out her hand. Into it soars a pair of shears, which she grips tight. Turning to me, she holds it out. "Take these."

"What are they?" I ask the question to keep myself from wondering what happens if I fail again. I can't let Ella die. But I can't try and fail again.

"Shears. I used them for—well, it's not important. They're

enchanted." She thrusts them at me. "Take them. You will need them to cut her free. They should work."

"Why can't you save her? And what if they—"

"I told you, I cannot enter the palace without permission; we don't have time for that right now. Those shears are the only thing that will cut through Blanche's enchantment—if it's the one that I think it is."

"And if it isn't?" I demand in alarm, my skin going clammy. "You said the dress was gone?" I direct at Marcus. "Did you see Dalia leave with it?"

"No, Your Highness. If I had, I would have stopped her." He bends his head before me again. "I am sorry. I did not think the dress was made for anyone but you."

The shears are cold and heavy in my hand. I feel their magic, a twisting, writhing, living thing. I tighten my fingers around the blades. "I made it for her. Why would you think I made a dress for myself?"

Brunnea shakes her head. "We have no time for this. Winterberry, you must go. Quickly, now."

"But midnight—" I begin, motioning to the dimming sky.

"And if she's not there?" Brunnea interrupts. "What if she is not at the masque, but has gone home? What if she decides to stop at a friend's house on the way home? Or the temple? Or do some errands? What if—"

"Right, I get it." I glance at the sky. The moon is emerging, a white half orb in the darkening sky. "I have to go. I have to find her."

"You cannot be complacent," Brunnea says. "You must hurry. Hurry to Ella, and hurry to save your kingdom. The longer you wait, the more opportunity you give others."

I open my mouth to reply, but she shakes her head.

"Take Crystalli and race to the palace," she tells me. "As quickly as you can. Find Ella. I think she's there, but she could be on her way home even as we speak."

Marcus bolts to his feet, racing to his horse to grab the reins and hold him steady. I vaguely recognize the animal as the one I attempted to escape slavery on, the one I called Ice.

Thick, white skirts of my ballgown and clear, sparkling slippers hamper my ability to mount. I yank the dress up to my thighs and shove my slipper into the stirrup, then drag myself into the saddle, throwing a stockinged, sheer-white leg over the animal's back.

With a half glance at Brunnea and another at Marcus, who won't quite meet my eyes, I gather the reins with one hand, hold the shears in the other, and whirl Ice around. I kick him forward, and we leave the cottage behind while I pray to every god and goddess I can remember that I'm not already too late.

THE TOWER

"Your Majesty? Do you wish to find a place to set up camp?" Silvanus motions to the clear, blue sky with one hand while stroking his beard with the other. "It *is* growing dark, though slowly."

I allow my gaze to linger on my huntsman's brother. For all their similarities, they are quite different. One is so skilled I had to curse him to do my bidding, the other is so trusting of me that he begs to serve me.

"Have you left Canens before?" I ask him.

He purses his lips out and drops his hands to his thighs. "I have. Just twice. Once into Ostium, once into Heia."

"Never Ardor?"

"No." He shifts in his saddle, casting his gaze out across the Ardor countryside. We've been traveling through a dense, green glen with narrow game trails since leaving Nubilus by the southern gates. It's unlike anything in Canens, land of eternal winter.

And yet, we've gotten nowhere. I wiggle in my saddle, trying to shake myself free from the chains of these destructive thoughts.

"So how does Ardor compare? To your mind?" Curiosity overtakes my tongue for once. "Would you leave Canens for this?"

"For this?" Silvanus chuckles and runs a hand through his wavy blond hair as he scans the trees around us. "No. I couldn't give up Canens for this. What would I hunt here? Unicorns?" He snorts at the joke.

A breeze flutters through the leaves, lifting Silvanus' hair from his shoulders. I spare a moment to admire the image of this strong hunter from the homeland I love riding a well-bred horse from my own stables. My horse doesn't compare to the Gelu, of course, and should draw attention but for the variety of horses found in Ardor. Just like Silvanus doesn't compare to any Ardorite, and yet blends in seamlessly. His words and appearance are all Canensian. He refused to shave his beard, so it grows down to his chest. He's unlikely to be mistaken for an Ardorite until he takes care of that detail, even though he's traded his furs and heavy wools for the lightweight linen tunics and uncommonly tight breeches the men of this country wear. I scan his well-formed legs, appreciating the male Ardorian clothing for the first time.

If there's one thing that Canens cannot match, it's the liberty taken with clothing here in the heat. Even in warm ballrooms, Canensian men wouldn't wear such tight-fitting clothing and revealing attire. I glance down at my own clothing, the low-cut, though simple flowing gown of light linen, which makes riding even under the heat of the midday sun tolerable. Though my skin burns red from the sun and is peeling and itchy, I must admit it's a strange relief not to be wrapped in layers of furs and wools.

Another warm breeze lifts the mane of the horse and tugs at the hem of my dress, rippling the light fabric. I turn my face and allow the breeze to brush the blond strands from my face. The air smells like my growing house, except it's deeper and richer somehow, as if the earth and greens permeate every fiber of this world.

Something rotten rumbles to life inside me. Why should the Ardorites have such bounty while Canensians suffer? But it's not just Ardorites with their blessings, is it? It's Ostiites, Teporians, and the Heians. At least the Edormiscans earned themselves a curse. They did rather deserve it with their magic.

This *has* to work. The faery *must* know the way to break the Canens Curse, to bring warmth back to the north, at least for part of the year as it once did. Seeing this greenery in Ardor, witnessing the uninhibited growth of plants, sprouting out of the earth so carelessly that my horse trods on them and I care not, I cannot return to Canens and live in the cold again.

We start up a small hill, and when we reach the top, I halt my horse and peer down at a valley that is sparse with trees, lush with greenery and cradling a small river that runs into a still lake.

"How about there?" Silvanus points to the most picturesque spot where the river meets the lake.

Although I was hoping to find the princess before setting up camp tonight, I cast a smile at Silvanus. "That looks perfect."

His gaze lingers on me, shifting from my face and trailing down me in a brazen examination of his queen. I shiver under the heat of his stare. He makes me feel both like a woman and a queen.

"Let's hurry. I'm getting hungry," he says, nudging his horse down into the valley.

I suppose my search can wait until first light.

While I bathe in a secluded cove of the peaceful lake, Silvanus sets up our tepik and begins a fire. Within an hour, I stand at the lakeside, once again dressed, only in a loose-fitting, pale gold gown with lacy sleeves this time.

Footsteps behind me alert me to Silvanus' approach. I turn only my head and warn him to silence. Together, we watch the water's edge as a doe tiptoes out of the forest and toward the water, her ears swiveling. She darts a glance at us, watches a few moments, then creeps to the water's edge and lowers her head.

As she drinks, two fawns prance out from the woods behind her.

The slightest rustle at my side, followed by a quiet twang. An arrow slices the air and into one of the fawns.

The doe and second fawn flee. The other fawn flops, feebly trying to rise, then collapses and pants, heaving its last breaths with jumping sides. At the edge of the woods, the doe pauses, looking back over her shoulder at her fallen offspring. By the time Silvanus stows his bow, the fawn is still.

The doe bolts into the woods, her fawn already ahead of her, and Silvanus withdraws a knife from his belt with the slightest whisper of blade against its sheath. He strides forward and takes the fawn up with one hand at the nape of its neck. It lolls, eyes glassy and dim.

I silently admire the way he handles the knife as he finds a spot of dirt away from the water's edge and skins and guts the small animal. My attention shifts. I must say focused.

"I'm going to explore," I tell him. "Familiarize myself with the area."

His blue eyes, thoughtful and warm, meet mine in consideration. "Don't be too long. Dinner will be ready in under an hour."

"I'll be back by then." I raise a hand, hesitate, then let it fall upon his head, almost as though bestowing a blessing on a child. His eyes soften, darkening with longing. I withhold my smile and walk away, letting my hand fall from his head with the turn. I think I hear him release a tight sigh as it does.

In the woods, all is quiet. The deer and her remaining fawn are far from here now, a mother half torn with grief, a sibling half alone. I raise my head, but I cannot smell them nor detect their hearts beating. It's strange being in this place. My senses are off. And yet I feel so much more alive here than ever before. As if everything has more feeling. The trees nearly sing with life energy, while the animals are a gentle hum above them.

My skin burns, my nose tingles, and my eyes see colors I am

certain didn't exist before now.

I pause at a large elm tree and touch a bare hand to the rough, lined trunk. It hums under my hand. It's the magic. It courses through everything here. It's not just a feeling of awareness from the trees; they are even more alive. Everything has so much more life. I cast my eyes down to the ground where new shoots erupt at the roots, young ivy crawling up to embrace this tree, while bushy vines a half dozen feet away sag with purple grapes.

Tempted to give in and investigate the lush forest with my time, I instead close my eyes and focus on the tremble of life underneath my skin. The tremble of magic.

For my plans, I'll need more magic than I have in my stores, especially after casting such a complicated spell to change into my stepdaughter's appearance so recently. A thought is all it takes to siphon off some of the natural magic that all living beings contain. At the jolt of energy that enters me, my eyes fly open.

From high above in the tree, a bird squawks and flies from its roost, disturbed by the tendrils of magic that ripple from root to tip. Even the tree visibly trembles, shaking its leaves in protest at the theft.

I cling to the tree, gathering my balance as the magic from such an ancient life courses through me. A slow smile begins at my absorption of its energy. It's not something I can—or will—do often, but tonight, for my plans, this magic will be well used. I will not bind myself to others' magic, which borrowing magic too often will result in. I will not become dependent on another—any other.

The bird squawks from a neighboring tree, glowering down at me. With a serene smile, I meet its angry, bird glare, then with a flick of my hand and a muttered word, my entire body transforms. Instead of standing beside the trunk, I hover in the air, flapping my wings. With a screech, I propel myself into the trees. The other bird flees.

Above the canopy, I stretch my wings, marveling at the lightness of my bones and the way the air moves through the brown feathers and buoys me far above the trees. I tilt my wings and experimentally dip, dive, and spin, moving through the air with such speed I can't believe my own abilities. With one more loop, I settle into flight, scanning the ground, speeding over the lake and Silvanus, who roasts the speared fawn over the fire.

Smaller birds hop on the dirt, squirrels and mice dart across the grass and into their burrows as I fly over them. Within minutes, I've flown in a large circle around our campsite. Ceara said she'd heard the princess was somewhere near the lake south of Nubilus, but she hadn't been able to discover it. I should be close now.

Then I spot it. Amidst the green forest below, a small meadow with a gray stone tower reaches high into the sky. I angle my wings and circle it, closer and closer. It appears uninhabited but well kept.

There's no one in the meadow, no hint of a garden or other food source, and my hope sputters. Still, I circle once more, dipping down toward the tower.

Then I hear it.

From the tower comes a song, a voice as pretty as a bird, singing a tune I don't recognize.

I make another circle around the tower, dipping low to peer into the glassless windows as I pass, but see nothing. On my next circle, I land on the ledge of a small balcony outside and hop toward the stone archway. Although there are wooden doors that are able to shut, today they are open, allowing the breeze to flow inside and the female voice to drift out.

I cock my head to better see out of the bird's strangely placed eyes, then again to better hear the voice from its strangely placed ears. I hop closer, trying to catch a glimpse of the singer. Inside I spot a small place, and to the side, what looks like stairs to the turret.

I frown. The faery said the girl was locked in a tower when

she was young. Of course, someone has to have a way to reach her to bring her food. And there is a small square of a window in the turret below, which I saw when I descended.

Is the girl free to wander the meadow? Is there some enchantment on her or the clearing? An enchantment that prevents the Fae from being able to find her?

A bird chirp surprises me, and I flinch crossly before realizing it came from my throat. Trying to stay silent, I crane my head to see inside. The faery said I would recognize the girl by her impossibly long locks.

I lift my head in a twitchy motion. My bird ears hear movement inside, a soft scratching of soft fabric against stone. Then a short, slender girl passes in front of the door and starts down the stairs in the turret. If I were in human form, I think my jaw would drop to the ground below. The girl has long since disappeared, but her hair continues to follow, creeping across the floor like a snake. A long braid, the thickness of a man's arm, collects whatever is on the ground and drags it along with it.

How can she live with such *hair*? My wonderment turns to satisfaction. This girl will be easy. The sheer weight of it alone must cripple her.

I spread my wings and drop to the ground, where I perform a quick inspection of the lower portion of the tower. While it's house shaped, there are only two very narrow windows where I assume food is passed through. An iron pump runs from a creek nearby, and with fancy pipes and a pulley system, it runs water into the little cottage attached to the base of the tower through one of the windows.

The girl has no need to leave her tower except for food, for she could have no garden if she cannot leave its stone embrace. So someone must deliver food to her...which means someone knows of her existence here. Someone guards her.

I return to the air and swoop around the area for a few more minutes, searching for a trail or nearby home to explain the dependence of this girl in the tower. Nothing but a few deer and innumerable green trees. I sense many *animae*, but in my animal form it's much harder to do, and they're all weak. That is something I must determine in my human form, on foot or horseback perhaps.

Without much else to do in this form, I return to the lake, touching down on the shore as a bird before effortlessly reclaiming my human form.

Silvanus leaps to his feet when my bird feathers shudder and begin to fly, the amusement on his face turning to alarm. Then when the wings transform back into limbs, the scrawny legs into long, feminine legs that he just glimpses before my summoned clothing obscures it, the alarm crosses into shocked relief.

"Something wrong?" I ask innocently, enjoying the stunned glaze over his eyes and his parted lips. "Do I have feathers in my hair?"

"Uh…" His gaze flicks up to my head. "No. No, I—" He breaks off as I stride into camp and glance at the fire. The small fawn sizzles over the fire, dripping juices into the flames with a trail of hisses. He clears his throat and motions to it. "Are you hungry?"

I let my gaze drift to the cooking dinner, then slide it back to him, over his muscular torso under that thin tunic, over the sinewy muscles of his legs in his tight breeches. "Yes. Yes, I am."

He blinks, an uncertain smile creeping over his lips. "I've set up the tent for you, if you'd like to refresh yourself, change your clothes, or…?"

"Why don't you take that out of the fire?" I ask, moving past him toward the two-person sized tent. "I've scouted the area and there's no one within miles. We don't need to rush."

I pause at the tent's entrance, holding the flap back with one hand to look over my shoulder at him. He looks up from removing the venison from the fire, and his eyebrow lifts slightly in question.

With a crook of my finger, I invite him in.

BREATHLESS

I still can't quite believe it. Dalia arrived early in the afternoon, along with another few children that she seems to collect like bees to the sweetest, most vibrant flower. She and the three girls she came with bustled me off to force me into the dress, mask, and a pair of silvery dancing shoes.

The girls giggle as they drag me into the house and through the servant's quarters. My sisters and mother paid a team of women and men to turn them into beautiful exhibitions of womanly glory tonight, and then left without speaking to me.

The three little brunettes Dalia arrived with wash my hair and scrub my skin with rosewater until I shine, then twist my hair into some sort of braided updo and spritz a delicate perfume upon it.

"All right then. I think..." Dalia stands back from me as all three of the little girls scatter to form a semi-straight line behind her, beaming with pride at their work. "I think that's good. You just need this." She holds up the mask, a silver and gold thing with slightly feline eyes and a silver ribbon.

"Really?" I protest faintly as she steps behind me and gently but snugly secures it in place. "It's beautiful, but—"

"It's a masque, Ella," she says in exasperation. "Even *you* have to wear one. Especially you."

I smile wryly. "I don't think anyone could ever recognize me with how much you've done here in the last hour."

The three brunette girls, whom I finally placed as three of the tailor's six daughters, grin at each other proudly.

"Where is Winter?" I ask the question that's been bothering me all evening. "Did she stay back at the inn?"

Dalia frowns, pursing her lips out with annoyance. "No. She's been running off for days, but don't worry about her now. I didn't tell her about this."

"You didn't?"

She shakes her head, but I don't believe it. "Now quiet, I'm trying to examine you, and I can't think."

I bite back a chuckle along with more questions about Winter.

Dalia circles me, a critical twist to her lips as she presses upon them with one finger. "Missing something..." she murmurs. Then she snaps her fingers. "Girls! We forgot the jewels."

My eyes widen. "No—no, I can't take Lady Eleanora's jewels!"

"Lady Eleanora is already gone for the ball with her other daughters." Dalia sniffs and turns to the girls, the eldest of whom hurries to hold out a small pouch. "But I wouldn't dare put her nasty jewelry on you anyway."

Before I know it, a simple, sapphire necklace is laced around my neck and sapphires dangle from my earlobes. Then, apparently not hearing my protests, Dalia marches me out the front door, where we both stop short to find a beautiful carriage waiting in the carriageway, two well-bred horses in front of the driver.

"Where did this come from?" I ask Dalia. "Where did you find this carriage?"

Confusion creasing her brow, Dalia shakes her head. "This wasn't me. I have no idea who sent it.

"I was told to tell you 'his grace hopes you're ready to attend the masque,'" the driver says, face inscrutable.

Dalia's face breaks into a grin as mine prickles with heat. The duke has been visiting the stable nearly every day since his first visit, and somehow, whether he stays for five minutes or an hour, it's never enough.

"This is perfect," Dalia says, taking my shoulders with her hands and turning me toward her. She runs quick hands over my hair and readjusts my light cape, even inspecting the fingers of my gloves.

I press her busy hands between my own. "Dalia, you've done so much. Let me go now."

She pauses, then releases a tight breath. "Yes. Yes. Have a wonderful, magical night." She seems to think about pulling me into a hug but just squeezes my hands.

My pale blue dress shimmers in the moonlight of a bright half moon as the driver assists me into the carriage. The streets are quiet. We're an hour late to the masque and are out of place now. Those who watched the carriages carrying guests to the masque an hour ago have disappeared into their homes now.

At the palace, carriages sit with already bored drivers who eye us as we arrive late.

A man dressed in a button-up black overcoat with a white tunic underneath hurries forward to assist me in climbing down to the stone steps of the palace.

"Welcome, miss," he says. "Just give your invitation to the man at the top of the stairs."

"Thank you." As he bows his head at me, I lift my pale blue skirts and head up the stairs unescorted.

Flowers line the way, huge bouquets of cut roses, daisies, myrtle, living rose bushes, orchids, and other flowers my unknowledgeable eyes don't recognize. Torches burn above the steps, each protected by glass to keep them from sputtering out in the autumn breezes.

At the door, I hand over my personalized invitation, the first of the three. I adjust the mask hiding my features as the footman marks and stores my invitation in a huge basket of others and motions me inside. My heart thumps as this moment nears. Will they recognize me? How could they?

But how will I recognize Duke Orestes? I think of his hazy, blue-green eyes, his smooth, shaven cheeks revealing his strong jaw, his Ardor wheat-colored hair, his broad shoulders, and try to remember exactly what spot I came up to on his body. My eyes are about level with his shoulder, I think. We spent so much time on horseback that it's difficult to say. I will just have to note our heights if we dance. I scoff at myself and my hopeful thoughts. But him sending me a carriage means something, right?

A path of flowers and small lanterns lead into a ballroom the size of my entire stables twice over, which is filled to the brim with swirling ballgowns, vibrant and dull masks, gleaming gems, tapping shoes, and hundreds of lanterns. Squinting at the masked faces rushing by, I recognize a handful by their stature and hair, but most I don't recognize in the slightest.

There are so many people in Nubilus. I laugh, giddy with excitement at being here at the palace masque.

The ballroom is magnificent on its own, but it's decorated with even more flowers than those leading guests inside—maybe more than the palace gardens themselves. Tables of refreshments stretch out in several spots throughout the room with a wide empty swath in the middle for dancing. Musicians, at least two dozen of them, play near the dias for the thrones where two people sit, watching the swirling masses below them. I can't help but notice that Prince Brann is absent, probably dancing with a well-dressed noblewoman. I don't spare him another thought except to pray that neither of my sisters are that well-dressed noblewoman. My life would never be the same should they ascend the throne beside Brann.

Dancing, eating, and drinking are well under way, and the people around me chatter and giggle around their fluted glasses.

There are many young women, each having a difficult time keeping their attention on their food or their partners, each glancing toward the thrones as if hoping for a confirmed glimpse of the prince.

Wandering through the crowd, searching masks, hair, and shoulder width for the Duke of Orestes, I hear dozens of familiar voices, including Sir Erik Birch's. But upon hearing Sallust's deep voice, I redirect my feet, avoiding the spot where they stand near a table laden with a fountain of bubbly liquid. I hurry the opposite direction, searching for Orestes. Every step I take, my heart sinks a little bit more until I'm nearly treading on it.

Starting on my second lap, I pick up a flute of bubbling liqueur from the table to buoy my spirits for the fruitless search.

"Ella?"

With the glass touching my lips, I pause and slide my eyes to the side. The flute nearly slips from my fingers as my face breaks into a smile. I thought I wouldn't recognize him, but I'd recognize those eyes peering through that mask anywhere. Orestes wears a beautifully designed and yet simple mask looking like the face of a black panther. It covers his forehead, cheeks, and nose only, leaving his lips open to smile and reveal his perfectly straight teeth.

Even though my own lips are covered by my feline mask, I smile broadly, hoping he can see just a part of my excitement. "How did you recognize me?" I ask him.

He chuckles and lifts a hand to my head. "No one else has hair like yours, Ella."

Self consciously, I half raise a hand to it. "No?"

He tucks a curling strand behind my ear. "It gleams like the sunlight. Or like Chrysos," he adds, naming one of the Gelu Rigens founding sires.

Another grin parts my lips.

"I'm so glad you came." He takes my hand in his and tucks it into the crook of his elbow. "And that I've found you." As a group of richly dressed guests laugh uproariously at something one of them has said, Orestes tugs me away from them.

"I am, too," I say. "I don't think I would be here if not for my friend. And you."

"Oh?" His eyes smile behind his mask.

"Thank you for the carriage."

He grins. "Thank you for taking it."

As I smile, he tucks my hand into his elbow and we fall silent. I admire the red gown of a woman that looks vaguely familiar. Tilting my head, I think I recognize her as one of Nubilus' seamstresses. I half raise a hand in greeting before remembering I'm in disguise as much as she and everyone else is.

"Will you dance with me?" The duke's eyes shine out of his black cat mask.

"Yes. I'd love to." I try to smother my smile before giving up and beaming at him. I am hopeless.

He takes the fluted glass from my hand and hands it to a passing server. Then he whisks me onto the dance floor.

"I might not be any good," I warn him as he sweeps me into his arms. My body trembles at his touch, at his thinly gloved hands brushing against the bare skin of my arm.

He leans down and says into my ear, "I'm good enough for both of us." His lips curve into a thoughtful frown. "At dancing, that is."

A laugh slips from me, and his grin answers.

Dancing doesn't leave much time or air for conversation, and soon we are breathless. Half a dozen dances later, I have to beg him for a break.

"*You* need a break?" he teases. "You ride all day and tend horses all day, and yet dancing tires you out?" But he leads me to the edge of the floor, his upper lip damp with sweat.

"I also worked all day today," I retort playfully, reaching for the drink he holds out to me.

He sobers, his lips forming a tight line. "I wish you didn't have to work."

I glance at him, confused. "I love to work with the horses. I love them, and to see them grow and learn…I wouldn't trade it for anything." I sip from my drink to cover my wince. I would give it up for the right man, maybe.

"I know, that's not what I meant," he says. "I meant I wish you didn't have to work so hard for the same rewards of others. It's not fair. And someone needs to do something about it. The laws should change."

"Well, I…" A flush heats my cheeks and tears surprise me by stinging my eyes. I'm grateful I haven't given into the temptation to lift my mask, as now it hides my embarrassment as well as concealing my identity from any curious onlooker.

His lips thin into an angry line, but his anger makes me ashamed.

I pick at the fingertip to one of my gloves that cover my cracked, bloody fingers and dry skin. They complete tonight's illusion: that I am a noblewoman worthy of being here, not a hard-working businesswoman in danger of losing everything.

His frown softens, but his stare doesn't recapture its earlier joy. "You don't mind? That you have to sacrifice to come here tonight, when your title should make this sort of event normal?" He leans back and frowns. "How much have you slept this past week?"

"I— Well…"

"That's what I thought. You're single-handedly taking care of the stables and your family and you have the added pressure of trying to secure the future of your land through marriage." He shakes his head, his wheat-colored hair flapping around the top of his mask. "Is it my fault you haven't slept? Have my visits kept you up later? You should have said something. I can't believe—." He stops short as if he's gone too far.

"Well—"

"I—" he begins at the same time. "Go on," he urges.

"It wasn't your fault. Your visits gave me something to look forward to every day. But all that you mentioned, it's not something anyone but I think about, probably." I twist one of the fingertips on my glove. "The longer I do this business, the more I realize everyone is concerned with their own troubles, trying to find their own success. Some try to prevent others' successes, and some try to claim it. And I have done my best to survive alone, without anyone else's help. But I...I've been selfish."

Duke Orestes blinks down at me in surprise at my confession.

This mask has made me brave. Foolishly so.

"And what does your family think of your choices? Did you decide your path together?"

A bitter laugh escapes me before I can stop it. "No. No, my family? Oh, they would have me sell and gain them husbands. All three of them, if possible. They would..." I pause and glance at the moonlit sky. Stars twinkle amongst wispy clouds. "They would sell me to gain their own freedom."

I throw back the rest of my drink and walk toward the cool, night air of the balcony. For some reason, no one has stepped out of the ballroom, perhaps still looking for their prince in disguise.

Orestes trots to catch up with me, touching my elbow with his fingertips. "I'm sorry. I didn't mean to upset you. It's just...you are not like other girls, Ella."

His words ripple over me with a strange familiarity. I shrug and go to take a drink but find my glass empty. With a small grin, Orestes offers me his. After a moment's thought, I take it.

"Though I'm more sorry that your family thinks so little of you and all your hard work. It's horrible. They sound horrible."

Dipping my chin, I watch the floor turn from blueish-gray marble to dark gray as I walk. My toes, encased in those perfect, silvery slippers peek out from under the shimmering blue skirt of my gown. My eyes burn. How can I be crying now? Over Orestes' simple concern for my well-being? For me. I can't remember anyone other than Dalia and maybe Winter becoming offended on my behalf. But Orestes is more than that, he's...protective. The only man I've ever met like him before was Hadwin... I dart a look back at his profile. I am not like other girls. Once upon a time, Hadwin had told me that. My heart beats faster. Could it be him? His name has been on my lips a dozen times tonight, and yet each time, I lose my courage. But he must be. A smile grows on my lips. I know he is. My heart warms. It is him, he remembers me, but he's as afraid to confess it as I am.

I lift my head. "Hadwin?"

But the duke has moved off, farther into the garden, and he doesn't hear me.

A sudden sorrow washes over me, taking away my joy of discovery. If he is Hadwin, why hasn't he confessed it to me? Is he afraid I don't remember? Is he afraid I won't still love him?

"Ella?"

Orestes' voice is soft and concerned, but I don't want to lift my chin or turn and face him. I don't want to show him my sorrow or my weakness. I've only survived these last years on my strength. I've only ever let one person see how much it takes from me, how much of a struggle every single day is. And if Orestes isn't Hadwin...

"Ella?" With two fingers of his own, Orestes lifts my chin for me. "Ella." He peers into my eyes, his expression both warm and kind, but also full of anger. "Ella, I'm so sorry. I shouldn't have—I should have held my tongue. I shouldn't have..." He trails off, falling silent. An unvoiced question in his eye, he slowly reaches behind my head and loosens my mask.

He catches it in his hand as it falls off. My heart hammers in my chest faster than if I catch sight of a unicorn. Mouth dry, I let him tilt my chin up with his fingers again. Then without moving his mask, he leans down toward me, capturing my lips with his. I melt into him, my heart hammering so fast I can't breathe. He tastes slightly of peach, the same flavor of the liquor we've been sipping.

When we part, I inhale shakily. My entire body trembles, but not like it ever has before. A thrill of excitement courses through me, followed by a surge of joy.

"I'm sorry. I should have asked," he says.

"Don't ruin this moment for me," I reply, leaning my head against his chest and waiting for my body to solidify.

Under my ear, his body rumbles with laughter. "Right."

Still breathless, I pull back and lift my face to his. My intention is just to see him again, to make sure that this really happened, but our eyes lock and his mouth finds mine again. And I melt all over again.

"We should go back and dance some more," he says, but his gaze doesn't leave my face as I breathe shallowly.

"Sure," I whisper against his lips, touching them as light as a butterfly's wings landing on a rose.

"Well, the dancing will continue for another hour yet."

"Of course," I say, my legs weak. My dress seems so tight.

He kisses me again, gentle and sweet. Spots dance in my vision. This must be pure joy.

"You don't have to leave soon, do you?"

"No." I can't stop smiling, even though it's growing harder to breathe the more he kisses me.

He pulls me farther into the shadows of the garden. His lips find mine.

I try to inhale, a quick little breath between kisses, and I can't. I gasp, locking gazes with him. I push at his chest, my muscles weak and reluctant to obey. My knees wobble.

"What's wrong? Are you all right?" His words are laced with worry. "Ella?" He grips my hands as the edges of my vision go dark. I fix my gaze on him even as my legs go weak, and I sink toward the ground, my descent slowed only by his grip.

My eyes drift closed against the burning in my lungs. Then, with a tiny exhale, I collapse into darkness.

THE LOVER

*J*wake slowly to the sound of birds chirping and the wind rustling through the forest leaves. Turning, I find the sleeping pad beside me empty, the only evidence of Silvanus' presence a divot in the pack he used as a pillow last night.

Stretching out my arms like a cat might stretch her limbs, I inhale slowly, hold it, and exhale, listening to the world waking around me. With just a touch of my powers, I hear Silvanus stepping through the woods a short distance away, a fish jumping out of the lake and diving back in, a rabbit nibbling on a blade of grass, and farther away, a buck scratching his antlers against the bark of a tree.

It is a world alive. Sucking in a breath, I rise straight up, invigorated by the life around me. Magic courses through me like I've taken an energy draught or even stolen a full *anima*. The magical life in Ardor is so much greater than in Canens that every day I wake, I find my magical strength replenished.

Within minutes, I've risen, stepped out of the tepik, and taken to the skies. I swoop through the air in my streamlined, falcon body, formulating my plan as I dive and wheel. I don't want to kill the girl, for who knows what sort of war that might create.

Ceara wanted me to do this without death and without letting the princess or anyone else know of my presence in Ardor. After all, knowing where a trapped princess lives is valuable, and being able to find her again whenever we want invaluable.

My mind works as I fly through the sky, surveying the Ardor forest below. After circling the meadow a few times, I settle into a tree on the edge overlooking the stone tower to watch the girl for the day.

An hour into my watch, I nearly fall out of my roost in shock when a man rides into the clearing upon a dark-colored Gelu Rigens. His green, linen tunic leave his forearms bare and exposed to the warmth of the sun. His hair flutters in the wind with every floating step of his horse until the mare slows and stops, when the man's thick tresses rest upon his broad shoulders. He hardly glances at the tower except for a cursory inspection, suggesting that its presence doesn't surprise him in the slightest. He dismounts confidently, certain of where he is going and the reception he'll receive. He is expected.

My bird head tilts in consideration. He is expected? I came to this tower last night as a woman and felt the pull of magic upon me—or rather, the push of it. For there is an enchantment upon this meadow and the tower within. It pushes things away, people, animals, weather. If I had not been looking for the magic, actively working against it, I would never have sensed it. It is delicately done, this curse, subtle enough to deter even those who can recognize magic. I could give Silvanus instructions to the tower, and he would struggle to locate it.

All humans should avoid this area. So how is this man deliberately finding the tower? Who is he? What is he?

I tilt my head the other way, taking his strange image in my bird vision as he ties his horse to a tree on the outskirts of the meadow and starts across the flowery field. His booted feet leave ill-defined impressions on the soft grass and gentle flowers, but he goes straight to the base of the tower under the balcony, not bothering to circle it or inspect the lower house for a door. He's definitely been here before.

Stopping under the tower, he tilts his head back and calls out loudly, "Aeria! Aeria, it's me! Let down your hair!"

I chirp in surprise. Let down her hair? What nonsense is this?

There's a rustle in the shadows at the top of the balcony, then a long, thick rope falls from over the top of the railing and hits the ground.

I blink my bird eyes. That cannot possibly be the girl's hair. I know it's long, but—no, impossible.

While I'm distracted inspecting the rope, the man has grabbed on and begun to climb. He makes short work of the job, dragging himself up the rope with just his arms until he reaches the railing then kicks himself over it and disappears inside.

Stunned, I give another chirp, this one of annoyance. This certainly complicates things. What am I to do with a man inside there? I can't very well use magic to subdue him, not with the tower under enchantment. I can only hope he leaves as quickly as he appeared. And if he doesn't, well, perhaps Silvanus will make himself useful after all. Though I had hoped to do this without using magic at all, for a new curse could trigger the enchantment's protections on the princess.

I wait a minute after the man fully disappears into the shadows of the turret, then leave my perch and fly over, landing upon the slanted roof of the tower. Voices drift out of the door beneath me.

"The weeks are so long now," the girl is saying.

"I'm sorry, my darling. I cannot escape more often. Especially with the prince back in Nubilus. And we must avoid your mother, of course."

"I know." She sighs heavily, clearly heart wrenched. "But every day is so long."

"I know, my darling."

"If you would just consider leaving him…why does he need you?"

"I can't leave him, darling. He's my best friend."

"But how will we ever have a life together then? We could live here happily. You have no need of him."

There's a pause between them.

"Darling," the man says, "have you given thought to what I said? Perhaps you can leave the tower."

"I can't!" Panic captivates the girl's voice. "I've told you! I can't! I would die. And it would break Mama's heart."

He sighs. "You break my heart by staying. How can you expect to grow if you never venture outside?"

"I cannot. Why do you ask that of me? How could you? I can't!"

"All right, all right." The man soothes her with his words and sounds for several minutes.

"You see the tower," she says after a long silence. "How am I to escape anyway? Besides, you knew when you first met me that I would never be able to leave."

"I know…but things have changed."

"How?"

A little bird sigh slips from my beak. Get over your lover's tiff already and get on to something interesting. Inside, the two continue bickering about their refusal to give in to the other's requests. Growing tire of listening, I fly to a nearby tree and settle in more comfortably to wait.

A long time later, after some sobbing and some presumed hugs and kisses, followed by more sweet talk and soothings, the man reappears on the balcony, not looking nearly as mussed as I would expect, given their length of intimacy.

As he glances at the sun high in the sky, I hop down the branch toward the tower. Why leave now instead of staying the day? Does he know someone else approaches? Or does he have something to return to? Is this his typical pattern?

If only I had more time to observe him and his visits before I have to take action. Several weeks would be best, to see if he shows up the same time every day or every three days or just once a week. And see who else shows up every day. But the masques have me limited.

The man descends the tower the same way he entered. When his feet dangle a few feet above the ground, he lets go of her hair and drops with practiced ease upon the meadow. Walking backward part of the way so that he might wave goodbye to the girl above, he returns to his horse.

He mounts and rides away with several backward glances. Silent, I watch him go, as does the girl.

If I had lips and could smirk, I would. For a new plan has come to mind, and I couldn't have asked for a better man to build it on.

MIDNIGHT

I ride the Magister's horse as fast as he can run through Nubilus. He weaves through the town, receptive to my slightest touch, his hooves barely skimming the cobblestones. In no time at all, we're racing up the palace road.

As we approach the gates, I slow him, for the guards are already bracing themselves against us.

With a feigned, calm nod at them, I hope I look like nothing more than a girl afraid she's too late for the masque and her chance at meeting the prince.

One of the guards peers at my legs with wide eyes. Remembering that I ride astride with a ballgown on, I flush. My legs are exposed up to my knee. Scandalous, surely, but what can I do about it now? I give him a little nod and lift my chin before nudging Ice into a jog toward the front of the palace where hundreds of carriages wait.

At the door, I practically throw myself from the saddle and toss the reins at a footman hurrying my way.

"Wait, miss!" he cries as I sprint up the stairs into the palace. There's no one at the door, and I fly through, racing for the ballroom, the shears banging against my thigh in the pocket of my sparkling dress.

I burst into the ballroom and skid to a halt, gaping at the sheer number of people. How...how am I to find Ella here? There are hundreds of people.

Despair washes over me, making my knees bend at its weight. Heads turn at my abrupt appearance through the door, and I meet a few gazes before lifting a hand to my cheek. The mask covers my face almost completely, and I've never been more grateful. My fingers drift across the smooth leather and over the feathers fanning out from the cheeks of my mask.

Groups of well-dressed women eye me suspiciously. For a moment, I forget what Ella's mask looks like. I dismiss anyone with dark hair, for I know Dalia wouldn't have concealed her identity so much that the prince couldn't recognize her.

We gave her a feline mask, I remember, a silver and gold cat, thinking that her sisters would expect something equine. I had helped make her mask, using just a touch of magic to make it look like something even more fantastical than any other person could possibly have, so that the prince's attention might be drawn toward her.

I search the crowd, pushing through and looking for that silver and gold mask. There's a gold one with white accents, a white unicorn with a black horn, a bird-like brown one, a startling red bird, and a hundred others. Hers is not there. Not there.

My stomach squirms. Some of the groups are leaving. It's late, nearly midnight. How close to midnight? It must be only minutes away.

Stomach in knots, I dash through the ballroom, pushing through the groups, looking at masks with unashamed brazenness. Some have removed their masks entirely, and I dismiss all of them without further inspection. With her family present, Ella would never remove her mask, never.

Still, even with the help of many having their faces exposed, I cannot find her.

The seconds tick by, my heart beating loudly in my head. Where is she? The words pound in rhythm with my heart. Where is she? If it weren't for Brunnea's training, my hands would be bursting with light as I race through the room as fast as I can without attracting everyone's attention. Even now, I feel my control wavering. The last thing I need is for all of Ardor's nobility and anyone who is anyone to see me cut off Ella's dress with magical shears. That's the last thing *Ella* needs, too.

As the minutes tick by, my despair grows until it pushes at my ribs and threatens to make me explode. I've searched the ballroom twice, the faces I've seen three times, and she's not here. She's not *here*. She's *not here*.

She's not here.

I follow the movement of the guests. There's a commotion toward one side of the room. They're disappearing out through a wide archway, through a door that appears to exit into a garden. A garden? Did Ella step out for some fresh air? That would be like her, not wanting to be stifled in this stuffy palace room.

I'm running out of time. I scan the room again, searching for her blue dress and silver and gold mask, her golden hair and tanned skin.

No time.

My gaze skips across faces.

Another one you couldn't save, comes the snide little voice in my head. *How many does that make?*

I start to count before I can help myself. Des, Certa— Even as I think their names, the clock begins to strike. I race to the archway and grip its frame. "No. Please. Please let me save her," I whisper.

Then I feel it. Tendrils of magic wrapping around my middle. A slight tug from behind, nearly physical in its insistence. "This way!" it seems to say. "And hurry!"

Trusting it and abandoning caution, I race into the garden.

A few turns into the hedges, and then I hear him.

"Ella! What's wrong? Can you breathe?"

I lift my skirts and round a corner in the hedges then skid to a halt. Chills embrace me. Ella's collapsed on the ground like a fallen angel, her dress spread out around her like wings, and a man bends over her, pulling at the laces to her gown.

"Ella, I can't—they're too tight." The man tugs at them again, and this time I see a knife glinting in his hand. "Ella!" He saws at the laces, his face pale in the moonlight. "It's not working! Can you hear me? Breathe, darling!"

I sprint toward them and into him, pushing him aside as I slide onto my knees beside her. Her face is pale, her lips blue.

"Hey—" he begins.

I ignore him. She's not breathing.

"Her dress—I— She can't breathe—"

Ella's skin is cold and clammy, or maybe it's my hands that feel like that. I drag Brunnea's shears from my pocket and tug Ella onto her side, exposing the laces up the back of her dress.

"I already tried; it doesn't work." He holds out his knife.

"Get out of my way." I shove his hand aside and slide the shears under the laces. They spring apart at the blade's touch, slicing the fabric like a foot falling through fresh snow. I drop the shears and yank the laces apart, loosening the bodice of the dress. I roll Ella onto her back and lean over her.

"Ella, Ella, can you hear me?" I pat her face and shake her shoulder. I'm about to start breathing into her mouth when she gives a great, rasping breath and her eyes flicker open.

Relief courses through me in a rush of heat. "Ella?"

My friend pushes herself half upright. "I—what happened?"

"Your dress was cursed by the Queen," I tell her without thinking.

"Cursed? What?" she asks breathlessly. "Who?"

"I'm so sorry." Tears spring to my eyes at the release of my fear. "It was the Queen. She wants me dead."

A shuddering inhale sounds over my shoulder, and I turn to see Prince Brann staring at me with ice in his gaze.

"Why does the Queen want you dead? Who are you?"

Realizing my mistake, I open my mouth and shut it again. I hadn't planned on it like this. Not with Ella watching, not in front of just the prince. I need his father's allegiance more than his.

Brann points his knife at me. "If my mother wants you dead, tell me who you are and why before I kill you right here."

"Your mother?" Ella gasps, fixing him with wide eyes. "What?"

I slowly hold up my hands, showing them empty. "Brann, Your Highness, I did not intend to suggest that your mother, Queen Ada, wants me dead." I twitch my head to the side. "Well, she very well may once I tell you that my stepmother is…is the Queen of Canens."

For the space of several heartbeats, the air goes silent.

"Traitor!" He hisses the word, and although his gaze slices me, it's Ella that winces away.

"Please. I mean no harm coming here—I thought that—" I motion to Ella. "I came to save— And maybe…maybe we could unite against my stepmother. Against Canens. She—"

The prince's face twists in disgust. "We would *never* ally with Canens. I would sooner abdicate my throne than ally with you."

Fury meets humiliation in my chest. "You may very well have that opportunity." I rise and face him. "She's here, in Ardor, now, and I risk more than my life in coming to you."

A flush rushes to Prince Brann's cheeks. "One more word, and I'll have you arrested."

With a shake of my head, I say, "You don't have the power to arrest me. You might be heir to the throne, but—"

"Don't test me." Brann steps close, his dark eyes burning into mine. "You might think you know things, but you don't." His gaze shifts to Ella then back to me. "The only reason you're not under arrest right now is because of her."

I glower, but his words ring with honesty. Quickly, I turn to Ella and pull her to her feet, giving her a quick hug. "I must go," I whisper to her. "Before he calls the guards on me."

"I—" She wobbles as I let her go, putting myself between her and Brann. I grit my teeth at the hurt and confusion on her face. She passed out at a masque as a low noblewoman falling for a young duke and woke as a low noblewoman in love with a prince far above her station. A romance now doomed by her friendship with an enemy princess.

My heart twists in my chest like a deer in its death throes. "I'm so sorry, Ella."

At the commotion of Ella's faint and our strange meeting in the hedges, guards jingle and tramp their way toward us through the hedges. I bend and scoop up the shears, suddenly aware that I never removed my mask. It fits so well that I never needed to remove it. Is it because it's made of magic? Or because my disguise is so complete?

"Wait," Ella says as I straighten, tucking the shears back in my pocket.

But I can't wait; instead, as the guards round the hedge, I flee, not stopping even when I lose one of my slippers.

HOME

As Winter disappears around the hedges, I feel a strange numbness in my lungs, as though I am still trying to catch my breath. The Duke of Orestes takes a step after her, then pauses as a crowd of guests surges around with excited cries.

He abruptly turns, abandoning his pursuit of Winter, takes me in with wide eyes, and hurries toward me.

He whisks off his jacket. I frown. Then, as he swings it over my shoulders, I'm aware of how my dress is barely hanging onto my frame. His jacket smells vaguely of wood and leather, reminding me of his love for horses, reminding me once more that I shouldn't have come tonight, reminding me of everything that's happened.

Orestes hurries me in the opposite direction of the crowd, giving an odd jerk of his head toward the bushes.

As he takes me around a turn in the hedges, I look back and see the King's Guardsmen intercept the crowd from following us. There on the verdant floor is my silver and gold mask, kicked to the side by a guard's boot. And above a guard's arm is Haydée's face, flashing eyes narrowed in confusion.

I look away, forcing my feet faster even as we disappear from view. Orestes will protect me, right? No. My skin tingles. He's not Duke Orestes, but Prince Brann. Wait, he's always been Prince Brann. Always. But now, I simply know the truth. He's been lying to me. Every time I call him Orestes, I'm lying to myself.

The torches outside glitter in the night, their images smearing. Just minutes ago, I was so happy, dancing with a man whom I love, kissing the man who might love me in return. And now… it's as though it's all slipping away. As though reality has crashed back down. And I think I could weep for a week.

What has happened? The man I thought a duke is a prince. The woman I thought my friend is my country's enemy? Why did I come here tonight?

I stumble as my soft slipper catches on something rough. A rough sob escapes me before I can call it back.

"All right?" he asks, his hands tensing on my shoulders to hold me up.

"Yes," I whisper and take a deep breath to control my emotions. "Your Highness."

His grip spasms on me.

It takes me three steps before I realize he's released me and I continue on without him. Slowly, I stop and face him. He still wears his mask, but his eyes are grieved, his mouth twisted into a pained expression.

"Don't—don't call me that, Ella."

I lift my hands, palm up. "I—what should I call you?" I bite my lip. Hadwin? I want to ask. Because it seems impossible that it wasn't him all those years ago, and yet, now knowing he's actually Prince Brann, I no longer dare think it could be true. A prince would never come visit a young lady in the woods as Hadwin had done.

He closes his eyes and lifts a hand to his face. Finding his mask there seems to frustrate him, and he rips at it with one hand only to need the other to yank it from his face and throw it into the hedges. Face exposed, he steps up to me, earnestness in his eyes. "Ella, I—"

"You lied to me." My words come out small.

"Your Highness!" A deep voice finds us in the hedges, followed quickly by a pair of steps thumping our direction. "Reports of a woman fleeing the palace have reached us. Should we pursue?"

The prince's gaze lingers on mine.

"Sir?"

The prince turns from me. "Yes."

My heart leaps into my throat. Pursue? Winter? I fall back a step. Pursue Winter, who just saved me from sure death? My thoughts swirl. I don't know whom to trust. Everyone's been lying to me. Has she been lying to me about more than her identity, but about her sympathies as well? Could she be that deceitful?

The prince points toward the palace and says something to his guards, but it's all a swirl of words that don't make sense. I have to warn Winter. I have to help her. She saved me. She's innocent.

"Have the guests leave," the prince says. "Keep track of that girl —don't let her out of your sight."

"Yes, Your Highness."

"I must speak with the King and Queen. Make sure the gates to the city are closed. Let no one in or out of the gates until you receive further instructions."

My heart twists in my chest. He believes Winter? That someone is out to kill her? Not just someone, but a queen? The Queen of Canens? And that makes Winter a princess—the Princess of Canens.

I don't really know her at all, do I?

The prince rests a hand atop the hilt of his ornamental sword.

Or him. I don't think I know him at all.

With a stone-heavy heart, I give him one last, lingering stare, and walk away, leaving him discussing things with his soldiers.

He won't want me here, not when he really thinks about Winter being my friend.

Distantly, my body numb, I wind through the hedges and out the other side. My mind whirls as I make my way through the palace ballroom, following the other guests to the exit, where I consider asking for a carriage home.

But as I walk down the stairs, Gavin appears with Flora. Silent, he hands me the reins and helps me mount. I can't even look at him.

I avoid traveling by The King's Inn. Dalia will ask too many questions, and I'm simply not ready to speak. When I finally reach home, I don't dare go to the house. Besides, I have clothes in the stables that I'll change into before I risk seeing my family tonight.

When I tuck Flora into her stall, I finally meet her liquid eyes. Her concerned snuffling at my face informs me that I've been crying. And once I realize it, there is no more controlling it. I bury my face into her neck and sob for all the almosts of tonight.

QUESTIONS

I don't dare return to the inn that night. Nor do I dare seek out Ella again, though I hope and pray she's recovered from her near-death experience. She was fine when I left her, but memories of my losses haunt me so much I want to turn Ice around and check on her again. But I can't.

Riding through town in the midnight moonlight on a silvery stallion as I do, with my dress up to my thighs and one shoe missing, all left in Nubilus watch me. Though there are few eyes to watch. Most are at the palace, others have gone to sleep, not expecting a single rider to be leaving the ball alone. A couple people dressed in their masque attire wander toward their homes shoot me shocked glances, a few stumble along on foot or weave on horseback and holler inappropriately at me, while another rides in their fancy carriages driven by well-dressed drivers and ignore me. I nudge Ice faster until we're trotting through town.

I find the gates of Nubilus open, not shut at curfew as they typically are, but with triple the usual guards. Slowing Ice to an extended walk, I exit the city and aim him toward the forest where Brunnea's cottage hides. She will protect me. She'll tell me what I must do.

Ice picks up his pace until we're almost cantering into the woods, but as I pass into the trees, I hear shouts and the gates clang shut behind me. I shudder at the sound but don't dare turn and acknowledge them. If they were shut early, it was because of me.

Ice takes me through the forest, confident of his path. I give him his head, too exhausted to think of much except what happened at the masque. I saved Ella. I finally saved someone I care about—without magic. It wasn't a repeat of Des or Certa. It wasn't someone else saving me. Brunnea helped me, but I saved Ella with my own strength. I bite my lip. Though I could have left her in more danger than she was in before, revealing myself as I did.

That spell was meant for you. That little voice pipes up again, the one I've begun thinking of as the magical part of me.

How dare you take credit for saving someone from harm when it's you who put her in harm's way, it continues.

My heart crumples against my ribs. You're right. I can't take credit for this at all, can I? I shouldn't even stay here.

I pull on Ice's reins. Confused with the cottage almost in sight, he tosses his head up. He snorts, clearly wanting to reach the cottage and his bucket of grain and bin of alfalfa. Twisting in the saddle, I look back at the path we've taken. I could leave. Now. Run away again. Leave them behind. It would protect them, wouldn't it? Protect Ella, protect Dalia, protect…Brann.

It wouldn't protect your people. It will only help kill them.

I suck in a breath.

"I could find another way. Find someone else to help."

The voice snorts.

Surely someone else—anyone else—would fight Canens? The King of Ostium? Tepor? Rus?

Coward.

I ignore the voice. If I leave, where do I go? And should I go now, before Prince Brann has me arrested? Or do I try again? Try to talk King Greggory and Queen Ada? There are two more masques, two more chances to get near them. The cursed dress ruined tonight's plan, but perhaps the next two…

In my distraction, Ice has resumed walking, and now Brunnea's cottage looms ahead.

"Princess?" a male voice asks out of the shadows.

There is so much question in his voice that I touch my face and jolt to find the mask still covering my cheek.

I tug the string and it falls to the ground.

"You return safely?" the Magister asks.

Do I imagine the surprise in his words? His wolfish face is hidden in the dark, so I can almost pretend that he is not the same man who bought me in Merise and enslaved me. The one who worked for my stepmother for years and killed people upon her whim. My thoughts bring the sting of magic to my palms.

"Yes," I murmur. Without another word, I slide from Ice's back, landing on my slippered foot on the patchy grass.

"And is your friend safe?" he urges, compassion evident in his voice.

For a moment, I grip the saddle with both hands, tempted to lay my head against it and weep. I'm pretty certain I've lost her forever as a friend.

"Yes," I say. "She's alive."

"Thank the gods," he murmurs.

I don't answer but leave him with Ice. Without knocking, I push my way inside the cottage.

Brunnea looks up from the large table in the kitchen when I enter. "You're back." Her gaze is calm, unworried, as if she expected my return earlier, but sympathy creases around her eyes. "Come, have a seat. I'll make you something to drink."

Too tired to argue, I limp across the room and collapse in the chair across from hers and kick off the other slipper.

For a few minutes, the cottage is silent as Brunnea bustles around heating water and setting tea to steep as I stare into the small but cheery fire across the room, my mind strangely empty. A few lanterns burn in the cottage but none seem to be burning oil. I suspect magic, but I'm too tired to test the theory.

"Drink up," Brunnea says, putting a mug of steaming tea in front of me. "It will help, I promise."

I ignore it.

"I didn't poison it; you don't have to worry."

Pulling the mug toward me, I inhale the steam.

"I take it things were not a total victory?"

"No." I bend my head over the mug, letting the steam caress my face.

"Tell me."

"I saved her. But the prince was there."

"Oh."

"And I accidentally told him who I am."

"Oh."

I prop my head on my hand, weariness overtaking me. "What do I do, Brunnea?"

"Well, dear, I'm afraid there isn't a certain answer to that."

"But don't you know? Can't you divine the future or something?"

"Even if I could, there are many possible futures ahead of us, princess. And it's only our decisions that determine which one takes hold."

"Then tell me what to do. What must I do to save my people? Tell me the future I must seek and the actions to get there." My eyes brim with tears as I beg her, clasping my mug in front of me to keep my hands from trembling. "Please."

Brunnea shakes her head sadly. "Winterberry, I cannot. It is against the Fae law. We do not interfere with prophecies or dare to tell the future. All I can do is help you on your path."

I purse my lips.

Brunnea motions to my drink. "Drink up, dear. I promise it will make you feel better."

Shoulders slumping, I take a drink. The tea is sweet and sharp at once, while also delivering a quick jolt of energy and calmness through me. It's the strangest thing I've ever tasted.

My thoughts churn. Here I am, looking for an ally, when I might already know one. I have saved a prince and a princess' lives, haven't I? They might not have a country, but...what about Heia? Rus and Elaina, if they make it back to Heia, could be great allies. They have an army, and they know me. They know who I am. They have the loyalty of their people, right?

I stare into the tea, watching the leaves swirl around the top just like my thoughts swirl in my head.

"Brunnea."

"Yes, dear?"

"What do you know about the Prince of Heia?"

The faery smiles mischievously. "I was hoping you'd ask about Prince Ruslan. What would you like to know, princess?"

For the first time all night, a tremor of hope rises in me.

PART III

PASSED

$\mathcal{W}$inter is gone. I don't know where, nor does Dalia. She must fear for her life after revealing herself to Prince Brann as she did, but I wish she would have at least said goodbye. Neither Dalia nor I have seen her since the masque.

But I don't have any time to weep and mourn, even if I wanted. With the auction in less than a week, there is far too much to do. Every minute I spent with Brann in the past week haunts me this week.

Two days after the masque, The Crown Inspector arrives, his pencil flashing and quick to find errors. I've corrected them all; I corrected them immediately after he found them, spending my evening and nights doing so. The ledgers hold the correct numbers—checked and rechecked until my eyes cross—the problems in the stable have been fixed, and I'm even wearing a simple work gown when the Crown Inspector arrives. Though I wear breeches underneath so that I can ride more easily, the inspector doesn't need to know that.

At least when the man arrives for his follow-up inspection, Gus and half the pack greet him with ferocious barks and threatening growls, so I know we've passed that requirement. The other dogs roam the property today, as required.

The Crown Inspector greets me with nose raised, and his coolness continues as he completes his second inspection of my stables in an unusually short time. He dismounts, thankfully not into a pile of manure this time, and hands me the reins to his gelding. He doesn't ask for oats this time either. Perhaps he's in a more generous mood this time. Or perhaps he's simply in a hurry.

With another glance his way, which tells me nothing except that he remains aloof, I stable the gelding and return to the Gelu Rigens Equine Crown Inspector's side. He stands in the court-yard, tapping his toe and peering over his notepad and pencil at the well in the center, as if trying to come up with a statute of the law that it's breaking.

"Are you ready, sir?" I ask him.

"What's that? Oh, yes, of course." He jerks his head to me with narrowed eyes as if I've pulled him out of a deep reverie.

For the first time with this Crown Inspector, I recognize a distraction from his job here. If I look at him like I look at my horses, try to determine what might be preventing them from focusing on their task, whether a pebble in their shoe, or a too agressive bit, or something else entirely, perhaps I can convince him to pass my stables.

He removes a sheet of paper with a carefully penned list of my stable's flaws on it. "Dirty courtyard appears to have been addressed." The sharpness of his tone belies his irritation at my success and determination to find other flaws in its place.

"Yes, of course, sir. That was a misfortune the last time you were here," I say with an overabundance of pleasantness.

He snorts at his list as he crosses it off. "Rest assured I will be completing a full check again this time, not just address your prior indiscretions."

I inwardly grimace but keep my tone sweet. "Of course, sir. I wouldn't expect you to do otherwise."

Nose hovering over the list, his eyes dart across and down the page until they find the bottom, then scrutinize the courtyard again. Wordlessly, he marks one more thing off the list. He narrows his eyes at a shadow near the barn. I follow his gaze to Gus.

"What is that?" He points his pencil at it.

"Oh, that's Gus."

"He's looking a bit old, isn't he? There's an age limit on the guard dogs you keep, you know." The inspector's pencil waggles on his ear as he speaks.

"I— Yes, I know."

"How old is he?"

"Oh, he's…" I hesitate, not wishing to lie, but knowing that Gus nears the end of his official guard dog duty. "Well, I don't know exactly. He's partially retired anyway, but I cannot keep him away from his duties for long." I smile fondly at the large dog.

"Do you have his papers?" The narrow-faced man wets the tip of his pencil with a long tongue.

"Yes, of course." I clamp down on the inside of my lower lip. "In my office."

He crooks an eyebrow and scribbles something on his paper.

I bite harder on my lip. It's been years since I looked at Gus' papers. But I remember he was born at least a year before Father died, and that was seven years ago. Legally, all guard dogs must be retired before reaching age ten, though it is traditional to let the dogs live out their lives serving their purpose and then retire them to the home when they can no longer act as guards.

The inspector hasn't stopped scribbling. This isn't going any better than the last time. We haven't even made it inside the stable, and already I have a *new* fault.

"Inside then?" he questions, his tone a bit more cheerful.

Resigned, I nod, forcing the smile to remain on my lips. "You'll be pleased to know that I checked into the price of oats, as you had suggested. Mr. Arator said that he would guarantee me a price of seven coppers a kilogram for the next six months."

The inspector blinks at me through the darker interior of the barn. "He guaranteed you that?"

"Yes, well, he's a long-standing friend of my father." I readjust a lead rope hanging from a hook in the aisle.

"That's…a wonderful deal."

I shrug. "I drive a hard bargain."

His eyes narrow. "Indeed."

"If you'd like to save time, I can show you how I've corrected each of the items you found—"

"I'd prefer to complete a full inspection again," he says coolly.

A sigh threatens to escape my throat, but I swallow and nod. "Of course. But I do have a great deal of tasks to complete today. So if I can show you those corrections and perhaps leave you to it then?"

His eyes round. "You're aware of the rules, Miss Saevus. This will take as long as it will take."

I press my lips together, tempted to remind him of my limited staff—due to the Crown's absurd extra rules for me to follow— and remind him how much work I have to do. Instead, I dip my head and pick up my pace.

Finally making it up to Father's office in the house, I open the door to find Haydée curled into a corner chair inside the room.

She scowls and me and opens her mouth when the Crown Inspector nearly runs into me from behind.

"Oh, I wasn't expecting anyone here." She tosses her feet to the ground and brushes wrinkles out of her skirt.

Every time I see her, I expect her to tell me she saw me at the masque, fleeing from a suspicious scene. Sometimes when she looks at me in the halls, I can see a glimmer of suspicion beneath her usual hatred. Despite the looks, she never says anything.

Either she didn't recognize me or else she thinks I didn't see her and will only reveal it when it benefits her most. My stomach dips and churns. Between her and the inspector, I'm going to be off my feed soon.

"I had no idea Ella was entertaining a guest!" Haydée says, batting her long lashes at the inspector. "Ella, dear, you should have said something."

"The Crown Inspector is here on business, Haydée, not amusement," I mutter, even though Haydée is too smart to not realize this.

"Well, there's always time for a little amusement, isn't there?" She sets her book down on the side table and flounces up out of her chair toward us. "Hello, sir."

Ignoring her, I cross the room to my desk and pull out the ledger. I don't have time for her and her silly ideas, nor do I have more time to waste with the Crown Inspector. "Here are the ledgers, updated and corrected," I tell him, opening to this and last month's figures.

"What's that?" He turns from Haydée's flopping eyelashes and coy smiles to me. "Oh." He clears his throat. "Of course. Excuse me, miss."

Haydée narrows her eyes at his back as he walks toward me.

Please leave him alone, Haydée. I don't want to be in here for the next two hours...

Instead of answering my silent plea, she makes a show of selecting and removing a book from the shelf and sitting down in a comfortable leather chair that's closer to Father's desk. She carefully tucks up her legs underneath her, making sure to give the inspector a nice flash of her ankles but also making it appear accidental while making a show of properly covering herself.

Rolling my eyes, I run a hand through my hair and sigh as softly as I can while the Crown Inspector takes my usual seat behind the desk and recalculates my columns. If I try to speak with him right now, I don't think I'll be able to keep from mentioning Haydée's ridiculousness. Instead, I pick up the books she's abandoned on the tables and shelve them.

"Aren't you humbling yourself a little bit?" Haydée remarks without looking up from her book.

"What?" I ask.

"Nothing. I'd just expect you to have a bit of a big head now." Haydée turns the gold-gilt page in her hands.

"I don't know what you're talking about."

Haydée adopts an innocent expression and lifts her gaze to me. "Don't you?" Keeping hold of my gaze, she sets down her book in such a deliberate way that my gaze falls to it. One of our many collections of faery tales that our nanny used to read to us as children, and spread across two pages is a beautifully painted picture of a girl dressed in a gown dancing with a prince. It's eerie how much that painted picture resembles the masque.

I stiffen. She can't be going to tell about my attending the masque here, in front of the Crown Inspector, of all people?

"Sometimes life is just like a faery tale, isn't it?" She flips a page in the book. "Unhappy endings and all." Her eyebrows flicker as a smile plays on her lips. Then she sweeps herself to her feet and crosses the room to the inspector.

Trembling, I stand in the spot for several seconds, staring down at the next picture, where a girl runs down a set of steps, leaving one of her slippers behind. With an annoyed huff, I snap the book shut and shove it onto the shelf above the chair, not caring if that's the right spot or not.

"Sir, did you happen to hear about any more break-ins this auction season?" I ask, trying to keep Haydée from attacking the inspector with her feminine wiles.

"Break-ins?" the inspector asks. "Of course there have been. My colleagues have been dealing with insurance claims all week."

"Oh?" I finger my skirts.

"That's why I almost fined you for not having armed, mounted guards. It's rather foolish, asking for trouble."

I flash him a subdued smile. "Gus and his pack are more than enough for the average intruder."

He raises his brows. "Yes, well, he can't shoot arrows at an intruder, can he?"

Agreeing, I dip my chin and fall silent. If only there were a way for me to hire someone to act as guard. Perhaps I ought to start sleeping in the stable. All the horses are locked in their stalls every night, so it's difficult enough to get to them at night, and the dogs are there, and I sleep with my window open to hear them, even with the autumn chill now invading, but perhaps that's not enough. A true breeder and owner would sleep in the stables with his horses.

"So how long have you been Crown Inspector?" Haydée asks in her most seductive voice, jarring me from my thoughts.

Haydée hovers near the inspector's arm, batting her lashes and trailing a hand toward the ledger suggestively.

Inwardly, I shake my head. She's ridiculous. I know she's only doing this to bother me, for she wants nothing more than the prince's ear. The prince whom I danced with. At that, I feel a surge of pride that I wince at.

Without sparing her a glance, the inspector answers, "Mm, about five years."

"Must be quite the illustrious job, getting to visit all the stables."

I roll my eyes at the bookshelf. "Haydée, could you help me?"

She ignores me.

"Haydée?"

"I have something to show you. Something I found for your next mask."

"What are you talking about? Leah is making my mask."

"Yes, but I saw it, and I think I have an idea for it." I'm making this up as I go, and all I saw of her mask was the base of the gold and blue tiger face. But I am familiar with Leah's famous mask work, since masques are popular events in Ardor. Her name also makes me shudder; she's the most expensive mask-maker in all of Nubilus.

Haydée rolls her eyes and walks over to me as I pull out a basket of ribbons and assorted scraps I've collected over the years.

"So, I found these," I begin, digging out a long, pale blue ribbon. "And I was thinking—"

"Ella, shut up. You have no idea what you're talking about."

Shocked into silence at her tone, I stare at her, the ribbon dangling from my fingers.

"You can't stop me from telling people about your lies. Not now, not ever." She leans closer, and though she's several inches shorter than me, she looms over me. "And you can't stop me from doing whatever I please." With that said, she turns, pauses, snatches the ribbon from my hand, and leans over the basket to steal another. She turns and seats herself back at Father's desk, immediately drawing the inspector back into conversation.

My face burning, I rearrange the ribbons and scraps in my basket, then sink down in the chair and take up a pair of stockings I need to mend while I wait for the Crown Inspector to finish.

Half an hour later, he slams the ledger book closed with a sound that startles both Haydée and me. I jump to my feet.

"I'm all finished," he announces, pushing the chair back with a scrape across the weathered wood floor.

"Excellent," I answer, my heart jumping at my throat. *Please tell me I've passed.* "Sir, I know you must be quite busy, and it's late. Is there anything else I can show you before you must leave? Or would you care for a light lunch before leaving?"

"Please, stay for lunch," Haydée agrees, shooting me an angry glare that I ignore.

"No, I couldn't." The Crown Inspector straightens, tugging down his jacket at my words. "I am quite busy." He pulls out a pocket watch, and pops it open. His eyes widen. "Indeed! I must get going. Excuse me, young lady," he says to Haydée, then crosses the room toward me standing near the exit. "You can pick up your formal paperwork tomorrow afternoon at the Gelu Rigens Rules Office." He pauses next to me and extends a sheet of paper to me. "Congratulations on passing your inspection."

My lips spread into a smile before I can stop them. "I—thank you, sir."

Lips pressed together, he gives a quick, decisive nod, then with another glance back at Haydée, leaves the office.

Haydée's soft footsteps sneak up behind me. "You're welcome."

"Excuse me?" I turn to her, my joy at the news of passing this re-inspection dampened by her presence. I choke back more aggressive words, not wishing to anger her further. Surely Haydée will tell our mother eventually, but hopefully not until after the auction. If she just waits until then, I'll be fine. As long as I can sell the horses…

"Without me and my flirting, he was going to fail you." She flips a strand of her hair off her shoulder as she flounces by me. "If you aren't grateful enough, perhaps next time I'll make him fail you."

Sadly, I'm not entirely sure whether she's right or not.

SEARCHING

The Magister is intent upon proving his loyalty to me, even giving me Crystalli, his white horse that I call Ice. He promised to stay with Brunnea, and he told me everything he knows of Blanche's plans. And though it isn't much, it's more than I knew before.

Perhaps there's another answer, a simpler one even. I could send him to her with my heart. At least, something similar to my heart. I allow myself a grim smirk. A pig's heart should do quite well. And if it doesn't, well, it's only the Magister's life that will be forfeit.

My grin slips as my stomach squirms. If he's loyal to me, I don't want him to die. Because if what he's said is true, he's one of my most powerful allies in this fight against my stepmother. He changes everything.

If it's true.

I squint up at the sun from under my broad-brimmed hat, wincing when I realize the sun isn't even at full height yet. For being autumn, supposedly the coolest season next to winter, it's still hot throughout the day, and today is especially warm.

Blanche would simply cast a spell to keep herself cool, just like she enchants the palace and her sleighs and her growing houses with spells to keep her and her plants warm. My stomach turns. Isn't what Brunnea has trained me to do make me like her already? How is bringing flowers back to life and into bloom any less trivial or…selfish?

Feeling my unease, Ice hesitates and flicks his ears back at me in question. I put a hand to his shoulder. "It's all right. It'll be all right. Somehow."

Groaning, I shift in the saddle. Even now, the right decision is elusive. Why couldn't Brunnea just tell me what to do? Why must she be so mysterious? What laws is she talking about?

The village nearest to Nubilus takes less than a day's journey. Its streets are dusty and dry when I enter that afternoon. It's a far cry from the cobbled streets of Nubilus and the charm of the shopfronts. There, the merchants have brightly colored awnings and beautiful fabrics and jewels, exactly what I always imagined a town to be. But here are ramshackle homes half falling down with dusty, gaping windows, a hole-ridden road, and rusty water troughs.

I peer into the first trough as we pass and turn up my nose. The water is stagnant and hardly acceptable for animals, let alone me. Perhaps there's a well or creek nearby though.

I ride slowly through the village, peering at the homes and looking for life and a better water source. But the homes are skeletons devoid of flesh, and the streets bones with broken, dusty joints. It's halfway down the single road before I catch any movement out of the corner of my eye.

I hesitate, letting my gaze linger on the window. The top of a head pops up. Human.

My hands tingle. Light shimmers around my fingernails, and I concentrate on pushing away the magic, drawing it back inside. I can't reveal myself, especially to Blanche. Not yet anyway. I pull Ice to a halt and dig into my saddlebag, I watch them from the corner of my eye.

Feigning that I can't find something, I dismount and pretend to dig deeper into the bag. Instead, I attune my hearing to the slightest sound around me. Ice's breathing is deep and heavy but steady and unconcerned. Everything in the village is amplified. And everything without, too, I realize.

Very slowly, picking through every rustle of leaves and whisper of nearby winds, I locate a human's rapid breathing a short distance away from me.

I jolt. I'm using magic. Despite myself, I marvel at this power that comes so naturally. Is this what the Fae can do? And more?

I shake my head. Perhaps, if I ever return to Nubilus, I can ask Brunnea more about her powers. Right now, I must deal with the heartbeats I hear besides my own. One belongs to Ice, the other is human, and it sounds very similar to mine: fast and uneven.

We're both nervous.

Footsteps near, crunching on the dry road and rock. I inhale sharply. They snuck up on me.

I close my hand around the knife hilt in my bag. Ice snorts and I turn, knife at the ready, magic stirring in my chest and bleeding into my hands.

A gasp escapes my mouth and the mouth of my would-be attacker.

The bearded man gapes at me as my tongue refuses to form words.

Finally, I burst out, "Cito? What are you doing here?"

Of all the people to be here now.

The man's knife drops to the ground with a thump. "Winter." He motions to the horse behind me. "I thought... How do you have the Magister's horse?"

Though he grows a beard like a Canensian, he wears Ardorian clothes, a light linen tunic and leggings in dark blue, but as my magic continues to pulse through my veins, I sense something else about him, something I never noticed before.

"Where are Rus and Elaina? Did they leave you? Are they—" I can't finish my thought.

"No. Well, yes, but— Well, they're fine. I think." He shrugs and clears his throat. "They returned to Canens."

"What? Why?" Despair prickles over my neck. I need them!

"We left Ino—a maid of Elaina's—back in Merise. Elaina insisted upon returning for her after finding out. We stumbled upon this village when we entered Ardor, as we were going to Nubilus, and then I fell ill. Elaina kept insisting that they turn back, but His Highness wanted to contact the royals in Nubilus first. Instead, I insisted they leave me to recover alone."

"The royals? His aunt and uncle?"

"Yes." Cito picks up his knife and sheathes it at his side.

Tentatively, I reach inside myself for my magic, following the glow that is somewhere near my center. I grasp it and imagine it spreading out like vines, reaching around me and searching for the magic tendrils she mentioned. From Cito comes faint traces of its touch, as if a perfume. But it is also different...somehow.

He walks up a set of nearby porch steps and plops down upon the dry, wooden bench.

"Cito, how did you escape the frozen lake?" I call from the street.

His brow furrows. "What do you mean? Don't you remember?"

I hesitate.

"Oh. You wish to check my identity?" Cito smiles. "You saved us all. Rus fell through the ice after the earthquake...the Magister was on our heels, I could see him fifty paces away, it was hopeless. Then the quake..." He spreads his hands palm up as he leans forward to rest his elbows on his knees. "You were so brave and selfless. You dove in the water after him. You both almost died. You almost died for him."

My cheeks heat.

"Yes. And when we came out, you..." He motions to my hands,

his gaze lingering there. "You healed him. Or warmed him at the least, which amounts to the same thing in his case."

My breath releases from my chest. No one but Cito and Rus saw me do that. We were on the green banks of Ardor by then. "It's really you."

He smiles gently. "Yes."

"I thought—" I shake my head. "Never mind. What are you doing here? Why do I feel magic upon you?"

He straightens. "What?"

I walk to him and grasp his hands in mine. The touch of his magic sends needles through my entire body.

"You have tendrils of magic upon you, Cito. Has someone been here?"

"No one." He frowns again, shaking his head as if trying to think back. "I've been alone."

"You told me…after I healed Rus…you know of magic; you could recognize it. Does that mean…"

He waits patiently for me to complete my thought, a strange expression on his face.

"…you have magic of your own?"

A twitch of Cito's lips betrays his emotion. "You have found a mentor, haven't you?"

I hesitate. "I've learned a bit."

"Good. You need to learn as much as you can. You have…" He coughs and leans back against the house. "You have great power in you. I believe the prophecies now."

I shrug.

"In fact, your level of magic is impressive." He aims a wry lift of his brow at me. "If we were in Heia, I'm afraid I would have to ask you to leave the country for fear of your life."

"Would you?"

He chuckles. "So…it seems much has happened in a short time for you. What are you doing here?"

My lips twitch. "I was actually looking for you."

3: ELLA

BETRAYAL

Still annoyed by Haydée's interference with the Crown
Inspector, I lock the study behind me this time and
hurry back down to the stables, where I'm relieved to find Dalia's
gaggle of children hard at work, cheerfully mucking stalls and
filling up water buckets.

"Gavin?" I call down the aisle.

He pops his head out of Letifer's stall.

"Do you need me here? I have to go into town and talk with
Sir Birch."

He shakes his head. "No, miss."

I touch him on the shoulder in appreciation. "Thank you. I'll
be back as soon as I can."

"Take your time." He nods his head behind me down at the
cheerful children. "I've plenty of help."

I grin. "They are getting pretty good, aren't they?"

"Would you like me to tack up Flora for you?"

"No, I've got it, Gavin. Thank you." I give him another appre-
ciative smile before heading out to the pasture to find Flora.

When I make it into town, shocking rumors flit amongst the
townspeople.

"Did you hear about Anabell Trippet? She danced with the prince, then got thrown out for trying to kiss him," one girl says to me.

"And did you hear what that other girl did? She threatened the prince and then got arrested!" another young woman says.

"Did you hear of the girl that died at the masque?" a third girl says.

Each rumor is crazier than the last. Rumors of Winter and me, but no one names us or looks at me any differently than before the masque. No one suspects me, except for Haydée. No one even asks if I was there, but each person is eager to tell me what I missed.

Even Sir Birch bypasses the usual reprimand about me choosing to enter the autumn auction when I enter his office. Instead he says, "I saw Lady Eleanora and her daughters at the masque, Miss Saevus. My son and I were there. With Sallust." He raises one eyebrow at me. "He said he spoke with you."

"I wasn't at the masque. He must have spoken to someone else," I tell Sir Birch with a smile to cover my lie. Instead of waiting for him to correct me, I hold out my temporary inspection paper. "The Crown Inspector passed the stable. So all my horses are confirmed? You'll sign this?"

He frowns at the paper then sighs and sits back in his leather chair, surveying me over his steepled fingertips. "My son said you turned his marriage proposal down."

Lifting my chin, I try to think of a way to avoid repeating to Sir Birch what I told his son. "Sir, with all respect due to your position, what I told Sallust is between him and me."

He removes his glasses. "Your rejection of my son doesn't concern me? Is that what you're telling me?"

I try to smile, but my lips won't move into position. "Sir Birch, if you'd like to know what I told your son, ask him. I only came here today to have you sign off on my auction entry. I have the Crown Inspector's paperwork, as he just left Aeneas this morning—I'll stop by the office on my way out of town today and have them send over the full inspection report when it's completed—but I wanted to confirm with you my entry first."

Sir Birch doesn't move either to speak or sign, but remains staring at me over his fingertips.

"What is it?" I ask.

He drops his hands and leans over his haphazardly papered desk. "I'm afraid I've got some bad news for you, Miss Saevus."

"What is it?" My dry tongue sticks to the roof of my mouth.

He taps an index finger on his ledger, as if trying to find the right words, but he won't look me in the eye.

"Wha— Just tell me, please." My stomach clenches into a knot as hard as a horse's hoof. Did Prince Brann say I couldn't enter? Did he name me a traitor and decide I cannot be master of my own life? After all the conversations we had, it seems impossible to believe, but if he thinks me in league with the Princess of Canens, perhaps his views toward me have changed.

"Your mother found out about your entry into the autumn auction," Sir Birch says, reaching for a fancy feathered quill.

I inhale slowly. That's not quite as bad as Prince Brann removing me, but... "What did she tell you?"

He replaces his glasses on his nose. "She withdrew some of your entry fee."

My jaw goes slack as the breath in my lungs escapes with a rush. My knees fold. I'm lucky there's a chair behind me to catch my fall, for I thud into it ungracefully. "Yo-you let her take the fee?"

"Not all of it." He grimaces over his ledger at me. "I told her I could only give her back fifty percent."

"Fifty percent!"

"She's not a fool, Miss Saevus. She knows she cannot afford to not sell your horses. But she borrowed against me. And I need that money back by tomorrow. I thought—I hoped—she would tell you, so that I wouldn't have to. I thought it was why you were here now."

"No. No, she did not tell me, Sir Birch. Why would she?" My tone deepens in anger. "She doesn't have that money. I don't have that money. I gave you *all* I had—and I gave it to you so *she* couldn't get it!" Tears prick my eyes. "I thought it was safe with you—where it was supposed to be, set aside for the purpose it was saved. Instead, you betrayed me?"

He straightens in indignation. "I did not betray. Legally, she has as much right to that money as you."

"Does she?" I challenge, glaring at him. "I wager she doesn't, and you know it! She was my father's wife, *not* the hereditary owner of Aeneas Stables. That stable lies in trust with me until I produce a male heir or the Crown seizes it from me. It is neither your decision nor my mother's!"

His lips thin so they almost disappear behind his short-cropped moustache, though his eyes are wider than usual at my outburst. He clears his throat. "I do apologize, Miss Saevus."

"I don't *have* more money, Sir Birch." I fight the urge to stomp a foot. "Now you've made it so that I must remove three of my six horses."

A chasm deepens between his eyebrows. "You don't have anything else to sell? Perhaps we could take something as collateral for a small fee."

"A small fee? So it will cost *me* more than it will cost everyone else? Am I not penalized enough, Sir B—"

"I apologize, again, but Lady Eleanora owns—"

"She owns nothing!" I snap, losing my patience. "Keep your apology. Nothing of that stable is hers. It is barely mine! She has no legal control over that land since I am my father's sole heir under the law, which means she also has no control over whatever money I handed you for the sake of this auction! Need I show you the legal statute *again*, as I did when I began running Aeneas Stables?" I stop, panting slightly and glaring at him with imperialism I must be channeling from witnessing Prince Brann speak to Winter as he had.

Sir Birch blinks at me in surprise, holding my gaze, and just when I'm about to close my eyes and turn away, he breaks.

"You're right, Miss Saevus."

I barely catch my jaw before it falls, but I cannot control my tongue enough to speak.

"You're right that you shouldn't have to pay more. Your money should have been safe with me. I...cowed to your mother at her insistence."

I bite the inside of my cheek to keep my agreement inside. Perhaps if I'm graceful about this, he will do something I don't expect.

"And Miss Saevus, if you accept Sallust's proposal, I will cover the entirety of the auction fee, from my own pocket."

For several seconds, I think I misheard him. But the smug turn of his lips betrays that there is nothing wrong with my hearing. Slowly, I straighten my spine and lift my chin, injecting all my authority into my tone. "Then I suppose my only choices are to withdraw three of my horses or come up with the auction fee."

HEART

The Queen's trail is easy enough to follow in the afternoon sun. Though autumn clouds play with the sun, floating before and behind it, casting occasional shadows on the ground. When I crest the hill on foot, the expansive green valley interspersed with trees is dappled with sunlight and shadows. To the left is a thick forest of trees, while the right side of the valley is sparse with trees and has a small river flowing into a clear lake. In the crook between the river and shore of the lake is a tepik the color of grass.

It's not surprising to see only one tepik; Silvanus has always been a flirt, unable to control his urges and using whomever he can find to satisfy them, including Reds—the younger the better.

I shudder. Perhaps it is simply the breaking of the curses upon me, but the idea of returning to Canens and the slave trade no longer appeals to me, but I cannot quite pinpoint why. It doesn't matter at the moment, and perhaps won't matter at all, if I cannot convince the Queen of my trustworthiness.

Skipping along the shelter of the copse of oaks and behind a line of dark green bushes, I slip down the hill toward the camp. Pausing halfway down to survey the scene again, I spot my brother kicking dirt over their small cooking fire as a half-packed bag waits for his attention beside him. Although he seems distracted, he has a tilt to his head and a strange stillness to his expression that I recognize as him paying more attention to the sounds around him than his task at hand.

I wait, quiet as a deer watching a wolf from the grasses and wondering whether the wolf will scent him.

Silvanus finishes packing the bag and shifts it onto his shoulders, and with a final glance at the fire and around the campsite, heads off in the opposite direction.

In silence, I turn back up the hill and survey the path I've taken, then do the same with all other nearby routes. An excellent hunter in his own right, Silvanus might have sensed my arrival and now plan to circle around behind me. But my brother should not endanger me, not when he believes me to be working on his side.

Silvanus' form disappears into the surrounding trees below, and I wait a few minutes before leaving the safety of my hiding space. Then I slip from behind the dark green bush with pink flowers, darting from one tree to another bush, using the shadows of the trees to hide me, knowing I'm nearly impossible to spot unless my brother looks up at exactly the right moment. I let my feet fall on the hard ground whenever possible, making it more difficult to track me. A couple of minutes later, I stand on the opposite side of the campsite, watching my previous hiding spot.

For many minutes, I stand as still as a gargoyle on the Merisian palace, only my eyes scanning my surroundings. I see nothing. Then…something.

The only hint of his presence is a shadow that wasn't there before. My lips twitch. My brother knows all my tricks—or thinks he does. He knows where I might go and what I might do, for we have hunted together since we were children. We have even hunted the vicious white bears alone together since I was thirteen and he eleven.

The shadow ripples, deviating from the tree's straight line then disappears back into the tree.

I watch a few seconds before moving from my own position, jumping silently through dark patches of the woods until, a few hundred feet away, I find a spot behind a thick, low bush to watch my second hiding spot.

This time, it takes Silvanus a full quarter of an hour to find it. When he reaches it, he inspects the ground and stands, throwing his hands into the air.

"Come out, brother, I know you're watching."

I wait.

"Brother!" Silvanus calls in exasperation. "I surrender!"

I continue to wait.

He leans his head back to the sky. "You are the superior hunter. Please emerge."

Smirking, I slip out from the bush, from its shadows and slip around to pop out from behind a wide tree. "You're growing sloppy, brother."

Jumping, Silvanus scowls my direction and runs a hand through his long, blond hair. "You really are an arrogant, insufferable boar."

Despite it all, I laugh a deep, rusty laugh. "Brother."

Silvanus clasps my hand and pulls me into his chest in an embrace. "What are you doing stalking us?"

I shrug. "Have any food?"

"'Course." Silvanus shrugs and motions toward their campsite. "Her Majesty has gone off somewhere, but you're more than welcome to await her return." He casts me a sidelong examination. "As long as you have what she waits for?"

"Of course."

Silvanus' eyes narrow, but he merely motions me toward the campsite.

Out of habit, I inspect our surroundings. Silvanus follows, his steps light but audible. As we emerge from the trees and into the campsite, his steps stutter.

A crunch sounds before pain blazes through the back of my head. A grunt escapes me, but I turn just in time to see the rope in his hands. He only hit me hard enough to stun, but Silvanus pushes me to the ground and wraps the rope around my wrists. I struggle, yanking one arm free, but he is strong and caught me by surprise. He already has the rope around one wrists and wrestles my other behind me, into the waiting loop.

"Silvanus, what are you doing?" I demand when he ties a tight knot and straightens over me with a pant.

"Did you think you could deceive me?" He sneers at me.

"I—" Hesitating, I curse inwardly. Of course Silvanus, my brother who knows me so well, could tell of my duplicity. "I promise you, I have deceived no one," I say to him with forced calmness.

"No one?" He crooks a blond eyebrow.

"No one but the princess," I say with a shrug made awkward by my tied wrists. "Who am I meant to deceive?"

Silvanus snorts and reaches down, yanking me up to my feet. "The Queen will be pleased to see I've caught you." He drags me up and marches me into the camp only to push me down beside the smoking fire pit. "You think I'm a fool, but I'm not. Nor is the Queen."

"I have her heart, brother," I say, shifting my shoulders to indicate my bag.

Silvanus snorts. "If you killed her you would be dead."

"Why?"

"That's what the prophecy says," he snaps. "You know it as well as I! You grew up hearing it."

"The prophecy?" I shake my head. "It doesn't matter what the prophecy says. The girl fell from a spell, and I live."

A shadow of doubt crosses my brother's face. "You'll stay here until the Queen returns. She'll decide what to do with you. In the meantime, I have a job of my own. And I don't intend to neglect it like you have."

I sigh. Whatever job the Queen has given him, he will take it seriously.

Silvanus shifts his pack onto his back and grabs a second length of rope. He crouches down and loops it quickly around my ankles, tying it securely enough that I won't be able to escape. "You'll be staying here until Her Majesty returns."

Flat on my back, I gaze up at my brother, irritation brimming over. "You know, I'm rather surprised that you still call her that. I would expect you'd be calling her 'Blanche' by now. Being as intimate as you are."

With blazing eyes, Silvanus lunges at me and grips me by the front of my tunic. "Don't speak disrespectfully of our queen." His nose brushes mine. "If you want to keep your life, you'd best prove your loyalty when she returns." He drops me, steps back, and glances at my pack, which hangs haphazardly from my back. "I hope, for your sake, that you have what you say in there. And rest assured, she'll know the truth."

I will my pulse to remain steady. Silvanus knows me better than the Queen, but the Queen has skills of her own to decipher truth.

Instead of answering, I shut my eyes and turn away, listening to my brother's disappearing footsteps. Then I settle in to wait.

FAMILY

Sir Birch's ultimatum destroys the remainder of my hope. Anger and grief pull at me so that I'm halfway home before I realize I forgot the rest of my tasks in town. I am in desperate need of bandages for the horses, extra salve ingredients, as well getting carrots from Dalia for the horses, if she can spare them.

Stopping Flora a few strides before the Nubilus gate, I sigh. A couple of people entering the city shoot me an annoyed look as they go around us. I offer a weak smile at the dusty travelers who look like potential bidders.

I don't want to do anything but run home and weep, but I've done that too much already. Or search Mother's room for any money she's hidden away—although that's a useless endeavor. Perhaps I can find some gaudy jewelry to sell though.

I rub a hand over my face. I have to go to Dalia's and at least tell her thank you again for sending her daily army of children and feeding them. I should have brought some apples to start repaying her. Slumping in the saddle, I turn Flora and return to town.

After I buy what I need, I find myself in Dalia's kitchen as she smugly compliments my riding trousers and uneasily reports that Winter is still missing in the next breath. Her forehead creases as she says it, and she slams her knife down on a hunk of beef.

"She shouldn't have run off. She should know that we'd take care of her. We wouldn't betray her." Dalia chops the meat into little bite-sized bits and throws it in a bowl nearby, separating out the gristle into a smaller bowl as she always does for Gus and the pack. She tosses the last handfuls into their respective bowls and rests her bloody hands on the counter, turning her head to me. "Is she really the Princess of Canens?"

Thankful for the distraction from my other problems and not wanting to discuss them with anyone yet, I nod and lean my hip against the large table in Dalia's kitchen. "That's what she told the prince. But I don't know."

Dalia shakes her head, grabbing another hunk of beef and dragging it in front of her before attacking it with her knife. "I can't believe that. A princess. What in the Great Fae's good earth is she doing *here*?"

"Exiled, running from the Queen of Canens," I remind her. I filled Dalia in as soon as I could after the masque. She'd tracked me down at the stable when I hadn't come here immediately, and she'd wiped away the rest of my tears. While I'm surprised by the depth of Dalia's concern for the girl she didn't want to save, I know Dalia is soft-hearted underneath her exterior.

"But that doesn't make any sense," Dalia complains. "Why would she go running to the prince?"

I try to remember what she said when she saved my life. "I still can't believe the Queen cursed my dress. She was here, Dalia. In the inn. She cursed it before you brought it to me."

Dalia worries at her lip with her teeth, and to my surprise, a pair of large tears roll down her cheeks. She sniffs. "I'm so sorry, Ella."

"What? For what?" I hurry to her side. "Why are you sorry?"

Dalia sniffs again and grabs a nearby cloth to wipe at her

nose. Looking up at me, she shrugs, her eyes brimming over with tears. "I saw her, Ella. The Queen."

It's like a fist has reached in and grabbed my guts and twisted. I reel backward from her. "You saw the Queen of Canens here, in your inn? And you didn't tell anyone?"

Eyes wide and sparkling with unshed tears, Dalia dips her chin hastily up and down. "No. Yes! I spoke with her. But she looked exactly like Winter in appearance, except…"

"Except what? What is it?"

Eyes closed, she takes a deep breath. "I knew there was something wrong. I knew it wasn't her."

"I don't understand. How did you know?" I sink onto a nearby stool.

"I sensed it. Somehow." Dalia lifts a shoulder, her expression clouding like there's something she's holding back.

"If she looked just like Winter—how is that even possible?"

"Winter's tattoo…it took me a while, but I realized it was missing."

"Missing? She otherwise looked like Winter?" I feel numb at the idea. "So, are we talking magic and changing your own appearance? Witches can do that?"

"I don't know if she's a witch," Dalia says matter-of-factly. "There are many different names for people with magic."

I gape at Dalia. "Does that really matter? She's trying to kill her stepdaughter, and she has magic that can apparently turn her into a person who looks like Winter!"

She studies me for a long moment. "Most witches can only do little spells or brew special potions. Queen Blanche must have a great deal of power—probably Fae power—if she can appear to be someone else and fool even me. So, it does matter, if she's coming after Winter."

"Even you? What experience do you have with magic?"

Suddenly, Dalia's task chopping up the meat becomes vital, and she turns from me to resume chopping.

"Dalia—"

"I should have recognized that that person wasn't Winter." Abruptly, she changes her grip on the knife and slams down into the countertop so that the tip of the blade sticks an inch deep into the wood.

"Dalia!" I gasp.

"I shouldn't have ignored it. I should have gone to Brunnea immediately." She turns to me, and her eyes ripple with tears again. "I almost got you killed. I'm so sorry, Ella. I failed…you."

I return to her side and squeeze her shoulders reassuringly. "Dalia, there is nothing to forgive. Unless you cursed the dress yourself, then there is nothing to forgive." Pulling her into a tight hug, I feel her relax a little under my touch. When I step back, I smile wryly and shrug a shoulder. "Besides, at least I would have died after kissing the prince."

It takes a second, but Dalia's eyes round. Of all the things I told her about that night, I hadn't confessed that.

"You're kidding me!" A wide grin splits open her mouth. "You kissed—"

"Shh!" I hiss, looking over my shoulder.

She lowers her voice. "You kissed Prince Brann?"

An uncharacteristic giggle escapes my lips. I can't keep the smile from my face. "Yes. Yes, I did. A couple of times, actually."

Dalia giggles with me. "That's amazing. That makes everything worth it."

I laugh at that. "Well, I suppose I would have died happy at least. The only downside is that the horses would have gone to the Crown. Or to Haydée."

"That's a thought." Her lips twist in disgust that she quickly shakes off. "But, still, I can't believe—what a night. You almost die, thanks to me, but thanks to Winter, you're alive. And then you danced with—and kissed!—a prince!" Dalia grins and sweeps me around into an impromptu dance in the middle of her kitchen. "What a night!"

I laugh with her, embracing the giddiness she's brought up in me. Even though there are so many things to worry about right now, and I shouldn't be thinking about the relationship with the prince that ended the same night I danced with him... My thought brings me down a little. "It was certainly a night to remember."

As Dalia returns to her chopping, I lose myself in those memories, remembering how the prince found me amongst the crowd, how we danced for a dozen dances, how he drew me outside, and how he kissed me...memories that can never be taken from me, but which won't ever be repeated. My joy dampens.

"Dalia..."

"What is it?" she turns to me, alerted by the change in my tone.

Quickly, I fill her in on Sir Birch's ultimatum.

"He what? How dare he!"

If I thought I had ever seen Dalia angry before, her expression now puts me in doubt. Her face heats red in an instant, and I almost imagine I can see steam like from a kettle emerging from her ears.

"I'll have a few things to say to him about this— How dare he abuse—"

"No, Dalia! Don't, please." I latch onto her forearm. "Please don't make a scene about it."

"Well what do you want me to do then? Chop off his hands?" She snatches her knife from the counter and holds it up suggestively. "Or some other appendage?"

"Dalia!" A shocked giggle escapes me.

She grins, but it's the darkest, most sinister grin I've ever seen on a person's face.

"No. Don't do anything that will get you sent to prison. Agreed?"

"Don't worry—they'd never catch me." At my answering look,

she lowers her knife with an exaggerated pout. "Fine. How about something just worth a fine or a flogging?"

"No!"

She sighs. "All right. What do you need then?"

"I need to figure out how to come up with two hundred and twenty-five silver coins by tomorrow."

She wrinkles her nose, then shrugs. "Done."

"What?"

"Don't worry about it. It's done."

"No, I have to worry. I can't be involved in anything illegal or suspect. How's it going to be done?"

She scoffs. "Would I do that?"

I cock an eyebrow at her, and she shrugs with a smirk.

"You know Noemì pays me, right?"

"Sure, but—"

"What do you think I spend my money on?" She chuckles lightly. "Besides a bit of fabric and ribbons, most of which Sara gives me from her scrapes or gives me a great deal on."

"Wait, so you have two hundred and twenty-five silvers?"

"More than that." She shrugs and dashes a few spices onto the chopped beef in the bowl. "Just pay me back when you can. If you can."

"Dalia, I can't believe you would do that for me. I'll pay you back out of the auction earnings."

She shrugs again and takes her final piece of meat to begin chopping. "It's not a big deal. So we'll be hard at work on your next dress, and we'll make sure that—"

"Dress?" I shake my head to readjust my thoughts from auction to masque. "I'm not going back, Dalia. I can't."

Dalia fumbles her knife and winces, dropping it with a mutter. She inspects the tip of her index finger before pointing it at me accusingly. "What do you mean you're not going? That's my deal. I pay, you go."

"I'm sure he thinks I'm a traitor, to be friends with an enemy to the Crown."

"You're not an enemy to the Crown."

"How does he know that? All he knows is that I'm a stubborn young woman who insists on running her dead father's business when there are dozens of men who want to do it for me or else marry me just so they could take it from me."

"So you're desirable. You're not a traitor for it!"

I sigh and motion to the bowl of gristle. "Are you almost finished? I really have to get back to the stable."

Her lips twist to one side as if she wants to say something more, but she refrains, instead resuming her task in silence and packaging up the gristle for me in the meat's bloody butcher paper.

"Thank you. Gus and his pack thank you for this. Oh, which reminds me, do you have any spare carrots?"

She nods, then impulsively pulls me into a hug. "You're not a traitor, Ella. You never will be."

I give her a squeeze, even though my heart remains heavy. "Thank you, Dalia." I step back and let her go. "And thank you for this meat."

"Pull some carrots from the garden on your way out."

"Thank you."

"If you really want to thank me..." She trails off, eyebrow raised.

"What?" I ask warily.

"Must I say it?"

"Go to the masques?"

She smirks.

"I can't, Dalia."

She huffs and grabs her knife again, turning her back on me. "Think about it. Maybe not the one auction night, but the final one."

"I'll think about it."

A snort is my only answer, but it makes me smile anyway.

Back at the stables, I pick up a pitchfork and set to work. After that, I saddle up to check the fence lines and work with one of the younger horses at the same time. Though the inspection is passed and I am looking forward to sleep tonight, there is much to do before I can rest.

When I head up to the house, the scent of Bona's supper makes my stomach growl. I find the kitchen at a standstill, however, with Bona keeping the roast chicken warm in the oven and spooning grease over it to keep it from drying out.

"Where are…" I motion toward the dining room.

"I dunno," Bona replies, wiping her hands on her apron.

Distant hoofbeats catch my ears.

"That them?" she demands.

I go to the front door, Bona behind me, and peer out the side window. "Yes."

"Finally," Bona mutters, disappearing back into the kitchen to ready supper.

Watching out the window as my sisters and mother come riding up in the carriage with Gavin at the reins, I grimace, wishing I could run away too. But there's no escaping them. Instead, I open the door wide and stand at the front door, not going down to greet them as I ordinarily might.

To my shock, the three women disembark from the carriage with heaps of wrapped packages. They insist that Gavin carry them up the stairs, and when he nearly stumbles because he cannot see, I step forward and take pity on him.

"What is all this?" I ask Gavin.

"Gowns," he answers in his gentle way.

"Gowns?" My hands begin to shake. They bought gowns? With what money? With my *auction* money?

Inside the house, I dump the boxes on a table and take the top off one. "What is this?" I demand of Haydée, who is standing nearest. "What have you bought?"

"Hey! You have no right to open that," she snaps, reaching for it.

I'm too quick for her, and I lay my hands on the dress while she snatches at the box. When she rips it away, I'm left with a dress that is far too rich for her. It's far more beautiful than I could ever make, and from such exquisite fabric that I know a great deal of coin must have paid for it, probably enough coin to send another of my horses to auction. Gripping a fistful of the fabric, I whirl to face my mother as she enters the room, tugging her cream-colored gloves from her hands.

"What have you done?" I shake the dress at her. "Is this what you did with my auction fee? You've spent my money on dresses? On the foolish hope that your spoiled younger daughters will catch the eye of the prince?"

Her eyes round as she stills, a sure sign that her fury is growing white hot inside her, but this time, mine matches hers.

"Excuse me?" she asks in that arrogant way of hers.

"How dare you? You know that money is the only thing that we have to keep this stable afloat. If we don't sell those horses next week, then we have nothing. You'll be out on the streets."

"No. You might be, but I will sell this house, and I will get husbands for Haydée and Carmen. And we shall enjoy the fruits of our labors."

"You don't even understand the laws that affect you." I laugh darkly, my anger and frustration spilling over. "And what labors? You have labored over nothing! You have stolen what doesn't belong to you and you have taken *everything* from me."

Stepping closer, she towers over me in her height and her heels. "Taken from you? Let's discuss what you have taken from me. You have taken my husband. Stolen his life from me because of your petty little horses. Now, I have been patient. I have tolerated your hobby, just as I tolerated his. But I am finished. Haydée and Carmen will marry noblemen, and you will rot in your little attic room like the pathetic, selfish girl you are."

A chill runs through me at her words. "It was an accident," I murmur. "As you know very well."

She scoffs. "Accident? You foolish girl. You think I don't see the truth? You got what you wanted—a dead father and his horses to train. You're a fool if you think I didn't know what you wanted. You killed him, my dear husband, for his gold and his horses. And because of you, he never loved me. He left me long before you took him—all because of your shared obsession. I hated him less than I hate you, you little ingrate."

My hands loosen on the dress. As it flutters toward the floor, Haydée lunges for it, saving it from any dust and dirt.

Her words cut me deeper than I imagined they could. All these years of thinking that she blamed me, and now hearing the hatred spewing from her mouth and those very words I feared... Tears spring to my eyes and spill over, and ducking my head, I rush from the room.

6: WINTER

CONFIDENCE

To my entire story, Cito listens without judgment. He runs his hands over his beard, leaning onto his knees. "How are you certain the Magister is trustworthy, Your Highness?"

"I'm not," I say. "But now he has less magic upon him than you do."

A grimace flickers over Cito's face.

"You've been hiding your magic? How does yours work?"

He sighs. "It's not well known that all advisors of Heia are gifted with hereditary magic used only to discern if another person has magic."

"So you can find magic in anyone?"

"Theoretically, yes. Mine is a sensing magic rather than a performing magic. And certain types, like yours and the queen's, are easier to pick up on. I sensed yours as soon as you appeared before me. But some magics are nearly untraceable. Or unrecognizable to someone with limited powers like me." He shrugs. "I'm not particularly powerful, Your Highness, even amongst my family."

I flinch at the title. "Well...I suppose your kind of magic won't help against the Queen, then, will it?"

He shakes his head and offers me a hand, pulling me up from the ground. "Not as it is, I'm afraid. Though there are other ways of using magic that I might be able to assist with. But let's worry about your strength first, Your Highness. How are you feeling?"

"Cito, please. I'm just Winter. I'm no one. Not now."

"You are much more than no one," he corrects gently, helping me up from the bench I've been sitting on for the last hour and leading me into the house.

The house inside is rather bare with a rickety table, a chair, and a thick layer of dust over everything. He leads me to the chair, swipes a hand over it to remove most of the dust, and sets me down.

"Where have you been staying?" I ask him.

He motions out the door. "Another house has a cot. I think I have fleas now, but... It's kept me cool and warm, whatever I require. Now that I am feeling better, thank you, I will bathe and rid myself of these vermin."

I take another drink of the water he offers me. "So...do you think Rus will help me?"

Cito considers his answer. "I think you have more of an ally in him than you realize."

I open my mouth to argue.

"But if you are concerned, perhaps if you offer your reasoning in the correct way, you might be able to gain a true ally in him."

"And what might be 'the correct way'?"

"Perhaps if you help him reclaim his own throne, he'd be convinced that you don't mean him or Heia harm."

Of course. If I help Rus return to his throne— "Wait, he's been usurped?"

Cito dips his head into a regretful nod. "Yes. We've learned, since entering Ardor, that His Majesty's uncle Karl has taken over the throne in our absence. He has declared himself king and announced that Prince Rus has abandoned his throne. The royal family of Ardor is outraged, from what I've managed to glean, but that's being kept very quiet."

"Karl did what? Took Rus' throne?" Though the information means little to me, it is still crippling if I expect Rus to be able to help me. "How did you find all of this out?"

Cito smiles wanly. "Ears in the right spot."

And maybe a touch of magic, I think as I consider him. "You're a clever one, aren't you, Cito?"

He half sits against the table. "Sometimes."

I rub at my neck, feeling the bump of my tattoo under my fingertips. "Will you help me convince Rus? Please. He's my only hope. Unless you know how to convince Prince Brann? I'm afraid I might have already ruined that opportunity."

"Well, if you convince Rus, there's a decent chance you can get Prince Brann on your side. Rus is the one you need to win."

"And I do that by…?" I throw up my hands. "He hates me, Cito. Hates me."

"No, he doesn't hate you, Winter. He owes you. And he is… afraid of you."

I scoff. "How could that be?"

"You are the heir to Canens, Your Highness. You have great power, even if you don't believe you do."

"Yes, but he's the heir to Heia. He's much more respected than I—"

"If he were, would his uncle manage to unseat him so easily?" Cito remarks calmly. "Would his uncle be able to spread lies so easily if he were?"

My mouth parts. I have no answer. "I don't understand, Cito. His people don't care for him?"

"You must understand. Rus is still young, and he did not expect to rule for many years. His father was a beloved king, but a, well, a slightly foolish one. Prince Brann has been very angry and bitter that his father passed and left him a country needing far more than his father ever told him. And as far as the country is concerned, Prince Rus is entitled and arrogant, and while his sister is sweet and perhaps a little flighty, it's undeniable that Elaina and Rus both disappeared, without prior communication to anyone in Heia. It has resulted in many who feel abandoned and angry with them both. They don't understand why either the prince or princess disappeared. It's created a rift, and without Prince Rus or Princess Elaina there to present their side or hold the throne—"

"Karl has taken it," I supply. "Of course. Abandonment issues. I certainly understand that."

Cito takes back my empty water mug. "Can I get you some more?"

"No. Yes. More information. What do we need to do in order to get Rus his throne and then rally his army against Blanche?"

Cito blinks. "That's right to the heart of the matter, isn't it, princess?"

"Well?"

"I don't know," he says slowly. "But it's something we must discuss with Rus. And you must soften yourself toward him. Do not be so agressive; he does not like it."

I bite my tongue. "All right then. Am I to be a demure little princess?"

He chuckles. "No. Just kind. Like…like Elaina, perhaps. She is far from demure, far from obedient, but her words and heart are kind. And he loves her for that."

"I am—" I break off, flinching at my own memories. I have not been kind to Rus, though I cannot say he has been kind to me. He has brought out my frustrations, found me at frustrating times. We have butted heads like sparring deer, exchanged words like shrieking foxes. I must curb my own tongue. And perhaps I could be a little more thankful that he saved me from the *oubliette*, despite his every intention of not wanting to. Gratitude is always appreciated, I remember that from my slavery days.

"You are a good person, Your Highness," Cito says softly.

"But not kind." I scoff. "Not to Rus at least." I rub at my neck. "And what about Brann? He is Rus' cousin, is he not?"

"Yes." Cito scratches at his beard. Ardor has perhaps been less pleasant for him even than Canens in terms of creature comforts. I never remember him having so much as an evening shadow on his chin before. "Rus' mother and Queen Ada of Ardor were sisters."

"And Rus' mother is dead?"

"Yes."

"So this is the last of Rus' family? Or are there more family members? Siblings, grandparents…?"

Cito considers me. "I believe there is one additional sibling of Queen Ada of Ardor."

"Oh? Brother, sister?"

"A brother. A count. But I do not believe they are particularly close with Queen Ada. Prince Rus does have a good friend named Tobiah, if that helps."

"Perhaps." A smile pulls at my lips as a plan forms. "Tell me, Cito, is Prince Brann a good man? One who fights against evil and loves good? Whose friends and family are good men and women?"

Cito lifts a brow at my words. "Well, yes, Your Highness, to the best of my knowledge, he is. Why do you ask?"

"I have a plan, but part of it requires your assistance."

"Oh?"

"Yes. Because, as you know, there's an auction in Nubilus coming up. My friend has had a bit of an interaction with the prince."

Cito's brow descends, then lifts. "She's fallen for him?"

"Yes. And I believe he's fallen for her. But there are difficulties." I quickly fill him in on the masque and the cursed dress. "Had it not been for my interference—for my stepmother's foiled attempt to kill me, I believe the prince would have confessed his love for Ella."

Cito nods, still listening attentively.

"Instead, he abandoned her without so much as an apology. From what I can gather through Brunnea, he's not contacted her, and he seems to be pretending that their relationship—their *kiss* —didn't happen. But I didn't take Prince Brann to be such a man."

"No. To my knowledge, he is not." Cito's forehead creases. "He is an honorable man. He wouldn't toy with a woman's affections."

"So then, it seems I was right." I slump. "He probably thinks Ella's attraction to him was my ploy all along."

"Ploy? Because you revealed yourself as the Princess of Canens?"

"Yes. Exactly. I think maybe he thought it was an attack against him, and I was using Ella. Or maybe that Ella was inno- cent, but I'm lying, or…I don't know. I don't know at all what he thinks, and I don't have time to wait for him to come to Ella, Ella can't contact him, and more than a romance rests on my reaching him."

"If you don't mind me asking then, Your Highness, why has Prince Brann not arrested you yet?"

I chew on my lip. "I don't know, Cito. That's what bothers me. That's part of the reason I found you here—because I was leaving Nubilus before he could decide to do so."

"But—" Cito breaks off and pauses. "I still don't understand."

"That's why I need you."

"Why?"

"He doesn't know you know me. But he would trust you, right? You're Heian, and you're his cousin's advisor."

"Well, yes. Exiled along with the prince, but, yes, in theory, you are correct on all that."

"You must go to the prince and tell him the truth. Tell him everything—tell him that I do not lie, and that I want to remove

Blanche from the throne, that I hate her more than they do, if possible.

"Tell him I want peace between our countries, but I cannot accomplish it if he refuses to listen. The palace has been barred, except for the masques, and I cannot enter. Brunnea, the Fae I've spoken with, cannot enter without express permission, which she's unlikely to get right now, given the current relationship between her and the royal family."

"Fae? What's happening with—?"

"I don't know. She won't tell me." I wave a dismissive hand despite the confusion creasing Cito's brow. "But it doesn't really matter. Not when I have you." I grin at him. At his look of discomfort, my grin widens.

"I'm afraid I haven't seen any of the Ardorian royal family for years, Your Highness. I don't know that they would recognize me. And surely, with the knowledge that Karl is on the throne in Heia…"

"They will know that you—and Rus and Elaina—need their help, Cito. That's exactly what we need."

"But—" He breaks off, closes his mouth, and sighs through his nose in defeat.

I pat his hand in reassurance. "And while you're in there, Cito, there's one more thing. Tell Brann that if he cares for Ella at all, then he can make everything up to her in one way."

Leaning forward, I outline my plan in full.

7: MAGISTER

THE LIE

When the Queen returns to the campsite, she stumbles out of the forest as though she's had too much wine. I ache all over from the awkward position Silvanus left me in, the embers of my fury stoked by each passing moment. How dare my brother suspect me of betrayal?

The Queen blinks twice when she comes upon the cold fire with a tied-up man prone next to it. "And what do we have here?" A smile dawns on her lips. "Who left you for me, my dear huntsman?"

I offer her a lopsided smile of my own. "Your Majesty. Rarely have I been more eager to see your return."

She laughs lightly and points at the fire. The coals turn over but no flames emerge. She scowls and glares at it, pointing at it again with wavering fingers. Flames grow out of the embers, then sputter and spit. She throws a log atop them, and the fire takes over.

She sinks down onto a large rock nearby and leans over to warm herself at the flames before saying, "I wasn't expecting you like this, I must admit. Silvanus loves to leave me little surprises."

I am not surprised by the declaration in the slightest. "Are you all right, Your Majesty?"

She stares into the dancing flames for so long that I almost think she didn't hear me. Then she begins to murmur as if to herself. "All right. Yes. I'd have to say I'm better than all right. With a plan developing, someone to assist me, and everything coming together, yes, I'm all right."

I wait a few moments before speaking. "Excellent. Then do you mind untying me? I brought you a gift, but my bother insisted that I wasn't trustworthy enough to wait for you on my own." I attempt a shrug that twists my body into a highly uncomfortable position on my elbow. "Or something like that."

"Oh?" The Queen turns to me with only mild interest and waves a hand.

The ropes around my wrists loosen just enough for me to pull my hands out of their bindings, and I set to work removing the ropes from my ankles. I take my time, dragging myself to my feet and brushing the dirt off my pants and shirt before slipping my pack off my aching shoulders. I must be getting old.

"I have been waiting to deliver this to you, Your Majesty." My heart gives an uneven thump despite itself. I expect her to notice any second.

She holds her hands over the fire, uninterested in me. "What is your gift?"

"It is what you've asked for." I remove a plain, wooden box from my pack.

She stares at me blankly. "What?"

I kneel before her and extend the box between us. When she does not move to take it, I set it at her feet.

"She—" The Queen takes the box into her trembling hands. She opens the clasp and peers inside, her face cast with the disbelief that could be my downfall. "She's dead?" She lifts her gaze from the heart and the vial of blood inside the box. Suspicion laces her next words.

I incline my head. "I live. She does not."

"How did you get her heart?" She reaches a finger for the bloody mass.

"I followed her to the masque." The Queen does not answer or look up, so I continue. "I disguised myself, so she did not see me. When it neared midnight, she left, and I followed her. I watched her die in an alley near The King's Inn."

The Queen lifts the finger she touched to the heart and puts it to her lips, running her tongue over the tip.

"And when she died, I took her heart."

The Queen's eyes pinch around the edges. "What did you do with her body?"

"I put it in the cesspool."

The Queen chuckles. "A fitting end." She snaps the box closed and looks up. "I am most impressed, Sir Marcus, with your ability to see a job through to the end. In fact, you might have earned yourself a promotion." She smirks. "Of course, you'll have to prove your loyalty to me."

"Prove it?" My stomach muscles cramping, I motion to the box with forced unconcern. "Does that not prove it?"

"This?" She lifts a brow as she raises the box slightly from her lap and set it back down with a shake of her head. "No."

I resist the urge to stretch out my limbs. Despite my discomfort with lying to my Queen, my muscles ache enough to provide distraction. Perhaps Silvanus' betrayal is beneficial after all.

"Did you see any indication of the King's Curse when she died?"

"I don't understand."

"Did you feel anything? Like magic?"

"Your Majesty, I have, of course, heard of the King's Curse." Risking a glance up at the Queen, I find her gaze intent upon me. Lines crease her otherwise youthful forehead as she scrutinizes me. I duck my head again. "Your Majesty, I felt nothing out of an ordinary slaughter."

"Hmm."

When I pause, there are several slow heartbeats of silence. "How annoying. I shall never know if the rumored curse was true or not."

I force my eyes to remain upon the dirt beneath me and speak not a word. There is still a great chance she will not think twice about taking my offering and killing me.

She rises, carefully setting the box to the side, and throws a fresh log on the fire. The older log snaps and spits in distaste at the intruder. "Thank you. You have no idea how useful this heart is."

"I live to serve you, Your Majesty," I answer, trying to keep my muscles as relaxed as possible.

"Yes, I am seeing that, more and more." Her voice is thoughtful, and though I long to move from my kneeling position, she has not released me, and I refuse to break the stance against her will.

"And so," she continues, "I think I have a new job for you, since you have proved yourself so capable in this one."

I don't yet risk a sigh of relief, but bend my head further in submission. "I am at your service, Your Majesty."

"Excellent." She clears her throat. "Take watch tonight. We will be executing a very important job in the next few days. We have much watching to do."

"Yes, Your Majesty." I rise and, trying not to let her see my curiosity, head toward the outskirts of the camp to the best lookout position.

8: ELLA

THE COTTAGE

It's been too long since I really rode. So midweek, after morning chores, I tack up Attonitus, a horse who needs a touch more work, and ride out to explore the forest. As the day peaks, I know I should turn around, but racing across the pastures with the freedom that only comes from being atop a horse is too enjoyable. It's only when I come across the witch doctor's cottage that I realize how far we've ridden.

"Oh no," I mutter, pulling Attonitus down to a walk and glancing around. When my sisters and I were young, my parents warned us to never go to into the witch's land or else she would curse us. I'm not entirely sure how much of it is a threat from adults to keep their children in town, or how much is fact. But I've never been tempted to break that rule, even now as an adult. There are some rules you don't break.

There appears to be no one there, but I stop the colt and turn him around. As he's completing the turn, a man steps out from the trees and a woman's voice speaks.

"Eleanora." A woman appears beside the man. "I haven't seen you in many years."

I blink at the woman. I've never feared the witch healer, not like my sisters did, but I've also only had two conversations with her in my entire life.

Once when I was five and Father called her to assist our mother when Carmen was arriving via a breech birth. The second, I was with Mother in her room. Mother had been gravely ill for a week, and the town healers suggested there was no hope for her. As I stood by the bedside, the witch examined Mother. When she was finished, she mixed a tonic and had Mother drink every drop. Mother had fallen into her first calm sleep since being so ill she could hardly breathe.

Staring at the woman now, I remember how Mother had been so pale, so close to death, until this woman's arrival.

"You remember me, I see," the woman says, her expression thoughtful, and if I'm not mistaken, compassionate.

I dip my chin into a nod. "I'm sorry. I didn't mean to come here." Tugging on the reins, I nudge Attonitus back into motion, turning him away from the cottage.

She cocks her head at that, her brows descending. "You mean you didn't come to see Winterberry?"

My spine straightens, and I yank the reins. The horse's jerks his head up, mouthing the bit until I force my fingers to release the pressure. I twist in the saddle and face the witch. "What?"

"You didn't know?"

"She's here?"

The woman adjusts a basket full of greenery in her arms. "Come in, dear," she says in such an inviting voice that I find myself following. "It's time you learned just a little of the truth. But she won't be back for an hour yet. I assume, with all the help sent your way, you have plenty of time to help me now. Come on." She disappears into the stone and wood cottage.

Help? Has she been talking to Dalia about sending the children?

When I hesitate to follow, the man emerges from the woods and grasps Attonitus' reins. Hardly knowing what I do, I dismount and let the man lead him away. In mere minutes, I've been given an empty basket and ushered into the backyard of the cottage, where the woman sets me to work pulling weeds while she digs neat, new rows with an ancient hoe.

"Isn't it a little late to be planting?" I ask as I heap more weeds atop the others in my basket.

"Not when you know what you're planting," she says with a twinkle in her eye.

I eye her seeds curiously as I tug another handful of greens out of the earth.

"Dearest, I'm sure you have many questions for me. Why so silent?"

I shake my head at a healthy plant with a few sneaky weeds growing up underneath it. I lift the leaves tenderly and grasp the invaders with my other hand.

"It's all right to ask them, you know. It's healthy."

My mouth twitches. I was never allowed to ask questions.

"No, you weren't, were you?"

Slightly panicked, I glance at her. Had I spoken aloud?

She smiles softly and sets aside her hoe. "No, dear, you didn't speak aloud."

"Then how—?"

"I'm a faery, Eleanora."

"A what?" My hand spasms and the weeds I clutch in my hand go plopping to the dirt.

"Faery. We're magical beings, with the ability to heal different sorts of hurts and even change the course of people's lives."

"What are you doing here, in Ardor? I thought Fae only lived in Edormisco… Do the King and Queen know?" I snap my mouth shut.

She hums a soft laugh and picks up her cloth bag of seeds. "Oh yes. Yes, my sisters and I have a long-standing relationship with the royal family." Her lips close into a line as her smile fades. "But it has been strained since…of late. But things are changing, and I hope for a different future."

My hand stills upon a stubborn weed, then I pinch down lower along the stem and give it a mighty tug. "Maybe that will be good for Ardor." We fall into silence, each working on our task.

"You know, magic can change the course of people's lives. Aren't you curious about that?" She pauses, leaning on the handle of her hoe.

"We aren't supposed to dabble with magic. I'll change my future by myself. With hard work. Perseverance. Honor."

She sighs and resumes her work. "Magic does get a bad reputation. I've been telling the princess all about that, what with her abilities and all."

Abilities? I look up, then shake my head. "So she is a princess?"

"Why, yes, dear. Why did you doubt it?"

"Princes, princesses…magic? My life was simple before all this arrived in Nubilus."

She tosses back her head as she laughs. "I wouldn't say that. You have a mother that hates you, sisters that make your life miserable, and your only friend has been an Edormiscan girl who runs an inn twenty minutes away."

My mouth parts. "How do you know all that?"

She motions a hand down at herself, and for the first time I take in the peasant gown made from linen and how she looks nothing like either a witch or a faery. "I'm fae."

"Yes, but I thought faery were tempestuous creatures that didn't like humans very much." I almost clamp a hand over my mouth at my nerve.

"Lore. Myth. We're actually quite nice. Well, most of us."

"So…you know all about Sir Birch and his theft then?"

"Ah, Sir Birch." She sighs. "Yes, he is a troublesome character, isn't he?"

"So you know he wants me to repay my mother's debt by marrying his son."

"Yes, of course he does."

"What must I do? Can you make it so I don't have to marry Sallust to keep the stable?"

"Are you honestly considering that?" She straightens and sets her hoe down at the end of the rows.

I frown at the plants. "Well…it's that or lose the stables."

"There are other men. Some who might treat you better."

"I think I've rejected them all too often." I sigh down at the weeds. "*Why* did I have to meet Prince Brann?" The question slips from me before I can stop it.

"Dearie, you do start with the difficult questions, don't you? You're surprisingly like Winter in that respect."

She takes her hoe and begins to cover up the line of seeds she's spent the last five minutes planting. "Well, all I can say about that is that there's an important reason you had to meet him."

"Oh?" A surge of hope lifts my heart. "Does it involve me going to the other masques?"

"Brunnea, all I could find was this sorrel, I hope it'll do. I—" Winterberry rounds the edge of the cottage and stops short, gaping at us. "Oh, I— Hello."

I offer an uncertain smile.

"I— Brunnea, why didn't you tell me?" she asks.

The faery, Brunnea, pats the dirt over the last of the row. "Well, that ought to do it. Oh, I'll take that sorrel, dear." She sets the hoe aside and swoops over to Winter, taking the large basket filled halfway with plants. "I'll take this inside. Can you finish up here? Just a bit more weeding. Winterberry, be a dear, and help your friend."

Winter purses her lips and we both follow Brunnea with our eyes as she disappears into the cottage. Turning back to me, Winter gives a little huff and surveys the weeds.

"I'm almost finished," I say. "I can finish without you, if you…if you need to go."

She crooks an eyebrow at me, then sighs and heads to the

next row, where she falls to her knees in the dirt. "Why do you take so much upon yourself, Ella? And why do you do so much for others?"

Ducking my head, I tug at another clump of weeds without answering.

"You work so hard to keep the stables, yet you let your family live at your father's home, take your money, and tell you what to do. Why? What is it that makes you care about their well-being when they're so cruel to you?"

Her words are a kick to my soul. My hands tremble as I grab the next clump of weeds. "They're my family."

"Yes, but...they're also cruel." There's a tenderness to the anger in her words that I can't quite fathom.

I'm quiet for a moment. "I want them to love me." I blink back the moisture on my lashes. I hadn't meant to admit that.

Winter pauses, a soft breath passing over her lips. "No thing you do will make them love you."

"That doesn't make mistreating them right," I say a bit stubbornly.

"You'd just be giving them what they deserve."

"What would that be?" I return, more curious than angry.

She shakes her head. "They are not the lawful heirs to the land, right? Why not send them away? Or, if you don't wish to exile them, make them do their share of work?"

"How might I do that?"

Winter sits back on her heels, chewing on her lip. "If they don't work, they don't stay," she says simply. "Everyone does their fair share of work in my country."

"Do they?" My words come out far more biting and cold than I intend, but my apology won't come to my lips as I call it.

"Almost all of us. We have to. It's impossible to live in Canens without work. To live is to work in Canens..." Winter rubs at her neck, leaving a streak of dirt over the dark numbers tattooed there.

"What is that from?" I ask. "That tattoo?"

Winter jerks her hand away from her neck then flinches as if realizing how guilty she's acting. "It's…my slave number."

My eyes widen. "Slave number?"

Pain ripples across Winter's pale face. "My stepmother sold me into slavery. Before she tried to kill me." A rough laugh escapes her.

"I had no idea." I can't imagine having a stepmother do something so evil. But Mother's face as she told me she hated me comes back to me now. Hatred leads to such acts, doesn't it?

Winter scoots down the row.

"And so…because Blanche has hurt you when she ought to love you, I should strike at my mother before she can kill me?"

Winter's shoulders tense.

"I'm sorry," I say again, and this time the apology comes easily. "I shouldn't have said that."

"No. It's…it's all right." After a second, Winter's body relaxes. "I…I'm sorry for not telling you the truth. I wasn't sure I could trust you."

I dump a handful of weeds into my basket and to the final row of weeding. "I didn't ask you to confide in me."

"No. But you took me in and provided for me, and…" She picks up a red beetle and watches it climb over her finger. "I lied to you."

"You don't confide in others often, do you?"

She snorts, and the bug flies away. "No. The only times I have, I've gotten those people…punished."

She's been lonely—as lonely as I have. Whereas my loneliness has been an odd one, one where I have been isolated by the necessity of my work, without the time or opportunity to meet others, hers has been of a different sort.

She rips at a handful of greenery so when she lifts it, dirt clings to the roots and falls to the ground with a plop.

"Your stepmother tried to kill you?"

"Tried. And tries." She scratches her cheek, leaving a smudge of dirt across her pale skin. "I didn't..." She glances at me. "I didn't think she'd attack me magically like that."

"So...is she some sort of sorceress? Like Brunnea?"

A frown creases her brow. "Yes. But not like Brunnea. They both have magic, but I do, too. But Brunnea is...different."

"So the abilities Brunnea mentioned you have...it's magic?"

Winter turns to me, wariness written on her face like she's said too much and regrets it. She sits back on her heels. "What do you know of magic?

"Magic? Nothing. Nothing but lore, I suppose." My gaze flicks toward the cottage.

"What kind of lore?"

"Well, faery godmother lore, that sort of thing. The fae would help those who do good for other people, those who are deserving of their help, I suppose. Like princes and princesses, or poor boys and girls who are good inside, like in the tale of the Sleeping Talia. But those are just myths from Edormisco. Legends."

"I never heard faery godmother lore. For us, magic is always something frightening. Even the gods are frightening and cruel, punishing humans as much as each other." She tugs at a stubborn, stringy weed, digging the roots out with her fingertips. "My stepmother has always had magic, but she wouldn't tell anyone. I knew though. There was something off about her, and shortly after she married my father, I spied on her and saw her working a spell. I think it was a beauty tonic or something, because she drank something afterward. And after she did, she turned to a hand mirror of hers, nothing really ornate or elaborate, but nearly the only thing she brought into her marriage. I know because I saw the contract. She spoke to the mirror. When she held it up, the glass didn't show her anymore though...it showed me."

Winter drops the weed in the basket and sits back on her

heels, staring at the row of beans before her. "It showed me at that moment, peering at her. As she realized what I was doing, I fled. She threw something at me; I never found out what. She raged so loud I heard her halfway down the hallway. I ran to my rooms and hid under the bed, I was so terrified. I never returned to that room. I was afraid to even eat the food I was given, almost afraid to smell it, thinking she'd poisoned it or something worse." She leans forward and tugs at a weed. "It took me another couple years to realize that she didn't need to make a potion or peer a mirror to cast a spell. She didn't even need to speak. And by then, she had killed my father, she had taken almost everything from me, and I knew she was far more evil than I thought."

Watching her clear the last of the weeds from the line of beans, I realize that I have stopped my own task to listen. Her life seems, if possible for a crown princess, worse than my own. No wonder she doesn't think there is goodness left in Blanche. I can't even think of Blanche as queen anymore, knowing such things about her.

Winter rubs the back of a knuckle over her temple.

"What are you going to do, Your Hig—" The narrowed, slanted gaze she gives me halts me mid-word.

"Winter. I'm hardly a princess."

"By birthright you are."

"Yes, well, birthright doesn't mean much these days, it seems." She gives me a wry look. "It hasn't helped you, has it?"

I frown. "Of course it has. I mean, by birth, I'm a lower noble-woman. I may not look like it, and I work harder than any noble-woman I've ever met, and it hasn't shielded me from pain, but… being a princess can't shield anyone from pain." I knock dirt off the roots of a weed. "I wouldn't trade my life for the world."

Winter blinks at me. "You wouldn't?"

I shake my head. "It's what I was made to do. You asked me why I am so kind to my family when they treat me so awfully. And the truth is that I feel there is goodness in them still, and perhaps by my being kind to them, they will change. I've been put in this spot not just to provide for myself but for them.

"I have a passion for the animals I breed, train, and sell, and my mother and sisters do not. They would let these animals suffer to the death but for me. And I have been blessed with skills that prevent that from happening.

"My family has suffered much as I have. With fewer skills to survive it, however. My life before Father died equipped me to survive his death and endure it. They were not so lucky."

I sense Winter's disbelief more than see it.

"Isn't there always more to the story? Another side? If I knew nothing of your past, I would have thought you cowardly to flee your home. Or take tomorrow's auction for example. I must sleep in the barn now because of some thieves. Now, I could hate those thieves, and though I hate what they do taking what is not theirs, I don't hate them. I don't think I could hate anyone."

"We're staying in the barn now?" Winter asks.

"I am."

"We are?" she repeats, a small glint to her eyes.

"I—" Thrown off, I pause. "I can't ask you to put yourself in danger for me."

"Yes you can. And you should." She yanks at a handful of weeds and a bean plant comes out along with it. "Don't be afraid to ask for help, Ella. Some people want to give it to you, they just don't know how." She shakes the plant a little harder than necessary. "Do you really think I'm a coward?"

"No! Definitely not. I said what you did might *appear* cowardly, if people didn't know that you weren't running in order to save others. You are a princess—a queen—through your core, Winter. I feel it. You might be just surviving now, but soon you'll return home and free your people from oppression. So to leave is not cowardly at all, not when it ensures your future and that of others. And maybe you shouldn't keep from asking for help either, when you need it."

She cocks a brow.

I chuckle. "You still think I'm foolish, that I should give my family what they deserve, don't you? At first, I thought so, too. But as I built up the stables, I didn't have time to remain angry or bitter.

"No one is perfect. Each of us is just doing the best we can with the hand we've been dealt. Father was obsessed with the horses. I've been given that obsession and it's given me purpose. But my sisters and Mother? They have only been taught to think for themselves, and that is their purpose. While I have been taught to think about another first, to think about the horses before myself, they weren't. Father was even more obsessed with the horses, and he never cared half as much about his family. And I…I can't make that same mistake and earn their hatred. If I have their hatred, it's not because I earned it." My eyes tear up as I speak, for despite my words, I know they despise me. "But you probably think me a fool."

She shakes her head. "And what of Queen Blanche?" Winter's bitterness cuts through my introspection. "Is she just doing the best thing she can think to do? Or is she just evil?"

I tilt my head in thought. "There's always another side to the story."

She grunts. "The problem is that some people only think about themselves, some only about others, some war between self and others, and others fear to give in to either. And who of those are fit to wear a crown?"

The strange acidity dripping from her words leaves me wondering if she's condemning Blanche, Brann, herself, or me.

She clutches a weed in her fist between us and gives it a shake as if imagining it to be Blanche's head. "And I think I'm tired of the evil in this world winning. It's time for that to change."

Considering her fierce expression, I almost pity the evil forces she's got her eye set on.

9: BLANCHE

BLOOD

After a week of watching and waiting, of camping and eating off the land, the man finally returns to the tower. I have been patient, but I would be more patient still if I had the time. Instead, I have only days before the auction and next masque in Nubilus. This short time has at least informed me of the girl's two visitors, one her lover, and one an older woman, and neither appear to know about the other.

Anxiously, I settle into my spot amongst the branches. Although the week has been long and all but two days empty of visitors, it has not been fruitless. I have spent most of each day experimenting with how long I can appear as another. Two days ago I spent the entire day as a man, a rather awkward experience, but well worth the effort. I became my huntsman and hid in the forest as he might. My experiment did not extend to stalking through the underbrush as I watched the tower, for my skills as a hunter are not his. However, setting my true huntsman to surveille, I snuck away and learned to exist in a man's body.

Now, I perch atop a tree branch, resting from my morning of circling to await the man's arrival. When I sighted him, I flew above him for a couple of minutes, confirming that it was the same man who came before. Then I flew ahead, found my perch and settled in, waiting for him to arrive at the tower.

His arrival is expected today, and he doesn't have to call up to the waiting girl before she throws her hair over the ledge. She greets him on the balcony with a huge smile and hug that throws them both staggering into the railing. For being a small thing, she certainly seems to have power. Or maybe it's just her obscenely long hair that makes her look small, though the man towers over her.

He stays the greater part of the day. Whenever I grow restless, I stretch my wings by flying around the tower, not daring to go out of sight of the window for long. Finally, he reappears on the balcony. Mid-flight, I land gently on the roof of the pointed tower.

"Do you have to leave so soon?" the girl asks.

"So soon?" the man chuckles. "I will not be home before dark as it is."

"Then why not just stay?" she asks through a pout.

"Darling, I would if I could. But there is far too much going on back home for me to stay any longer."

"Home," she murmurs. "Yes, I suppose you ought to go home, since this isn't your home."

"Darling," he says again, this time with warning in his voice.

There is no more answer from her, but he murmurs a few words in her ear that do nothing to ease the pout to her thick lips before he descends the rope.

Within minutes of his departure, I have cast the spell that transform my womanly form into the male form of the girl's lover. The act drains energy from my own body, from my muscles to my bones. I shouldn't have been a bird this morning is all, I tell myself. It's simply that flitting between species is more difficult than flitting between human appearances.

I grimace at the lie. Both are exhausting, just in different ways. I don't bother to cast the illusion of the man's horse; the girl won't be looking outside the balcony when I arrive, and it's part of my excuse. As I pass a thick bush, it shudders slightly and a small pack appears at my feet. Without missing a stride, I stoop and lift it, tossing it over my broad shoulders and crossing forward toward the base of the tower.

At the base, I stop and call up, lifting a hand to my mouth, "Aeria! Let down your hair!"

A head peeks above the top of the balcony railing. "Tobiah?" Confusion laces the girl's face as her mouth moves again.

I cup a hand to my ear. "What?"

She shakes her head and says something else, and I squint at her.

She half rolls her eyes and disappears from view. A moment later, a rope of hair nearly hits me on the head.

I grunt and toss the strap of the pack across my chest to avoid dropping it, grab the hair and begin the journey up the tower. The man's muscles make the climb surprisingly quick as I pull myself hand over hand to the balcony and then drag myself over.

"Tobiah, what happened? Why are you back?" Aeria asks, her heart-shaped face ripe with worry.

"I'm sorry, my love," I say, "but my horse threw me and I had nowhere to go, with it being so late and all. Staying in the forest tonight would get me attacked by a wolf, surely."

A small furrow appears on her brow. "Did you say… Did you just call me…"

I blank. What had I called her?

"My love?" she whispers. "You love me?"

"I—" Before I can argue, she throws herself into my arms and hugs me so tightly that it's difficult to breathe, even in this man's body.

I cough and disentangle her as gently as possible, but she's like a sticky creature with eight arms. Every time I move one arm, another appears. "Darling," I begin, realizing then that *that* was what this man had been calling her, not "my love." I hold back a sigh. "Darling, you must let me go. I'm absolutely parched, can you get me a drink of water, please?"

"Water?" She pulls back and blinks her large eyes up at me. "Oh, of course, Tobiah. Of course." Grinning, she all but runs off, her every move alight with energy and excitement.

She dashes to her bedside table and pours a generous serving of water into a cup sitting beside the pitcher.

"Thank you. My dear—darling," I add belatedly. I take the drink and sip it.

"So," Aeria says, not giving me time to empty my glass. "What happened? Why are you back?"

I smile soothingly at her. "I told you, my horse threw me."

"Oh." Her shoulders slump slightly, and she turns away, as if to hide her disappointment.

I swallow the last of my water. "May I have another cupful?" I am, truthfully, quite thirsty. In all my surveillance as a bird today, I couldn't deign to drink the polluted rain water laying in the gutters.

"Of course, darling!" She jumps to fulfill my request.

"Thank you."

"Did your horse get frightened?" Aeria glances back at me as she pours, as if unable to keep her eyes off her lover for longer than a few seconds.

"Yes. It was an animal in the underbrush. Frightened him and threw me." I wave a hand through the air. "I feel like a fool."

"Him?" Her brow furrows. "You weren't riding your palfrey?"

I blank. He rides a mare? "Oh, yes, of course. That's what I meant."

Aeria opens her mouth, but I continue.

"Darling, I had to come back and tell you that I loved you. That's why the mare threw me. I was so distracted at how we parted—"

The water spills over the cup, and she hastily sets it and the pitcher down on the bedside table. "Do you really? Love me?"

"Have I never said so before?" I edge toward her and the bed. "Don't you love me as well?"

"Of course! Yes!" Her little face breaks almost in half with her smile. "I've been waiting for weeks for you to say this, Tobiah."

"Then let's celebrate. Do you have anything to drink? Other than water? We'll make a toast of it."

Raising herself onto her tiptoes in her excitement, she hesitates then nods and darts toward the stairs. "Stay here. I'll be right back." She disappears down the spiral stairs, her hair dragging along behind her so that when only the end remains at top, it stops.

I shift the pack from my shoulder and drop it atop the foot of the bed. This potion, once she swallows it, will take effect immediately but only be effective for an hour.

I ready the vial as she lingers down below. While I wait for her return, I gaze out the balcony window. The meadow is empty. No chance of being discovered, as there is no one to discover me. The man—Tobiah—must never come on the same day as the woman. I wander around the room, peering at the bookcase and feeling a strange pull of magic from the items there. Before I can investigate it, a clanking sound rises up the stairs. I flinch and step back.

What's wrong with me? I'm acting quite guilty. I must stop indulging myself and focus. Yet this tower has piqued my curiosity for these past days.

"Here we are!" Aeria reappears at the top of the stairs, holding up two clear glasses and a bottle with something red in it that could be either wine or juice. She beams at me. "I found this in the back of one of the cupboards."

"Oh? What is it?" I despise feigning such pathetic interest in this girl, but it's just for a few more minutes, that's all.

She goes to a small table beside the balcony door. "Oh, I think Mama brought it a few years ago and it got forgotten. I was mad at her for something then, and she brought it as a peace offering.

Elderberry juice, I think. Should be several years old by now, so maybe it's fermented." She gives a mischievous twinkle of her eye my direction.

I raise a brow.

She pops the top off and begins to pour, but I reach out to still her hands. "I'll do that. Oh! Sorry," I force the apology off my tongue as I bump my hand into the bottle and half knock it over. "I'll do this. Why don't you go and get a towel?"

"Right." The girl hurries across the room and disappears through a doorway.

Quickly, I fix my back to her and pull the small vial from my pocket, where I moved it from the bag earlier. I uncork it and pour a the entire amount into the second cup, then tilt the bottle over the second cup and return the empty vial to my pocket just as the girl rounds my shoulder.

"Here." The girl hurriedly presses the towel to the spilled juice, casting me a quick, adoring look as she does so. She's so in love with this man, it's utterly pathetic and weak. If she hadn't invited him inside in the first place, I wouldn't be standing here, able to trick her. She has made my job so easy.

I pick up both glasses and hold out the doctored one to her. "To us."

She abandons the towel on the table, her eyes locked on mine, and with slightly pink cheeks, she takes the cup from me and clinks our glasses together so enthusiastically that I wince. "To us," she says breathlessly.

Smiling, I put the glass to my lips, tilting it back just enough to look like I'm drinking, but instead watch her.

She takes a deep gulp and her mouth twists in distaste. "Ugh. This is awful!"

I take a tiny sip of my own glass. As my nose informed me, the juice has fermented. Could it honestly be that she has never had any wine in her life? What an innocent.

Laughing, she holds out the cup from her body as though it

might attack her. "You don't think that's a bad sign, do you?" Worry suddenly creases her forehead.

I take the glass from her hand and set both of them upon the table. "No, darling, I don't think that's a bad sign. Not at all."

"No? You didn'n…" Her words begin to slur. She blinks at me and tries again. "You did—done." She squints at me.

"Are you all right, my darling?" I inject concern into my tone. It's impossible to tell how much of this she will remember when she wakes, but I must pretend in case she remembers it all.

"I—" Her eyelids flutter, and her knees go weak.

I catch her before she hits the ground, though it's unnecessary for me to do so, I suppose a chivalrous bone must be lent to me from this man I impersonate. However, I don't bother to sweep her into my arms, instead I drag her toward the bed and deposit her unceremoniously atop it.

The girl's eyes are closed, her mouth parted in her drugged slumber as I stare down at her.

From my bag, I remove the other vial hidden inside along with a third item. Without hesitation, I press the tip of the short-bladed knife to her throat, and as blood pours out from her porcelain skin, I exchange my knife for the vial and catch the crimson liquid in the clear tube.

Something, some magic that is not my own, stabs at me like a knife to my own throat. Alarm flares in my gut. Hands still held to the girl's bleeding throat, I lift my gaze and slowly turn my head. No one here. I listen for sounds outside the tower, but I hear nothing, not even the sounds of the forest. I shake away my unease. It is simply the magic of the tower and the enchantments upon it.

Despite the wound to her throat, the girl remains asleep, her pulse thumping steadily next to the cut I made. She will be sense-less until morning. She will not know what happened, but I will make it look as though we spent the night together. I stopper the vial and press my fingers against her wound. Magic flows out from me and the cut ceases to bleed. I push a little more magic out and the blood that didn't enter the vial disappears. A vein my head throbs at the magic used. Tomorrow will not be a comfortable day.

I replace the knife and both vials in the pack and shoulder it. Debating my next move, I glance at the girl. Then I pull back the covers from her bed and wave my hand at her body, simultaneously exploring the depths of my own magical stores and groaning silently at what I find. I must be going; I won't have much longer, especially considering the physical requirements of my escape.

At my spell, the girl rises from the bed and hovers over it. I give another wave and her clothes slip off, revealing a delicate frame beneath. With another flick of my wrist, she's half covered in blankets, her long braid twisting around the bed and throughout the tower room. It will have to do. I tighten my pack across my chest and stride to the balcony. Outside, the tremble of magic is strong. Something has triggered a reaction in the magical protection this tower has. Whether it's what I've done or something unrelated, I have no time to waste. At the edge of the balcony, I pause and peer over. It is a long way down.

A wave of magic courses over me so that I have to fight to retain the man's image. I push back against the invisible, magical onslaught, throwing up a protective barrier around myself. Someone—or something—powerful protects this tower. And it has set up protective spells to inform upon any magical interference here.

The magic is calling to someone; I cannot be here when they answer. I throw my leg over the balcony rail. Then I hear the familiar birdsong of my huntsman.

10: ELLA

BREAK-IN

uction day arrives too quickly. Even though it's useless, I stay in the stables the final nights leading up to it, worried that something might happen, that someone might attempt to sabotage me or otherwise prevent me from getting to the auction. The final night before, I have such a bad feeling that I ask Winter and Gavin to stay up with me.

"I'll be at the front of the barn, then?" Winter asks me, refastening the broach at her throat that holds a beautiful dark blue cloak Brunnea gifted her.

"Yes, that's perfect." Checking the horses on my way, I head toward the back of the stable, my mind elsewhere.

For despite the auction and all the preparation, and the break-ins that risk everything I've worked for, my thoughts are with the prince.

He's a prince. How could I not have known? And—I tremble at the thought—I kissed a prince! Now that I've had time to think about it though, I realize how foolish it was to let my guard down and let him in. I hadn't known who he was. And that was foolish. I should have realized he wasn't who he said. I shouldn't have kissed him.

As I near the feed room, any remaining enthusiasm I had about Brann is brushed away like a wisp of smoke. Nothing will come of it—nothing *can* come of it. I won't be attending the next masque with it being scheduled the same day as the auction, and even if I find a dress for the final masque, why would I go? What is there for me now except a man who doesn't want to see me again, the friend of his enemy?

Yet…something tugs inside me, pulling me toward that masque.

I want to go…

I climb the ladder to the loft and find a hay bale with tines broken and the flakes slightly apart. I sink down against it.

I want to see him again.

Just one more time.

Just to say goodbye.

Yawning, I nestle into the hay, my eyelids heavy.

I imagine myself dancing with Brann in the ballroom. Swirling gowns in a rainbow of colors.

I lean into Brann's embrace, nestling my cheek into his firm chest.

A horse nickers.

I jolt upright. I can't fall asleep. If something happens, it will be tonight.

Where is Winter? Oh, downstairs at the front of the barn. I fall back against the hay, careful not to get too comfortable this time. At least I'll have backup.

Around midnight, after I've daydreamed a million endings for me attending the masque, each worse than the last (which is the only thing keeping me awake), a creak breaks the silence. The small door in the back of the stables.

Soft footsteps tap down the dirt and straw aisle.

As they near underneath me, I slowly sit up. Silently, I crawl to the edge of the loft and, lying on my stomach, I peer through the trapdoor.

A small, cloaked person tiptoes through the stable, peering left and right as they go. Why are the dogs not barking? What have they done to them?

Squinting and inching a little farther out over the trapdoor, I try to catch sight of the intruder's face.

The person passes the loft and goes down the stable toward where the auction animals are stabled. They seem almost familiar with the stable, and none of the dogs have sent up an alarm.

I wait a minute after the cloaked person disappears then sit up and slide my legs around. As silently as I can, I slip my feet onto the ladder rungs and climb down.

The intruder is nowhere to be seen. My feet hit the soft ground of the stable floor, and I hesitate, peering into the shadows. They could be hiding somewhere, ready to attack. Gelu thieves have never been unwilling to hurt people in order to steal a horse or two.

I grab a pitchfork from the hook on the wall and hold it, tines up, in both hands. My heart thumps heavily in my throat; the wooden handle slips in my sweaty hands.

As I walk along the stalls, the horses make soft sounds of unease. Ahead, a stall lock clicks open, to my surprise. How did the intruder get my key? I pat my pocket, but my key is there.

A horse snorts. Attonitus. I grimace. He might work better on the ground now after all that I've done with him lately, but he's certainly not the best horse for a stranger to grab in the dark.

I peer at the person as they step into the stall. They seem uncertain...a little too uncertain for doing this. Recognition washes over me, followed quickly by dread.

"Haydée?"

The person starts and whirls toward me. Attonitus snorts and backs up into his stall.

"How dare you!" I'm too shocked to do much more than wave the pitchfork at her. "Come out of the stall before he kicks you."

Haydée sets her jaw but obeys, sliding the bolt home with an extra loud click.

"How did you get my key?" Pitchfork pointing at my sister, I glance toward the front of the stable, wondering if Winter hears any of this.

"What are you going to do, spear me?" Haydée taunts, sneering at my weapon.

"Maybe," I snap. "What are you doing? Don't tell me you're the one letting horses out and sabotaging everyone in Nubilus?"

"Of course not." In the moonlight filtering through the stable windows, I can see the offense passing over her face. "Why would I be doing that?"

"I don't know. Why are you trying to let him out now?"

She sighs and sets her jaw at me. "I don't have to tell you anything. You work for us."

I cock my head at her. "Actually, I'm the legal heir to this land."

She steps close. "Only if you get married and have a son. You and I both know that Carmen and I are far more likely to catch a man that you are, with your trousers and your dirt." She snorts in my face and sneers, revealing her teeth. She looks so much like a stubborn mule that I want to snap her lead to reprimand her.

"Then why haven't you married already?"

Her mouth opens and closes. "I'm just of age. You know that. And you know you don't have much time to produce an heir anymore."

"The laws could change," I say stubbornly. "And there's still time."

"You're so sad." She grins with twist to it that makes her seem at once sympathetic and hateful. "The difference between us is that there's nothing of this land I want—except the gold it's worth."

"Well let me clue you in, Haydée. If you hurt my horses before they're sold, they won't be worth any money to you, and they are worth more than this land. So I wouldn't do anything to them—

I'd instead make sure they bring in lots of money at the auction tomorrow."

She lifts her nose in the air. "I have a dozen men vying for my hand, Ella, what do you have? Gavin?" She snorts. "He's nothing."

I shrug at her misconceptions.

"You can't think the prince would want you." She laughs, long and hard so that, despite my resolve, I flush.

When she finally stops laughing, I say, "Even if I married Gavin, I'd still inherit." I offer her a pretty smile. "That's the difference between us, Haydée, I know that whomever I marry, I will value them for more than their money."

Haydée snorts, her nose wrinkling. "You value all the wrong things."

"One might say the same about you." I motion her down the aisle with the pitchfork. "Now get out of my stable before I decide to spear you."

The stable door slides open quietly on its track, and Haydée's eyes glitter smugly in the moonlight.

"Did you bring someone else?" I demand.

She smirks.

I narrow my eyes, but she refuses to do more but stare back. Where is Winter? I peer toward the front of the stable again, and pitchfork in hand, head toward the entrance. In front of me is a shadow within the shadows. A male shadow.

"Stop right there!" I call out, aiming my pitchfork his way.

The figure freezes in the shadow. Out of a pale face, a pair of eyes glint fearfully.

"What are you doing in here?" I step closer, bolder with Haydée behind me than I would be alone. Winter and Gavin must be sleeping, curse it all. "Who are you?" I demand.

The burly man hovers in the shadows, shoulders hunched.

"Who are you?" I repeat. "Why are you doing this?"

He stares at me, then turns toward the stable door. He takes a few steps, then a growl fills the air, formidable and low. Gus. At least *some*one else is here.

"Tell me who you are." I say hold the pitchfork higher, emboldened at Gus' arrival. "Come out of the shadows."

"He'll eat me," the man says.

There's something familiar about the voice, distinctly so. "He won't unless I say so. Come forward."

He gives Gus another look and then steps out of the shadows into the soft light of the aisle.

"Sallust?" I gape at Sir Birch's son. "What—why— I don't understand?"

He throws a mutinous look at me, then his gaze shifts to Haydée.

I gape. "Haydée? You— You—and *him*?" My pitchfork sinks a little toward the ground. "Why would you do this?"

"Because," she spits venomously. "Because Father never loved me. And you can't have it all. You just can't."

From the end of the stable, a pounding of hooves interrupts our conversation. Letifer, growing angry at the nighttime disturbance.

"Come on, Sallust," Haydée says. "I have the keys. Let's let them out like we planned. She has to have them there in a few hours—she might have enough time to catch them all if they don't run too far." She laughs.

"Haydée, do you really hate me so much that you would ruin your own future? Do you think he would want you without all this?"

She lifts a cloaked shoulder. "What can I say? Perhaps my hatred for you grew when you kissed a prince."

A chill scuttles its way down my spine.

"Her? Kiss a prince?" Sallust laughs cruelly. "What a farce. The little stablehand kissing a prince. How embarrassed the prince must be. Wait until the town hears about this! Why didn't you say, Haydée?"

My cheeks heat at Sallust's mocking.

Haydée's laugh joins Sallust's. "I think that's a fabulous idea, Sal."

His teeth, slightly crooked, shine in the dim light.

"Let's go," Haydée says, striding toward me.

From behind Sallust, Gus growls. Several other dogs have moved into position, flanking Sallust but confused by Haydée's confident, familiar presence. Although I don't know exactly what any of them will do if Sallust threatens me, if he just wants to leave, I can't stop him. And who will believe me that Haydée would dare do this to her own stable?

"I don't think you're going anywhere, actually," comes a voice from behind Haydée.

Haydée whirls to face the new voice, and Sallust starts, squinting into the darkness.

"Who is that?" he snaps.

Winter. About time she shows up.

From the darkness, a glow swells.

I shift my grip on the pitchfork as Haydée leans back and Sallust leans forward. The glow illuminates the shadows, lighting Winter's face, framing her head with a black halo, while her face glows as pale as the moon.

REVELATION

I know I shouldn't reveal myself to Haydée and Sallust, but their words to Ella are so hateful that I can't help it. I only hope the shadows will hide what I intend to do.

Brunnea didn't teach me how to take a life, and I'm grateful. Right now, I don't trust myself.

"You won't be telling anyone anything," I tell them. They both disgust me. I want to at least mute them for life, but I won't darken my heart for them. And so I won't give them what they deserve here, not even close.

Haydée's sharp laugh breaks the stillness of the night. My appearance shocked them, but nothing shocks Haydée enough.

"I'll tell everyone. Everyone what *she* is"—she points to Ella —"and how she thinks herself so amazing and then all about you."

She turns such a cold glare on me that my urge to curse her returns.

I summon the magic to my fingertips, but the glow comes with it. I struggle against the glow, not wanting them to see more of my face. I cannot have them identifying me and risk everything simply for revenge. I hesitate, then the answer comes to me.

Conceal my identity from them, I ask of my magic, ignoring the wince of guilt I feel at such a self-serving magical request.

"You will say nothing to anyone about Ella's presence at the masques, nor about my presence here." My voice is lower and bolder than before, and I know without asking by the confused expressions on their faces that they don't know who I am, and have forgotten if they ever guessed. I continue, "If asked, you will admit only that you tried to break in to sabotage Ella's horses. You will admit it freely and accept your punishment for your actions. Do you understand?"

The pair gape at me. Behind them, Ella's face is equally shocked and a bit bemused, but she doesn't interrupt.

"I asked you a question." My fingertips flame, and Haydée stumbles back a step with a yelp, then lunges to the side and grasps Sallust's arm.

"Do you understand?" I growl the question through my teeth this time.

"Yes!" they both say together, the notes of panic in their voices a duet to my ears.

But only a moment later, Haydée tilts her head in that defiant way of hers, as if reason is returning.

"Then go," I insist before she can speak. "And if you disobey these orders, you shall be mute until you accept responsibility for your actions—all of them." I grind my teeth. And go before I lose control and really curse you, you stupid girl.

"But—" Haydée begins, her eyes slightly wide.

"Don't tempt me," I reply before she can continue. "If you fail this test, I will make you mute until your heart changes."

Confusion on her face, Haydée snaps her mouth shut. Sallust glances at her and then at me.

"Who are you?" he asks, something like wonder in his voice.

"Not your concern. Test my command and you shall see the power behind my words." I don't know what makes me say that, but they look suitably frightened by it. "Go. And behave yourselves." I wince at the way those words come out. Not at all faery-like or regal even, more motherly.

But it seems to work. With a glance at Ella, and a lingering look from Sallust to Gus, the pair hustle out of the stable without another word. Perhaps a stern mother is just what they need then.

When the back door snaps shut, I extinguish the light in my hands and step out of the shadows.

"Do you think they'll listen?" Ella asks, her gaze lingering on the exit.

"Yes," I say. "They aren't fools."

"How did you…" Ella motions to my hands.

Oh. I never actually told her. I bend my head in guilt. Then, deciding it's only fair, I lift my palm and an orb of light bursts into being, filling the stable with such sudden light that she jumps.

"It's true then? You have magic? You did magic? For me?"

"I've only told you the truth," I say softly. "But no. I cast no magic for you. Other than this light." I half grimace, half smile.

"Are you…are you like Brunnea?"

"No," I say quickly. "No. Not even close. I don't…I don't know what I am, exactly. Fae-gifted, she called it." Like Blanche, I think but can't say. I shake my head. "Ella, I didn't tell you because I fear that if anyone else finds out about me, no one I know will be safe here any longer. Even Dalia could be at risk as your friend, as having aided me."

"I won't say a word," Ella rushes to say, her words coming out breathless. "I wouldn't dare."

"It's too late. Haydée and Sallust…" My magic only seems to divide me from others, marking me different, just like my tattoo does. But there's something more in her tone, like she feels she's under a spell as well, or afraid of being enchanted. "You're not bound, Ella. I would never use magic against you."

She gives an uneven smile, an unusual display of nerves for

her. "Oh. Right." She steps toward the stable door and cracks it open. A pink light under a dark sky fills the fissure.

I follow her out of the stable and together we watch Sallust's silhouette walk along the road toward town.

A minute later, Sallust pauses at a thicket of trees and collects a horse out of them. He mounts and, with a glance over his shoulder, aims his horse toward Nubilus.

"You know," Ella says conversationally. "Not everyone with magic abuses their power. Just like not every king or queen abuses their privilege."

I snort. "And who are these people?"

Ella pauses, then shrugs. "The Great Fae, I suppose. Like Brunnea, they're good. And they're the most powerful magical beings anywhere in the Seven Kingdoms, right? If they can control their magic for good, then so can you."

She's right, I realize with a shock. They have much more magic than I could ever could contain. And, being Fae-gifted, Blanche is also weaker than the gifter, right? Our magic came from the Fae, began there. There's no possible way that it could be greater than them, could it?

I should have asked Brunnea about that. There's so much I hope I get a chance to ask her.

"But it must be easier for them to resist the pull of evil, mustn't it?" Ella muses. "After all, none of them have gone bad, have they?" As Sallust atop his horse disappears, she walks toward the well, and I follow. She reaches for the pulley and begins to pull up the bucket on the well.

"I don't know. Brunnea suggested one of her Fae sisters had…" I rub at my neck. "I wish Brunnea had more time to tell me about them. About everything." I reach for the bucket as it nears the top, pulling it up the rest of the way onto the ledge.

Ella picks up the ladle hanging on a nail near the pulley handle. "Ask her when you get a chance."

"If I get a chance." I push the bucket toward her on the ledge at the same time as she offers me the ladle. I motion to the bucket to indicate her first.

Ella downs an entire ladle of water. "Well, it's late enough in the morning that I think I'm going to start mucking stalls. Do you want to help?"

I crook an eyebrow up at her. "Want?"

She grins and wipes the back of her mouth with her sleeve.

"I'll help do whatever you need, Ella. You know that."

"I know," Ella says. "And believe me, I've never appreciated it more."

Smiling, she nods and offers me the ladle. Making empty threats is thirsty business, so I take it and drink deeply, shivering in the early morning chill. I hand it back. She dips it into the bucket again.

A prickling premonition makes me turn. I catch my breath.

A rider comes across the grass from the King's Forest. Sallust? No, he went the other direction, and then I see second rider. I squint through the dawning light then suck in a breath. "I must go."

"What?" Ella turns, forehead creased in confusion, holding out the ladle toward me.

"Don't mention me. Please." Briefly, I beg her with my eyes to remain silent before dashing into the barn and up into the loft, hoping that Prince Brann didn't see me. Whatever his reasons for coming here, I don't think it was to find me.

THE PRINCE

The ladle still dangling out toward Winter, I watch as she dashes into the barn and disappears. What on earth?

Quiet hoofbeats reach my ears, and I check the road, thinking for a moment that Sallust has returned, but it's empty. The hoofbeats continue coming though, dulled as though on grass. I turn. Two men ride across the grass, clearly having just emerged from the King's Forest. One sits straight and tall on his impressive, coppery Gelu Rigens, the other rides comfortably upon a dainty dark chestnut Gelu mare.

Prince Brann. And...someone else.

Trying to slow my racing thoughts, I drink another ladle full of icy water from the well, trying and failing not to spill it down my chin.

Prince Brann rides up to me with solemnity on his face that puts a pang into my heart. The animal he rides is quite a magnificent Gelu, such a perfect display of male features in the breed that I am already imagining what sort of colts and fillies he might make with some of my mares, though I will never get a chance, I'm certain.

"Hello," he says softly, his tone and slumped shoulders suggesting his uncertainty at my reception.

Try as I might, words don't want to form on my lips. So I press them together and dip my head in a nod that welcomes both men equally.

The prince scans my face, his lips pinching at what he seems to find. He motions toward the watering trough near the stable. "Would it be too much to ask if we could water our horses?"

"Of course not," I answer then add, "Your Highness."

A wince creases his nose, but he doesn't correct me. He dismounts instead in silence.

I should have curtsied to him. He's here, undisguised, and I know who he is this time. He's practically dismissed me along with Winter, so why is he here?

Not knowing what else to say, I lead the way to the watering trough.

"Hi," says the second man, his gaze slipping from Brann and me and back several times. He juts out his hand, palm up. "I'm Tobiah, Brann's best friend."

I stare at his hand for a moment, then reluctantly put my dirty hand with dirt-caked fingernails into it when he doesn't withdraw. Tobiah smiles and, as though my hand is that of a duchess and we are at a ball in the palace ballroom, he presses his lips to the back of my hand. "I've heard much about you, Miss Saevus. I am honored to meet you."

My lips turn up at the edges at his mix of frivolity and decorum. I even feel the tension slip from my shoulders.

"I hear you have more than a few admirable specimens here on your property," Tobiah says as his mare noses the water. "Do you mind if I leave my most beautiful girl with you and take a walk around?"

Surprised at his audacity, I glance to Brann, who shrugs. Though I would never allow a stranger to wander my stables alone, this man is a friend of Brann's.

As if he reads my thoughts, Brann's lips twitch in answer. "I vouch for him."

"Well, if that's the case," I answer. "I suppose you may. Just don't try to touch the silver stallion in the paddock with the tall fence. If you value your life."

Adopting a serious expression, Tobiah snaps his heels together and salutes me sharply. "Yes, ma'am."

A reluctant giggle escapes me. "But I'm serious," I say as he hands his mare's reins to Brann.

"Oh, I believe you," Tobiah calls over his shoulder, already a dozen paces away. "I wouldn't dare test you. Not after what I've heard."

I bite my lip, wondering if I ought to go after him after all.

"Are you prepared for the auction?" Brann asks, diverting my attention back to him.

"What? Oh, yes, I think so. As much as can be."

"Any more troubles?"

Sallust and Haydée's names are on my lips, but I bite them back. "No, no troubles." I long to tell him, to confide in him, but can I? Should I?

He watches me over his stallion's lowered head, his shoulders slumping. "I'm sorry."

For what? For kissing me? Ignoring me? Trying to arrest my friend? I don't know what he's supposed to be sorry for, but I can't very well ask the prince so blatantly. No, I must speak as politely as I can, keep everything neutral, and unless he brings up another topic, keep our conversation to the horses.

"I heard about all your difficulties with the Crown Inspector when discussing the autumn auctions with Sir Birch and the Crown Inspectors." The prince shakes his head and gives an annoyed little sigh. "How did your re-inspection go?"

A part of me is disappointed at his chosen topic of conversation. He doesn't want to talk about the masque, that much is clear. Perhaps he wishes to forget what happened. "I passed," I say, just the words giving me relief.

He lets out a long sigh and tilts his head against his horse's neck. "Thank the Lord."

I chuckle. "Yes, I said a few thank you prayers myself."

He grins at me, and I'm reminded again so strongly of Hadwin that I blink and have to recover myself.

"And so everything is all right then? You'll…Aeneas Stables, I mean, will be all right?" he asks.

My smile fades. "Well, no. Not exactly."

"What do you mean? You can sell them, right?" He pauses and shakes his head. "Forgive my ignorance. I've never understood all the laws and rules and regulations surrounding the Geli. And the auction rules are not something I have had much of a chance to learn. My schooling has focused on geography, territorial disputes, writing charters and political agreements, on learning the history of our country…"

He trails off, and halfway through a nod of agreement, I look up at him, but his gaze slides away from me.

"So there is a lot that I feel I should know, but I don't. Would you mind explaining it to me? From your point of view?"

I hesitate, but what is the harm in speaking of these general terms? That is probably safest after all. "Well, there are a lot of factors for my success—for anyone's success—in this auction. It depends on the order the horses are drawn in. If my horses are drawn to be sold later in the auction, then most likely we won't have anyone who has money left to bid. The later horses in the auction usually don't go much above their reserve price." I press my lips together. "And my reserves might not be enough to fund me until the next auction."

"Why not choose a higher reserve?"

"Because it's better to get some money and try to supplement through other areas, than to get no money at all."

For a second the prince looks shocked at the idea, then he

nods. "I can understand that." His horse pulls against the prince's hold, toward a patch of green grass alongside the fence.

I motion to it. "You can let them graze, if you'd like."

"May I? Thank you." He leads the horses over as I trail behind. When his horse lowers his head and tears at the grass, the prince half glances at me. "How, um, how well do you do at the auctions?"

I lift one shoulder. "Usually I manage just enough to keep the stable afloat."

"And so your reserves are lower than anyone else's because you can't afford to gamble on not selling a horse," the prince says slowly. "And yet it doesn't help you sell your horses."

I bite my lip, but he's right. I nod.

"Then there's something wrong with the laws, isn't there?"

I look up at him in confusion.

"I mean." He flushes but clenches a fist next to his thigh as he directs his gaze out at the pasture where several almost-yearlings frolic away from their mothers' sides. "It's foolish to expect you to deal with more laws and regulations and yet be unable to earn more money for doing so. This prejudice against women should stop. It must stop." He stops, and when he doesn't go on, I look to him. "Am I not right?"

All I can do is shrug.

"What is that look on your face?"

I sigh. "Well, it's a kind thought, but attitudes are difficult to change, as I've realized over the years. At first, the other breeders were kind. But too quickly, every breeder with an eligible son offered them in marriage. Or noblemen offered their sons to me —or to my mother on my behalf." I curl my lip in distaste. "Then when I refused them, when I insisted I would run the business myself and wait for someone whom I might care to marry, their true intentions came out. They only wanted my business."

There is a moment of thought between us. "And how much longer do you have? Should you not marry?"

"Not two years," I say softly.

The prince leans against his horse's shoulder, gazing steadily down at me. "And what future do you see for yourself?"

"Future?" I trail a hand across the animal's coppery flank, not daring to look at him. "I imagine I will refuse the marriage offers I am given, in the hopes of finding a match with a man who might treat me as an equal. And then if I cannot find such a man within fourteen months, I will enjoy my last nine months with my horses and pray that whoever buys my stable might let me stay on as a groom or rider."

The prince fingers a strap of leather hanging from his stallion's saddle. "That would be a sad future indeed." He untangles a leaf from the stallion's coppery hair and twirls it between his fingers. "I was imagining you saw a more hopeful future for yourself."

"Hope is a dangerous thing, Your Highness," I murmur, running my fingers over a bump in the saddle pad. "Sometimes it feeds you lies even more than despair does." I reach under the pad and remove a twig that must have gotten lodged there in their ride through the woods.

I drop the twig on the ground and let my hand fall. As it does, it brushes the prince's. I jerk back, my hand tingling and cheeks burning at the unintended touch. "I'm sorry. I must—I have many chores to complete before the auctions. And I must check on your friend. And Letifer. Make yourself comfortable, feed and water your horses as much as you wish, Your Highness."

"Ella?"

I look back.

"Good luck on the auctions."

Cheeks hot, I hurry away, leaving him on the edge of my land, certain it will be the last conversation I'll have with him. It must be so. I could not risk my heart again.

Behind me, I think I hear him call, "Good luck...Ella."

13: BLANCHE

THE TUNNEL

The man's human strength is my salvation now, for it takes most of my magical concentration simply to keep his form. I focus the remainder of my magic on repelling the invisible threads seeking me out by throwing up magical distractions.

I impersonate the man further, calling for my very being to absorb my magic and shield my outer form from magical inspection. I call upon my magic to make me appear normal. It won't work for long, but something seeks me, and I cannot let it find me. It will ruin everything!

I dart back into the tower's shadows as the huntsman's bird call sounds again, warning me. Someone comes to investigate this disturbance.

Nowhere to hide. Nowhere to go. Nowhere but down.

Undoubtedly the person who comes now has magic that seeks me out. I either drop all pretenses and flee as myself, without magic, or I take a chance on what is below. She must have some sort of kitchen in this place, and perhaps there is somewhere I could hide. The ridiculous girl doesn't even own a wardrobe.

I hear a woman's voice calling from the meadow, and groping for the doorway, I throw a look over my shoulder.

"Aeria! Let down your hair, dear."

I fly down the stairs. The spiral steps are dark and slick, and my man's body is not familiar with them. I trip, stumbling against the wall and barely catching myself before I topple head over heels down stories of unforgiving stone.

My fingers come away from the tower's sides slippery with blood. I take a breath. The woman's voice is dim. She will not keep calling long. She will find a way inside.

I must be near the bottom now. Dirt mixing with the stench of blood from my fingertips assails my nostrils.

My foot collides with something other than stone, softer but not dirt. Wood. I push through an archway, blinking at the room before me. Small but rectangular, it's a kitchen with a stove, oven, icebox, and some counter space.

Nowhere to hide.

I fight to quench the panic rising in me. This man must be taking over me. Even if there is nowhere to hide, I have my magic.

I take another glance. Nothing living to take magic from, not even a plant.

Where might I go? I risk the tiniest amount of magic to aid me in answering my question. Find me an exit.

Three answers call to me. I turn to the narrow windows. One has a pipe taking up most of it. Another is empty but far too narrow for even my woman's body to fit through. But the third answer is the most interesting.

I stare at the floor before the stove. It looks impenetrable. Wood that appears exactly as the other pieces. And yet…

At a noise outside, I hasten atop it.

Show me.

The slightest shimmer in the middle of the floor appears. I'm about to fall upon it when I pause. I must leave no trace for the woman outside to follow.

I reach for the handle and find none. Either it answers to magic, or it's not meant to be an escape for this girl from her tower. I curse inwardly. Magic. It will answer to magic, of course. And the woman will trace it.

With a jolt of annoyance, I magically open the trapdoor. And then I scramble down the ladder into the cavernous depths below, shutting the door as quickly and quietly as possible.

The darkness envelopes me. I seek out any magical traces without success. How strange. I can't wait for my eyes to adjust, so I stumble forward, feeling with my feet to make sure I don't walk off a cliff. After a few minutes of this, I know that either the woman hasn't entered the tower, or she has and is distracted with reviving the girl, or…she is searching for me. But if she searches for me, she won't worry about coming in secret. She will come down with magic, light the room I hide in, and give me no chance to defend myself.

I am trapped.

With another muttered curse, I make my decision and cast a spell. Light bursts out of my palm, a spell that allows light only for me. If she is seeking me, she will have felt that use of magic.

I glance around the illuminated room, and a grin breaks free. It's not a room, but a tunnel.

"Show me," I murmur. "Show me the way to what I seek."

With a surge of light, my spell goes to work, and I follow.

Nearly an hour later, my feet are tired, but my magic is strong. I surrendered the man's image, and in my queenly body, I am strong. Tree roots go deep in this land, and they have offered me some strength, along with only the slightest regret for requiring life from another…again. This will be the last time, I promise myself. I won't steal another's *anima* again.

The path begins to slope upward rapidly.

Ahead, for the first time, I see an ending to the tunnel. Instead of blackness outside the light's reach, there is gray. Stone.

My pace speeds up, and yet I become more cautious, sending out magical hands to sense danger.

Reaching the stone, I inspect it carefully with the light. There —a handle. This door is not meant to open magically. It is intended for a simple human. So…whom?

With my hand on the handle, I let the light die. Then I grasp the handle and, heart thumping in my throat, I turn it.

14: ELLA

THE AUCTION

Dark clouds hover over the not-too-distant mountains. In Nubilus' town square, people already crowd the auction blocks while my stomach twists and writhes. People chatter and laugh, waiting for the opening prayer to bless the auction, followed by the drawings for names and numbers from two hats. One hat holds the horses' names, and the other hat contains numbers; together they determine the order of the horses to be auctioned today.

I, along with the rest of the crowd, wait anxiously as they begin drawing the forty-seven horses' names.

Dalia appears at my side, a cloth bag in her hand. "Here. Eat."

"I can't," I mutter, but I accept the pastry she stuffs into my hand anyway and begin to nibble on the edge. "Where's Winter?"

"Back at the inn." Dalia shrugs, her eyes on the platform as they draw the first horse. They draw the number eight. She grimaces. "Said she had to check on someone...or something. I don't know. Said she'd be here soon."

I nod and take another bite, this one bigger than the last. I must be hungry after all.

"Allucea, Aeneas Stables!" The man drawing names from the first hat announces.

I nearly inhale a crumb.

"…will be auctioned…" The man announcing waits for a teen boy to pull the number from the second hat. "Eighteenth!"

I grimace but nod. Having Allucea eighteenth is decent. She's a solid mare, a bit on the high end of value, and she'll be respected in that spot, provided the audience is good.

Soon most of the horses have been drawn and the order arranged, but I still have Letifer's filly. I glance at the board with growing dread. There are three spots remaining: forty-seventh, fortieth, and twenty-sixth.

"Espoir, Aeneas Stables!" calls the announcer. "And let's see what number she—oohh. Forty-seventh."

I groan. Someone claps me on the shoulder.

"Don't worry 'bout it," the man says. "She's a good horse. She'll sell. As a broodmare if nothing else."

I cast him a quick, awkward smile, recognizing him as a groom at one of the other stables. Of course he wouldn't worry about it—all his boss's horses will be auctioned by then. But even if Espoir does sell, it won't be for as much money as I hoped. She will have no chance of being the top bid.

Not until people begin talking and milling around me do I realize the final horses have had their order announced and marked on the large board before us. Some in the audience are wandering off toward the food stands. Their horses probably aren't due up soon, or else they won't be bidding at all.

Dalia reaches for me. "Are you all right?"

"Forty-seventh?" I reply. "That's—"

"Fine," she says firmly. "It will be fine."

I fix her with incredulity. "How? Dalia, no one will have money to spend on Espoir. She's my best—"

"You don't know what—"

A couple of passersby glance our way.

"Just watch and see," Dalia says.

I bite back the complaint on my tongue. If everyone holds back, it hurts the entire auction, not just Espoir.

"Come on, Ella, things will turn out fine. Just wait and see. And if not all of your horses sell today, you sell them in the spring auctions." Dalia squeezes my arm reassuringly. "Trust me. You won't end up here. You'll be running your stable until the day you die. Now come on."

Her words don't make me feel better. If my horses don't sell today, then I won't have enough money to keep the stable going until the spring auctions. I let her pull me along to the market stalls, where she buys me a hot, sweet cider to ward off the chill of the autumn morning and the worry of the encroaching clouds. By the time the auction has begun, Winter has found us and says that Gavin's keeping an eye on the horses to make sure they're not spooked and that spectators are leaving them alone.

I shudder. Where is my head?

"Don't worry, Ella," Winter says calmly, her face implacable. "I made sure they are safe."

Given her example of power this morning, I don't know how to take her words. Does she lie to make me feel better? Or has she cast a spell to keep them safe? Neither reassures me.

Winter tilts her head. "They're safe. And you're…very worried." She smiles and pats my hand in a grandmotherly sort of gesture. "It will be fine. Your horses are the prettiest here today."

As the two of them drag me to an empty market stall where we can view the entire city square, Sir Birch steps up to the podium and spreads his hands wide. "Welcome, residents and visitors of Nubilus. It is lovely to see you all gathered here to support the town and to, I hope, buy exactly forty-seven horses."

A chuckle ripples through the crowd.

"I won't talk too long, but today we have forty-seven excellent horses for you. We have eight stables participating in the autumn auctions, one more than last year. A big welcome to Aeneas Stables for joining us."

A scattering of applause answers.

I flush, averting my eyes from the audience. They don't mean it. At least, Sir Birch doesn't. I wonder if anyone else hears the bitterness in his voice or if it's just me. But judging by Winter's narrowed eyes and Dalia's thinned lips, they hear it, too.

Sir Birch says a few more words, talking about the history of the auctions and its importance to the city of Nubilus, how it was founded on horses and by the work and skills of the horses we breed. "So without much more ado, and in the hopes that the rains stay at bay for the next several hours, I'm going to hand the podium over to Mr. Priseur, who will be leading us through this auction for the twentieth year in a row."

Cheers go through the crowd at this, along with cries of "Let's get started!" and "Bring out the first horse!"

I sip my now-cool cider, trying to calm my nerves, glancing at the shadowed clouds only a few miles away.

"Don't worry," Winter repeats from beside me. She seems to glow a little as she says it.

Somehow, as I hold her ice-blue gaze, I find my worry lessened. When my first horse prances up to the auction block, admiring whistles flit through the spectators. Winter's hands twitch and I think I see a hint of a glow to her skin. A surge of hope lifts my heart.

"Let's start the bidding at"—Mr. Priseur consults his list and a twitch crosses his face—"at three hundred."

A murmur runs through the crowd before the first hand is raised by a thin, well-groomed man. "Three hundred," he calls in a quavering voice.

From either side, hands slip into mine. One Dalia's, one Winter's. Gripping them both, I watch the bidding rise from three hundred to just reach the one thousand reserve I placed on the mare. I need my six horses to bring back no less than ten thousand coins today. A thousand is nowhere near enough. Panic rises in me again, thick and grasping as quicksand.

When the bidding ends, I let go of Dalia and Winter's hands, wiping my sweaty palms on my trousers.

"That mare should have sold for twice that," Dalia mutters angrily.

Winter doesn't reply but peers at the crowd, searching faces as though she's looking for someone in particular.

"Is something wrong?" I ask when she begins to scowl.

"What?" Her eyes round and fix on me. "Wrong? Oh, nothing. I mean, except for the fact that your mare should have brought in two thousand coins instead of one. If that's wrong, then yes."

Impulsively, I lean forward and wrap my arms around her in a hug. I don't dare admit my disappointment to myself—not yet. But her loyalty when she knows nothing of Ardor means the world to me.

When I let go of her, a frown creases the pale, smooth skin of her forehead. "Are you all right, Ella?"

I laugh; I cannot help it. "Yes, Winter. Thank you. I am."

"If you say so," she muses, turning her gaze back to the crowd, but interjecting a glance toward me every now and then, checking.

Her protection and her confidence in my animals, whether misguided or true, lifts both my spirits and my hope.

"If you had all the money in the world, Ella, what would you do with it?" Winter suddenly asks.

I blink at her odd question. "What?"

"Just tell me. If you had all the money you needed—more than you needed—if you never had to breed another horse, what would you do?"

I contemplate my answer as the horse before my next one prances across the stage and sells for fifteen hundred coins. Winter doesn't prompt me again, patiently waiting my answer. Then the bidding on my second horse begins. "I would breed horses," I murmur as the auctioneer announces the starting bid. "Geli or not, I don't think I could stop."

Winter grins but doesn't take her eyes from the auction stage. "I was hoping you'd say that."

It takes only until the seventeenth horse to present one that doesn't meet his reserve and returns to the pens unsold. Dalia tucks her hand into mine. "Allucea will sell, don't worry," she murmurs as my mare is led into the square.

When bids close for Allucea at nearly two thousand, my hope rekindles. Dalia pulls me into a huge hug.

Hours later, we still have five horses to go, and I have one horse left to pull in a full third of the money I need. All my hopes are on Espoir, yet the sky has darkened ominously, and the crowd is already thin and purse-poor. Many of the big bidders have gone to celebrate in the pubs or to ready themselves for the next masque. Some who haven't gotten the horses they want are already checking out of their inn rooms on the edge of the square, tying bundles to pack horses. New purchases aren't handed over until the morning, when all paperwork is completed and Sir Birch signs their exit papers. Then they are checked again at the gates.

A heavy wind whips through the square, rustling cloaks and dresses. Several people glance at the clouds and exchange worried looks. Tonight, even nature is against me. Clouds have been darkening all day and now gather what must be only a few miles away.

My hope in a mere flicker now. There's no way Espoir will be the highest-selling horse of the entire auction. I might not have questioned that sum if she had been one of the first ten horses to sell, or even the second set of ten, but she's the very last horse. There are less than a dozen men remaining in the square, the sun dips toward the horizon, and dark clouds obscure what little light it gives.

My stomach growls. Even though Winter and Dalia have

brought me food throughout the day, skirting in and out of the crowd to visit the merchants selling foods and drinks, I haven't been able to eat with my stomach in such knots. Now I wish I had, but the same idea turns my stomach into another knot.

I twist a lock of my hair around my finger so tightly my fingertip goes cold.

Horse forty-six, one of Lord Sarcina's horses is called and led to the block. Of course. His horse being next to last explains the crowd. Even though Espoir is flashy with her silvery coat and muscled body that makes a sheen every time she moves, there is no way that a dozen men are interested in my mare, despite her sire.

My lip is bloody where I've been chewing on it for hours, and so I turn to the inside of my cheek. Lord Sarcina's horse creates a flurry of bidding with half the men, and when it ends, several of them throw up their hands.

"Too rich for me!" one announces, laughing with another who hadn't been bidding.

I look to the auctioneer. The stallion, a reddish roan with a golden hue to his coat and a slight wildness to his eyes, surveys the crowd and tosses his head in the air.

"Sold!" the auctioneer cries, pointing to the man who's purchased him. "For the sum of two thousand coin! An astonishing sum for so late in the auction. And a steal for a stallion of such bloodline."

My body has gone hot and cold at once. "I'll never get it," I murmur.

"Shh," Winter says, glancing around the square, some men are moving to leave, while a half dozen men mingle at the departing merchants' tables. "You must have faith, Ella. In yourself and in your country."

I turn to her in despair. "Faith? I know what my horses are but does anyone else?" The skys above swirl and darken as the distant clouds that have been threatening all day continue their advancement.

She smiles in a strangely infuriating way. "Have faith. I think you are more beloved than any of the other stable owners."

I blow out a breath through loose lips. What does she know? She's been in Nubilus for mere weeks, while I have spent my life here. Small raindrops plop on the ground a few feet from me, then one hits my cheek. Not now. Please not now.

"Wait, don't go, gentlemen! It's just a little rain, and it's now it's time for our final sale of the day!" Mr. Priseur calls out as the winner steps forward to take care of the details of his purchase.

A couple men wave dismissively at him.

"No coin left!" another jokingly calls.

I shake my head. If I wouldn't be penalized at the next auction, and if I didn't need the coin, I would remove Espoir now in the hopes of a better auction next time. But all my hope lies on her.

I don't look behind me at the buyers left; I can't. Even if there is only one buyer, I can make my reserve.

"We'll be starting this animal—wow, this impressive mare of four years' age—at the very reasonable bid of seven-fifty."

I grit my teeth. I should have set a higher opening bid. I hadn't expected her to be last. Now, if there's only one buyer, she won't fetch more than this opening bid.

"Are there any takers?"

There's stoney silence in the square, except for the rustle of animals and a soft wind that blows through.

"Seven-fifty? You, sir? You, ma'am?" the auctioneer attempts. "Seven-fifty? This animal is granddaughter to the legendary Mythos. A breeding like that is worth at least seven-fifty alone. The dam was a prized sporting horse in her youth, and the sire is an up-and-coming stud through Nubilus—"

"One thousand coin," a man's voice says.

The auctioneer stops speaking, peering over his half-sized glasses to locate the bidder. "I'm sorry, who—"

I turn as well, scanning the crowd.

"Fifteen hundred coins," a second voice says.

This time, I find the speaker, a well-dressed man that I haven't noticed before, a man who must be a visitor to Nubilus, but who I don't think was part of the twelve that participated in the bidding of the last horse.

"Two thousand coins," the first speaker says.

My knees go weak and I grab for Dalia before I fall, hardly registering the grin splitting Dalia's face.

"Twenty-five hundred," the second man says.

My eyes dart between the two.

"Three," the first answers with a cavalier shrug.

"Four," the second answers simply, a twitch of a smile to his lips under his well-groomed beard.

My knees tremble. Only two horses have passed the four thousand mark in this auction, and both of them belonged to Lord Sarcina and his stables.

"Five," the first answers, turning to the second man with challenge in his eyes.

The second meets the first man's gaze and his jaw flexes. Then it smoothes and he crooks an eyebrow at his competitor. "Six."

The first man's stoic expression breaks and he grins, nodding once to the other man, then turning to Mr. Priseur with a congenial and oddly satisfied look upon his face. He shakes his head at the stunned auctioneer's face.

"Oh, I— Uh, sold! To the man on my left, for…six thousand coin." The flummoxed auctioneer bangs his gavel down, then Dalia and Winter erupt into cheers and grins, drowning me with hugs.

15: BLANCHE

THE STUDY

The door opens into a library. No, a study.

It's empty at the moment, and yet I know with one glance that I have stumbled upon the thing my success needs the most.

I only wish I absorbed more magic on the way here, for now I am exhausted and cannot risk using more from my own stores. No life here either, not yet at least.

A table sprawls out almost immediately before me, spread with papers, quills, and ink, as well as a locked wooden box that reminds me of the one that sits upon my desk at the Merisian Palace.

A slow smile works its way upon my lips. The Ardorian seal? Could it be?

And there, on the table nearby, another box with a lock left unlocked. Curious, I flip it open. A fist-sized wax seal with, yes, the Ardorian seal of King George upon it. I remember it. I have received a message with that seal before. A refusal to trade or sell, I recall. My lips thin before curving upward at my good fortune. I am in the King's study. Too bad he's not here.

A chill of anger caresses me as I examine the room more

closely. Bookshelves full of leather-bound books, titles like *Ardorian Land Laws*, *The History of the Gelu Rigens*— My gaze stutters to a stop upon a book with golden letters. *The History of Edormisco?* What in the Seven Kingdoms would possess King George to keep such a book in his study?

A sound outside turns my head sharply. Footsteps. Booted footsteps, and many of them. The door opens a couple of inches.

"Your Majesty, we're very late as it is," a voice says.

"Yes, yes, I'll just be a moment," the voice nearest the door answers. "I need my papers from my study."

Quickly, I remove the Edormiscan book from the shelf and duck behind a screen in the room. Behind it is a door, and inside, another one of those rooms to relieve oneself. There's nowhere to hide, not if someone enters this room.

I stand, immobile, listening through the closed door as a lighter set of footsteps enter the room. They go to the opposite side of the room. The person rustles around on the table or somewhere around there, and then the footsteps cross toward me. I hold my breath.

The main door squeaks open. "Your Majesty?" a man prompts, his voice daring to be impatient with his monarch.

The King sighs. "Yes?" His voice is alarming near the door to this room.

"We must go. They're waiting."

He inhales as if trying to control his temper. "Fine." His footsteps recede and the door squeaks again before clicking shut.

I wait a moment before emerging from behind the screen. The door is closed tight, the room empty. And the locked box atop the King's desk, gone.

I turn the Edormiscan book over in my hands. Then, tucking it into the pocket of my cloak, I slip out of the room the way the King left. I walk out of the palace without any disguise but an act of pretending like I belong here.

Perhaps one day, I will.

RUINED

The stables are quiet when I put Flora to bed tonight; even Gavin has gone to bed, judging by the dark room he keeps at the front of the stable, and I don't blame him. I complete my work in the stable as quietly as I can and walk up to the house in the burgeoning dark.

The house is quiet when I step inside, with my sisters and mother at the masque, but a low light from the drawing room catches my attention. Bona must have left it on for me when she went to bed, but it's not something she would ordinarily do.

As I near, a low murmur of voices and rustling fill the hall, as though there are many people behind the door. Shadows flash in the crack of light underneath the door. My feet pause. Did Lady Eleanor and my sisters stay home instead? But inside I hear Bona's voice chattering; she would not be with Lady Eleanora or Haydée, or even Carmen. I turn the handle.

"Ella!" Bona's enthusiasm pulls me inside. She grins and reaches for a fluted glass with an over-eager hand. "Pour her a drink, Gav."

His own hand is steady, but a twinkle lightens his eye as he pours me a generous serving of whatever they're drinking.

"What is this?" I ask.

Bona gives me a feigned offended look. "Celebration, girl! Psh!"

I laugh, my giddiness at the success of the day returning as I accept the glass. "Thank you."

"Every horse sold! And *over* their reserves," Bona continues, leaning toward me. "Gavin told me everything."

I grin into my cup. "It's amazing. I couldn't have done it without Gavin, or you, Bona. You kept the house running smoothly, and Gavin, you did so much…"

He raises his glass to me, and we all drink, Bona not stopping until she's emptied her glass.

"For the first time, I'll have enough money to settle all our debts and get us through the winter…maybe even paint the barn."

"I'll drink to bein' paid!" the cook says with a cheery smile.

Her eyes twinkle so I know she's kidding, at least half so. I always make sure the animals are fed, the help is paid, and then pay the rest of the bills—if there's anything left, thanks to my mother and sisters.

"Or maybe a bonus for you two," I say, daring to dream of how much money we'll have left over after paying bills.

"Ach, no, that wouldn't be right," Bona says, shaking her head into her glass with a frown and swaying on her feet as her glass continues to sway though her head is still.

"I'll drink to that," Gavin murmurs and raises his drink.

Giggling, I tap it with my own, then try to tap Bona's moving target.

The bell on the door interrupts us. Gavin rises. "I should go?"

"No, no. You're fine." I wave a hand at him. "Sit. You're here at my invitation. You're in *my* house, remember?" I grin at him, feeling cheeky, perhaps thanks to the liquor. "And who makes the money in this house?"

A true grin lights up his face as he sits back down. Bona slaps him on the knee. "You know better than that."

Gus gives a gruff bark from his place by the door, waiting for me to answer the bell.

"I'm coming," I tell him, brushing a hand over his head as I open the door to the sitting room. His old limbs seem to complain as he trots ahead of me to the front door, but he seems insistent on being in front, and I let him.

Swinging open the door, I blink at a half dozen people from town standing on the doorstep looking wet and rumpled. Gus' growl jars me out of my surprise. "Can I help you?"

A man, the jeweler, I finally recognize him as, steps forward. "Mistress, may we come in? It's a bit damp out here tonight."

"Of course," I say, stepping back to allow them inside the tiled foyer. "Back up, Gus."

Reluctantly, Gus moves, a gruff growl rumbling in his throat. "Hush," I tell him, putting my hand on his head. He licks his lips and sits down, but the tension doesn't leave his body.

As I face the jeweler, he removes his damp hat and beats it on his knee to rid it of the rain.

"How can I help you, Mr. Gemmari?"

"I think we have some business to discuss, Mistress Ella," the wiry-haired man answers.

"Yes, it's been brought to our attention that you've had a very good day at the auction, Mistress Ella," Leah, the mask maker, says.

My breath catches on my lips as I scan the rest of the crowd. I recognize them all. The mask maker, the seamstress, the jeweler, the cobbler, a bar owner, and a shopkeeper who sells trinkets and knickknacks.

"Right." They're here to collect my debts. Or my mother's debts. Not mine. "Well, I'm sure first thing in the morning, we can—"

"We're not waiting any longer," Leah says, crossing her arms. "I won't wait. By morning, you'll have settled every debt but ours. You owe me for six masks already and three more—"

"I wouldn't—" I begin, but overlapping conversation cuts me off.

"That's right," the jeweler says over all the people crowded into our foyer, and the others fall silent to let him speak. "I've extended as far a credit as I can—for too long. But Lady Eleanora—" He breaks off and looks at me, his expression softening. "I tried to believe she'd repay me, Mistress, but if you can't settle this debt, then I'll send my bill to the constable and have your mother arrested for her debts."

I gape at him. "You would turn in my mother as a debtor? Turn *me* in as a debtor?"

"Yes!" Leah agrees, her gaze narrowed. "Your mother has put me into debt—"

"Why continue to sell to her then?" Anger flickers in me, heating my words.

The seamstress looks uncomfortable, her gaze sliding from me to linger on a vase in the entryway.

"Your mother has influence in this city, Miss Ella," says the jeweler. "She has great status in Nubilus, and we…" He trails off with a darting glance away.

"What has she promised you?" I ask.

All the merchants avert their gazes, and realization dawns over me.

"You fear her. All of you."

The jeweler glares at me. "Of course we do. We live on the goods of this city, and your mother holds great power."

"Does she? *I* am the eldest daughter, Mr. Gemmari, the heir. So why has your fear never extended toward me? Am I too kind?" I glare at them, trying to meet each of their gazes in turn, daring them to tell me, challenging them.

All my frustrations of the past weeks, Winter's duplicity, the stress over the auction, the prince's deception, and everything else starts to boil over in my stomach.

"Tell me, please, am I too kind?" My voice cracks.

The seamstress softens. "No, Miss Ella. No. I—it's not that. It's that we all must live. We cannot keep extending credit to your mother when she—"

"She doesn't control the money," Mr. Gemmari says bluntly. "You do."

"So why do I not have your respect? It's your own fault if you know who controls the money and then don't refuse a line of credit to the one that doesn't."

A shopkeeper and the cobbler exchange glances.

From behind, Gavin's clomping boots announce his arrival. I half glance at him, emboldened by his calm presence.

"I— Miss Ella, please, understand that we all must live—" the shopkeeper says.

"My mother holds no power over you." I glower at them. "Or does she?"

Gavin steps up beside Gus. His even breathing is peaceful and reassuring, but I don't let it calm me. I want to be strong on my own, to come into that strength and respect that I deserve. I'm tired of cowering and being cowed.

My hands clench into fists at my side, even as I war with regret. I don't want to pay them their money, but they are no different than I. They have simply trusted the wrong person, just as I trusted Sir Birch to keep my money safe for the auctions, they trusted Lady Eleanora to pay them. Should I punish them like Sir Birch punished me? At the thought, my stomach clenches further. In addition to paying these creditors, I have Dalia to repay for half my auction fee.

None of these people have done wrong—Mother has. She is the one who has opened lines of credit without any money, who has purchased things she hasn't needed, who has—

I close my eyes. "How much do I owe you?"

"Miss Ella," Gavin says from beside me, his voice a warning.

I face him and find Bona standing behind us, her arms

crossed and expression mutinous, but worry underneath her demeanor.

Gavin leans closer to me and says in an undertone, "Tell them to bring their charges to the bank. The bank will sort it out."

I shake my head before he's even done speaking. "They will report us to the debtors, and then..." I clench my fist to keep from motioning at the home we stand in, as I imagine not it, but the stables outside as I speak. "They'll take it all, Gavin. The horses will go first."

His gaze darts at the crowd of merchants, at once fearful and resigned. "They wouldn't..."

I don't answer, but give him a sad smile and turn to the merchants. "What does my mother owe you?"

A couple of them flinch at my wording, but each put forth the debts to me, and by the time I've paid them each, I want to weep. They've not left me enough to live on, not enough to feed the horses for the year and pay the bills.

My mother has ruined us.

PART IV

1: WINTER

A QUEEN'S PLAN

Thanks to Dalia's quick, skilled work with a needle throughout the week, along with her uncanny ability to sneak into Ella's manor house and steal dresses from Carmen and Haydée, all three of us girls have ready-made dresses for the third masque, once we make a few critical alterations, of course.

Dalia sits in a corner of her bedroom, squinting down at the hem of a maroon dress she shortens for herself. As the shortest of us, she had her choice of any of the dresses, but she insisted on taking whatever dress was left, saying it would be easier to shorten a dress than to lengthen one.

I chose one from Haydée's trunk: a golden dress that could almost be fit for a princess. Ella's dress is shimmery blue, voluminous dress that Dalia found in Carmen's room. I anticipate it bringing out the blue of Ella's eyes with flattering precision.

The third dress is a slightly matronly maroon gown with lace for Dalia. Though she claims it came from Carmen's rooms, I wonder if it was actually Lady Eleanora's at some time. Somehow, the motherly look suits Dalia, though she spent the majority of yesterday ripping off the lace and sewing glass beads on it instead. Pleased with the state of my dress and its fit, and convinced that Ella's will flatter her, I spend most of my time changing a few key components to the gowns in case Haydée and Carmen recognize their former dresses.

"Ouch." Dalia grunts and pops her finger into her mouth with a wrinkle of her nose.

"All right?" I ask, glancing over.

"Hmm." Dalia checks her finger and resumes her work only to throw it down into her lap a moment later. "Do you think Ella will even go?"

I grimace. "I…I think she wants to see the prince again." I pull a string of thread off its spool and sever it with my teeth.

"You do?" Dalia stabs her needle into the hem and tugs it out again.

"Yes." I inject more certainty into the word than I feel and thread my needle.

Dalia snorts. "She's hardly mentioned the whole thing to me. You've told me almost everything I know."

I lift my head and study her, but her expression is closed, guarded, as usual. "Should I not have told you?"

"No, you should have." Dalia sighs and tears off the thread with her teeth. "I want to help her, and the best way is to bring her to the masque. Isn't it?"

I open my mouth to reply, but she doesn't wait for my answer and pushes ahead.

"But there's no chance of getting her there without her knowledge. She has to get dressed…" Dalia points at Ella's dress, finished and waiting on the bed.

"Yes." I frown at my own hemming and tie a knot in my thread. "If she doesn't want to go, then we won't force her."

"We won't?" Dalia seems surprised at my response. Her gaze skims over me from head to toe, as if sizing me up.

Something uncomfortable prickles over me, and I shift in my seat. It felt almost like…magic. I narrow my gaze at her and the feeling stops. "No," I say. "We won't force her. I don't want to force my friends to do anything." I spread the fabric between my fingers to pick the next spot for my needle. "Even if I think it's for her own good, I'm not going to make her go. I think we owe her that, don't we?" I meet Dalia's gaze. "For all the things she's done for us and the questions she hasn't asked?"

Dalia lowers her hands to her laps and looks at me. "How much do you know about me?"

I lift a shoulder. "Not much, why?"

"What have you been told though? Or what have you…guessed?"

I turn my attention back to my sewing. "You're not from here. I'm guessing you're Edormiscan, or as close to it as you can get these days with the country under the sleeping sickness. And you've run from something. Family, enemies, I don't know. But I recognize that look in your eye. You don't want to get close to people because you don't want to hurt them, whether because someone finds you, or because you have to leave one day. You're abrasive because of it. It's why you first hated me. Oh. And you have magic." I lift my gaze. "Am I close?"

Dalia is sitting back and staring at me with something like admiration. "Not at all."

I tilt my head, but she doesn't elaborate, and I almost laugh. Instead, I resume my tiny little rows of stitches that are nearly invisible along the sleeve.

"You're spot-on," she whispers.

Rapid footsteps in the hallway outside the room turn our heads. Dalia jumps, but before either of us can react, a quick knock on the door precedes a familiar voice.

"Winter? Winter are you in there?"

"I—yes." I stand and set aside the dress. Before I can make it to the door, it opens and Brunnea steps through, shutting it quickly behind her as though she's been followed.

Dalia frowns up at the Fae. "What are you doing here?"

Brunnea gives her a look that seems to tell her to be quiet, almost like a mother uses to warn a child.

"What's happened, Brunnea?" I ask.

"Blanche. She's near."

"Yes, I know—" I begin.

"No. I know what she's doing now. I know why she's been after you. And I know who she'll go after next."

A chill as cold as Canens runs its hands over me. "What do you mean? Why is she after anyone else? She's just after me, isn't she?"

"She's trying to break a spell." Brunnea shakes her head and paces the room, ignoring Dalia as if she's not even there. "There's a spell in place to prevent any one person from becoming ruler over all the Seven Kingdoms."

I stay silent. I know of the law, but I thought it was just law, not a law backed by a spell. Back when I wasn't sure about spells and magic, I assumed those things were simple laws, put in place by man and enforced by man. "Am I supposed to believe now that the Fae put spells in place to prevent the land from being ruled by one ruler?"

"Of course we did, princess!" Brunnea snaps.

I start and flush. I hadn't meant to speak aloud, especially not with such a disrespectful tone. "I'm sorry, Brunnea. I didn't— I'm just confused. I don't understand what she's doing. Or why."

"My dear, why did you not learn these things as a young princess?"

I open my mouth, but she cuts me off.

"Oh, dear, I'm not really asking. It just would have been so much easier if all the royals were, like the Edormiscans, taught about the magic that constantly affects their days."

"I didn't even know magic could be good." I lift a shoulder and try not to think of the lines I've already crossed knowing what I know. How dark is my soul already? "At least, you claim it can be good. I'm still not entirely convinced."

Brunnea pauses her pacing to give me a sad look. "Yes, dearest, I know."

"But what is Blanche doing? Why are you so worried?"

"She's trying to break the Seven Kingdoms spell. She's trying to become the Empress of the Seven Kingdoms."

"How? Is that even possible?" Dalia interjects.

Brunnea ignores Dalia's interruption. "The spell is a closely guarded secret, but many things have changed since it was first cast. Alliances have been forged and broken. Countries have risen and fallen. Not on this continent, of course, but elsewhere."

"What—?" I begin, mind reeling.

She waves away my confusion with an impatient strike of her hand. She's talking completely over my head, and she knows it.

"There is no possibility of Blanche knowing of the curse except through Fae intervention," Brunnea continues. "No one but one of the thirteen could tell her what's needed, of course. I didn't put it together until just now, until poor Aeria..."

"Fae intervention?" I ask. "You mean that Blanche has a Fae helping her? A faery like you?"

Brunnea's jaw sets and her lips thin. "It is the only solution. But I do not know who might dare... Not unless..." Her face pales and she closes her eyes, putting a hand to her forehead. "I pray it is not so. If it is, it will take the remaining twelve sisters to defeat her."

Brunnea turns as if to depart, her mission clear.

"Wait, Brunnea!" I hurry toward her, reaching out a hand. "You haven't told me— What must I do?"

She gives me a confused look, like she isn't quite sure how I came to be there. "You continue what we talked about. But you must get them all to ally with you. All the kings, all the royals. The only hope we have is to unite against Blanche and..." She trails off.

"And what?" I ask, my stomach utterly filled with dread now. "What do you fear so much? Whom?"

A long moment passes where Brunnea neither answers nor

moves. Her shoulders droop, her spine curves, and her chin dips toward her chest.

Then she raises sorrowful eyes to me, which slide to linger on Dalia before returning to me, unmoving. "One of my sisters let the lure of dark magic captivate her. She is a Great Fae turned evil. And she would like nothing more than to rule all the Seven Kingdoms herself, despite the Fae laws. I have no doubt she intends to break the spells put there to protect all humanity and place your stepmother as Empress. Fae law states that no one man or woman can rule the Seven Kingdoms. But we never intended to guard against the Fae themselves—we all made vows that have their own consequences should we break them. If Blanche succeeds, if the other countries fall, then all is lost, Winterberry. All. No life would be worth living should Ceara ascend to any throne. Man or Fae."

Her words chill me to the bone. It's only when Dalia's eyes go to my hands that I realize I've lost control. Every surface of my exposed skin glows.

"Don't lose heart, dear." Sadly, Brunnea gives me a pat on the cheek and leaves as quickly as she entered.

"What do I do?" I whisper as the glow slowly fades.

"Let's use those advantages to our advantage and convince Ella to go to the ball," Dalia answers for Brunnea. "If you intend for Prince Brann to ally with us, I think it's Ella who holds the key."

A reluctant yet unhappy smile on my lips answers Dalia, and the light continues to fade, taking my anxiety along with it.

"You're right," I say. "That's how we'll get her there. And how we'll convince an entire kingdom to fight evil. And then we'll get another kingdom to fight her. And another. Until we all unite against Blanche."

Dalia grins, exposing her sharp teeth.

Before evil overcomes us all, I add silently.

Aloud, all I say to Dalia is, "Let's get started."

MASKED

As soon as Mother arrives home, I confront her.

"How could you spend so much money on frivolous things?" I demand.

Her eyes round in amazement, then narrow in anger. She drops her fur-lined cloak onto a chair. "You don't understand, Ella, you never have."

I glare at her. "Understand what?"

"That appearances must be kept. Relationships must be developed. If those men we already know will not accept your sisters —or *your* hand in marriage, then I must carve out *new* relationships and impress *new* men to take you on. How do you think I am to do that in tattered, threadbare dresses? It might work for you at the stables," she says, sneering at my work clothing, "but it cannot work for me in town. A man might look past that attire for you because of what you offer, but they won't for me or your sisters."

"You—?"

"Of course I look for myself as well. What am I to do if my daughters don't make good marriages? I have nothing to bring to a man, Ella, think!"

For the first time I can remember, worry dances over her features, darkening her high cheekbones and wrinkling her brow.

"I cannot depend upon your mercy, can I? And if neither Haydée or Carmen make a worthy match?" She shakes her head and leans back to look at the ceiling in despair. Outside a dog barks. And then a sly smile slips onto her lips. "The prince announces his fiancée on Sabbath's Eve, and I intend to have him name one of my worthy daughters."

My stomach drops. Brann is going to announce…?

"And do not delude yourself into thinking that you are worthy of him."

Mother sweeps away, her soft shoes making her departure a mere whisper on the tiled floor.

Through tears pricking my eyes, I watch her disappear, knowing she will never forgive me for Father's love, when it is only because of her own preference for her younger daughters that I strayed outside in the first place.

In the week that follows, I do not speak to Mother or my sisters. I don't know what I will say to them when I see them. I'm ill at the thought of having to give up the horses and my only home, but I cannot think of any other solution. I know Dalia and Noemì would let me live at the inn; I know Dalia would willingly share her room with me, but leaving the stables will break my heart. It already breaks my heart.

The morning of the final masque, I wander into town on Flora. I have to start accepting the truth.

Outside the temple, I tie Flora to the hitching post and give her an absent stroke. I can't imagine a life without horses, but if I sell the stables, if I give up on Father's business, then I will have to give them all up. Even Flora. I won't be able to keep her at the inn—or wherever I go.

I slip inside the temple and find it empty and cool. Just over a week ago, this place was filled with people asking the Lord for a good auction showing or a good horse to buy. Now, they seem to have forgotten to thank him. Or perhaps they already have and I'm too late.

Sighing, I kneel before the altar and pause to reflect on the dancing horses carved on it. The altar dates back several hundred years, or further, I'm not entirely sure. But it goes far beyond my knowledge. Even then, Ardor was built on the backs of horses and, some say, unicorns.

I bend my head, focusing my thoughts more appropriately and silently pray my belated thanks for a successful auction. Then I pour out my heart, confessing my fears of losing Aeneas Stables and having to marry a man I don't love. Is that what I am to do? Marry someone I don't love? I can see no other answer.

Finally, I pull myself off the floor, wiping my eyes and sinking into a pew.

"Miss Eleanora?" a soft voice calls.

I jump to see Father Ciprus emerging from the corner room.

He approaches and stands beside me. "Is there something wrong?"

I sigh. How to start? What to say? I know he would never betray my confidence—he couldn't—but to say my worries aloud makes them too real.

"May I?" He motions to the pew beside me, and I nod, scooting over.

"I'm sorry, but I'm not in a talkative mood, Father."

He smiles and clasps his hands upon his knees. "I know, Miss Ella."

My eyes smart with tears again. "I don't know what to do. I was hoping…" Trailing off, I nod at the altar.

"You were hoping for some answers?"

"Yes," I whisper, tears pricking my eyes.

"Sometimes answers don't come in voices or even images or events. Sometimes it's that little feeling inside of us that suggests the right path." He pauses, staring at the graven horses just as I am. "Is there anything in particular you wonder about, dear? Something I might be able to help you with?"

"Father..." I pause to consider my words. "I don't want to marry."

His brow lifts slightly, but otherwise he shows no indication of shock or dismay like I expect from a fatherly old man. "Are you considering the nunnery?"

"No, Father." I hesitate. "I just can't marry without love."

"Is someone insisting that you enter a loveless marriage, Miss Ella?"

"The law." I shrug as he frowns, trying to follow my thoughts. "If I want to keep the stable..."

"Ah, yes, of course. The Possident Laws." He grimaces. "They are not exactly helpful to you in your state. Is that truly what they say?"

"Yes. 'An orphaned young woman might not legally inherit until she marries and produces a male heir.'" I lift my eyes to the thick, wood-beam vaulted ceiling. "'If a man dies with no male heir, his eldest daughter may inherit in trust until age twenty-two, when the land reverts to the Crown for public sale. Or, if by that time, the female has married and produced a legal male heir of her own, her husband may then control the estate until the male heir comes of age.'"

"And you have found no man in Nubilus worthy?"

I hesitate, thinking of the men in town. "There is no one here that I would marry. No one here that I think I could love."

"Not one?"

I wince thinking of the prince. "No one who would take me, Father."

"Ah." He taps his still clasped hands upon his legs. "So the rumors are true?"

I turn to him. "What rumors?"

"There was a young lady who attended the first masque. A beautiful young lady, with a beautiful gown, full of grace and poise. She conducted herself so like a princess that rumors flew about this town that one of the Ostiite or Teporian or even Heian princesses had come to visit. I even heard a rumor that the Abbatian princess had snuck across all the continent to attend the Ardor masques." He chuckles lightly, although his humor doesn't seem to be at the stupidity of someone thinking me a princess, but someone thinking that real princesses would be interested in coming here in secret. "So tell me, Miss Ella, what is it that concerns you? Has the prince found out?"

"I still don't understand how you knew that it was me... Am I that obvious?"

"My dear. There are few graceful and poised young women in this city that compare with your beauty."

I blink. "I'm sorry, Father, but there are many beautiful young women, such as my sisters..."

"Oh Miss Ella, it's not quite the same. Your hair is very distinct, after all. To anyone that knows you and saw the girl in a mask, you could not have hid."

My frown deepens. "Honestly?"

He winks. "I also might have seen you return home that night."

My shoulders sink in relief. "I see."

"Your mask might have loosened a little bit." He shrugs then smirks. "And after all the rumors I heard, I knew it was you." He tilts his head at me. "But it doesn't explain why you didn't go to the second masque. Or why you aren't at home preparing for the third? Is it not tonight?"

My shoulders slump further. "I don't think—"

"Did something happen to make you flee?"

I weigh what to tell him. "If I tell you, you won't tell anyone, right?"

"It's my oath as a priest, Miss Ella, you know that. I must stay silent and keep your confidence."

Biting my lip, I study his quiet patience and then abandon caution and confess everything. He listens in silence, his hands clasped on his lap, expression soft and gentle, betraying neither shock nor disappointment, not even outrage.

Until I say, "And then the merchants came to the house that night, asking for me to settle Mother's debts."

"What?" His voice is slightly hoarse, as I have spoken for so long.

I explain what happened.

"And you settled them all? All the foolish things your family purchased, you bought them for them?"

"What else was I to do?" I spread my hands. "I couldn't see another option. The debts had to be paid."

"So now you have no choice but to surrender your animals, let them starve, or to turn over your land to the Crown?"

I bow my head.

"Miss Ella, you are a good lady."

"What?"

"Please don't make any decisions until you promise me this one thing."

"What?" I squint at him.

"Go to the masque tonight."

"But, Father—"

"While you have been speaking to me, I have been praying. Go to the masque tonight. I feel strongly that you must go. It may very well change things for you. At the very least, promise me that you will make no decisions about your stable for the next... oh, week. You can wait a week?"

"A week?" I shake my head then shrug. Nothing has to be done today. We have enough money to feed the horses for a month or so. I do not have to make any decisions tonight. "Of course, Father. If it's that important to you, and you feel that strongly, then I will not."

"Thank you, Miss Ella. Now, if you'll excuse me." He rises and smiles down at me. "I have some things I must see to."

Frowning, I rise as well. "Of course, Father. Thank you for listening. I feel a bit better now."

"Don't forget, Miss Ella, go to the masque. And why don't you visit Miss Dalia on the way out of town? I think she's hoping you'll drop by." Before I can say much more, he's hurried me to the exit.

A touch shocked, I leave the temple behind and glance at the town clock tower. It's already past five. The masque starts in only a couple of hours, with tonight being a huge feast followed by a ceremony where, rumor is, Prince Brann will announce his fiancée. My shoulders sag as I glance back at the temple. I promised Father Ciprus I would go. And that I'd visit Dalia before going home.

Oh well. It's not like I need to be on time anyway.

I don't bother mounting Flora on my way to The King's Inn. It's just a few streets over, and I could use the walk after sitting in the temple talking to Father Ciprus for so long. I tie her at the back door so she won't get into the garden and let myself in.

The kitchen is empty but smells of dinner, so either Dalia is out in the pub or else she's set up the pub as a buffet for the few remaining guests. I shrug and head into the hallway toward Dalia's room, calling her name.

"Ella?" Noemì's voice comes from her room. "In here, darling."

With a glance at Dalia's room, I turn instead to the one across from it, and find it empty.

Thinking she is in the garderobe, I return to the kitchen. As I push open the door, my jaw drops to the floor. "Mrs. Caupo!" I exclaim. "What are you doing in here? You shouldn't be making breakfast, you—"

"Oh, Ella, I feel fantastic!" Noemì beams at me, pressing pastry dough out with a rolling pin. "Ever since your friend, Winter, visited me on auction day, I've been able to walk around without pain; it's simply amazing. She has such a gift."

I blink at her, as shocked by her words as I am by the sight of her aged body bustling around the kitchen, slow still, but bustling nonetheless. She reaches for a large pot, but I hurry there first. "Please, Mrs. Caupo, take it easy. I wouldn't want you to injure yourself because you worked yourself too hard back in the kitchen."

"Oh, dear, you're so sweet."

I grab hold of the large, cast iron pot and lug it over to her table. Even for me it's heavy, and I shudder to think of her lugging this full anywhere. "Call me when you want to move this, Mrs. Caupo. Please don't do it yourself."

"Oh, dear." She chuckles. "I'll have Eddie do it."

I frown, wondering who Eddie is, but don't comment as her knife flies over the meats and vegetables just like it used to years before.

"Oh, Dalia's upstairs. She told me to send you up should you happen by. Forgive me, I forgot with my excitement of telling you my news."

"It's fine, Mrs. Caupo, don't worry. I'm just grateful to see you so energetic and…healthy again." There's no other word for it. She appears like the picture of health. I know it's impossible, but she even seems to have put some weight on since I last saw her. I give her a lingering glance before heading for the kitchen door.

"Room four, dear," she calls after me, tossing me a smile that has a definite glimmer of mischievousness in her eye.

Confused, and feeling a bit like I'm walking into a trap she's orchestrated for me, I head up the narrow, wooden steps to the top floor of the inn. At room four, I knock. "Dalia? Are you in there?"

"Ella?" Dalia's voice answers a second later. The voice precedes a flurry of rustling and tapping from inside.

"Yes, it's me. Mrs. Caupo said—"

"Hold on, Ella, just a second!" Dalia answers.

More rustling and tapping, a muted voice, and then the door

flings open and Dalia jumps out, grabbing my arm and dragging me inside before kicking the door shut with a toe after us.

"Where have you been?" she demands, hands on her hips. "I've been searching all over for you, and just returned to the inn now."

"What—what is going on, Dalia?" I half laugh at her indignant stance.

Then my laughter fades at the sight before me. The double bed is spread with three gowns, three masks, and at the base of the bed are three pairs of dancing shoes, which have a distinctly magical whiff to them.

Winter stands off to one side, looking determined, but with the faintest lines of dread creasing her face, as though her stomach is knotted.

"What is this? Why…?" I spread a hand at the gowns. "Dalia, Winter, I—" I shake my head but stop when Winter steps forward. Her hair has small, white flowers laced into impossibly tiny braids that pull it back from her face.

"Ella, I need your help." She motions to Dalia. "We need your help."

"My help?" I shake my head again. "You must have the wrong person. I'm just a horse breeder."

Winter raises a brow. "A very successful one. Whom the prince loves."

"Well, not anymore. I'm not even a horse breeder anymore."

"What are you talking about?" Dalia asks.

I shake my head. I promised the Father that I wouldn't make any decisions for a week. "Wait…" I glance between them. "Did you talk to Father Ciprus?"

Dalia and Winter both remain stoic, but I think I sense a touch of guilt in Dalia's eyes.

I sigh. Even if they did, they're probably right—all three of them. No one will win by me rushing into a decision. I should at least wait until after the masque, until after Brann announces his fiancée. My stomach twists as I look at my friends and make my decision.

"What do you need me to do?" I ask.

Dalia and Winter exchange a look, then Winter says, "We need you to go to the masque tonight."

I open my mouth, then shut it. "All right."

"I—" Winter gapes at me. "All right?"

"Yes. I'll go."

She shakes her head, confusion knitting her brows together.

"What?" I ask.

"I thought it would take much more than that to convince you. At least take explaining our plan to you," Dalia says.

"An hour ago, it would have. Wait, what plan?"

Winter's brows creases deeper, but Dalia shakes her head, steps forward, and pulls me farther into the room. "Come, we must get you cleaned and dressed for the masque," she says. "And we have to fill you in. We'll already be late as it is."

Nearly two hours later, they have told me their intentions, the three of us are dressed in our gowns with cloaks concealing us entirely, and we are climbing into a small, covered carriage out front of The King's Inn.

I smirk to recognize Midnight and Moonlight at the helm, matching Ardorian geldings I usually put my sisters on when they wish to ride. Peering through my mask at the driver, warmth floods me to recognize Gavin's broad shoulders and dark, slightly wavy hair brushing his neck.

"Have the invitations?" There's the slightest tremor in Winter's voice as we near the palace. She has grown more withdrawn the closer we get, undoubtedly worried about our plan. So am I; I have just as much depending on it.

Dalia answers by holding up three invitations, which shake in the motionless air of the enclosed carriage. Her black masque is decorated with silvery faux jewels and lines of silver, finished with unmoving silver lips, all lightening the darkness of it. Her eyes, dark, forest green, shine out from the slits, brimming with determination.

"How did you get three—?" I begin, then hold up a hand and shake my head. "Never mind. I probably don't want to know."

It's odd not to see Dalia's answering grin. I'm not entirely sure I like masques…but it does at least hide my nervousness. I think.

In another few minutes, we're disembarking with the help of a palace servant. Standing on the palace steps waiting for Winter and Dalia to join me, I can't help but think of the first masque, when hope overflowed from inside me. Tonight, there's a fair share of dread mixed with that hope. I'm not sure what will happen, but it won't be like that first ball.

"Ready?" Winter's quiet voice startles from beside me.

"Yes," I say before she can say more. "I'm ready."

"Good." She pats my arm and then leads the way up the steps with certain steps.

THE PALACE

The Nubilus palace is bedecked with lights, candles burning in sconces, hanging from the ceiling on long chains, setting the palace aflame. The light glitters off the sparking jewels on the guests, lighting up hair and necks, even dresses, whatever is laced with gemstones. My gaze skips ahead of the crowd toward the raised dias where three thrones crouch. They are simple chairs, not at all like the glittery, carved, gemstone-riddled honor of Canens' throne, nor with half the history of my throne.

But for now, it's the man and woman sitting in the two larger ones that catch my interest. The man is large and modestly bearded and stoic in appearance. He has forgone a mask tonight, though he wears a flowing black tunic that reminds me of some sort of fowl. The woman beside him is his foil: small, with a round face and large eyes, hair that goes to her waist and an innocent appearance to her face despite her age. Yes, I can see them as the princess' parents quite clearly now.

Silvanus touches my elbow, his question evident in his fingers as if I can read his thoughts through them.

I nod and leave him at the door, gliding closer to the throne to complete the task that only I can do as he stands a discreet guard behind me.

Slowly, blending into the chattering crowd of Ardorites, I make my way toward the front of the ballroom. The third throne remains empty throughout my approach. The prince must not plan to reveal himself until later tonight.

I scan the crowd for him, but with everyone wearing masks, it's an impossible game, especially not knowing his attire. I'm not sure I would recognize him even if he were unmasked; his image has never been widely circulated, like his parents could ever have protected him.

A line of guards before the dias prevents me from getting within a dozen feet from the royal family, but I can accomplish my task from that distance.

Snagging a flute from a passing servant, I briefly admire the glittering pink liquid before taking a sip. It bubbles on my tongue, exploding in a rush that makes me gulp in surprise. Trying not to cough, I peer at the raised dais where the King and Queen of Ardor sit upon their thrones, gazing down their noses at their people with all the arrogance their natural births allotted them.

My gaze slides from the royal couple to where Silvanus stands alongside the door. My vision of him flits through dozens of dancers, and I squint against the gems caught in the lights to see him better. He raises his hand to scratch his ear, and I place my half-empty flute on a passing servant's tray.

Feigning that I've dropped something, I edge backward toward the line of guards before the King and Queen, bumping into the closest guard.

"Are you all right, ma'am?" he asks.

"Oh, I apologize. I dropped my fan." I step past him, to the foot of the dais as I speak. My hand with its applewood bracelet extends, and I whisper the words I've planned for weeks.

"Oh, ma'am, you must not cross this line." The guard repositions himself between me and the occupied thrones.

"Oh, I apologize," I repeat as I move back onto the correct side. The spell is already cast; it matters not where I stand now. Through my mask, I bat my eyes at him, acting demure. Even without my magic, the guard hesitates and half smiles in answer.

Before he can otherwise respond or recapture his ground, I move away through the crowd, my imaginary lost fan forgotten.

As I pass through the entrance to the ballroom, Silvanus is gone, preparing for the next step in our plan like an intricate dance to which only we know the steps.

A smile plays on my lips.

Only we know.

4: ELLA

THE MASQUE

Winter weaves through the guests, pausing every half dozen groups only to pause and point at a man who resembles the prince in body type or color hair. "Could that be him?" she asks.

The answer is always, "No." It's easy for me to identify him. So easy that my heart breaks, and yet I can't find him.

Then there's a gentle squeeze on my elbow, and Winter leans close.

"There."

This time, it's not a question.

Following her gaze, I suck in a breath. There he stands. His midnight-blue tunic crisp and clean with silvery and golden threads along the hems. He stands beside another man, taller than the prince, with a white mask half hidden by golden feathers. I recognize him by his hair as Tobiah, the man he came to the stables with last time, his best friend, he called him.

A half dozen women stand around the men, engaging Tobiah in conversation as much as they engage the prince. The noblewomen are richly dressed, and I can't help but glance down at myself in comparison. But where I keep my mask tight on my face, at least half the women have exposed their faces, some removing their masks completely, others pushing them up over their hair. Better to reveal their beauty now that they know he's looking for a wife, for perhaps their beauty will be what turns them from a lady into a princess. The thought saddens me.

"Come on." Dalia pulls me forward.

"No." The word escapes me before I can tell it not to. This is what I'm here for.

Dalia halts. "What?"

"I—I can't. He—" I lift a limp hand toward him and let it fall back down. "I can't. He could love one of those women…"

Dalia steps back to me, facing me. "He loves *you*. And it's time you acknowledge that."

"No, I— What do you expect him to do? How can I matter in this plan? Do you really need me?" The words slip from my lips, unbidden. I want to help Winter, but I don't want him to break my heart and extinguish the flame of my hope.

Her eyes narrow behind their mask. "Just wait here." In a moment, she darts through the crowd and appears at Brann's side as if through magic. When she bobs a curtsy, he barely glances at her. Then he lifts his chin, his shoulders tense, and he searches the crowd. When he sees me, he stops.

I half lift a hand to him, ignoring the people floating through in the distance between us. A woman swathed in a golden gown pauses before me. When she moves, he is leaning his head down toward Dalia, but his eyes are still on me.

I want to call out to him. My heart aches, as if the muscle itself swells and not just the emotion contained within it.

He nods brusquely at Dalia, then moves through the crowd toward me without so much as a look back at his party.

He stops in front of me. I look up at him, tears pricking my eyes. I want to see his face, to see the man that I fell in love with, but the mask makes it impossible. He speaks, but his voice is so muffled that I tilt my head in confusion.

With an annoyed huff, he rips off the mask and throws it into a nearby group of guests. A few startled women look over before they shriek and scramble for the abandoned mask. He tries to speak again, but I cannot hear. He glowers at the guests and takes my arm, leading me out to the balcony. I let him; I cannot tear my gaze from him, trusting him to take me through the crowd parting before us. Every few steps, he looks down at me, searching my face and only tears his gaze away when forced.

Outside in the cool autumn air, he guides me to a quiet corner of hedges. He gently disentangles my arm from his, only to immediately take both my hands in his. "Ella." His face softens.

I flush behind my mask at the emotion in his voice. I duck into a deep curtsy. "Your Highness."

"No. Don't—" He pulls me up from my position, his body slumping, his smile disintegrated behind his frown. "I'm so sorry, Ella. I should have— I nearly— I just—" He stops and fixes me with agony on his face. "Curses, Ella, I don't know what I've been thinking. But, seeing you here, seeing you in the middle of all these beautiful women—" He pauses, tipping my chin up and my head back. "Ella, I made a grave mistake."

"No, Your Highness—"

"Brann. Call me Brann. I know I've given you other names, but call me Brann." The earnestness in his words is so clear that I cannot deny him this.

I smile faintly at his use of "names," as if he has admitted outright to being Hadwin as well. I knew I was right all along. It could only have been him. My hope surges back into an inferno. "Brann. All right."

His lips curve into a smile, but the pain still remains.

"But I must...there are many things to explain, I think. Before you continue."

Brann nods. "Yes. I agree, I—"

"No, Brann, I mean that I have things to say."

"Oh. Of course. Go on."

I hesitate, torn between what Winter told me to say and what I actually want to say. "Brann, I love you."

"Oh, Ella, I love you, too. I'm so relieved to hear you say that. This time apart has given me such clarity—"

"I have loved you almost since I first saw you," I continue. "After my father died, and we spent so many long evenings in the woods, escaping our responsibilities."

A grin splits his face. He opens his mouth.

"But you are currently mortal enemies with my friend."

He shuts his mouth with a snap.

"My friend who saved my life at the masque."

He makes a scoffing sound, but I hold up a hand.

"If you love me, you will listen to me." I wait for him to speak, but he only presses his lips together. "Winter risked her own life, confessed her own identity to find me and save me, and then explained to me why, risking my hatred and yours, to save both our lives." My heart stutters in my chest at what I am saying, at how close to treason it is. "If you love me, you will listen to this."

He draws in a deep breath, his hands still clutching mine firmly. "I'm listening, Ella. But I don't have to agree with you."

I hesitate, then push up my mask and inch up on my tiptoes. Before I can change my mind, I kiss him gently on the lips. Pulling back, I open my eyes and smile a small smile at him. "I had to do that just once more."

A fierce look creases his face, then he dips his head and captures my lips with his, clutching the back of my neck with one hand and pulling me against him with the other around my waist. I don't know how long passes, but finally he pulls back only to rest his forehead against mine.

With tears streaming down my cheeks, I pull away. He

watches me, pain on his face, but I don't wait to hear what he might say. I can't. Instead, I look toward the edge of the balcony where we agreed that Winter would wait.

Through my tears, I see her blurry image step out of the shadows.

5: WINTER

ALLY

I emerge from my hiding spot, my mask dangling from my hand.

Prince Brann's eyes round with fury, his face moving so quickly from adoration to hatred that I flinch inwardly.

"I let you go last time, but why would you ever think I'd let you go again?" he growls.

My gaze slides to Ella with tears streaming down her face. Those kisses weren't in our plan, and while I was pleased, thinking she was convincing him of her love for him and how she wouldn't harm him or their country, now I'm not so sure. He seems ready to kill me simply to protect Ella.

"Brann," she says. "Please listen. She is here for the good of us all. You must listen."

He spares her a glance, and his expression softens just for that moment. I allow myself the smallest measure of hope I haven't felt since Ella's success at the auction. Brann loves her, whether he's confessed that to her or not, whether she believes it or not. But now I stand before him, vulnerable. His love does not extend to me.

"I saved Ella's life," I remind him now. "And the life of someone else you love."

He squares his shoulders at me. "What are you talking about?"

"We have a mutual friend. His name is Cito."

"Cito? Yes." Brann straightens, his mouth turning down in suspicion. "I spoke to him recently…"

I nod. "And Cito has two mutual friends of ours: Rus and Elaina Solem?"

He huffs. "I wondered how he knew about the masques. He did not give me many answers." A small smile twists his lips, but it is not a pleased smile. "You sent him."

"He didn't tell you?" I feel a surge of smugness. "I expected him to break. He wanted to confess everything. To trust you right away."

Brann blows out a breath. "No. He didn't tell me."

"I told him to wait."

The muscle in his jaw flexes.

I glance toward the ballroom where the doorway is filled with dozens of onlookers. They've been surging out onto the balcony almost the whole time, obtusely watching the prince kiss Ella, despite Tobiah's best efforts to shepherd them away. I wish she had let him propose before she called me out. It would be better if she were his fiancée rather than his love.

"Well," I say, "it's vital that you listen now. I've saved Cito, Rus, and Elaina's lives. More than once for some of them."

The prince's brow creases into three distinct wrinkles. "What does that matter?"

"Do you *want* Karl to reign in Heia?"

"Karl?" Brann laughs outright. "That man is—"

I tilt my head in the direction of the balcony.

He breaks off and follows my indication to our audience, held back by the presence of a line of guards at the stairs to the balcony. "Let's go farther into the garden." He motions us away from the guards. "There we may speak in peace."

Ella trails back, indicating for me to precede her, but I take her arm and bring her alongside me. She smiles weakly, clearly feeling as though she doesn't belong in this discussion. But that's not true—she is my ally, my first, my truest ally. She is also the one who can influence Brann the most, whether she believes it or not.

Brann leads us to a clearing in the garden where he turns to us. His gaze lingers on Ella for a moment before returning to me. I can almost hear her pulse increase at his scrutiny.

He must not reject her because of me. I couldn't bear that.

"I'll give you two a moment to speak," Ella says, stepping back from us.

"Ella, you don't have to—" I begin.

But Brann says at the same time, "Thank you."

She meets his gaze instead of mine, and Brann gives her a surprisingly gentle smile. Ella smiles back with a little nod of understanding then disappears around a topiary.

Watching her go, Brann squares his shoulders and peers down at me. "What do you want from me, Winterberry?"

The change in his expression and tone is alarming. Perhaps using Ella to soften him was not the best plan after all.

"Brann, I sent Cito as an emissary of sorts. I hoped that he would remind you what is actually important." I lift a hand in the direction Ella disappeared. "Ella loves you. And you love her."

"That has nothing to do with you being here, or what you're asking from me. Does it?"

"No."

"Do you think me a fool?"

I purse my lips. "I saved her life, Brann."

He rolls his shoulders back, but his face softens slightly. "Yes. I do owe you for that." He lifts a brow. "Though you didn't do it for me, did you?"

I ignore his question again. "And Cito mentioned something

else to you. Something you acted on. Something that proved your heart—to yourself if not to others."

Brann's lips purse. "Yes." He holds my eye, staring me down and searching. "But what does that have to do with you?"

"It proved to me your nature. That you are a good man who wants to do good—for the people you care about but also for your city and country. I don't know if you want to change the country and the laws that oppress those you love, like Ella; I don't know if you care about more than Gelu Rigens. But I hope that it hints at how much you love your country that you would act upon a Heian's advice." I clasp my hands together. "Brann, if I am right, and you love Ella like you love your family—more than you love your family—then you owe me."

"I owe you?" His eyes widen incredulously.

"Yes. You love your cousin, don't you?"

"Of course," he mutters.

"Then you owe me—for saving all of their lives. You seem to forget, when it pleases you, that I am Canensian. You would not expect one of my culture to save a countryman from any other kingdom, but I have. And some of them are not even people I particularly like."

His lips press into a thin line as if he's torn between a smile and a scowl.

"But there are, to be blunt, far more important things happening in our worlds right now, Your Highness."

The lines on his forehead deepen.

"Our countries will be at war soon, if we aren't already." The air chills around us at my words. "If we don't save the Seven Kingdoms from Queen Blanche, then all is lost, possibly even your future with Ella. Or any future at all."

"Go on," he mutters darkly.

"My stepmother tried to kill me—she's tried several times now—and the last time she nearly killed Ella instead. But I have spoken with the faery Brunnea, and she agrees that Blanche is on a destructive path. Not just for me, but for all of the Seven Kingdoms."

"Faery?" Brann crosses his arms over his chest. "What are you talking about?"

"Blanche intends to make herself Empress."

"What?" He snorts. "That's impossible. Everyone knows the laws; no one man can rule all seven kingdoms."

I lift a shoulder. "She has Fae help. She's going to break that spell and declare herself Empress over the Seven Kingdoms. Unless we stop her."

He laughs a long, mocking laugh. "I don't know what you think you know about the Fae, Winterberry." He rolls his eyes. "And if you do think they even exist, what do you think we can do that they can't? Queen Blanche is…terrifyingly powerful. She strikes fear into all the royal families—not just mine. Every kingdom fears her. There have long been rumors of her magic, and if she's allied with a Fae—with more magic—then what are we to do? Better to throw you to her and beg for mercy!"

I cross my arms. "Is that what you would do? Do you really expect mercy from her? Not for me, but for you? After you have been so good as to harbor me for these past weeks?"

His face tightens and pales. "No."

"She will flay you alive for knowing about me and not killing me. She knows I'm here. If she suspects at all that you protected me—and you have—then she will peel your skin off while your mother watches."

He swallows. "Then what do you suggest?"

I pretend that I don't hear the tremor in his voice as he imagines the scene I paint for him. "You ally with me. Against her. Our enemy."

"Why would we do that?" Brann retorts. "*You* are the enemy."

"I will give anything to protect my people. My adamas mines, my country…anything."

He tilts his head slightly.

"Even my crown."

Brann releases his breath in a long whistle. "Well, I wasn't expecting that. Mother might approve of you after all. If that's the case, I might as well offer you back the glass slipper you left behind when you fled like a coward. It's the least I could do."

I stiffen. "If you want my country, Brann, I will offer it to you…" I pause. "As long as you marry Ella."

"Well how—" His gaze flicks to the direction Ella took then back to me. "Why do you demand that?"

"Because she has shown me kindness I've never known. Because she loves you, and I have faith in her judgment of character. I know that if you are with Ella, she will not let you mistreat anyone. You will be made worthier by your union with her." I lift a shoulder. "And I'm pretty well convinced that you already meant to propose to her."

His lips turn to the side, softening as he peeks in Ella's direction again.

His heart is written so plainly on his face, but this is a matter of state. Sending Ella in before me was a mistake. I offered Ella for the safety of my people. Though she's hardly mine to offer, she agreed. And outside of myself, she is all I have to barter with.

He looks uneasy, and as his gaze lingers not on Ella but on his hands, I suddenly realize where his thoughts are.

"I didn't tell her about this part of my plan, Brann."

His eyes fly up to meet mine. "You didn't?"

"No." I can't help but be amused at the relief written on his face. "I only asked her to soften you toward me. I never told her that I would demand you ask for her hand in marriage." My lips quirk. "I also didn't tell her about your part in the auction bidding." I shrug at his cocked brow. "I figure there are some things you ought to be the hero on, should you decide that's the right path to take with a woman like Ella."

Brann takes a deep breath and slowly releases it through thin lips. A slow smile tugs up one side of his mouth. "Then I accept your blackmail, Winterberry, with a grateful heart."

My smile is pained.

"But just as you are not the one who must agree to marry, I am not the one you must convince."

My lips twist into a half frown, half smile. "I know." I motion to where Ella waits for him. "But know this, Brann," I say when he has taken one step. He pauses and looks over his shoulder at me. "Because I grew up with very little love, I recognize it when I see it. I have never seen such love as I have here in Ardor."

His mouth parts in confusion. "Between…?"

"Your parents love you, Brann. They would give anything for your joy and safety. Just as you would for Ella and she would for you. Keep her safe. And together we can keep the Kingdoms safe."

His chin lifts as he inhales. "I suppose you are wiser than you look."

I grin. "And since I am, I—"

Shouts break out from the palace doors. At the sound of screams, we whirl.

"Protect the queen!"

My heart flies into my throat as a chill runs down my body in cold fingers of dread. Blanche. She is here.

6: BLANCHE

DEATH

*A*s I pass through the doorway of the ballroom, I stumble on the hem of my gown, catching myself on the arm of a guard nearby.

"I'm so sorry," I say, the words sounding tired in my mind. I've never apologized so much in my life as I have lately. I grunt as my knee hits the ground.

"Are you all…right…ma…da…?" The guard's words trail off as I lift my gaze to him, magic ebbing out from my fingertips into his arm. His eyes are blank, and as I watch, they shift to the ballroom, scanning the crowd and locking onto their target.

I lift myself to my feet, and without another glance at the guard, walk down the hallway, deeper into the palace. I slip through a door about halfway down, enter another hallway, and from there through another door. The room inside is empty but with a glassed-in flame flickering on the desk and glass-covered candles upon the chandelier hanging from the ceiling. Books on mahogany cases line the walls, and a large desk commandeers the room.

I smirk and step into the spot behind the door, waiting for the

King and Queen to answer their guard's summoning. Or rather, my summoning.

When I hear heavy footsteps in the hall, I flatten myself against the wall behind the door. Footsteps tap through the hallway, urgent and decisive. A hand rattles the doorknob; I hold my breath.

For a few annoying seconds, I think the wrong person has come, then I feel the tug of magic in my navel, and my annoyance melts.

The door shudders. Only it is not just the King that steps inside. By the sound of the footsteps, three rushing guards follow on his heels.

"Your Majesty! You must let us go first."

I bite back my impatience and remain in place.

"Your Majesty, I do not think this is a wise idea," another guard says.

The King scoffs impatiently. "If she needs me, I will be there."

"Your Majesty—" The guard attempts, but he is set aside again by the King's insistence.

"Where is she?" A pair of footsteps thump through the room.

A hand reaches for the edge of the door, level with my face, and the door swings away. The guard shutting the door stares at me, his eyes large as copper coins in his shock. A breath hisses across his lips, giving me long enough to cast my spell. His eyes glaze over as the door clicks into place. With a thought and twitch from me, it locks.

"Sire!" A second guard says, jumping toward me.

As the King turns, I hold out a hand and all three guards freeze in their places. Only their eyes remain able to move, and I revel in the fear they emit. The one nearest the King, I realize, was not moving toward me at the first guard's alert. His eyes flick toward the King.

King Greggory stands near the bookshelf along the far wall,

standing like a foolish bird who thinks I cannot see him because he doesn't move.

I tilt my head and move out from behind the guard, giving the King a considering look as his guards struggle in vain against the grip of my magic. The other royals really should look into at least one magic-wielding guard.

"What's back there, Your Majesty?" I ask him, knowing full well it's the tunnel to his daughter's tower.

He shifts away from the wall, squaring himself to me. His hand goes to the hilt of the sword strapped to his hip.

I raise a brow. "I wouldn't. Unless you want to be frozen flesh and bone just like your guards."

His gaze flicks to the men standing in various poses of urgency. "What do you want?"

I reach a hand to my face and tug the string on my mask, allowing it to fall to the warm, wooden floor beneath my feet.

The King's eyes narrow.

"Your Majesty," I mock, spreading my hands as if I might curtsy if he weren't so far below me.

A breath rasps over his lips as he takes me in. "Queen Blanche of Canens, I presume?"

"I'm pleased to hear my reputation precedes me." My lips turn up on one side. I'm impressed, despite myself, at his presence of mind and courage in this exchange.

"It doesn't," he answers harshly. "My son warned me you might be in our country."

My eyebrows lift, then descend. How did he know—? The dress. I barely refrain from shaking my head in self disgust. "How long have you known?"

He opens his mouth to answer, but I slash my hand across the air.

"Never mind. At least now, we don't have to waste time with introductions, and you can hear what information I have for you." I step around the nearest of his guards. "After all, I'm sure you want to hear how your daughter fares."

His mouth drops open above his well-trimmed beard. "My—" He snaps his mouth shut and straightens. "How do you know about my daughter?"

"I am the Queen of Canens, you know. And my reputation precedes me." I step toward him, smirking at the trembling in his hands.

He tightens his grip around the hilt of his ceremonial sword to stay the shaking, but his lips give him away, wavering as though he's crying.

"I see." The king draws in a shaking breath, but straightens under my gaze. "So I suppose you have attacked my daughter in her tower."

My lips twitch. "Quick, aren't you? Yes. Your cursed daughter, the one you were so ashamed of, that you exiled to a tower for life. That daughter."

"What have you done to her?" His eyes gentle as he stares at me in an unkingly manner. "Tell me, please. Does she live?"

I tilt my head at him. "She does. Although you shall not live to see her again."

"Please, don't...don't kill me." He holds his ground, but he doesn't draw his weapon. Instead, his gaze darts to his frozen men once again, who watch and hear this exchange, but can do nothing to stop it. "I have never hurt you."

My amusement fades. "You abandon your daughter and heir to a tower? You gave her life and made her life not worth living. You should die shut behind bricks, slowly and desperately. The same life you're giving to your daughter. A father should love his daughter, not abandon her."

Tears squeeze from the king's eyes as he sinks to his knees before me. "I know. Every day, I know I have failed her. But what were we to do? Her life is in danger as long as the one who cursed her lives. And then our people would have revolted to have a cursed princess, a princess so touched by magic. It was to save her life. To save us all."

"And yet she has no say in the sacrifice she makes, does she?" I shake my head, soul-heavy darkness rising inside me. "The world is changing, King Greggory. You must change with it or die outside of it."

"I won't live in a world where you take what is not yours." He lifts his chin as he speaks, and though his words tremble, his expression is fierce and determined. He is a fool.

I run a hand over my chin. "Your daughter lives. And you would die? For...what? Respect?" I laugh at the indignant expression dawning on the King's face. "You have no respect, King. You are devoid of honor, and you should die without honor."

I walk past a particularly young guard and pause. "He's old enough for your special guards? Hmm."

The King glowers up at me from his knees. "What do you know of anything human? Do you even need guards to protect you?"

"If you can give me a true, sympathetic reason for locking your daughter away, perhaps I will spare your life." I shrug as if it doesn't much matter anyway. "I won't spare your body and mind, but I could spare your life."

"We tried to save her," he whispers.

I shake my head. "You tried to save yourself from guilt."

His brows quiver, but he resolutely jumps to his feet and draws his sword. "Queen Blanche, do what you will to me. I refuse to bow to you. Now or ever."

My smile slips into a frown. I raise my hand and point at him. "Then you are nothing to me."

Before he can reply, I cast my spell. The King's eyes widen in shock as it hits, encasing him with ice from the inside out. The initial blow shocks him, freezing him, and then it wraps his every cell within in ice until his body teeters and falls like a tree in a frozen forest.

For several seconds, I stand over him, not bothering to indulge the myriad of emotions that nudge at my awareness. They hardly even register anymore. In my many years of being queen, I have pushed such trivial things aside.

One king down. One throne nearly freed. Too bad he didn't bring his wife. Or his son.

Slowly, I bend over the King and remove his signet ring from his finger. This might come in useful. I glance toward a sound at the door.

Then it begins with a scream from the study, and footsteps thunder in the hall as someone screeches, "Dead! The King is dead!"

"Protect the queen!"

"Lock down the palace!"

I jolt at the alarm, taking stock of the three, still-frozen guards in the room beside the fallen king. Who in the Seven Kingdoms raised the alarm?

I swoop to the ground and pick up my mask. Displeasure squeezes a grunt from me. An alarm ruins the remainder of my plans.

No matter. At the King's death, Ardor is crippled anyway. And even if the prince thinks he can rally his people—the signet ring on my thumb glitters and I grin—I will cripple him.

"Intruder in the palace!"

Cursed Silvanus. He must have done something to alert them.

I race to the door, reaching for it just as it bursts open. I reel backward.

A woman in full ballgown and mask stands in the door, her ice-blue eyes flaming with fear and fury.

For once in my life, shock overtakes me.

He lied to me. *My.* Huntsman. Lied. *To me.*

She lives.

7: WINTER

FACING THE QUEEN

"*P*rotect the queen!"

Guard's cries break the stillness of the night.

"Mother! *Father*," Brann whispers. He fixes a fierce gaze on one of his nearby guards as he draws his sword from his side. It's a ceremonial blade, not intended for battle, but it will do if it must. Except, I have no doubt that the attack right now is not from blade or bow. It's from magic.

My skin tingles with its presence, my fingers alighting with the burn from within me.

Brann, halfway out of the clearing, turns back to me. "Protect her!" he demands. "Take her to the safe room."

I glance to the guard nearest us, who snaps out a sharp salute and a, "Your Highness!" then draws his sword and positions himself near Ella as several others flank her. Her eyes round in panic, but they're fixed on Brann's departing back.

Hastily, I replace my mask and dart into the palace.

"Brann! Winter!" Ella's fading cries are difficult to ignore, but the din of the panicking crowd helps.

I dodge behind Brann, squinting through the slits in my mask as I do. At first the guards start toward me, but then rally around

Brann, taking him by the arms, despite his cries of protest, and whisking him away, out of my sight. I'm almost certain that he and the guards disappear through a wall to my right as I trace Blanche's magic.

My feet fly through the halls of the Ardorian palace. I follow the tendril of magic blindly, skidding past doors and hallways, tracking the trail only I can recognize.

My heart has lodged low in my throat. If she is here, as the fresh remnants of her magic warn me, then Brann, the King, and the Queen are all in mortal danger.

Slippered feet sliding as I race down the marble-floored hallway, I fly past door and skid to a halt as the tendrils of magic loosen and weaken.

I missed it. I go back, pausing at every door until the magic tugs like a hand inside my ribs, tugging so strongly that it almost pulls me straight through the door. What magic has she cast that leaves such a trail? I rip open the door and burst into another hallway lined with doors. I curse and dart down the hall, slowing at each door just long enough to tell whether the magic goes through it or trails across in front of it.

Finally, I halt before a pair of wide doors and rip one open, expecting another hall behind it. Instead, I come face-to-face with my stepmother.

She snatches her hand back toward her as though she were reaching for the door.

We stare at each other with unconcealed shock. I knew she would be here and yet still the horror of meeting her overwhelms me. I am not ready for this. I am weak compared to her; the stench of the magic in this room tells me that.

But here I am, and we must fight. I square myself before her as magic rises in me, burning in my palms. I clench my fists, fighting it back, not ready to have her see the truth about me or to condemn myself simply to kill her. Perhaps she can sense my magic already, but she shows no sign of it. Racing here, I had been too concerned about following her magical trace to find her. Now, I have to defeat her. Only, I had not anticipated meeting her this soon. I am not prepared. Not even close. How do I defeat her? Brunnea has not taught me to fight with my magic, and I have only ever healed with it before.

Now Blanche stands before me with her shock rapidly turning to arrogance. I brace myself. I will not cower before her. Not today.

"Well. It would appear you still live."

Taking a tight breath, I hold it before spreading my palms open before her. "It would appear so."

"I must have a discussion with my huntsman then." Despite the smirk on her lips, there's a tightness there that betrays her fury.

I loosen my fingers. He is no longer hers, but I won't tell her that. Instead, I take in the room around us with a hasty glance. Three guards stand in various poses, frozen, only their eyes darting around. Then I see him. Behind her, King Greggory lies prone on the lush, blue and gold rug.

"What have you done?" I demand as a chill seizes me.

"What have I done?" she asks innocently as she strides away from the Ardorian king, stepping behind his large desk as though she is here for nothing but to find a book or scroll. "I've only done what too many generations of Canens queens have been too afraid to do."

I hurry to the King's side, keeping half my attention on her. At least enough to note that she ignores me, moving papers around the desk with mild interest.

The King is obviously dead, his eyes glassy and glazed, a strange sheen coating them almost like frost forms on a window. I bend to him and touch his neck. He's cold to the touch.

I remain in place, but my attention is no longer on the King. Blanche has hardly glanced at me since she moved from the body, since I surprised her. She doesn't consider me a threat. And why would she? I am a copper coin that you find when you need a gold coin; I am worthless to her.

Several heartbeats of time fill the space between us as my mind races. What am I to say to stop her? How do I stop her? Do I fight? Or should I just let her go? I know that's the exact thing she's asking herself. She's asking whether she should let me go or kill me now. Only, she can't kill me herself.

The reminder of the King's Curse straightens my spine, and I lift myself from my kneeling position beside King Greggory. I can kill her, but she cannot kill me or else she will die.

Empowered, I turn toward her and meet her ice-cold gaze with a smirk of my own. If I can kill her without retribution, what's stopping me? Certa's face flashes before my eyes, then Des', and then Elaina, Cito, and Rus. And now…King Greggory's as well. All those who died in various ways. If only I had known of my magic before, perhaps I could have saved them all. But now their dead faces haunt me in my dreams and waking. Would her face haunt me as well?

"They're coming for you. You won't kill them." I inject as much confidence and certainty into my voice as possible.

Her eyebrow lifts, but her eyes flicker over me, lingering on my hands before returning to my face. "I won't? I thought for sure I had you in the palm of my hand." Without warning, she makes a slashing motion through the air, and I feel the touch of her magic upon me. Her spell is ice, injecting my bones with a deep freeze.

My body reacts automatically. I force her magic out of me, pushing against the touch. As abruptly as it attacked, it disappears.

Blanche blinks and lowers her hand, her head tilting.

Footsteps echo in the hall; her eyes shift toward the door.

"They come for you," I repeat coldly, trying to distract her from recognizing the defense of my own magic. They are searching the entire palace, not knowing the King's location. I raced here, knowing that wherever Blanche was, the King was. Only I was too late. His frozen stare, condemning me. *No.* I can't think of my failure now.

Her eyes narrow, but her feet shift, drawing her out from behind the desk, toward the far end of the room.

"They're coming," I mock.

"Then I'll kill them all." She laughs mercilessly, but it sounds hollow, fearful.

"You won't." I step toward her. "You are not invincible, Blanche. You are not all powerful. You cannot survive should a sword find your heart. How many of them can you freeze?"

Her face pales, and she glances at the immobile guards around us.

"Here!" a voice calls outside the door.

"You have no escape."

When her gaze darts to the door this time, I seize my chance. As the door opens and Brann's friend, Tobiah, with sword drawn, bursts inside, I attack. Fighting every magical instinct inside me, I charge at her and catch her in the middle, pushing her off her feet and landing atop her.

She hisses like an angered cat, baring her teeth. With a flip, she rolls over on top of me, growling in my face as she straddles me like a snow leopard pouncing on its prey.

Wildly, I grab at her, pulling at her hair in a desperate attempt to keep her at bay. She screeches in fury as her hair falls into her eyes. I struggle under her, striking her hand and the wooden bracelet on it. My hand shudders at the impact, but I'm rewarded when the bracelet flies halfway across the room and slams into something with a snap.

Screaming, she shoves me with a burst of magic. I skid across the room and into the stone behind the door, my head cracking against the surface. Blackness flashes before me, alternating with bright spots as I blink.

"Stop right now, or I promise you, I will skewer you with my sword," Tobiah threatens.

Dazed, I blink at the two facing each other.

Blanche glares at Tobiah and points her closed fist at him. Light shines out between her fingers, and Tobiah freezes.

"Not today, boy," she spits, slashing her hand through the air with a flash of light.

Squinting across the room, I see Blanche reach for something on the bookcase and move it. The bookcase glides out from the wall, and without a backward glance, she disappears behind it.

My head pounds. Surely I didn't see what I just saw? Where did she go? I blink then sigh, losing my battle against the darkness.

THROUGH THE TUNNEL

My wand, my applewood bracelet wand is broken, nearly crippling me magically. My eyes itch. The first wand I made myself, and my favorite.

Anger burns from deep inside me. This wand, made shortly after I gained my magic, has been more friend to me than anyone. It's kept my magic private and yet gave me power to cast it well. It was admired, even by the Fae once. I must repair it. Somehow.

At my anger, light blossoms in my palm, and my feet slip in a clump of wet dirt. I glance at my hand, then around. It's been a long time since I lost control of my magic like this, but right now, I can use it. The light illuminates the tunnel, showing me what I already know, except, as I run on, that there are other tunnels off this one.

I dig deep for my magical stores. Doing magic without a wand isn't impossible, some do it all the time, but it is less controlled. Instead of hitting my target and enchanting Silvanus to kill Winter, I might hit whoever stands next to him instead. Now, there is no one but me to hurt, and the light is harmless enough, a burning of emotionally tied magic. There's a whisper in my head, a whisper long forgotten that seems to come along with it, but I ignore it, pretending it's the whisper of a wind in the tunnel.

Still, at the next fork, I murmur to the light, "Show me which way will save me."

The glow in my palm pulses then pulls me to the right. I allow myself a grin.

At every fork, I continue this, but soon I become aware of someone's jingling footsteps behind me. I pause, slowing my pace and listening over my own steps. Tobiah. The fool of a lover who burst in when I was about to destroy Winterberry.

I grit my teeth. He still pursues me, and I failed to make my light invisible for others. Either I hide my light, try to outrun him, or I slow and draw him in.

I must deal with him, now. I cannot have someone following me. In minutes, he is near enough that I hear his panting breaths. He is intent upon catching me. He must have loved his king. I scoff.

"Halt!" he calls out, and though he huffs, his word is firm, betraying the energy he has to follow through with a fight.

Unarmed, I will die at his hand.

Slowly, I halt and turn. He holds out his sword, pointing it at me with a steady hand.

Tilting my head at him, I call my magic to swell and create a burst of light so bright even I squint at it.

He gasps as I throw a handful of magic at him, a spell that might not obey my wishes without a wand.

It doesn't.

I curse and jump backward at the sting of magic against my own skin. As the magic flares through the tunnel, the man falls backward on his bottom with a heavy thud against the hard-packed dirt. Refocusing my magic before the man can recover, I throw another spell his way, cursing when it misses again. I advance, calling for my magic to rise, ignoring the twinge that comes when I dig too deep for what isn't there. This time when I throw the spell, the man chokes.

"Ha!" The grunt of satisfaction escapes me through a gasp. I squint through the dimming light at him, barely able to make out my finally effective spell that binds him ankle, wrist, and around his mouth. I would much rather kill him, but my magic is unpredictable and might kill me instead.

I lean over him. "Don't follow me; you will never win."

He glares at me over his gag, but I just offer him a smirk, then turn and leave him in the dark, huddled against the wall in a cove that no one will ever find. He deserves his death. My step-daughter—if she dare pursue—will race past him and never know she could have saved my enemy's life.

An hour later, my grin is long gone, but my light still burns dimly. It tugs me down another tunnel, this one cobwebbed and full of slithering creatures I sense rather than see. I bite back a sharp inhale at the sight of a snake slithering out of the light, more afraid of me than I am of it. I dart around it. If animals are here, then the exit is near.

Almost without warning, a ladder appears before me. I barely manage to stop before slamming my nose upon it.

9: WINTER

FOLLOWING BLANCHE

*L*ight burns through my eyelids, digging into my eyes with sharp needles.

Blanche. Tobiah.

I force my eyelashes apart, gasping at the pain, and lower my head to the ground. My stomach churns, threatening to raise my last meal, but the nausea passes with a moment's rest. I lift my head again, squinting into the room. The bookcase is back in place, but I saw how she opened it. If I wasn't imagining the entire thing…

Stumbling my way across the room, I reach for the statue Blanche had touched. I can't pick it up. I grope at it, my fingers depress the horn of the unicorn, and the bookcase opens with a creak. Behind it, the blackness Blanche disappeared into. I take a deep breath and plunge inside.

The tunnel is dark, cold, and damp. At first, with my head throbbing and vision blurring, I can barely stumble into the darkness. My hands outstretched, I fully expect to run headfirst into something any second. Instead, as I walk, I find that the tunnel lightens just enough to see a few feet in front of me.

At first the tunnel is made of stone and rock, cool and damp after the heat of the fire in the King's library. But it quickly turns to dirt, wet and miserable.

I should call upon my magic, only I can't. If Blanche is watching, it would reveal me in the most dangerous way.

But would she? She can't kill me because of the King's Curse, even if I come at her, untrained as I am. With one spell she can curse me like the King, and there's nothing I can do to prevent it.

But I can't. I still can't risk using magic so recklessly.

I grimace and do the only thing I can: pursue Blanche through a midnight-black tunnel, without a plan should I catch her. Perhaps she won't be there this time, or perhaps she waited for me to pass then slipped out the way we entered. But that isn't like her.

My head swims, and I stumble to a halt. I put a hand to my temple as it throbs. I cannot keep on like this. The next foot down the path is overwhelming. Tears prick my eyes. Do I just let her go? If I don't, and Tobiah catches her, she'll kill him.

Hesitating just another moment, I release a sigh that makes my head pound harder. I reach for my magic. A tiny flash heals the aching and pounding in my head, but only in part. My head still feels strange, and probing it, a large bump remains, but at least my thoughts are clear again. Perhaps healing oneself requires a different sort of magic?

My stomach churns at my use of self-serving magic. But this is so that I can fight evil. It's necessary. Isn't it?

I don't know any more. But I do know that if I don't stop her, all will suffer. Better to end it now.

I close my eyes and seek out the tendril of Blanche's magic.

A tangle of magic pulls at me. When it lead me to the library, the path got stronger and remained strong until I found her, but this...this is both weaker than normal and strangely fierce. It's wild, untamed. A mixture of old and new traces. The new magic is...different. More chaotic and less refined. What happened? Has Tobiah injured her? Did I?

Whatever it is, I can't focus on it now.

I lose track of time as I follow her path. Sounds are both amplified and dampened in the tunnel. I think I hear someone scuffling up ahead, the clinking of a soldier's armor, but I never seem to reach the sound.

As I follow the magical trail, the clinking grows more frequent. Then a muffled groan of outrage and despair.

Wary of a trap, I slow.

Drawing on my courage, I continue, hesitant to divide my magic between Blanche's magical traces and the source of the sounds.

But the jingling is up ahead and the magic seems even more concentrated here, a muddle of fresh magic with a slightly acrid smell, like something has been burned.

Someone nearby groans and gives an odd sound, almost like a muffled shout.

I bite my lip then whisper, "Tobiah?"

The motions stop, then renew with more urgency.

I tiptoe near the sounds and crouch down before Tobiah, barely able to see him through the dimness. "Is she near?" I murmur.

He shakes his head, his eyes wide and the whites glowing in the darkness.

My gaze slips to his mouth, gagged with a thick rag. "I'm going to untie you." He nods vigorously as I reach behind his head and begin to work blindly at the knot. It takes a silent minute for me to remove the gag and free his mouth.

He opens and closes his mouth as though stretching it out before saying, "She left me some time ago and headed farther down the tunnel. We have to stop her."

"Are your hands and legs tied, too?"

He nods. "If you untie my arms, I can do my legs."

I grimace into the darkness. "How did she do this?"

His head remains downcast, as if he stares at his outstretched feet. "I don't know, exactly. I came up on her, then this light just erupted, and—" He raises his chin to look at me as I work on his arms, which are bound in two places, not just around the wrists. "She didn't touch me," he confesses.

I bite my lip, not looking up at him, instead digging into the bindings with my fingernails. I grimace and finally glance at him, trying to read his expression in the dark. "Magic," I mutter like a curse.

In the darkness, his head tilts to the side. "That would have been my guess, but…"

"Magic isn't supposed to exist?" I say wryly, my eyes on his face as I abandon caution, summon my magic, and my hands burst into light.

He inhales sharply and squints, leaning back from me. "You too?"

Asking my magic to untie him, I scoot back, keeping the light burning and glancing around at what it illuminates. Roots and rocks glitter in the dirt walls, hinting at life not far above us. Chunks of dirt and rock are blown out nearby, leaving deep gouges in the walls.

Farther down the tunnel, my light illuminates the path another ten feet before it returns to black. No sight of Blanche, but then I didn't expect her to stay, not after binding him like this. She wouldn't care to see him rescued. She would expect me to stop for him if I happened by. It's mere chance that I did, only able to follow because I traced her magic.

Tobiah stands and brushes himself off, running hands over his wrists before settling his hand familiarly on his sword's hilt.

I tilt my head at him. "This isn't your first run-in with magic, is it?"

A crooked grin appears on his lips. "I've seen magical items before. But nothing like this." He motions at me and around us in the tunnel, his grin turning down with worry. "Most impressive, I admit."

Small smile on my lips, I let my light dim so that it barely illuminates the two of us. We both take a moment, blinking at our surroundings, as our eyes adjust to the dimmer light.

"Do you know where she goes?" he asks me.

"No," I say, "but I follow her path."

"She's long gone. Can you tell where she goes? There are multiple tunnels in here; it's a maze. I've been following a light she has—well, a light like yours, I suppose." He frowns at my hands.

"Well, I do something similar, but I don't need light. I can follow her magical traces."

"Then why are we waiting? Let's go." Tobiah tugs down his tunic's bottom hem and starts down the path. "I owe her a fight, and you even the odds."

Grimacing at his back, I follow.

ADA

In all the confusion in the garden, I watch Brann rush away with his guards, then suddenly several guards are there at my side.

"Are you Ella?" one of them demands.

I nod automatically. At my confirmation, all them close rank around me.

"You're to come with us at Prince Brann's orders," one of them says and grasps my elbow. Quickly, he leads me through the garden and into a side door into the palace.

"Where are we going?" I ask, but no one answers me. Thoughts race through my head faster than a unicorn, too fast to catch or even entertain.

After ten minutes of racing through abandoned hallways and winding secret passages, we emerge in a plain room with half a dozen other guards and a woman in a masque and gown.

The guards drag me inside and shut the door after us, which closes so tightly that I can't tell where it is. Although I know there's at least that door, if not another, in this small room holding nearly a dozen people, I can't help but feel trapped.

"Where is Brann?" a woman's voice asks. "Where is my son? Who is this?"

My panting breaths catch. Her son? I'm in here with the queen?

"He has other guards with him, Your Majesty," one of my guard says. "He instructed us to bring Miss Ella here for her own safety."

The Queen turns and focuses her gaze on me, drawing herself to her full height a head beneath my own. "So you are Ella?" Despite her lack of stature, her queenly bearing does not suffer for it.

I sink into a deep curtsy, bowing my head. "I am, Your Majesty."

There's silence in the room except for the breathing of the guards and my own, still slightly more rapid breaths than normal from our sprints through the palace.

"You may rise," Queen Ada says with a tired sigh. "If Brann sent you here with me, then he must have ignored me."

Uncertain, I rise, but I avert my gaze. I've never met a queen before. Do I look at her or fix my gaze on the floor?

She waves me toward a plush but masculine chair. "You should get comfortable. We'll be here for awhile."

As the guards station themselves around the exterior wall of the room, I sink into the chair and fold my hands in my lap, trying not to rub the fabric over in my hands as I do when I'm nervous.

The Queen ignores me; only the occasional clearing of a throat or cough from the guards breaks the silence. My own heart quiets and resumes its normal pace, and just when I am becoming bored with the wait, the Queen speaks again.

"He didn't see anyone else, you know."

Frowning, I turn to her. "I'm sorry, Your Majesty?"

She considers me with her large, sad eyes. "My son. He couldn't see anyone besides you. Not for years."

What should I say to that? My heart lifts in relief, but the expression on Queen Ada's face is impossible to read. She sits upon her comfortable leather chair, a living statue, with no warmth in any part of her.

I choose not to answer.

"He had his choice of every unmarried woman in this country, plus all the unmarried princesses in the Seven Kingdoms." She pauses, her long lashes sweeping up and down as she takes me in. "He chose you."

The earlier Ella would apologize to her, but I can't find it in myself to do so. Instead, I raise my gaze to hers. "Yes, he did."

Our gazes lock. Though the Queen is small, at least a foot shorter than me, I can see a bit of Brann in her. The intensity of her gaze hidden behind a layer of reserve, the shape of her eyes, the texture of her hair. As I study her, she examines me. And when her lips twitch on one end, I think she's reached some conclusion about me that isn't entirely unflattering.

She drops her gaze to her folded hands in her lap, speaking to them when she says, "They say the King is dead."

I inhale gently, not sure what to say.

"They say the Queen of Canens killed him."

I press my lips tight over my lower lip.

"Do you think they're right?"

"I fear so, Your Majesty." When she looks at me, pain in her eyes, I add, "But I pray that it is not so."

Her eyes shine with tears. "Are you a woman of faith, Ella?"

"Yes," I reply softly.

"Would you pray with me?" she whispers. "I fear…"

I don't make her continue, but instead I scoot my chair closer to her and reach for her hands. They are cold and clammy in my own as I squeeze them. "Of course I would. I would be honored."

I bow my head and close my eyes, fighting back the emotion in my throat for the man I never met. I hardly know the words I am speaking as I say them, but pour out my heart's desire to find the King healthy and alive and to protect Brann and Ardor from harm at Queen Blanche's hands. Still, a part of me knows we are too late for the King. I can only beg the Lord that we are not too late to change Brann's path.

As I struggle to find more a more poignant way of imploring the Lord for help, a door bursts open into the room.

Queen Ada shrieks, and I leap to my feet, placing myself between the Queen and the door, as if I could possibly protect her or stop an attack. The guards are quicker than me, whirling on the intruder with weapons raised.

AERIA

As abruptly as I found the ladder, a wooden ceiling appears above me, and I nearly ram my head into it. After a moment's inspection, I smother my light and push up on it.

I emerge into the small, stone kitchen of the tower with its wood-burning cooking stove and cupboards.

But this time, I am not alone. A shriek has me whirling, hands raised and dwindling magic ready.

My hands hesitate long enough for the girl to turn around at the base of the stairs and race up them, only her hair left behind, but even that steadily disappearing.

I stare at the trapdoor in the floor, still yawning open. Hastily, I shut it, for it allows light into the tunnel that would be a beacon to anyone following, and I could have a host of Ardorian guards following me by now.

Curse it all. I told my magic to bring me to an exit, not to the princess. I must have taken a wrong turn. There must be an exit I missed. But still, my magic tugs at me, telling me my exit lies here.

A sound in the tunnel below has me flinching toward the

stairs. Without a choice, I follow the princess' hair up the steps, this time as myself.

At the top, the girl stands in a pool of her braided locks with a poker raised above her head.

I cock a brow at her.

"Who are you?" she demands in a wavering voice so fear-filled that I almost don't recognize it as the one she used when I was impersonating her lover.

I almost laugh but my bone-weary exhaustion robs me of humor. While I want to collapse on the girl's four-poster bed and sleep for days, I give her a scathing look instead. "Don't worry, princess, I have no need of you."

The girl blinks. "What did you call me?"

I realize my mistake. Curses. Did I really just reveal to this girl who she is?

"I have no need of you. Just your hair."

One of her hands leaves the poker to touch her head. "What?" If possible, even more fear enters her voice.

I roll my eyes and motion to the tower balcony. "Your hair, girl. I must get down and am too exhausted to do it as I otherwise might."

Her brow furrows. The act gives her the wrinkles her face is lacking in comparison to her mother's. "No."

"No?" I laugh outright. "You want me to stay in this tower? With you?" I step toward her, watching fear darken her large, gray eyes. "Trust me, you don't, girl, so I wouldn't tempt me to do something you would regret, like cutting off your hair and using it without you."

"You can't," she says automatically. "No one can cut it."

I crook my brow. "Then I'll just kill you and use you as an anchor."

The girl pales, and her poker weaves over her head.

"So which will it be? I've given you three choices, which is two more than I usually give."

The girl backs up as I advance.

"I warn you," I growl, "I don't have time to waste."

Stepping farther back, she slowly lowers the poker and gathers her hair, glancing out the balcony door at a hook above the railing. But then she hesitates. "*Can* you cut my hair?"

I grit my teeth. "What?"

"Can you try?"

"Why would I do that if you're going to let me use it now?" I demand shortly. I must get away from here, and she's stubbornly preventing me.

Her brow furrows. "Well then I won't let you use it now." She wraps her arms protectively around her hair. "Not until you try to sever it."

I laugh darkly. "You said nothing will cut it."

"You have magic. Magic can cut it, that's what Mama said."

"How—" I break off. I haven't used magic before her. "How can you tell I have magic?"

She dips her chin at me as if it's obvious. "You have an aura about you."

I crook a brow. That's one I haven't heard before. "And if I cut your hair, you won't prevent me from escaping?" Cursed princesses and their stubbornness—and the arrogant faery's insistence that none be harmed, but only blood be taken for her spell.

The princess nods twice.

I consider her. I could attempt to cut it and have her willingly help me, or I could fight with her and waste more energy, magical and otherwise. It would be a gamble either way, but a severing spell is less magic than fighting her, especially if she has magic of her own, despite my inability to sense it. I will use a minor spell in my attempt, and if my unpredictable magic happens to do something, I can blame no one but her.

"Lay it out on the floor. I promise nothing though."

She hesitates only a second before dropping her armful. The

heavy, dark locks thump to the floor with a *whoomp*. She backs up onto the balcony behind her, stretching out her hair between her head and my feet.

I inspect the girl's braid. It's as thick as my arm, clearly enchanted to grow faster than normal and never break. What spell should I attempt? A common severing spell would never work; it would certainly be enchanted against that. But there are spells that could break the enchantment perhaps without cutting the hair, or even a spell that would age the hair and make it fall out. What has this girl's pretend mother attempted already anyway?

I shake my head. "I will try one spell. If that doesn't work, then I cannot try another."

The girl frowns and opens her mouth, as if to argue, but I hold up my hand.

"Do not ask for more or my one spell will be to strike you down."

The girl shuts her mouth with a click of her teeth.

I dig into my pocket for my broken applewood wand. I will need whatever precision I can gain at this point if I don't want to send the girl and my escape up in flames. I grip the bracelet in my hand and point it at the hair before her toes. After a moment's consideration, I step closer until she's an arm's reach away.

Then I take a deep breath and release it. The magic runs out of my core like water rushing down a waterfall. I stumble, going to my knees as the magic pools around us, glowing as it touches the girl's hair. It bursts into fire, flaring two feet high and then down to patches. The girl shrieks.

My stomach clenches; I retch but produce nothing.

"It burns!" The girl runs from the balcony past me toward the room, still crying as her hair glows with magical flames. "It's burning!"

I force my eyes to stay open and peer at her, irritation rising. Her screeches are decidedly uncomfortable, driving into my ears like metal spikes into my brain. Forcing myself up to my feet, I stumble toward her and reach out a hand, using what feels like the rest of my strength to quench the fire.

"Stop!" I erupt when the girl doesn't stop screaming. "The fire's out," I gasp.

She halts, staring at her hair and patting her head with both hands as if to check if her hair is in place.

My vision doubles, and I bend over, retching emptily again until my sides ache.

"Are you—are you all right?" The girl's voice comes from near me, too near.

I lean back, fighting for control. "Let me down now," I manage through a gasp. "I must get out of here."

The girl glances at her hair and then the balcony. "Yes, all right. A promise is a—"

We both turn as footsteps thump on the stairs. Curse them all to Sheol. They've found their way inside. And me, magically expended, with a traitor for a huntsman.

My heart pauses in my chest. I will only have one chance to borrow the strength I need from this girl before she realizes what I do. I force myself upright and stumble toward the balcony. "Quickly."

The girl hesitates.

"Now!" I thunder with my remaining strength and authority.

Jumping, the girl sprints and stumbles her way to the balcony. Then her lover bursts out of the stairwell with Winterberry following on his heels.

SHOWDOWN

I stumble out of the stairwell behind Tobiah and skid to a halt in the middle of a room with a fireplace on one side and a bed on the other. On a balcony in front of us stands Blanche and a small girl that could be anywhere from a few years older than me to a few years younger than me. She reminds me vaguely of someone I can't place.

"Tobiah!" she exclaims, her face lighting up in excitement before her brows descend in worry and confusion. "What's going on? What are you doing?" She looks to Blanche, fear dawning on her face. "Who—" Her face goes the color of snow.

"Aeria, step away from her," Tobiah says in a tone of forced calm, as if the girl stands near a wild animal she can't see and he's trying to talk her away from it.

I pause to see both Queen Blanche and the girl, Aeria, glance at Tobiah with curiosity. He knows this girl? And for that matter, where on earth are we? I risk a quick glance around. No weapons, no armor. It seems to be a young woman's bedroom.

My stepmother looks green around the edges, but also like the trapped animal she is. Judging by the girl's reaction, Blanche has done something to get Aeria to help her, but I cannot tell if the girl is magically coerced or just confused. Magic is so thick in the air that I want to choke, but I cannot betray that I sense it.

Blanche isn't waiting much longer though. She grabs the girl's wrist and points to the balcony. "Let me down now, follow through on your promise," she growls, "or I will carry through on my threats."

As the girl frowns and slowly looks to Tobiah, I grab his elbow and murmur, "We can't let her go."

"I know that," he mutters without turning to me. To the girl he says, "Do not listen to her Aeria. She…she is pure evil."

I tighten my grip on his elbow. "She can't know about what I showed you."

At that, he pauses and tosses me a glance. But there are no time for questions right now.

"Let her go, Blanche," I say.

At my address, Blanche draws herself up and tries to stare me down, but there is very little strength left in her, and it's clear. She needs this girl's help because she can't do what she would normally do. She needs this girl's hair. She leans on Aeria so heavily the girl staggers.

I begin toward her, one deliberate step at a time. When I'm halfway across the room, she moves. Life jolts back into her, lighting her from within, and she suddenly stands with a short, sharp knife at the girl's throat. The girl's eyes bulge as large as coins.

Tobiah draws his sword, starting for her before I can put out a hand stop him.

"Don't give her a reason," I say. "She doesn't need much of one."

Blanche grins at my words.

Tobiah halts just behind me, and out of the corner of my eye, I can see his face pale with worry. I spread my hands before Blanche and address her. "You know there is nothing I can do to stop you."

Her knuckles whiten around the hilt of the knife. Aeria's breath stutters as she tries to suck in a breath through her terror. Tobiah growls behind me.

Aeria leans backward against my stepmother. The girl's eyes plead with me to help her. My words didn't make Aeria feel any better. I have to do something, act somehow. *Without* magic. I take another step forward, my hands held out palm up again. "Please, Blanche, do not take innocent life."

Blanche's laugh is more a low and throaty growl. "Do you think she's innocent? This girl is no more innocent than you or I."

At the comparison, I almost laugh with her. "How innocent are you, Blanche? How long have you *not* been innocent?"

Blanche's amusement falters at my question, and her grip loosens enough for Aeria to squirm. Then Blanche recovers, tightening her grip, and Aeria gives a little squeak of terror.

"I don't understand what you're getting at *stepdaughter*, but I do none of this for myself."

"No?" I scoff. "You do what you do you for your own power and glory, no thought of anyone else. That makes you innocent? You are so guilty I can hardly look at you. You are— You have killed so many innocents simply in the name of what? The name of Canens? You have killed without mercy and destroyed all hope of peace between us.

"There cannot be peace between us, Winterberry," she snaps at me, disgust and derision feathered across her face. "Or even Canens and this country you sell yourself for. You are a fool to think that you could ally with Ardor. You are a fool to think you can ally with any of them. And that foolishness will destroy our country and destroy you. If you value your life and the lives of all Canensians, then you must take control of it and stop giving it to others."

With that, Blanche throws the girl's hair over the balcony. "Fix it," she demands to the girl. She releases the girl's neck enough to allow her to fix the hair with trembling hands by throwing it over a wooden out jut above the balcony.

When Aeria does this, her face contorts with something like confusion, or perhaps it's just nerves at being held at knife point. Blanche grabs hold of the the hair and throws her legs over the balcony.

Aeria puts both both hands to her head. "Wait, something feels wrong," she gasps.

Then as Blanche leans out over the balcony, putting her weight on the girl's braid, fear consumes Aeria. She screams, grabbing her hair and holding it with both hands as if trying to hold the strands in place. At the sound, Blanche startles and the knife slips from from her grasp. She slips off the balcony, fingers grasping desperately for Aeria's braid.

The girl's screams continue, so high-pitched that it drives panic into me. But Tobiah reacts with a soldier's quickness, rushing for the balcony.

He snatches up the knife in his hands and without hesitation saws at the girl's locks. The knife goes through them like a blade through dirt as she sobs and cries out.

Blanche grasps at Tobiah's belt, pulling at him and threatening to draw him over the balcony with her.

He barely spares her a sharp jab with his elbow and is halfway through the girl's hair when Blanche screams in a voice that jolts me from my stupor.

I lunge for the trio.

Blanche scrabbles with Tobiah, grabbing at him as though he is her rescuer. Through Aeria's continued sobs, Blanche battles Tobiah while trying to maintain her grip on the girl's hair, and Tobiah tries to force Blanche off him to cut Aeria free of her braid.

Blanche grunts and yanks his hands off the girl's hair.

"No!" Tobiah cries as his knife slips over the balcony. He curses and the girl grasps the remainder of her hair that's attached to her head in her fists. Tears flow in rivers down her cheeks.

"Help him," she weeps, reaching for him with one hand despite her agony.

The girl grabs his arm with her free hand, but Blanche rips mercilessly at her fingers. I rush to the balcony and grip Tobiah with both hands. He cannot go over. I cannot have another death on my hands.

"Help me with him," Aeria begs.

I grab him just as Blanche twists along the hair rope. The girl screeches her pain and stumbles sideways, letting go of him to grab her head. My reaction barely keeps her from going over the railing.

Blanche grunts and something in her expression changes. She won't endure this human struggle much longer if it all possible. As I think it, I see her put her hand on Tobiah's face.

"No!" I realize her intentions a moment too late. The life-taking spell Brunnea mentioned, the one that could save my life if I am weakened.

Tobiah's eyes widen, his grip loosens, then his eyelids flutter. At the same time, Blanche again strengthens. Is that what she did earlier? She stole from Aeria? The jolt of energy Blanche received earlier suddenly makes sense.

I gasp involuntarily. "How dare you!"

She meets my gaze. At the fleeting apology in her expression, my fingers hesitate reaching for Tobiah.

"There are things you must sacrifice for," she snarls at me.

It only takes a second for my shock to turn to anger, but by then it's already too late.

With alarming speed, Blanche's body begins to transform. She twists and writhes until it becomes the shape of a raven with a strangely misshapen foot.

Suddenly it's just Tobiah hanging onto the girl's hair with one hand and looking increasingly weak.

I blink.
She's gone.
Tobiah's head lolls. His fingers loosen.
The girl's hair severs.
He slips through my grasp.
This time the girl's scream is one of grief.

SAFE

Several men burst into the secret room, drawing a gasp from me and a muffled shriek from Queen Ada.

The guards react quickly, placing themselves between the intruders and the Queen and me before they suddenly relax.

"I'm sorry," comes a familiar voice. "I—I didn't mean to startle you, I'm—I—"

"Brann?" I murmur.

"Son?" Queen Ada steps out from behind me, her one word trembling through the air.

Brann appears behind a tall guard, his gaze taking in the room and lingering on me before encompassing his mother. "You're both safe." He lets out a little sigh of relief as the door shuts behind him and the three guards who entered with him.

Queen Ada rushes to him, gripping his forearms with her small hands and peering up into his face. "Your father, where is he?" There's terrible hope and fear in her words.

The calm in Brann's face cracks, revealing his grief beneath the surface. "I...I'm sorry, Mother."

Queen Ada's intake of breath shudders through her entire body, shaking her shoulders so violently that I think she might fall. Brann grips her by the elbows, holding her up and drawing her into his arms as she falls against him with a sob.

My own legs tremble. The King is dead? A mixture of emotions flood through me. I remember losing Father, the shock that hadn't allowed the pain to settle, the grief that followed, the agony of emptiness. Now the same pain will rip through a nation. Because of me and my friendship with Winter? No, Blanche would have come for him anyway... wouldn't she?

I clamp down on my lip, waiting for Queen Ada and her son to turn and blame me just as Mother did for Father's death. But all of a sudden, Brann is at my side, his mother still in his arms, but he's reaching for me, drawing me in as if to give me comfort.

I meet his gaze, the gaze of the new king of Ardor, but right now, he's only a son who has lost his father. I slip into his embrace, resting my head against his shoulder, and realize that tears stream down my cheeks.

Eyes closed, I start at a soft hand touching my face. Opening my eyes, I find Queen Ada gazing at me with her grief-stricken expression already in control and gratitude in her gaze.

"Thank you," Brann says, and I look up to see him addressing me.

"For what?" I whisper.

"For staying safe," he murmurs. "Both of you. I couldn't go on if either of you had died, too."

Queen Ada transfers her hand to her son's cheek, a moment of intimacy that makes me feel out of place in Brann's arms alongside her. But his grip doesn't loosen on me, and he seems to want nothing more than to hold us both.

Finally, Queen Ada disentangles herself and dabs at her face with a pale pink handkerchief. "We must get out of here." She turns to the guards. "When is it safe to leave?"

"We are conducting a sweep of the palace, Your Majesty," one of the guards who entered with Brann answers. "When that is complete, and we are convinced that Queen Blanche is no longer here, then we will allow you to leave."

Brann sighs and squeezes my shoulders. "I'm sorry about this," he murmurs to me.

I look up at him in disbelief. "Brann, you have nothing to apologize for. I'm sorry for..." I shake my head, unable to complete my thoughts. Every word I speak in here is overheard by a dozen others, and I can't bring myself to say the hundreds of words on my tongue.

"Come and sit down," I tell Brann, tugging him toward the small grouping of chairs. "There's not much to do here, but at least there are a few chairs."

He glances at the three seats, his bottom lip trembling slightly, and his eyes glisten. "Yes. Three chairs. One for each of us."

My heart twists in my chest in realization.

At his other side, his mother appears, and she pulls him into her arms like he's a child in need of comfort. I watch as he bends his head to her shoulder and weeps quietly. Feeling out of place, but no longer feeling like I can claim what might be the King's intended seat in this room, I wander around the perimeter, battling my own grief in silence.

14: WINTER

SPY

"And what happened to Queen Blanche?" Queen Ada asks me as I stand before her in the Ardor throne room, dressed in my tattered ball gown, my mask lost somewhere along the way.

"She transformed and disappeared." I sweep my hands out between us.

A small gathering of advisors and high-ranking soldiers stare me down, as if expecting to decipher my lies from half-truths. Guards flank every exit to the room, and the King's special guards stand beside the Queen and Brann. I shudder to remember that these guards are now no longer King Greggory's but Brann's. In that, I have already failed.

"And then what happened?" Queen Ada asks.

Her voice is strong and steady, but I detect the grief under it that she suffers to hide. I don't know if it's my magic or if it's simply empathy for her.

"Tobiah fell from the tower's balcony," I begin, then explain how I brought him up to the bed using some rope, leaving out the part where I healed him as best as I could.

Tobiah stands in the throne room off to the side amongst the advisors and nobles, watching the scene with his arm in a sling and his eyes strangely unfocused. I don't know exactly what went wrong or what prevented me from healing him completely, but it had been difficult enough to make him what he is now. I can only guess that the spell Blanche used to take his life strength affected him just as much as the fall. Only I don't know if anyone can give him that back.

I close my eyes briefly, and the moment returns to me. I crouched on the ground next to his crumpled body, debating the risks of using my magic. I didn't know if Blanche still watched. Had she only been able to fly a few trees away through her exhaustion? Or had she stolen enough of Tobiah's life to fly home?

Then I decided it didn't matter. I asked my magic to bring us into the tower, and it obeyed. Inside, I healed him as well as I could, but something is strange. He is somehow different, distant, not quite the man he was before, even allowing for the injuries I couldn't heal.

I can't tell the palace that though; I can't reveal my own magic to Queen Ada or Brann or neither would trust me ever again. Though Tobiah might tell them, he hasn't even told his best friend about the woman he loves who lives in a tower. That is not my story to tell, but his. And hopefully, he understands that my magic is not his story but mine.

"After Queen Blanche fled, transformed into a raven—"

There's a murmur of unease in the room amongst the audience.

"—Tobiah and I returned through the tunnel to the palace," I continue. "I have marked the way in the tunnel so that we might return, should you wish to investigate the scene." I direct a questioning look at Tobiah. As I had tended to Tobiah in the tower, trying to heal him, Aeria had confessed their past, how Tobiah had found her a few months ago and begun to visit her. They are in love. But, out of necessity, we left Aeria in the tower, and now

I leave her out of my narrative. Tobiah blinks dully at me, making me wonder if he's heard any word I've said.

"And this tower," the Queen begins, her voice wavering, "you say it's empty?"

I hesitate and glance to the guards flanking her. "I think so."

She seems to shrink on herself, pale as the black dress she wears. I consider her face, the paleness at my information and even the shape of it. She is quite similar in appearance to Aeria, now that I think of it. I remember what Brunnea said, how Blanche would need the blood of the seven princesses, and how Ardor had a princess, a girl…locked in a tower. I close my eyes, reeling at my own stupidity. All it should have taken me was one look at Queen Ada and Aeria. The girl looks much like her mother, if you take away the obscenely long hair.

"Go on," Brann barks at me from the side.

Jolting, I glance at him, then back to the Queen. She struggles to collect herself, but Brann is oblivious. He knows nothing about the princess in the tower. His sister. As quickly as I can, I finish telling them everything else that happened, leaving out Aeria and any use of my magic. That will be for private, later. If need be.

When I end, the Queen is gripping the arm of her throne. Brann does not sit on his father's throne yet but paces between me and the Queen.

Brann stops and faces his mother. "This is what I told you before, Mother. It is time to choose our side. Do we stand against Queen Blanche, and do we join forces to avenge Father's death? Or do we wait for her to steal our throne as she stole Princess Winterberry's?"

I straighten slightly at his words. Considering how he has spoken to me in the past, it's difficult for me to believe that he agrees with me now. Perhaps Ella has spoken to him, convinced him that I tell the truth.

The air in the room is thick, almost too thick to breathe, and I long for a quick answer, but Queen Ada takes her time.

Finally she speaks. "We must stand against evil, Brann, you know that. But that does not mean that we do it unwisely."

"No, of course not," Brann says quickly, almost too eagerly.

"So we do not rush into this," the Queen answers. "We consult with our experts, and we discuss these things, and then we will give our answer."

I gape at the queen. "Your Majesty, forgive me for saying this, but you don't have that time to waste. She goes to eliminate the other kings and queens, and you'll be left with nothing. You will be destroyed. If you don't at least warn the other kingdoms and take precautions for yourself..." I shake my head and shrug. "There is nothing but death for you and your people if you delay."

"We must not rush into this decision." Queen Ada gives me a regal look that is clearly intended to put me in my place. "And if you try to lead me down another path for your own purposes, I will have you arrested."

Biting my tongue, I dip my chin. "But Your Majesty, I am here to help you—"

"I don't care what you claim you're here for," the Queen interrupts in a hard voice. "Right now we have a funeral to plan." Her voice, contrary to my expectations, doesn't break.

"Your Majesty," I attempt again, "if you don't listen to me, then you'd best have your own funeral planned."

A gasp goes through the crowd and the Queen stands from her seat. "Arrest her. I've heard enough of these threats."

Guards step toward me, glints of satisfaction in their eyes.

A murmur from the side is, at first, ignored as a result of the Queen's words, but as the guards grip my upper arms, Brann's voice, sharp and alarmed slices the air. "What is it, Tobiah? What's happened?"

"I cannot see." Panic laces Tobiah's words, though I can tell he's trying to stay calm.

"What?" I hear Brann ask as the guards start to whisk me out from the throne room.

"Where is Winter?" Tobiah asks. "She can help me."

"Bring me to him," I command them, pulling away from their grips. "Let go of me. You must let me help him."

"Let her go, let her come here," Brann commands of the guards.

In his expression, I see confusion mingled with hope that I can fix whatever ails his friend, though I do not hold the same belief.

Silence descends as I reach Brann and we both lean over his friend.

"You cannot see?" I ask.

"Winter?" Tobiah's eyes blankly scan the area above him.

"Yes," I say, gripping his searching hands. "I'm here."

"I cannot see—just dark shapes. Some of you look no different." He gives a half-hearted attempt at a chuckle.

I ignore everyone else in the room and put my hands on the sides of Tobiah's head. "Just be still," I murmur. "I'll do what I can, but I cannot promise anything."

At my touch, Tobiah calms. "I trust you."

Pressing my lips together, I focus on his face. I gasp as my magic penetrates into him, sucking warmth from me like a cold breeze. I feel Blanche's dark magic at work in him, as though the very evilness of her act stealing his *anima* continues to work even though she is gone. She cannot do this from a distance, can she? I wish I had allowed Brunnea to teach me how to take an *anima* instead of interrupting. Perhaps I would know what to do now to return one.

I squint, nudging at the darkness, reaching for it within his body, seeking it out. I suck in another breath as I find a cluster of her evil like a knotted muscle behind his eyes.

Gritting my teeth, I pour myself and my magic into it until my hands begin to shake and tremble. Still, the darkness does not move.

My grip loosens on his head. I waver.

"What's wrong?" Brann demands. "Winter? Are you all right?"

Panting, I rip my hands free and fall back against Brann, blackness threatening at the edges of my vision.

Brann holds me up, his gaze alternating between Tobiah and me. Tobiah sits immobile, his hopefulness ebbing from his features.

"Tobiah! What has happened to him?" a quiet voice asks in my ear.

"Aeria?" Tobiah asks. "Is that you?"

"Yes, my darling," she murmurs, kneeling beside him.

Startled, I look up to find Aeria gazing down at Tobiah. "He… Queen Blanche's…spell continues to hurt him," I answer her.

Tears prick her eyes as she goes to Tobiah's side.

Then a second woman's voice speaks. "Aeria?"

Aeria lifts her head, her face tearful and pale, to examine the speaker.

Queen Ada asks, "Is that you? Aeria?"

A murmur ripples through the crowd around us. Queen Ada looks as though she's about to faint as she creeps closer. Brann jumps to his feet and goes to his mother. "What are you talking about, Mother?"

"Aeria," she whispers. "My daughter."

Brann's eyes go wide. He looks to his sister and then back to his mother. "It appears we have a great deal to talk about, Mother."

RESOLVED

It has been five long days since the masque, and I have not left the palace.

I attended the King's funeral yesterday, only glimpsing Brann and his mother and the rumored Princess Aeria of Ardor. Since the King's death, rumors have flown that Brann's elder sister, the child long thought to be deceased shortly after birth, has returned from the dead.

The King's funeral only confirms that. While she did not walk behind the carriage through the city as Brann and his mother did, her rumored presence beside the Queen and Brann at the private funeral can only confirm her identity. The small girl is undoubtedly related to the Queen and Brann. They all have the same eyes, and the women have the same, heart-shaped face.

But after the funeral, there is no discussion of my returning home.

In the few conversations we have had, Brann acts as though I am under attack as much as he is. The more I think of it, the more I think perhaps he is right. For if he does love me like he says, as he proclaimed the night of the masque, then I would be the target of his enemies. I can easily see how one might take me in the hopes of getting him. But how would anyone know? We are not engaged, and we have not even had the privacy to discuss that together.

A part of me longs to return to the life I had. Not life without Brann, but the complicated life of a woman running a stable. I have been isolated since the last masque, except for notes and questions from Gavin reporting on my horses. Meals are brought to me in my room by the maids I've been assigned, where I'm to eat alone.

Though I'm allowed to leave my room and take walks through the palace and its grounds, everywhere I go, a half dozen guards accompany me, and I quickly tire of the excursion. Nothing makes these days any shorter or me less trapped. I pine to ride Flora or Letifer through the woods or even stand in a paddock and work the horses.

Has Brann changed his mind about me? I have so many doubts and so many questions, and yet there is no opportunity to voice them except to myself. I am tired of reconsidering them from every angle.

With a grimace at the sky, I sink down onto a wooden bench in the garden. The guards position themselves a respectful distance from me, giving me the pretend privacy they think I desire. Perhaps they just pretend to be trees, I don't know. I rub the fabric of my gown's skirt between my fingers. The gifted gown is nearly the same color of my last ball gown, and it recalls the entire evening to me, from the hope I had when Winter and Dalia dressed me to speaking with Brann in the garden, kissing him, and everything after. At the path of my thoughts, winding and twisting like a garden hedge maze, I clench my skirts in both fists and look up.

I'm tired of this game; I can't stay here like this much longer. If I cannot talk to Brann, it's time to go home. I lift my chin and open my mouth to address the nearest guard when my jaw drops.

Brann? Do I really see him or am I just imagining this?

He gives a lopsided smile. "Ella." He spreads his arms to me, and I run into them.

My cheek collides with his chest and he wraps me in his embrace, hugging me tight before settling in to stroke my hair. Tears well up on my lashes, but I fight them back. If we only have a few minutes together, I won't waste them crying.

"I didn't know where you had gone," I tell him. "I didn't know if you were even here."

He touches my hair with a gentle hand. "I'm sorry. I've had so much to do these past few days."

"What has happened since the funeral?" I pull back from his arms to search his face. "How is your mother? Is she all right?"

He blinks at me, as if confused that I ask about his mother. "She's doing as well as one could hope," he says finally. "Tonight is the public memorial supper for the country, and I wanted to talk to you before then."

"Of course." I take his hand, feeling as though I might be taking liberties in doing so, but I lead him to the bench where I was sitting and pull him down next to me. "What did you want to say?" My heart thumps in my throat, an unbroken yearling desperate to escape the saddle.

He takes both my hands in his and wraps them up with his palms. "Ella, I appreciate you."

Through my pang of disappointment, I try to keep my expression immobile, but I have to bite my lip. He appreciates me. Not loves. Appreciates.

"You have been my strength for more than just the past few weeks, but years."

"Hadwin," I murmur.

He gives a little chuckle and rubs his chin. "I never forgot you, Ella, but I thought you'd forgotten me. I sent years of letters you never answered."

"What? No." I shake my head. "I answered every letter you ever sent, Brann. You stopped writing to me."

He presses my hands between his. "I found out shortly before I returned to Nubilus that my advisor was withholding letters from you and not posting my letters to you."

My mouth twists in distaste. "How could he?"

"The man has been dismissed, Ella." Brann waves away my complaints. "It's done; we cannot change it." He sighs and gazes down at our hands. "But then I returned, and when I came to Aeneas Stables, you didn't seem to recognize me. I was certain your friend knew I was the prince, and you...didn't. I was... confused. And I was so disappointed that I gave you another name, another lie." He lifts his gaze, though embarrassment trickles across his features. "But you were still the same Ella I remembered, lovelier than ever, but Ella, nonetheless."

I flush.

"I couldn't imagine a future without you almost as soon as I saw you again."

He squeezes my hand and slides off the bench. He bends over, and I think for a second that he's going to get down on one knee, but he adjusts his trouser leg and offers me his hand instead. "I've been sitting too much these days. Would you like to visit my stables?"

"Oh, uh, yes. Yes." I nod so eagerly that he chuckles. But there is a part of me that would have given up a trip to the stables for a proposal.

He takes me through the garden, out through a door I never noticed before and to a dirt path between a hedge and a stone outer wall of the palace. I follow him along the dirt path, then through a second and third garden. Finally we come to a wide expanse of pasture land that must be at the backside of the palace.

I cannot help myself: I stop and gasp. For in front of the pasture is a sprawling stable made of gray stone brick with a clay-shingle roof. I can imagine being inside and listening to the autumn rains falling alongside the nickering horses rustling in their straw beds. I can imagine the sweet smell of alfalfa and horse and leather—

"I take it you approve?" Brann asks from beside me.

I turn to find him beaming at me. "Well, I'll have to see the inside, of course. And a beautiful stable is nothing if the horses inside aren't even Geli."

He chuckles and squeezes my hand in his. "They're Geli, Ella. Would you expect to find anything else in the King's stables?" Even though he smiles, there's a hint of sadness in his eyes at the words "King's stables." These were his father's stables, and now his father is gone.

I take his hand in both of mine. "Of course. And I can't wait to see them."

Together we walk inside, greeted by half a dozen grooms who immediately ask if the prince would like a horse saddled.

"Two, actually," he says to the stable master, a man he introduces as Clemens. "The newest purchase, and one in the stall next to her." To me he says, "Come on. One of my favorite mares just foaled, and I want your opinion."

For the next quarter of an hour, Brann and I play with a golden mare and her brand-new golden colt. He's got one of the most promising appearances I've seen in a long time and a unique swirl of white on his forehead just under his forelock.

"Perhaps it's a remnant of the unicorn blood," Brann teases when I find it.

I grin, but before I can respond, a groom interrupts to announce our horses saddled.

"We'll be right out," Brann answers, then gives the mare a final stroke.

It's clear he loves his horses, and while the stable itself is made of the highest quality building materials, with glass windows for every stall that open to allow air in, there are still locks on the stall doors, preventing an unscrupulous servant from taking a horse out without permission.

"Come," Brann says, grasping my hand again. "I want to show you this new horse I bought."

I give the foal another pat and let Brann tug me out of the stall. He leads me down the aisle back out the door we entered. At the sight of the two horses, I stop short. "What is this?" I point to them. "Brann? Why are my horses in your stable?"

He faces me, a solemn crease to the bridge of his nose. "Ella, I love you, and that means caring about the things you care about. As soon as I realized you wouldn't be going home to your stable for a while, I had your horses relocated here to keep them safe. Your groom, Gavin, is also working at my stables while your horses are here. I asked him not to reveal it to you in his updates to you until I could speak with you, and clearly, he's a man of his word."

Gaping at him, I shake my head, but he waits for me to reply. "Brann, I don't know what to say. I mean, I knew you were kind and considerate, but this is amazing." I grin at him. "Are you thinking of going into the horse breeding business?"

He chuckles. "Ella, I must admit that I visited your stables when I got back in town because I wanted to see what kind of a woman you had become. You had plans to run your father's business after he died, and I thought for sure that it would change you. And when you stopped writing to me, I believed that change had happened, as I feared. I imagined this business had taken away your kindness and made you hard and bitter.

"But...I couldn't keep you from my mind. When I met you again, I couldn't stop thinking about you after I left, and how impossibly hard the Ardorian laws make every day for you. And how kind and considerate you were still. And how no one had one single bad thing to say about you.

"And I've been realizing that we're all wrong. This country is all wrong about Geli and women in business. And I want to change that. Because too many people think a woman can't do a man's job. But you prove them wrong every day, Ella.

"I admire you for it. You inspire me so much. I have plans to change the inheritance laws as soon as possible, even make it possible for your friend, Dalia, to inherit the inn should Noemì choose." He stops abruptly and inhales a deep breath that puffs out his chest, but his proud look slowly fades at my continued silence. "Say something, Ella."

"Brann, I—I don't know what to say." I pause and glance back to my horses. "You still love me?"

"Yes!" His eyes widen and light at my words. "Ella, my heart has always been and always will be yours. There is no one else. Especially not Winter."

"What?" I step back. "Winter?"

Brann's expression turns wary. "Winter didn't tell you…? She suggested…?" He trails off, uncertainty stealing his words.

"Brann, I've no idea what you're talking about." Suddenly something Winter said makes sense. "Wait—did Winter offer her own hand in marriage? For an alliance? Is that what you're saying?" My mouth goes dry. Is that what he's been trying to tell me all along? Has he given me a big speech on how he respects me and admires me and even loves me simply to tell me that he could never marry me when he's already betrothed to Winter? "And you can't…marry…"—my voice breaks into a whisper at the word—"me because…"

"No! Yes. She did. But I haven't betrothed myself to her." Confusion darkens his eyes, but he reaches for me with both hands. "You didn't hear?"

Pressing my lips together, I try to still my churning emotions. "She didn't tell me anything about marrying you."

He pauses a moment, searching my face, then smiles. "Then it's forgotten. I'll tell Mother it's forgotten."

"No, wait." I pull my hands from his. "Do you mean that your mother wants you to marry Winter?"

He presses out a sigh and drops his chin to his chest. "Yes. She does."

"Why?" As soon as I say it, I know the answer. "Because Winter secures your alliance, that's why."

He grimaces and rakes a hand through his hair. "Yes. She would. But it won't, because that marriage won't happen." He moves toward me. "Ella, I don't love her."

"But that doesn't matter with royal marriages, Brann, you know that."

"It does to me," he vows, his eyes narrowing at me as if he didn't expect something like that to come out of my mouth. "I'm not going to marry a woman just to get her kingdom. Ella, it doesn't matter who offers to marry me, because I love you." His brow furrows. "Ella, do you *want* to marry me?"

"Of course I do." The answer comes easily to my lips. "I love you, Brann. But I—" I break off. What if he changes his mind? What if, because he marries me, the kingdom falls? Or both kingdoms fall? What if all the Seven Kingdoms fall because he won't marry her?

"None of that's going to happen," Brann says firmly.

"What?" I start. Did I say all of that out loud?

His smile is gentle. "Ella, I can read your thoughts in your face. And that's one reason that I would never marry Winter, even if all the kingdoms were to fall. Even if she hadn't swore to me that, if I married her, any alliance would be void."

"What?" I blink. "I'm confused."

"She swore that if I didn't marry you, she would void any alliance between us."

Something like hope stirs in my stomach. "But why didn't you tell me? And why tell me now?"

He shrugs. "Because I don't want any secrets between us. I want us to be open with one another, including uncomfortable things like other proposals or flirtatious encounters. Ella, I want to share everything with you. You are intelligent, kind, and wise. You can see through falsehoods and into my own soul. I want you as my partner on the throne. I don't want just a pretty wife."

A flush heats my cheeks. "Well, in Winter's defense, she is no fool. And she's quite pretty."

He curls his upper lip. "All right, I give you all that, but I don't love her."

My lips curve upward.

"Your Majesty!" A guard appears around the corner of the stable, striding purposefully toward us.

Brann's expression is one of regret, but he pulls his shoulders back and faces the approaching guard. "What is it?"

The guard snaps a salute to his new king. "I apologize for interrupting, but urgent business requires your attention."

Brann crooks a brow and half motions to me. "You can speak before Miss Saevus."

The guard, standing at attention, flicks his gaze to me and then back to Brann. "There has been a sighting of the Canens Queen and her companions, Your Majesty."

His jaw tightening, Brann straightens. "I see." There's a moment of silence, then he turns to me. "I'm sorry, Ella. I had hoped to ride with you, but this must be dealt with. You'll be at the memorial dinner tonight?"

"Of course. If I am invited."

"I need you there."

"All right." I smile gently at him. "I'll be there then."

He pauses, then impulsively leans forward and kisses my forehead. "See you then."

It's only when he leaves that I realize he still hasn't proposed.

16: ELLA

MEMORIAL

Brann walks to the three empty seats at the head of the table. Hundreds of guests watch his every step, craning their necks to see what choice he makes next. My smile pinches as he takes, not the King's seat, but the seat beside it.

He holds up his hands for silence and makes a motion requesting everyone to sit. After a long moment surveying the guests, and perhaps noting the conspicuous absence of Winter, he smiles and stands behind his chair.

"Thank you for coming tonight to King Greggory III's memorial dinner. It's been four days since my father died, and what has become clear to me is how much you all, how much this community and this entire country, has loved my father. I will never forget how much you loved him.

"Now, though Father died unexpectedly, kings often do, and there were a few things my father wanted to get in order recently. Unfortunately, he was only part way through one of those things when he died."

Brann pauses and lifts his gaze to the ceiling. I wince to see the sparkle on his lashes, knowing the pain that lingers so close to the surface. I remember my own father's death, how deeply it affected me, how torturous that first week was.

"But one thing I was able to confess to him before he died, and for that I will be eternally grateful," Brann continues.

He glances at me, holding out a hand. I smile encouragingly, even as heads turn and crane toward me. "I was able to confess to him that I had found the woman I love and want to marry."

My heart races uncomfortably fast. I can't keep a slow smile from spreading onto my lips.

Brann waves his fingers at me. "Ella, would you stand? I have something I would like to ask you."

Murmurs go through the crowd. A flush burns my face as I stand, prolonging the motion to compose myself. Brann takes my hand and pulls me from the chair, leading me up to the spot in full view of everyone.

"Eleanora Saevus," he begins, kneeling at my feet and pulling something out of a small pocket. "I want you to be my wife."

A murmur built of both disappointment and excitement floats through the crowd. I ignore them all as an irrepressible smile splits my face.

"Brann, of course, I—"

"Just a moment, son." Queen Ada's voice cuts across my words. She pushes back her chair and stands. "There's something that must first be addressed regarding your choice in a wife."

His cheeks reddening, Brann bristles. "Mother, this is hardly the time—"

"This is exactly the time. And the most expedient way of determining her acceptability." She peers calmly up into her son's angry face, and her words are just as calm and quiet as her expression. "Son, ask your people if anyone objects to her. And if they do, this is their opportunity to speak up."

"And if they don't?" Brann gives her an incredulous look. "Mother, Ella is a kind-hearted soul who wouldn't hurt anyone. I don't think she's ever said a rude word—even to people who hurt her. I've talked to people about her already."

"Let the people speak. She is from Nubilus and they know her, but I do not. If they speak for her, I will say nothing more, Brann." She spreads her hands apologetically but firmly. "Brann, I do this out of love for you."

He inhales a thick breath then nods stiffly and tucks something back into his pocket. "Fine. You may present the question."

Her lips thin slightly, but she faces the guests.

My heart leaps into my throat. All it will take is one person to speak against me. I refrain from scanning the crowd for Mother and my sisters. If they dare to speak up against me, I have no hope. The Queen wouldn't trust me over them. Would she?

"Guests, citizens of Nubilus," Queen Ada begins, spreading her hands so much like her son does that I find myself distracted by them. "I have no objections to this woman, but I do not know her well. So I ask you, my subjects, who loved my husband and love our country so well, to protect this country and my husband's legacy. Tell us whether my son has chosen wisely."

My cheeks flame at her words as if I am a prisoner under trial. The room is deathly silent, people looking at each other. But as the silence lingers, I risk a glance around. Slow smiles appear on faces I recognize, followed by nods of approval.

"I see," Queen Ada says, sounding neither disappointed nor pleased.

The band around my chest loosens.

"Then—"

A voice cuts across Queen Ada's words.

"He cannot marry her, Your Majesty. She is an enemy to the Crown."

The band snaps back in place so tightly that my breath escapes me in a whoosh like Letifer has kicked me directly in the chest.

"Who said that?" Brann demands, stepping in front of me as if to protect me from the crowd. His shoulders are tense and squared, ready to challenge the speaker.

"I did." Lady Eleanora stands from the table, her bearing proud and arrogant, even as she dips a curtsy to Brann and Queen Ada. "She is your enemy, and I have proof to which my daughters can attest."

"She can't. They can't," I retort so softly that I doubt even Brann hears me.

"Approach, Lady Eleanora," Queen Ada says.

Standing, she smoothes her dress as she steps out from her seat then approaches from the far end of the table.

"What do you have to tell us, Lady Eleanora?" the Queen asks when my mother bows before her.

My sisters have risen from the table as well, each beautiful in their black mourning gowns, possibly more beautiful than any night of the masques.

"Rise, Lady Eleanora, and tell us what evidence you *think* you have of your eldest daughter betraying the Crown," Brann says, his voice dripping with sarcasm.

Mother takes another few seconds in her curtsy before rising, trying to make her ascension as dramatic as possible, then fixes the prince with a demure look. "Your Majesty, first I must say how sorry I am for your loss—"

"Thank you," he interrupts through tight lips. "Now tell me what evidence you have of your daughter's betrayal, Lady Eleanora."

"Well, Your Highness, my daughter has been friends with a woman who came into town mere weeks ago and immediately sought out my daughter. I believe she had plans from the very beginning to infiltrate herself into your circle and threaten your safety. My younger daughter told me how Winter is from Canens and has spent her time here manipulating Ella and convincing her to help our enemy. And now, my suspicions have been shown correct—here she stands, an enemy of state and guilty of King Greggory's death." Lady Eleanora lifts her chin.

Mother's words don't even make sense, but I know they sound good to those around us. "That's not true," I interrupt before Brann can even reply. "Winter came here ill and in need of help. It was mere chance she found me." I lock gazes with Brann. "She sought me out less than you did, Brann."

His expression softens for the merest moment, then hardens. "Enough of this." He turns to his nearest guard. A chilling silence has fallen over the crowd, bringing silence with it, one which Brann speaks into, his voice carrying with its wrath.

"You, Lady Eleanora, are a liar. A manipulative liar who hates your daughter without just cause."

"Brann," Queen Ada murmurs.

"Your Highness!" Lady Eleanora's voice rises in something like panic.

"It is 'Your Majesty,' now, Lady Eleanora." Brann fixes my mother with a stern look, and she looks both suitably chastised and fearful. He sighs. "What do you want, Lady Eleanora?"

She hesitates under his glare. "Your Majesty, I apologize if I have offended you. But I only wish to spare you the pain of an unhappy marriage—or marriage to a traitor."

Brann straightens, his face growing dark with fury, but it's the Queen who speaks.

"Those are bold words, Lady Eleanora. You should be able to support whatever you claim."

My mother blinks in an owlish fashion, gaping at the two royals before her. "I, well, I promise that that girl, Winter, has constantly been at our stables, and then her mother comes and kills poor King Greggory—what is more proof than that?"

For a dreadful moment as Queen Ada turns her gaze from Lady Eleanora to Brann, my stomach clenches and plummets to my feet. Then a wry voice comes from the side of the banquet hall.

"Oh, I don't know, perhaps witnessing who actually killed him?"

We all look over to see one of the King's guards step forward from a line and bows respectfully. "Apologies, Your Majesties, but I cannot sit here and listen to lies any longer."

Brann's lips twitch but he nods at the guard. "Go on."

"I was in the room when the King was killed. And neither Princess Winterberry nor Miss Ella were responsible for his death. Queen Blanche was acting alone in that room."

"Simply because you didn't see that girl in the room doesn't mean she didn't plot with her—" Mother begins.

"Excuse me, Lady Eleanora, but I did see that girl in the room," the guard interrupts. "And what I saw was a supposed enemy to the Crown of Ardor fighting against Queen Blanche. Now it seems to me that that is evidence of Princess Winterberry being on the right side of this fight, and not with Queen Blanche. If you have stronger evidence than my own report of witnessing her trying to save the King's life, then, by all means, produce it to King Brann. But if not, then I would say no more, if I were you." With his word said, the guard gives another bow to Brann and steps back in line, leaving Lady Eleanora once again the center of attention.

"And then there's my testimony, Lady Eleanora," Tobiah says, standing from where his seat across from mine. He blinks in our direction, his eyes still unseeing. Aeria holds his hands from beside him. "I fought the Queen with Princess Winterberry at my side, and she nearly died trying to save me and kill her. So if the princess was fighting on Queen Blanche's behalf, and Ella is friends with an enemy, that enemy is not Winter."

"And let me be the third voice to speak," a red-headed man says, pushing back his chair from farther down the table. "I am

Prince Ruslan Solem, and while I have no testimony to give of Ella Saevus, I have a great deal of testimony to give concerning Princess Winterberry. If she is considered an enemy to Ardor, then I must be one also. For she not only saved my life, but that of my sister and my advisor. I have shared with my cousin and aunt the circumstances surrounding those events, as have my sister and advisor. So I don't see this as a legitimate example of Miss Saevus' treachery, but rather support of her loyalty and good taste in friends."

My heart lifts as several more people rise and speak, all talking over one another until Brann raises his hands and asks for quiet. When the room falls silent, he turns to my gaping mother with a small smirk. "Well, Lady Eleanora? Do you insist on calling your own daughter an traitor? Because let me tell you what I have seen of you." He leans toward her and lowers his voice. "I have seen you treat your eldest daughter deplorably. I have seen you despise her, undermine her, and sabotage your own livelihood to spite her. You have driven up debts in town that you know you have no way of paying except at her expense. You have abused those around you and driven away those who might love and care for you. You are despicable, Lady Eleanora, so despicable that I remove your title from you and exile you to the Forgotten Isle."

Several people gasp at the pronouncement, though Queen Ada lifts her chin as if to support her son's judgment. My heart beats fast, fluttering so quickly in my throat that I think I might faint. But Mother looks even weaker than I, her knees folding under her and depositing her onto the ground as two of the King's guards step forward.

"Unless there is one person to speak for you, you are henceforth banished."

Mother closes her eyes, not even bothering to look around at the guests here. But I do. And I see faces withdraw, expressions closed off like shutters to weather a storm.

Nobles sitting at the table who leaned forward to see Mother denounce me now lean back and busy themselves with their place settings or take a drink. Merchants standing along the wall inch forward, searching the faces of the nobles, of Mother's so-called friends. But no one is speaking for her. No one at all.

"I speak for her." The words come out of my lips before I fully realize them.

Several gasps go through the room as Brann turns to me. "What? Ella?"

Pity wells up in me as I face Queen Ada and Brann. "My mother is many things. But she does not deserve a criminal's exile."

"She *is* a criminal," Brann says. But at my expression, he takes my hands in his, and his are surprisingly gentle. "Ella...are you sure? This is the only way to be completely free from her."

"But I won't be any more free from her if she's exiled to the Forgotten Isle than I will if she's exiled to the Distant Forest, to Canens, to Edormisco...or if she has her title removed and is removed from our lands entirely. Those places are for violent criminals, and she is not that. She is manipulative, bitter, and selfish, but please do not treat her like a violent criminal."

Brann's lips soften from the harsh line Mother's words have put upon them. "All right. If you're certain. I will trust you."

"Good. Because that's all I want."

"My trust?" He tilts his head. "Here I was thinking you might want something else." He pulls out the object from his small front pocket again.

I grin as he lowers himself onto one knee.

"Ella, will you be my wife?"

Despite everything that's been said, I read the nervousness on his face. Until I smile and nod—then his nerves flee like a frightened foal. "Yes, Brann. I would love to."

He takes my hand and slips the ring onto my finger. He

doesn't give me any time to gape at the hugeness of it before he pops to his feet and pulls me into his arms and kisses me.

And this time, I don't care who watches. He will be my husband. I've finally found the man I want to marry, the man I cannot imagine my life without.

17: WINTER

A LAST VISIT

Even during the King's public funeral dinner, I find myself surrounded by Ardorian guards. As I stroll through the palace grounds, every which way I turn there is another armed soldier dressed in blue and gold.

I casually take a left turn around the exterior of the palace. Within minutes, I'm near the garden where I first practiced magic with Brunnea and at the spot where Ardorites wait for an audience with the king. A pang stabs my side. Poor King Greggory, to meet such a tragic end. From all accounts, he was a good man and a wise king. His experience would have been helpful in the fight against Blanche.

I linger there for a little while, hoping to find a familiar face, but finally I give up and head toward the small garden and its maze. There, I can lose the guards, at least for awhile. Perhaps even practice my magic, as Brunnea would have me do.

I wince as if stabbed again. Despite all my thoughts over the past days, I cannot see how I am to defeat Blanche if I do not use magic. Armies will die before they reach Merise. And if I trap Blanche outside of Canens, her magic will be far greater. No, the best thing would be to take her by surprise and kill her with one spell. Give her no hint of my magic until I use it. So whatever spell I use must be great and powerful and… I sigh. This maze in the king's garden is not the place to even attempt such a spell. I need privacy, I need space, I need…

"Brunnea."

The old lady in the middle of the maze smiles serenely at me. I recognize her brown eyes instantly.

"I thought you had left, I thought—"

"Oh no. Well, I did, but I'm back."

"Did you warn the other Fae?"

"My sisters? Yes. I have warned as many as I could in such a short time." She sighs, and a great weariness passes over her face, adding so many years to it that I suddenly see her as a frail old woman and not a powerful Fae.

"So they're going to come help us fight her?"

"Fight her?" Brunnea's eyes round. "Oh no, dear. No, we can't — That is—" She pauses as if searching for the right words.

"You won't help fight?"

Her face wrinkles. "We can't help fight, Winterberry."

My knees knock together under my full skirts. "What do you mean, you can't? Isn't that what you're supposed to do? Help fight the evil in this world?"

"Oh, dear, I wish it were that simple, dear." She sighs and pats the stone bench beside her. "Come, have a seat."

"I don't want to sit. I want you to tell me why you won't help fight the greatest evil the Seven Kingdoms has ever seen!" Anger pulses through my veins so strongly that I feel the loss of my control.

"Dear, please. Calm yourself and let me explain something."

I cross my arms, willing my heart to slow and the magic in my blood to calm.

"That's better. You sure you won't sit?"

"I'll stand."

"Suit yourself." Brunnea takes a breath that lifts her shoulders and straightens her back. "Now, the Great Fae, as you know, gave the land of the Seven Kingdoms over to be ruled by humankind. When they did so, we crafted a peace treaty with the kings of the age. That treaty has since been lost by man. But what mankind did not know was that we also crafted a treaty amongst us thirteen Great Fae."

I frown. "So?"

"It was different from the treaty we had with man, Winterberry," Brunnea says gently. "It was a treaty that said we would not meddle in the schemes of mankind any longer. If we did, we would be subject to death at the other Great Fae's hands."

I blink as the truth washes over me. "So you cannot help me fight Blanche? Because you've already done everything you could." I frown. "But wait, you said you help people who deserve it all the time! You helped me save Ella. You gave me a dress, you live amongst humans and heal them when they need it! What do you mean you don't 'meddle in the schemes of mankind'?" I demand, my voice growing louder as my anger returns. Who is she to give such excuses for bowing out of a fight that no one else wants to fight either?

Brunnea holds up her wrinkled hands. "Just a moment, dear. Of course there are many more things to the treaty than just that. We agreed that we would act as lesser faeries. We would assist humans if they desired, but only with their permission."

"Well fine! I'm asking! We're all asking! Help us!"

"We would help in minor things, if required. But within the kings and their machinations, dear, we have all of us vowed to never meddle again."

My heart sinks to my toes and then surges right back up. "But wait, one of your sisters is helping, isn't she? She's helping Blanche, so that makes your treaty null, right?"

"It's not that simple," Brunnea says with a shake of her head. "Ceara broke the treaty long ago, in a different way. She has left the thirteen of us, and we have become twelve. But that does not mean the remaining Great Fae respect the treaty any less than we did before her departure."

My heart sinks again. "So I'm alone. You can't do anything." Bitterness seeps into my voice, and along with it, tears for all that I've risked and lost and what I risk now. I angle myself away from her as grief pushes at me.

"Just a moment, dear, I didn't say that." From her lap, Brunnea draws out a book and holds it up.

I shoot her an affronted look. "A book? That's supposed to help me? A bedtime story?"

Brunnea clears her throat. "Perhaps you should consider thinking before you speak, dear. When have I failed you yet?"

"You just have," I mutter, but reach out for the book and take it into my hands.

"Dear, if I were to assist you as you wish, and kill Blanche for you, I would forfeit my life, and Ceara would become that much more powerful against the remaining Great Fae. Her greatest power is division, Winterberry. Even now, I have no doubt that she infiltrates my sisters and asks them to ally with her."

I hold the book in both hands between us, my eyes on Brunnea. "Do you think they would do that? Your sisters?"

Brunnea's face tightens a bit before she can smooth away her worry. "I hope not. I have great faith in my sisters. But I don't know what sway Ceara holds over them."

I bite my lip. If she cannot help me or the Seven Kingdoms, and if Brann and Ada choose not to, all I have is my pitiful plan of confronting Blanche with my own magic. But even should I defeat her, that leaves Ceara. My gaze falls to the book in my hands. There is no title on the cover or the spine, but rather a picture drawn in gold of a wand with a swirl of something I presume to be a spell emerging from it. I cock a brow over it in Brunnea's direction. "A spell book? I thought I didn't need those."

"Dear, we all need to learn what our magic is capable of. Ordinarily, I would gift you with a wand as well. Instead, I have decided to gift you with this." She holds out her closed hand, makes sure I am watching, then opens her palm to reveal a thick, folded golden ribbon.

I cannot help but frown at the gift. "A ribbon?"

She smiles serenely and continues holding out her hand.

Tucking the book under one arm, I reach out and grasp the ribbon with two fingers. I gasp and drop it. Only, I can't. My fingers close around it, stuck to it like a tongue to frozen metal, burning and terrifying. Magic thumps through me like a heartbeat.

After a long minute, my fingers release and the ribbon falls back into Brunnea's palm.

"Wha—what was that?" I demand, snatching my hand back and holding it to my chest, staring at the innocent-looking ribbon.

Brunnea chuckles. "My gift to you." She holds it out again toward me. "As long as you hold this ribbon, you can summon me. And should you need me, I will move heaven and earth and Sheol beneath to come to you."

Hesitating slightly, I reach for the ribbon again. This time, when I take it, it warms under my touch and seems to purr like a friendly cat.

"All I must do is touch it?"

"Touch it, wear it, yes, however you prefer." Brunnea raises a finger. "And say aloud, 'I summon thee, Brunnea, Great Fae of the Ancient Kingdoms, to help me in my need.'" She nods at me. "Say it back to me."

"I summon thee, Brunnea, Great Fae of the Ancient King-doms, to help me..."

"...in my need," she adds when I trail off.

"...in my need." As I finish, a shudder runs through the ribbon and it lifts in the air, stretching out one end back toward Brunnea. Instinctively, I close my hand around it and prevent it from escaping.

Brunnea puts her hand over mine and the ribbon stills. "Do not use it except in dire emergencies. Life or death emergencies."

I nod and swallow. "Of course."

"But remember the words. It will not work unless you recall those words." Brunnea takes her hand away from mine and replace it in her lap.

I repeat the words in my head. The ribbon remains still. "I'll remember." I think for a moment, then take the ribbon and tie it around my head, looping it into a bow slightly to the side of my head. It fits perfectly, as if it was made to rest there.

Brunnea nods approvingly. "Now. That book will give you many ideas. Some you will not wish to risk, some you should not. I can only tell you that if you remain true to your heart, then your magic will not lead you astray. Seek to serve others, Winterberry, and your heart will stay true."

Despite her words, my stomach squirms. "I don't want to use magic, Brunnea. Not at all."

"My darling, my dear, sweet, good Winterberry." Brunnea stands and puts her hands on my shoulder. "Dear, there will soon be a time where you have no choice. And when that happens, you will have no regrets."

I chew on my lip. "And still you cannot tell me where to go next? What to do? Do I stay here or do I leave?"

Brunnea takes one hand and strokes a clump of wayward hair from my forehead. "Your future lies in the sleeping kingdom."

"Edormisco?"

She dips her head into a single nod. "I cannot tell you more. But to say that someone very important there depends upon you."

My shoulders lift. "The Edormiscan princess?"

Brunnea's face is impassive, but I think I detect a hint of pride in her eyes.

"I must go to her." I half turn before I remember myself and turn back. But when I do, she is already gone. My heart swells in my chest. "Thank you!" I call to the sky.

As I turn and rush through the maze, I half think that the flowers and hedges rustle their answer, despite there being no breeze.

18: ELLA

LAST UNICORN

I stand before the window at my room at the palace, staring down at the wet grass where my horses graze despite the autumn drizzle. It's been an exhausting week with the funeral, multiple dress fittings, adjusting the horses—especially Letifer—to their new stables, wedding plans, coronation plans, and a million other little things I never anticipated my life would bring.

"Ella?" Winter's voice breaks through my distractions. When I turn, my friend stands in the midst of my room wearing a simple purple gown.

"Winter!" I go to her and wrap my arms around her. Since the King's death, I've seen her only twice. Up until the proposal, I suspect she was a prisoner of sorts, though Brann denies it. He promises she was given the choice of attending the funeral and the memorial dinner, but chose not to. If that's true, I'm not sure what to think.

Winter leans her head against my shoulder a moment before pulling back and looking me in the eye. "How are you, Ella?"

"I'm good. Very good."

She smiles knowingly. "Congratulations."

I can't hide my grin and lift my fingers to show her my ring. "Thanks."

Winter takes my hand in hers and inspects the gem in a cursory way. "A dream come true?"

"More like a million dreams." My face still heats at the idea of marrying the man I love, or at even being in love and having everyone know it.

Winter pauses, her long lashes sweeping up and down as she examines my face with more scrutiny than she gave the only jewel I wear. "Do you have a date yet?"

"No." Sighing, I sink down onto the bench at the end of the bed. The nearby fireplace crackles, a reminder that autumn is in its final throes and winter will soon arrive. "But I'm thinking a midwinter solstice wedding would be pretty. Or perhaps an early spring wedding."

"That would be." Winter fingers the tall post of the overlarge bed in the room as if she doesn't want to come farther inside.

There is something she isn't telling me, but I have so much else on my mind that I don't have time to press her and figure out what. I give her another look and find our earlier positions swapped. She ignores me, lost in her own world, while I study her, waiting for her attention to return to me. "Winter, are you thinking of doing something…strange?"

A little laugh escapes her, and even I smile at my word choice.

"Strange? When have I been strange?" she asks.

I chuckle, for though she has been full of surprises, she is certainly not strange. "Perhaps not strange then, but dangerous?"

Ignoring my question, she motions to the swatches of fabric that I have lying on the table.

"Are those for your wedding?"

I nod and shrug, but can't keep the smile off my face as I think about my marriage. "Yes. My dress and also for the attendant dresses."

A slightly wistful look dawns over Winter's face as she reluctantly leaves the bedpost to stand in front of the fabrics. Perhaps she's jealous, and that's why she's acting so strange. Or maybe... I pause and go to pick dirt out from under my nails, but they are smooth and clean. I have grooms who take care of everything dirty now, and maids who clean my nails and gently reprimand me for the dirt and new tears they find.

"Brann told me about your marriage offer."

Instead of looking at me, Winter stares down at the fabric samples.

"Oh," she says, drawing out the syllable. "Did he?"

"Yes."

"And did he tell you of my agreement with him regarding his marriage?" Winter asks. "How much depended on your answer?"

"Yes, he did," I say and smile warmly, trying to show her the love I have for her that I can't properly put into words.

She lifts a cream colored swatch, one of my favorites, rubbing it between her fingers.

I reach for one of the blues that the seamstress gave me and turn to hold it up to Winter's face, trying to clear my head as I picture her wearing a dress in the fabric. "And yes, this is nearly the exact shade of your eyes."

A shadow drifts over her. "Are you asking me something?" she asks, as if trying and failing to find humor.

"Well I was hoping that you and Dalia and maybe Rus' and Brann's sisters would be my attendants at the wedding."

Winter's answering smile is tainted with sorrow. "Ella, I would love to, but I don't think that's a wise decision."

I frown. "Why ever not?"

"Because...because...because the country still doesn't know how to think about me," she answers too hurriedly, like she has another reason that she's not ready to tell. "I didn't go to the funeral for a good reason."

"Why—?"

She lifts a shoulder. "I didn't want to incite a riot."

My hand drops back to the table. "I suppose we have to think about those things now, don't we?" Frowning, I smooth the fabric back into its place next to the others. "Well, they'll get past that. This will help them get past it. If you're there, it's to support King Brann's marriage to his true love. If you're in the wedding, then they will especially see that you are trustworthy and you have been honest with us. They'll see how good you are and that you— dare I say?—you love us."

Winter's pale cheeks pink up at my words, but she glances away and won't meet my eyes. "I don't know, Ella. I'll have to think about it. I—I am afraid that they wouldn't take it like that at all."

I nibble on my bottom lip, trying to keep my disappointment at bay. "I haven't known you long, Winter, but I dare say I know you rather well. And you are more of a sister to me than my own sisters are. Please, please make this day the most special it can possibly be for me and be one of my attendants."

Winter finally meets my gaze at that. "Ella, this is going to be the most special day in your life no matter what…whether I am there or not. Even if it is just you and Brann exchanging vows before the priest, it will be your most special day."

"If you're not—"

Before I can get more out, she's given me a tight hug and turns away, talking over me.

"I've got some things to get done. Some people to talk with. I hope you're all right if I leave you be now."

"I—of course," I murmur to her retreating back, wondering what she has on her mind to be so distant.

"Oh, sorry," Winter, in her most polite voice, says in the hall. "She's inside, if you're looking for her."

"Thank you."

Brann appears around the edge of the door, and seeing me, his cool expression immediately falls off. It would appear that my friend and my fiancé have some things to work through still.

But when he says, "Hello," to me, such a smile brightens his face that a frenzy of butterflies erupt to life in my stomach.

"Hi." I start across the room for him. "I haven't seen you in about a day."

"I know." He pulls me into his arms. "It's been the longest day, too," he murmurs against my hair. He abruptly leans back and looks down at me in alarm. "It hasn't made you change your mind about us, has it?"

I laugh. "Not in the slightest."

"So you don't plan on taking all your horses back home?"

Leaning back from him, I give mock consideration to Brann's question. "Well, not immediately; that would be too much work, and I'm still awfully tired. I'll give this engagement a shot. Perhaps find a happily ever after."

His lips quirk into that familiar half-grin of his that I love. "Excellent. Because I'm pretty certain that once you begin to realize just how much I love you, and now that I can shower you with gifts and spoil you every day, I don't think you'll be going anywhere."

A handful of butterflies have gotten trapped in my throat at the fierceness in his gaze. "No?"

He pulls me into his arms and bends toward me, his expression solemn. "No. Not one bit." He gently lowers his lips to mine, and I have to catch my breath at his touch.

"Come, Ella, let's go on that ride I promised you. Maybe we'll see your unicorn again."

I look up at him. "I think I've already found my unicorn. But I'll settle for a ride on a Gelu alongside you."

PART V
EPILOGUE

EPILOGUE

BLANCHE

I descend from the tower with a frightful dip from the balcony and a surge of thrill as my spread wings catch the air and launch me upward.

The bird's body thrums with energy, reassuring me of my choice in escape. I must keep my raven form as long as I can. The life I stole from that princess and her lover will carry me home—but only if I do not transform.

Even in my bird's body, I sense the trailing magic of the tower, seeking me. Severing that girl's hair was a mistake. Once that happened, the magic, which had been a mere hum of distraction, roared. And it was that moment I realized the girl has two other enemies in her life. One cursed her hair, the other cursed her to the tower.

And now one—I cannot tell which—follows. And I cannot risk either finding me in Ardor.

But if I land in Canens and transform, I cannot expect to make it to Merise alive, not without supplies. I must remain a raven until I reach Merise; only that shall save me.

As I fly over the edge of the forest, long having left the tower and that fiasco behind, I catch sight of a white blur below. My former huntsman's white horse. That traitor. He will not survive long, but I cannot spare the magic to kill him now. Though I am sorely tempted, it would be at forfeit of my own life. My raven transformation did not go as smoothly without my wand, leaving me with a deformed claw and bad vision in one eye.

Killing him now is impossible; I must return home and hope the one who remains loyal to me will follow before his brother has a chance to corrupt him. Otherwise, I am in this fight alone but for Ceara.

Ceara. If ravens had lips, mine would be smiling now. I do not need any human's assistance. I simply need the Great Fae's.

With that in mind, I angle my wings and fly higher, into the mist.

BONUS MATERIAL

THE SILVER COLT

It was a warm day in the middle of summer when everything changed for the young girl who would grow up to run an empire.

Father pulled the girth on the saddle tight on the silver colt and shot his oldest daughter a stern look. "Are you ready for this, Ellie? Can you handle him?"

The girl grinned up at her father. "Of course, Papa. He's a darling; he wouldn't dare hurt me." To prove her point, she slipped the colt a carrot sliced lengthwise, which he made disappear with a quick inhale.

"Of course, darling, of course." Her father stepped back and checked the buckle on the colt's bridle. "But know that anything can happen when you're breaking a horse. Anything. You must remember to be prepared for it all."

Trying to lose her grin of excitement, the girl nodded, but the colt twisted his head to tickle her hand with his nose, and she giggled instead, leaning in and scratching his cheek. This colt had plenty of spirit, and both she and her father shared high hopes for him and talked of them often.

He would be the horse they built Aeneas Stables on, this son of

Mythos. Of the best bloodlines, somehow his mother slipped through the cracks at the last auction in Depono, a few towns away. Ella had learned at a young age that sometimes those small towns and their smaller auctions contained the best surprises.

Ciris, his dam, had been sold as a barren broodmare, one that had been bred multiple times without success. The owners had given up on her, but George Saevus had seen what the owners refused to see: she was already pregnant. If mares could glow while pregnant, it was her in her velvety gray coat shining silver, and in her warm amber eyes. She was sweet, patient, and the perfect broodmare. It was just too bad that she died during foaling.

They'd owned her eight months before the foal was born, a month early by the size of him. Weak as he was, he couldn't stand for the first day; George had expected to lose him. With the mare gone, George borrowed a neighbor's mare who had lost her foal recently in order to feed him. That mare rejected him too, refusing to let the tiny, silvery colt nurse. And so they resorted to bottle feeding.

Ella spent much of his early months living in the stall with him, feeding him when he was hungry, playing with him, brushing him, caring for him, and refusing to go to the house for dinner or even to sleep. She loved him more than anything. But Lord George saw him as profit for the stables. If he died like his dam had, they would have no future, and so he allowed his daughter her indulgence, for she cared for him far better than any groom would.

Deep down, although the girl was young and loved the colt dearly, she knew his value to her father was not sentimental. Her father was all business, which was exactly why he had married her mother. Lady Eleanora loved him, but their marriage was and always had been a loveless one that had failed to produce what her father needed: an heir.

Slowly over the years, Ella came to realize that her father's love for her was limited by the willingness she showed toward learning the family business. Unfulfilled in marriage, he lived for his horses. He loved them, and the older Ella became, the more she realized his love was limited by what something could do for him. Every day, the horses became more of his pride and joy; if forced, he would choose them over his wife or daughters any day of the week.

Even knowing this didn't make Ella's love for her father waver. He was her father after all. Her love for him was unrivaled, except by the little colt that gradually stole her heart. It was only when she reflected on Lord George's death years later that Ella realized how little love he had ever shown her.

For her attentions had been focused on bringing up the small colt, being his constant companion, and now, on being his first rider. Her father, after much contemplation, decided that allowing his eldest daughter to be the colt's first rider would be perfect. He'd always intended to train her to break the horses, and a colt that loved her was the best entry into that part of the business.

At thirteen, Ella was old and wise enough to control the horses, but light enough that she could ride young horses without stressing their bodies. She also maintained a way about her that made her less of a threat to them. They all trusted her—more than they trusted him, if he were honest with himself, which he rarely was, except when he considered his business. Then, only brutal honesty would do. And this colt had his place in this business, a place that had no room for error.

"Check the girth," he told Ellie. "Make sure it's tight." He held the colt by the bridle as the colt gnawed on the iron bit in his mouth. Although he'd spent plenty of time with the bridle on his head, the bit was less familiar, and he had a special aversion to it. Ellie had once suggested a bitless bridle, but Lord George refused to use one of those feminine things on an animal that would grow into a majestic stallion. The colt would submit or he would suffer.

He led the colt over to the mounting block and motioned Ella to step up onto it.

"Now lean over the saddle, put some weight there," he told Ellie.

The girl sprawled across the saddle as though she were a trick rider, leaning her belly across the saddle until she hung there with her feet dangling above the mounting block.

"Not that far, Ellie!" His words came out sharp. The colt tossed his nose up in the air and sidestepped.

Lord George snatched his daughter's ankle, steadying her and preventing her from falling headfirst to the ground as he tugged her back to the mounting block. "I said just lean *across the saddle, not* balance *on it. Haven't you watched me break a horse before?"*

Ellie grabbed at the saddle as she slid down it in her lightweight linen gown. "Sorry, Papa. I thought it might be okay if I—"

"Do as I instruct and nothing more, Eleanora," he said firmly. "If you will not listen, you will not ride."

"Sorry, Papa," she repeated meekly, giving the colt a pat on the shoulder.

At her touch, the colt craned his head around and calmed, blowing out a heavy breath.

"Now,"—her father snapped the reins of the colt—"mount up properly."

"Yes, Papa." She swung herself into the saddle, and the young colt tensed under her. She sat upon the colt with her hands smoothing his mane to the side. At the feel of his back arching under her, she leaned forward, speaking in a soothing tone.

"Sit up straight!" Lord George snapped.

As soon as the words left his mouth, the colt startled backward. Lord George fell forward, the reins slipping through his fingers. At the lunge, the colt gave a shrill whinny and reared high. As he lifted his feet off the ground, he lashed out in his fear and surprise, catching Lord George under the chin. Before the man hit the ground, he was dead.

Ella slid over the colt's haunches, landing hard upon the ground behind him as the colt bolted.

"Father!" she cried at the sight of his unmoving body.

Terror gripping her with cold hands, she crawled to his body. As she sobbed over him, the uncertain, frightened colt trotted back and forth on the opposite side of the ring, slowly calming himself until he came to a halt away from the two figures at the other end.

Only when the healer arrived and the grooms forcibly removed her from her father did Ella leave her father, her body aching and face swollen from tears.

The colt was put away in his stall, where he remained for days. No one wanted to touch him. And so no one but Ella did.

WOULD YOU LEAVE A REVIEW?

Did you enjoy this book? Don't be shy about telling a friend!

Indie authors, like myself, thrive upon the reviews of readers like you. Why? Because reviews sell books. Amazon and other online retailers take into account how many reviews a book has received when determining where a book shows up in searches and what book to promote to their readers.

I promise, leaving a review is not scary and it doesn't have to take a long time. Just a rating and a few words to say what you liked (or didn't like) about this book will suffice. And I treasure each and every review written, whether it's three words or three hundred, whether it's flattering or disappointing.

And thank you, from the bottom of my heart, for reading and reviewing <u>Fire & Frost</u>!

ACKNOWLEDGEMENTS

There's no better source of writer's block than having to write your acknowledgements page. I like to wait until the last minute so I'm sure to forget almost everyone that helped me, then I have some sort of procrastinator's excuse. (Just kidding. I hate to think I miss anyone who helps me out!)

So much work goes into a story that it's difficult to even look back and see who has helped turn an idea into a full-fledged novel, especially given as it takes so long to do. But because I don't want to turn this page into a novel itself, let's get started.

First off, I would be remiss if I didn't thank the Lord for allowing me to finish this book. He has put this desire to write in my heart and made me able to write it.

Secondly, there are a great deal of people who have helped me make this happen. Most notably, my husband. Thank you for your continued support and indulging my fantastical obsessions. And thanks to my parents who babysit far too often and give me extra writing time, especially while my husband is traveling. Thanks, Jen, for babysitting and giving me confidence that my kids are well cared for while I pound away on my laptop at the nearest Starbucks drinking my Nitro Cold Brew.

Then there are my writing friends who were so kind as to give their thoughts for this book: Bill Hiestand, Jen Edelmeyer, Kristy Perkins, and M.L. Yates. I appreciate your feedback so much.

And my readers (ARC and otherwise) from <u>Fog & Mist</u>…there are too many of you to list, but you guys are the ones who have kept me forging ahead on <u>Fire & Frost</u> even when the writing was hard and revising even harder.

And to those of you that I've missed, thank you! Even though you escape me right now, you hold a treasured place in my heart.

ABOUT THE AUTHOR

Kelsie Engen grew up in North Pole, Alaska, where the long winters taught her to love reading and writing of all kinds. Now she writes and edits all day long (or however long she can), escaping the subzero temperatures by delving into previously uncharted worlds.

She still lives in Alaska, now with her husband, children, cats, and dog, all of whom create a million distractions to getting her next book written. (But she wouldn't trade any of it for the world.)

You can sign up for her erratic newsletter here on www.kelsieengenauthor.com and stay up-to-date on new releases and other writing shenanigans. Or you can email her at scriptor.librorum@gmail.com or through this link.

Where to find her:
www.Instagram.com/KelsieEngen
www.Twitter.com/KelsieEngen
www.Facebook.com/KelsieEngenAuthor
www.Pinterest.com/KEngenAuthor

Websites:
www.KelsieEngenAuthor.com (for readers & writers)
www.KelsieEngen.com (for other writers)

An actress. Her daughter. And a long-buried lie.

Attending Oxford University for medical school is Adrienne Talbot's lifelong dream--and it's finally coming true. She's been accepted, and she's on the flight to London when a concussion changes everything.

Now, instead of traveling England before school begins, she must call upon her estranged, A-list actress mother for help.

An unenthusiastic greeting leads to an extended stay when Adrienne meets her mother's new fiancé and is dragged into a world of glitz and paparazzi--by a scandal that centers around her. This scandal could not only destroy any chance of reconciliation with her mother, but ruin Adrienne's close relationships with her sisters and father back home.

Desperate to find answers, Adrienne sets out upon a journey into her mother's past and begins to uncover the lies she once thought were truths.

Finding Home

(Available on Kindle)

Emma Chesworth is a happy wife to an NFL player. But that all changes in one moment when her husband unexpectedly asks for a divorce.

Supporting her four-year-old daughter, while grieving the loss of her marriage, Emma throws herself into restoring a dilapidated, Victorian home. Nothing about this job promises to be easy, and Emma is soon sure she's bitten off more than she can chew.

Yet in exploring the home, she comes across some of the previous owner's belongings, and in there is something that might just hold the key to both her relationship with her ex-husband and the new financial troubles she finds herself in. Until it disappears.

"Finding Home" is a family tale "wrought with highs, lows, pain, and joy."

Bernadette & the Stranger

(Kindle and paperback)

"The stranger hadn't moved from where she'd left him, not that she'd expected him to, but his chest rattled every now and then, evidence of life that scared her as much as soothed her."

When Bernadette Laurent suffers another loss in her life, she abandons humanity and moves to the island that her father left her. There she finds the solitude she hoped for. For awhile.

One day a storm rolls in, depositing a man in a lifeboat upon her shore, and thus destroying her island sanctuary. In this stranger, Bernadette finds more than she bargains for, including a ticket home—if she is brave enough to take it.

SHORT STORIES IN ANTHOLOGIES

<u>From the Stories of Old</u>

"The Bear in the Forest"

(Kindle and paperback)

In this international collection, new life is given to fairy tales, both classic and obscure.

Mythical creatures put the fairy in Fairy Tale. Mermaids, selkies, and ocean guardians experience the best and worst of humanity; sisters encounter an unusually friendly bear; a brave bride meets a silly goose; and a spinner of gold sets the record straight.

Urban fantasies modernize classics: a Frenchman learns the truth about magic, his past, and his girlfriend; a girl sets out to find love but receives a curse; and today's naughty list makes Old Saint Nick not-so-jolly.

New worlds bring a fresh sense of wonder! In the future, a young woman fights for her people and herself; a bastard son finds acceptance in a world ruled by women; and a farmer's wits win the heart of a frosty king.

Discover unexpected twists on old favorites, and fall in love with new tales and worlds to explore!

<u>Of Legends and Lore</u>

"Three Nights"

(Kindle and paperback)

New life is given to eleven old stories in this second collection of irresistible fairy tale retellings.

Royalty faces magical challenges: a prince uses his powers on a rescue mission and reveals a terrible secret about his people; a king takes drastic measures to save his daughters from a troublesome curse; and a princess befriends an unusual frog.

Mythical creatures can be friend or foe: three brothers face a depressed dragon with a legendary treasure; an ancient crow brings a child's wishes to life; and one young girl discovers dragons aren't always the enemy.

Heroes come in all shapes and sizes: a miser is in danger of losing everything one cold night; a struggling mirrorsmith meets an invisible recluse; a boy must relive the fairy tale based on his ancestor's life; a child is rejected because of his love of drawing cats; and an evil witch is sealed in a glass coffin.

Be transported to new worlds and enjoy fresh twists on old favorites.

<u>A Bit of Magic</u>

"The Scarred Shepherdess"

(Kindle and paperback)

The oldest story can be made new again, changed and altered until it is reimagined and restored.

Pride interferes with happily-ever-afters: a proud princess is tested and tests the prince in return; a young thief is caught red-handed and must make amends; and a vain queen struggles to save her stepdaughter.

Finding love is not a simple task: a hero searches for the ideal magical bride; an innocent librarian is charmed by a man with a menacing secret; a queen takes a spoiled prince as her sole deckhand; and a well-intentioned princess seeks to make things right with her father.

Change causes chaos, for better or worse: a scheming cat seeks to better the lot of his daydreaming master; a cursed pirate captain is given a second chance when he finds a young stowaway; a spoiled teenager suffers the consequences of turning her best friend into a toad; and a thief and a rebel hiding secrets meet at a ball.

Follow these characters on their journeys as eleven magical tales are turned on their heads and seen from new perspectives.

<u>The Magic Within</u>

"The Queen's Orchard"

(Kindle and Paperback)

Nine stories come to life in this fantasy anthology imbued with magic and mayhem.

Magic often comes at a heavy price: a ribbon dancer seeks a phoenix for the magic to right a terrible wrong; a young witch is punished after using dark magic she has no memory of performing; and a grumpy witch is forced to face her past when she inherits a baby in exchange for a spell.

But with magic, the impossible comes to life: children create magical worlds only to lose their powers as they grow older; a student helps her grandfather battle a squirrel army of his own creation; and a newly orphaned girl seeks a witch to resurrect her parents only to find another future in store for her.

And, as all tales go, actions have consequences: instead of studying for his exams, a teenager modifies his magical device and unleashes hidden dangers upon his classmates; after losing her temper, an orphan must learn to control her wild magic before the entire realm is doomed; and a past decision haunts an apprentice mage as a dark-eyed daemon preys on his fear.

Visit faraway lands and local neighborhoods in this collection of fantastic tales. Magic can be found everywhere, if you only know where to look.

www.ingramcontent.com/pod-product-compliance
Lightning Source LLC
Chambersburg PA
CBHW070731120726
47910CB00001B/56